A System Of Logic, Ratiocinative And Inductive
(Vol. 1 of 2)

John Stuart Mill

Contents

A SYSTEM OF LOGIC, RATIOCINATIVE AND INDUCTIVE (VOL. 1 OF 2)

BY

John Stuart Mill

A SYSTEM OF LOGIC,
RATIOCINATIVE AND INDUCTIVE,
BEING A CONNECTED VIEW OF THE
PRINCIPLES OF EVIDENCE,
AND THE
METHODS OF SCIENTIFIC INVESTIGATION.
by
JOHN STUART MILL.
In Two Volumes.
Vol. I.
Third Edition.
London:
John Parker, West Strand.
M DCCC LI.

PREFACE TO THE FIRST EDITION.

This book makes no pretence of giving to the world a new theory of the intellectual operations. Its claim to attention, if it possess any, is grounded on the fact that it is an attempt not to supersede, but to embody and systematize, the best ideas which have been either promulgated on its subject by speculative writers, or conformed to by accurate thinkers in their scientific inquiries.

To cement together the detached fragments of a subject, never yet treated as a whole; to harmonize the true portions of discordant theories, by supplying the links of thought necessary to connect them, and by disentangling them from the errors with which they are always more or less interwoven; must necessarily require a considerable amount of original speculation. To other originality than this, the present work lays no claim. In the existing state of the cultivation of the sciences, there would be a very strong presumption against any one who should imagine that he had effected a revolution in the theory of the investigation of truth, or added any fundamentally new process to the practice of it. The improvement which remains to be effected in the methods of philosophizing (and the author believes that they have much need of improvement) can only consist in performing, more systematically and accurately, operations with which, at least in their elementary form, the human intellect in some one or other of its employments is already familiar.

In the portion of the work which treats of Ratiocination, the author has not deemed it necessary to enter into technical details which may be obtained in so perfect a shape from the existing treatises on what is termed the Logic of the Schools. In the contempt entertained by many modern philosophers for the syllogistic art, it will be seen that he by no means participates; although the scientific theory on which its defence is usually rested appears to him erroneous: and the view which he has suggested of the nature and functions of the Syllogism may, perhaps, afford the means of conciliating the principles of the art with as much as is well grounded in the doctrines and objections of its assailants.

The same abstinence from details could not be observed in the First Book, on Names and Propositions; because many useful principles and distinctions which were contained in the old Logic, have been gradually omitted from the writings of its later teachers; and it appeared desirable both to revive these, and to reform and rationalize the philosophical foundation on which they stood. The earlier chapters of this preliminary Book will consequently appear, to some readers, needlessly elementary and scholastic. But those who know in what darkness the nature of our knowledge, and of the processes by which it is obtained, is often involved by a confused apprehension of the import of the different classes of Words and Assertions, will not regard these discussions as either frivolous, or irrelevant to the topics considered in the later Books.

On the subject of Induction, the task to be performed was that of generalizing the modes of investigating truth and estimating evidence, by which so many important and recondite laws of nature have, in the various sciences, been aggregated to the stock of human knowledge. That this is not a task free from difficulty may be presumed from the fact, that even at a very recent period, eminent writers (among whom it is sufficient to name Archbishop Whately, and the author of a celebrated article on Bacon in the ***Edinburgh Review***) have not scrupled to pronounce it impossible.(1) The author has endeavoured to combat their theory in the manner in which Diogenes confuted the sceptical reasonings against the possibility of motion; remembering that Diogenes' argument would have been equally conclusive, though his individual perambulations might not have extended beyond the circuit of his own tub.

Whatever may be the value of what the author has succeeded in effecting on this branch of his subject, it is a duty to acknowledge that for much of it he has been indebted to several important treatises, partly historical and partly philosophical, on the generalities and processes of physical science, which have been published within the last few years. To these treatises, and to their authors, he has endeavoured to do justice in the body of the work. But as with one of these writers, Dr. Whewell, he has occasion frequently to express differences of opinion, it is more particularly incumbent on him in this place to declare, that without the aid derived from the facts and ideas contained in that gentleman's *History of the Inductive Sciences*, the corresponding portion of this work would probably not have been written.

The concluding Book is an attempt to contribute towards the solution of a question, which the decay of old opinions, and the agitation that disturbs European society to its inmost depths, render as important in the present day to the practical interests of human life, as it must at all times be to the completeness of our speculative knowledge: viz. Whether moral and social phenomena are really exceptions to the general certainty and uniformity of the course of nature; and how far the methods, by which so many of the laws of the physical world have been numbered among truths irrevocably acquired and universally assented to, can be made instrumental to the formation of a similar body of received doctrine in moral and political science.

PREFACE TO THE THIRD EDITION.

Several criticisms, of a more or less controversial character, on this work, have appeared since the publication of the second edition; and Dr. Whewell has lately published a reply to those parts of it in which some of his opinions were controverted.

I have carefully reconsidered all the points on which my conclusions have been assailed. But I have not to announce a change of opinion on any matter of importance. Such minor oversights as have been detected, either by myself or by my critics, I have, in general silently, corrected: but it is not to be inferred that I agree with the objections which have been made to a passage, in every instance in which I have altered or cancelled it. I have often done so, merely that it might not remain a stumbling-block, when the amount of discussion necessary to place the matter in its true light would have exceeded what was suitable to the occasion.

To several of the arguments which have been urged against me, I have thought it useful to reply with some degree of minuteness; not from any taste for controversy, but because the opportunity was favourable for placing my own conclusions, and the grounds of them, more clearly and completely before the reader. Truth, on these subjects, is militant, and can only establish itself by means of conflict. The most opposite opinions can make a plausible show of evidence while each has the statement of its own case; and it is only possible to ascertain which of them is in the right, after hearing and comparing what each can say against the other, and what the other can urge in its defence.

Even the criticisms from which I most dissent have been of great service to me, by showing in what places the exposition most needed to be improved, or the arguments strengthened. And I should have been well pleased if the book had undergone a much greater amount of attack; as in that case I should probably have been enabled to improve it still more than I believe I have now done.

INTRODUCTION.

§ 1. There is as great diversity among authors in the modes which they have adopted of defining logic, as in their treatment of the details of it. This is what might naturally be expected on any subject on which writers have availed themselves of the same language as a means of delivering different ideas. Ethics and jurisprudence are liable to the remark in common with logic. Almost every writer having taken a different view of some of the particulars which these branches of knowledge are usually understood to include; each has so framed his definition as to indicate beforehand his own peculiar tenets, and sometimes to beg the question in their favour.

This diversity is not so much an evil to be complained of, as an inevitable and in some degree a proper result of the imperfect state of those sciences. It is not to be expected that there should be agreement about the definition of a thing, until there is agreement about the thing itself. To define a thing, is to select from among the whole of its properties those which shall be understood to be designated and declared by its name; and the properties must be well known to us before we can be competent to determine which of them are fittest to be chosen for this purpose. Accordingly, in the case of so complex an aggregation of particulars as are comprehended in anything which can be called a science, the definition we set out with is seldom that which a more extensive knowledge of the subject shows to be the most appropriate. Until we know the particulars themselves, we cannot fix upon the most correct and compact mode of circumscribing them by a general description. It was not till after an extensive and accurate acquaintance with the details of chemical phenomena, that it was found possible to frame a rational definition of chemistry; and the definition of the science of life and organization is still a matter of dispute. So long as the sciences are imperfect, the definitions must partake of their imperfections; and if the former are progressive, the latter ought to be so too. As much, therefore, as is to be expected from a definition placed at the commencement of a subject, is that it should define the scope of our inquiries: and the definition which I am about to offer of the science of logic, pretends to nothing more, than to be a statement of the question which I have put to myself, and which this book is an attempt to resolve. The reader is at liberty to object to it as a definition of logic; but it is at all events a correct definition of the subject of these volumes.

§ 2. Logic has often been called the Art of Reasoning. A writer(2) who has done more than any other living person to restore this study to the rank from which it had fallen in the estimation of the cultivated class in our own country, has adopted the above definition with an amendment; he has defined Logic to be the Science, as well as the Art, of reasoning; meaning by the former term, the analysis of the mental process which takes place whenever we reason, and by the latter, the rules, grounded on that analysis, for conducting the process correctly. There can be no doubt as to the propriety of the emendation. A right understanding of the mental process itself, of the conditions it depends on, and the steps of which it consists, is the only basis on which a system of rules, fitted for the direction of the process, can possibly be founded. Art necessarily presupposes knowledge; art, in any but its infant state, presupposes scientific knowledge: and if every art does not bear the name of the science on which it rests, it is only because several sciences are often necessary to form the groundwork of a single art. Such is the complication of human affairs, that to enable one thing to be *done*, it is often requisite to *know* the nature and properties of many things.

Logic, then, comprises the science of reasoning, as well as an art, founded on that science. But the word Reasoning, again, like most other scientific terms in popular use, abounds in ambiguities. In one of its acceptations, it means syllogizing; or the mode of inference which may be called (with sufficient accuracy for the present purpose) concluding from generals to particulars. In another of its senses, to reason, is simply to infer any assertion, from assertions already admitted: and in this sense induction is as much entitled to be called reasoning as the demonstrations of geometry.

Writers on logic have generally preferred the former acceptation of the term; the latter, and more extensive signification is that in which I mean to use it. I do this by virtue of the right I claim for every author, to give whatever provisional definition he pleases of his own subject. But sufficient reasons will, I believe, unfold themselves as we advance, why this should be not only the provisional but the final definition. It involves, at all events, no arbitrary change in the meaning of the word; for, with the general usage of the English language, the wider signification, I believe, accords better than the more restricted one.

§ 3. But Reasoning, even in the widest sense of which the word is susceptible, does not seem to comprehend all that is included, either in the best, or even in the most current, conception of the scope and province of our science. The employment of the word Logic to denote the theory of argumentation, is derived from the Aristotelian, or, as they are commonly termed, the scholastic logicians. Yet even with them, in their systematic treatises, argumentation was the subject only of the third part: the two former treated of Terms, and of Propositions; under one or other of which heads were also included Definition and Division. Professedly, indeed, these previous topics were introduced only on account of their connexion with reasoning, and as a preparation for the doctrine and rules of the syllogism. Yet they were treated with greater minuteness, and dwelt on at greater length, than was required for that purpose alone. More recent writers on logic have generally understood the term as it was employed by the able author of the Port Royal Logic; viz. as equivalent to the Art of Thinking. Nor is this acceptation confined to books, and scientific inquirers. Even in ordinary conversation, the ideas connected with the word Logic, include at least precision of language, and accuracy of classification: and we perhaps oftener hear persons speak of a logical arrangement, or of expressions logically defined, than of conclusions logically deduced from premisses. Again, a man is often called a great logician, or a man of powerful logic, not for the accuracy of his deductions, but for the extent of his command over premisses; because the general propositions required for explaining a difficulty or refuting a sophism, copiously and promptly occur to him: because, in short, his knowledge, besides being ample, is well under his command for argumentative use. Whether, therefore, we conform to the practice of those who have made the subject their particular study, or to that of popular writers and common discourse, the province of logic will include several operations of the intellect not usually considered to fall within the meaning of the terms Reasoning and Argumentation.

These various operations might be brought within the compass of the science, and the additional advantage be obtained of a very simple definition, if, by an extension of the term, sanctioned by high authorities, we were to define logic as the science which treats of the operations of the human understanding in the pursuit of truth. For to this ultimate end, naming, classification, definition, and all other operations over which logic has ever claimed jurisdiction, are essentially subsidiary. They may all be regarded as contrivances for enabling a person to know the truths which are needful to him, and to know them at the precise moment at which they are needful. Other purposes, indeed, are also served by these operations; for instance, that of imparting our knowledge to others. But, viewed with regard to this purpose, they have never been considered as within the province of the logician. The sole object of Logic is the guidance of one's own thoughts; the communication of those thoughts to others falls under the consideration of Rhetoric, in the large sense in which that art was conceived by the ancients; or of the still more extensive art of Education. Logic takes cognizance of our intellectual operations, only as they conduce to our own knowledge, and to our command over that knowledge for our own uses. If there were but one rational being in the universe, that being might be a perfect logician; and the science and art of logic would be the same for that one person as for the whole human race.

§ 4. But, if the definition which we formerly examined included too little, that which is now suggested has the opposite fault of including too much.

Truths are known to us in two ways: some are known directly, and of themselves; some through the medium of other truths. The former are the subject of Intuition, or Consciousness; the latter, of Inference. The truths known by intuition are the original premisses from which all others are inferred. Our assent to the conclusion being grounded on the truth of the premisses, we never could arrive at any knowledge by reasoning, unless something could be known antecedently to all reasoning.

Examples of truths known to us by immediate consciousness, are our own bodily sensations and mental feelings. I know directly, and of my own knowledge, that I was vexed yesterday, or that I am hungry to-day. Examples of truths which we know only by way of inference, are occurrences which took place while we were absent, the events recorded in history, or the theorems of mathematics. The two former we infer from the testimony adduced, or from the traces of those past occurrences which still exist; the latter, from the premisses laid down in books of geometry, under the title of definitions and axioms. Whatever we are capable of knowing must belong to the one class or to the other; must be in the number of the primitive data, or of the conclusions which can be drawn from these.

With the original data, or ultimate premisses of our knowledge; with their number or nature, the mode in which they are obtained, or the tests by which they may be distinguished; logic, in a direct way at least, has, in the sense in which I conceive the science, nothing to do. These questions are partly not a subject of science at all, partly that of a very different science.

Whatever is known to us by consciousness, is known beyond possibility of question. What one sees or feels, whether bodily or mentally, one cannot but be sure that one sees or feels. No science is required for the purpose of establishing such truths; no rules of art can render our knowledge of them more certain than it is in itself. There is no logic for this portion of our knowledge.

But we may fancy that we see or feel what we in reality infer. Newton saw the truth of many propositions of geometry without reading the demonstrations, but not, we may be sure, without their flashing through his mind. A truth, or supposed truth, which is really the result of a very rapid inference, may seem to be apprehended intuitively. It has long been agreed by thinkers of the most opposite schools, that this mistake is actually made in so familiar an instance as that of the eyesight. There is nothing of which we appear to ourselves to be more directly conscious, than the distance of an object from us. Yet it has long been ascertained, that what is perceived by the eye, is at most nothing more than a variously coloured surface; that when we fancy we see distance, all we really see is certain variations of apparent size, and degrees of faintness of colour; and that our estimate of the object's distance from us is the result of a comparison (made with so much rapidity that we are unconscious of making it) between the size and colour of the object as they appear at the time, and the size and colour of the same or of similar objects as they appeared when close at hand, or when their degree of remoteness was known by other evidence. The perception of distance by the eye, which seems so like intuition, is thus, in reality, an inference grounded on experience; an inference, too, which we learn to make; and which we make with more and more correctness as our experience increases; though in familiar cases it takes place, so rapidly as to appear exactly on a par with those perceptions of sight which are really intuitive, our perceptions of colour.(3)

Of the science, therefore, which expounds the operations of the human understanding in the pursuit of truth, one essential part is the inquiry: What are the facts which are the objects of intuition or consciousness, and what are those which we merely infer? But this inquiry has never been considered a portion of logic. Its place is in another and a perfectly distinct department of science, to which the name metaphysics more particularly belongs: that portion of mental philosophy which attempts to determine what part of the furniture of the mind belongs to it originally, and what part is constructed out of materials furnished to it from without. To this science appertain the great and much debated questions of the existence of matter; the existence of spirit, and of a distinction between it and matter; the reality of time and space, as things without the mind, and distinguishable from the objects which are said to exist *in* them. For in the present state of the discussion on these topics, it is almost universally allowed that the existence of matter or of spirit, of space or of time, is, in its nature, unsusceptible of being proved; and that if anything is known of them, it must be by immediate intuition. To the same science belong the inquiries into the nature of Conception, Perception, Memory, and Belief; all of which are operations of the understanding in the pursuit of truth; but with which, as phenomena of the mind, or with the possibility which may or may not exist of analysing any of them into simpler phenomena, the logician as such has no concern. To this science must also be referred the following, and all analogous questions: To what extent our intellectual faculties and our emotions are innate-- to what extent the result of association: Whether God, and duty, are realities, the existence of which is manifest to us a priori by the constitution of our rational faculty; or whether our ideas of them are acquired notions, the origin of which we are able to trace and explain; and the reality of the objects themselves a question not of consciousness or intuition, but of evidence and reasoning.

The province of logic must be restricted to that portion of our knowledge which consists of inferences from truths previously known; whether those antecedent data be general propositions, or particular observations and perceptions. Logic is not the science of Belief, but the science of Proof, or Evidence. In so far as belief professes to be founded on proof, the office of logic is to supply a test for ascertaining whether or not the belief is well grounded. With the claims which any proposition has to belief on the evidence of consciousness, that is, without evidence in the proper sense of the word, logic has nothing to do.

§ 5. By far the greatest portion of our knowledge, whether of general truths or of particular facts, being avowedly matter of inference, nearly the whole, not only of science, but of human conduct, is amenable to the authority of logic. To draw inferences has been said to be the great business of life. Every one has daily, hourly, and momentary need of ascertaining facts which he has not directly observed; not from any general purpose of adding to his stock of knowledge, but because the facts themselves are of importance to his interests or to his occupations. The business of the magistrate, of the military commander, of the navigator, of the physician, of the agriculturist, is merely to judge of evidence, and to act accordingly. They all have to ascertain certain facts, in order that they may afterwards apply certain rules, either devised by themselves, or prescribed for their guidance by others; and as they do this well or ill, so they discharge well or ill the duties of their several callings. It is the only occupation in which the mind never ceases to be engaged; and is the subject, not of logic, but of knowledge in general.

Logic, however, is not the same thing with knowledge, though the field of logic is coextensive with the field of knowledge. Logic is the common judge and arbiter of all particular investigations. It does not undertake to find evidence, but to determine whether it has been found. Logic neither observes, nor invents, nor discovers; but judges. It is no part of the business of logic to inform the surgeon what appearances are found to accompany a violent death. This he must learn from his own experience and observation, or from that of others, his predecessors in his peculiar pursuit. But logic sits in judgment on the sufficiency of that observation and experience to justify his rules, and on the sufficiency of his rules to justify his conduct. It does not give him proofs, but teaches him what makes them proofs, and how he is to judge of them. It does not teach that any particular fact proves any other, but points out to what conditions all facts must conform, in order that they may prove other facts. To decide whether any given fact fulfils these conditions, or whether facts can be found which fulfil them in a given case, belongs exclusively to the particular art or science, or to our knowledge of the particular subject.

It is in this sense that logic is, what Bacon so expressively called it, ***ars artium***; the science of science itself. All science consists of data and conclusions from those data, of proofs and what they prove: now logic points out what relations must subsist between data and whatever can be concluded from them, between proof and everything which it can prove. If there be any such indispensable relations, and if these can be precisely determined, every particular branch of science, as well as every individual in the guidance of his conduct, is bound to conform to those relations, under the penalty of making false inferences, of drawing conclusions which are not grounded in the realities of things. Whatever has at any time been concluded justly, whatever knowledge has been acquired otherwise than by immediate intuition, depended on the observance of the laws which it is the province of logic to investigate. If the conclusions are just, and the knowledge real, those laws, whether known or not, have been observed.

§ 6. We need not, therefore, seek any farther for a solution of the question, so often agitated, respecting the utility of logic. If a science of logic exists, or is capable of existing, it must be useful. If there be rules to which every mind consciously or unconsciously conforms in every instance in which it infers rightly, there seems little necessity for discussing whether a person is more likely to observe those rules, when he knows the rules, than when he is unacquainted with them.

A science may undoubtedly be brought to a certain, not inconsiderable, stage of advancement, without the application of any other logic to it than what all persons, who are said to have a sound understanding, acquire empirically in the course of their studies. Mankind judged of evidence, and often correctly, before logic was a science, or they never could have made it one. And they executed great mechanical works before they understood the laws of mechanics. But there are limits both to what mechanicians can do without principles of mechanics, and to what thinkers can do without principles of logic. A few individuals may, by extraordinary genius, anticipate the results of science; but the bulk of mankind require either to understand the theory of what they are doing, or to have rules laid down for them by those who have understood the theory. In the progress of science from its easiest to its more difficult problems, each great step in advance has usually had either as its precursor, or as its accompaniment and necessary condition, a corresponding improvement in the notions and principles of logic received among the most advanced thinkers. And if several of the more difficult sciences are still in so defective a state; if not only so little is proved, but disputation has not terminated even about the little which seemed to be so; the reason perhaps is, that men's logical notions have not yet acquired the degree of extension, or of accuracy, requisite for the estimation of the evidence proper to those particular departments of knowledge.

§ 7. Logic, then, is the science of the operations of the understanding which are subservient to the estimation of evidence: both the process itself of proceeding from known truths to unknown, and all other intellectual operations in so far as auxiliary to this. It includes, therefore, the operation of Naming; for language is an instrument of thought, as well as a means of communicating our thoughts. It includes, also, Definition, and Classification. For, the use of these operations (putting all other minds than one's own out of consideration) is to serve not only for keeping our evidences and the conclusions from them permanent and readily accessible in the memory, but for so marshalling the facts which we may at any time be engaged in investigating, as to enable us to perceive more clearly what evidence there is, and to judge with fewer chances of error whether it be sufficient. These, therefore, are operations specially instrumental to the estimation of evidence, and as such are within the province of Logic. There are other more elementary processes, concerned in all thinking, such as Conception, Memory, and the like; but of these it is not necessary that Logic should take any peculiar cognizance, since they have no special connexion with the problem of Evidence, further than that, like all other problems addressed to the understanding, it presupposes them.

Our object, then, will be to attempt a correct analysis of the intellectual process called Reasoning or Inference, and of such other mental operations as are intended to facilitate this: as well as, on the foundation of this analysis, and *pari passu* with it, to bring together or frame a set of rules or canons for testing the sufficiency of any given evidence to prove any given proposition.

With respect to the first part of this undertaking, I do not attempt to decompose the mental operations in question into their ultimate elements. It is enough if the analysis as far as it goes is correct, and if it goes far enough for the practical purposes of logic considered as an art. The separation of a complicated phenomenon into its component parts, is not like a connected and interdependent chain of proof. If one link of an argument breaks, the whole drops to the ground; but one step towards an analysis holds good and has an independent value, though we should never be able to make a second. The results of analytical chemistry are not the less valuable, though it should be discovered that all which we now call simple substances are really compounds. All other things are at any rate compounded of those elements: whether the elements themselves admit of decomposition, is an important inquiry, but does not affect the certainty of the science up to that point.

I shall, accordingly, attempt to analyse the process of inference, and the processes subordinate to inference, so far only as may be requisite for ascertaining the difference between a correct and an incorrect performance of those processes. The reason for thus limiting our design, is evident. It has been said by objectors to logic, that we do not learn to use our muscles by studying their anatomy. The fact is not quite fairly stated; for if the action of any of our muscles were vitiated by local weakness, or other physical defect, a knowledge of their anatomy might be very necessary for effecting a cure. But we should be justly liable to the criticism involved in this objection, were we, in a treatise on logic, to carry the analysis of the reasoning process beyond the point at which any inaccuracy which may have crept into it must become visible. In learning bodily exercises (to carry on the same illustration) we do, and must, analyse the bodily motions so far as is necessary for distinguishing those which ought to be performed from those which ought not. To a similar extent, and no further, it is necessary that the logician should analyse the mental processes with which Logic is concerned. Any ulterior and minuter analysis must be left to metaphysics; which in this, as in other parts of our mental nature, decides what are ultimate facts, and what are resolvable into other facts. And I believe it will be found that the conclusions arrived at in this work have no necessary connexion with any particular views respecting the ulterior analysis. Logic is common ground on which the partisans of Hartley and of Reid, of Locke and of Kant, may meet and join hands. Particular and detached opinions of all these thinkers will no doubt occasionally be controverted, since all of them were logicians as well as metaphysicians; but the field on which their principal battles have been fought, lies beyond the boundaries of our science.

It cannot, indeed, be pretended that logical principles can be altogether irrelevant to those more abstruse discussions; nor is it possible but that the view we are led to take of the problem which logic proposes, must have a tendency favourable to the adoption of some one opinion on these controverted subjects rather than another. For metaphysics, in endeavouring to solve its own peculiar problem, must employ means, the validity of which falls under the cognizance of logic. It proceeds, no doubt, as far as possible, merely by a closer and more attentive interrogation of our consciousness, or more properly speaking, of our memory; and so far is not amenable to logic. But wherever this method is insufficient to attain the end of its inquiries, it must proceed, like other sciences, by means of evidence. Now, the moment this science begins to draw inferences from evidence, logic becomes the sovereign judge whether its inferences are well-grounded, or what other inferences would be so.

This, however, constitutes no nearer or other relation between logic and metaphysics than that which exists between logic and all the other sciences. And I can conscientiously affirm, that no one proposition laid down in this work has been adopted for the sake of establishing, or with any reference to its fitness for being employed in establishing, preconceived opinions in any department of knowledge or of inquiry on which the speculative world is still undecided.

BOOK I. OF NAMES AND PROPOSITIONS.

"La scolastique, qui produisit dans la logique, comme dans la morale, et dans une partie de la metaphysique, une subtilite, une precision d'idees, dont l'habitude inconnue aux anciens, a contribue plus qu'on ne croit au progres de la bonne philosophie."--CONDORCET, *Vie de Turgot.*

CHAPTER I. OF THE NECESSITY OF COMMENCING WITH AN ANALYSIS OF LANGUAGE.

§ 1. It is so much the established practice of writers on logic to commence their treatises by a few general observations (in most cases, it is true, rather meagre) on Terms and their varieties, that it will, perhaps, scarcely be required from me, in merely following the common usage, to be as particular in assigning my reasons, as it is usually expected that those should be who deviate from it.

The practice, indeed, is recommended by considerations far too obvious to require a formal justification. Logic is a portion of the Art of Thinking: Language is evidently, and by the admission of all philosophers, one of the principal instruments or helps of thought; and any imperfection in the instrument, or in the mode of employing it, is confessedly liable, still more than in almost any other art, to confuse and impede the process, and destroy all ground of confidence in the result. For a mind not previously versed in the meaning and right use of the various kinds of words, to attempt the study of methods of philosophizing, would be as if some one should attempt to make himself an astronomical observer, having never learned to adjust the focal distance of his optical instruments so as to see distinctly.

Since Reasoning, or Inference, the principal subject of logic, is an operation which usually takes place by means of words, and in complicated cases can take place in no other way; those who have not a thorough insight into the signification and purposes of words, will be under chances, amounting almost to certainty, of reasoning or inferring incorrectly. And logicians have generally felt that unless, in the very first stage, they removed this fertile source of error; unless they taught their pupil to put away the glasses which distort the object, and to use those which are adapted to his purpose in such a manner as to assist, not perplex his vision; he would not be in a condition to practise the remaining part of their discipline with any prospect of advantage. Therefore it is that an inquiry into language, so far as is needful to guard against the errors to which it gives rise, has at all times been deemed a necessary preliminary to the study of logic.

But there is another reason, of a still more fundamental nature, why the import of words should be the earliest subject of the logician's consideration: because without it he cannot examine into the import of Propositions. Now this is a subject which stands on the very threshold of the science of logic.

The object of logic, as defined in the Introductory Chapter, is to ascertain how we come by that portion of our knowledge (much the greatest portion) which is not intuitive: and by what criterion we can, in matters not self-evident, distinguish between things proved and things not proved, between what is worthy and what is unworthy of belief. Of the various questions which present themselves to our inquiring faculties, some receive an answer from direct consciousness, others, if resolved at all, can only be resolved by means of evidence. Logic is concerned with these last. But before inquiring into the mode of resolving questions, it is necessary to inquire, what are those which offer themselves? what questions are conceivable? what inquiries are there, to which mankind have either obtained, or been able to imagine it possible that they should obtain, an answer? This point is best ascertained by a survey and analysis of Propositions.

§ 2. The answer to every question which it is possible to frame, is contained in a Proposition, or Assertion. Whatever can be an object of belief, or even of disbelief, must, when put into words, assume the form of a proposition. All truth and all error lie in propositions. What, by a convenient misapplication of an abstract term, we call a Truth, means simply a True Proposition; and errors are false propositions. To know the import of all possible propositions, would be to know all questions which can be raised, all matters which are susceptible of being either believed or disbelieved. How many kinds of inquiries can be propounded; how many kinds of judgments can be made; and how many kinds of propositions it is possible to frame with a meaning; are but different forms of one and the same question. Since, then, the objects of all Belief and of all Inquiry express themselves in propositions; a sufficient scrutiny of Propositions and of their varieties will apprize us what questions mankind have actually asked of themselves, and what, in the nature of answers to those questions, they have actually thought they had grounds to believe.

Now the first glance at a proposition shows that it is formed by putting together two names. A proposition, according to the common simple definition, which is sufficient for our purpose, is, **discourse**, **in which something is affirmed or denied of something**. Thus, in the proposition, Gold is yellow, the quality **yellow** is affirmed of the substance **gold**. In the proposition, Franklin was not born in England, the fact expressed by the words **born in England** is denied of the man Franklin.

Every proposition consists of three parts: the Subject, the Predicate, and the Copula. The predicate is the name denoting that which is affirmed or denied. The subject is the name denoting the person or thing which something is affirmed or denied of. The copula is the sign denoting that there is an affirmation or denial; and thereby enabling the hearer or reader to distinguish a proposition from any other kind of discourse. Thus, in the proposition, The earth is round, the Predicate is the word **round**, which denotes the quality affirmed, or (as the phrase is) predicated: **the earth**, words denoting the object which that quality is affirmed of, compose the Subject; the word **is**, which serves as the connecting mark between the subject and predicate, to show that one of them is affirmed of the other, is called the Copula.

Dismissing, for the present, the copula, of which more will be said hereafter, every proposition, then, consists of at least two names; brings together two names, in a particular manner. This is already a first step towards what we are in quest of. It appears from this, that for an act of belief, **one** object is not sufficient; the simplest act of belief supposes, and has something to do with, **two** objects: two names, to say the least; and (since the names must be names of something) two **nameable things**. A large class of thinkers would cut the matter short by saying, two **ideas**. They would say, that the subject and predicate are both of them names of ideas; the idea of gold, for instance, and the idea of yellow; and that what takes place (or a part of what takes place) in the act of belief, consists in bringing (as it is often expressed) one of these ideas under the other. But this we are not yet in a condition to say: whether such be the correct mode of describing the phenomenon, is an after consideration. The result with which for the present we must be contented, is, that in every act of belief *two* objects are in some manner taken cognizance of; that there can be no belief claimed, or question propounded, which does not embrace two distinct (either material or intellectual) subjects of thought; each of them capable or not of being conceived by itself, but incapable of being believed by itself.

I may say, for instance, "the sun." The word has a meaning, and suggests that meaning to the mind of any one who is listening to me. But suppose I ask him, Whether it is true: whether he believes it? He can give no answer. There is as yet nothing to believe, or to disbelieve. Now, however, let me make, of all possible assertions respecting the sun, the one which involves the least of reference to any object besides itself; let me say, "the sun exists." Here, at once, is something which a person can say he believes. But here, instead of only one, we find two distinct objects of conception: the sun is one object; existence is another. Let it not be said, that this second conception, existence, is involved in the first; for the sun may be conceived as no longer existing. "The sun" does not convey all the meaning that is conveyed by "the sun exists:" "my father" does not include all the meaning of "my father exists," for he may be dead; "a round square" does not include the meaning of "a round square exists," for it does not and cannot exist. When I say, "the sun," "my father," or a "round square," I call upon the hearer for no belief or disbelief, nor can either the one or the other be afforded me; but if I say, "the sun exists," "my father exists," or "a round square exists," I call for belief; and should, in the first of the three instances, meet with it; in the second, with belief or disbelief, as the case might be; in the third, with disbelief.

§ 3. This first step in the analysis of the object of belief, which, though so obvious, will be found to be not unimportant, is the only one which we shall find it practicable to make without a preliminary survey of language. If we attempt to proceed further in the same path, that is, to analyse any further the import of Proposi-tions; we find forced upon us, as a subject of previous consideration, the import of Names. For every proposition consists of two names; and every proposition affirms or denies one of these names, of the other. Now what we do, what passes in our mind, when we affirm or deny two names of one another, must depend on what they are names of; since it is with reference to that, and not to the mere names themselves, that we make the affirmation or denial. Here, therefore, we find a new reason why the signification of names, and the relation generally between names and the things signified by them, must occupy the preliminary stage of the inquiry we are engaged in.

It may be objected, that the meaning of names can guide us at most only to the opinions, possibly the foolish and groundless opinions, which mankind have formed concerning things, and that as the object of philosophy is truth, not opinion, the philosopher should dismiss words and look into things themselves, to ascertain what questions can be asked and answered in regard to them. This advice (which no one has it in his power to follow) is in reality an exhortation to discard the whole fruits of the labours of his predecessors, and conduct himself as if he were the first person who had ever turned an inquiring eye upon nature. What does any one's personal knowledge of Things amount to, after subtracting all which he has acquired by means of the words of other people? Even after he has learned as much as people usually do learn from others, will the notions of things contained in his individual mind afford as sufficient a basis for a ***catalogue raisonne*** as the notions which are in the minds of all mankind?

In any enumeration and classification of Things, which does not set out from their names, no varieties of things will of course be comprehended but those recog-nised by the particular inquirer; and it will still remain to be established, by a sub-sequent examination of names, that the enumeration has omitted nothing which ought to have been included. But if we begin with names, and use them as our clue to the things, we bring at once before us all the distinctions which have been recog-nised, not by a single inquirer, but by all inquirers taken together. It doubtless may, and I believe it will, be found, that mankind have multiplied the varieties unneces-sarily, and have imagined distinctions among things where there were only distinc-tions in the manner of naming them. But we are not entitled to assume this in the commencement. We must begin by recognising the distinctions made by ordinary language. If some of these appear, on a close examination, not to be fundamental, the enumeration of the different kinds of realities may be abridged accordingly. But to impose upon the facts in the first instance the yoke of a theory, while the grounds of the theory are reserved for discussion in a subsequent stage, is not a course which a logician can reasonably adopt.

CHAPTER II. OF NAMES.

§ 1. "A name," says Hobbes,(4) "is a word taken at pleasure to serve for a mark, which may raise in our mind a thought like to some thought we had before, and which being pronounced to others, may be to them a sign of what thought the speaker had(5) before in his mind." This simple definition of a name, as a word (or set of words) serving the double purpose of a mark to recall to ourselves the likeness of a former thought, and a sign to make it known to others, appears unexceptionable. Names, indeed, do much more than this; but whatever else they do, grows out of, and is the result of this: as will appear in its proper place.

Are names more properly said to be the names of things, or of our ideas of things? The first is the expression in common use; the last is that of some metaphysicians, who conceived that in adopting it they were introducing a highly important distinction. The eminent thinker, just quoted, seems to countenance the latter opinion. "But seeing," he continues, "names ordered in speech (as is defined) are signs of our conceptions, it is manifest they are not signs of the things themselves; for that the sound of this word *stone* should be the sign of a stone, cannot be understood in any sense but this, that he that hears it collects that he that pronounces it thinks of a stone."

If it be merely meant that the conception alone, and not the thing itself, is recalled by the name, or imparted to the hearer, this of course cannot be denied. Nevertheless, there seems good reason for adhering to the common usage, and calling the word *sun* the name of the sun, and not the name of our idea of the sun. For names are not intended only to make the hearer conceive what we conceive, but also to inform him what we believe. Now, when I use a name for the purpose of expressing a belief, it is a belief concerning the thing itself, not concerning my idea of it. When I say, "the sun is the cause of day," I do not mean that my idea of the sun causes or excites in me the idea of day; or in other words, that thinking of the sun makes me think of day. I mean, that a certain physical fact, which is called the sun's presence (and which, in the ultimate analysis, resolves itself into sensations, not ideas) causes another physical fact, which is called day. It seems proper to consider a word as the ***name*** of that which we intend to be understood by it when we use it; of that which any fact that we assert of it is to be understood of; that, in short, concerning which, when we employ the word, we intend to give information. Names, therefore, shall always be spoken of in this work as the names of things themselves, and not merely of our ideas of things.

But the question now arises, of what things? and to answer this it is necessary to take into consideration the different kinds of names.

§ 2. It is usual, before examining the various classes into which names are commonly divided, to begin by distinguishing from names of every description, those words which are not names, but only parts of names. Among such are reckoned particles, as ***of***, ***to***, ***truly***, ***often***; the inflected cases of nouns substantive, as ***me***, ***him***, ***John's***;(6) and even adjectives, as ***large***, ***heavy***. These words do not express things of which anything can be affirmed or denied. We cannot say, Heavy fell, or A heavy fell; Truly, or A truly, was asserted; Of, or An of, was in the room. Unless, indeed, we are speaking of the mere words themselves, as when we say, Truly is an English word, or, Heavy is an adjective. In that case they are complete names, viz. names of those particular sounds, or of those particular collections of written characters. This employment of a word to denote the mere letters and syllables of which it is composed, was termed by the schoolmen the ***suppositio materialis*** of the word. In any other sense we cannot introduce one of these words into the subject of a proposition, unless in combination with other words; as, A heavy ***body*** fell, A truly ***important fact*** was asserted, A ***member*** of ***parliament*** was in the room.

An adjective, however, is capable of standing by itself as the predicate of a proposition; as when we say, Snow is white; and occasionally even as the subject, for we may say, White is an agreeable colour. The adjective is often said to be so used by a grammatical ellipsis: Snow is white, instead of Snow is a white object;

White is an agreeable colour, instead of, A white colour, or, The colour white, is agreeable. The Greeks and Romans were allowed, by the rules of their language, to employ this ellipsis universally in the subject as well as in the predicate of a proposition. In English this cannot, generally speaking, be done. We may say, The earth is round; but we cannot say, Round is easily moved; we must say, A round object. This distinction, however, is rather grammatical than logical. Since there is no difference of meaning between **round**, and **a round object**, it is only custom which prescribes that on any given occasion one shall be used, and not the other. We shall therefore, without scruple, speak of adjectives as names, whether in their own right, or as representative of the more circuitous forms of expression above exemplified. The other classes of subsidiary words have no title whatever to be considered as names. An adverb, or an accusative case, cannot under any circumstances (except when their mere letters and syllables are spoken of) figure as one of the terms of a proposition.

Words which are not capable of being used as names, but only as parts of names, were called by some of the schoolmen Syncategorematic terms, to predicate, because it was only **with** some other word that they could be predicated. A word which could be used either as the subject or predicate of a proposition without being accompanied by any other word, was termed by the same authorities a Categorematic term. A combination of one or more Categorematic, and one or more Syncategorematic words, as, A heavy body, or A court of justice, they sometimes called a **mixed** term; but this seems a needless multiplication of technical expressions. A mixed term is, in the only useful sense of the word, Categorematic. It belongs to the class of what have been called many-worded names.

For, as one word is frequently not a name, but only part of a name, so a number of words often compose one single name, and no more. These words, "the place which the wisdom or policy of antiquity had destined for the residence of the Abyssinian princes," form in the estimation of the logician only one name; one Categorematic term. A mode of determining whether any set of words makes only one name, or more than one, is by predicating something of it, and observing whether, by this predication, we make only one assertion or several. Thus, when we say, John Nokes, who was the mayor of the town, died yesterday,--by this predication we make but one assertion; whence it appears that "John Nokes, who was the mayor of the town," is no more than one name. It is true that in this proposition, besides the assertion that John Nokes died yesterday, there is included another assertion, namely, that John Nokes was mayor of the town. But this last assertion was already made: we did not make it by adding the predicate, "died yesterday." Suppose, however, that the words had been, John Nokes *and* the mayor of the town, they would have formed two names instead of one. For when we say, John Nokes and the mayor of the town died yesterday, we make two assertions; one, that John Nokes died yesterday; the other, that the mayor of the town died yesterday.

It being needless to illustrate at any greater length the subject of many-worded names, we proceed to the distinctions which have been established among names, not according to the words they are composed of, but according to their signification.

§ 3. All names are names of something, real or imaginary; but all things have not names appropriated to them individually. For some individual objects we require, and consequently have, separate distinguishing names; there is a name for every person, and for every remarkable place. Other objects, of which we have not occasion to speak so frequently, we do not designate by a name of their own; but when the necessity arises for naming them, we do so by putting together several words, each of which, by itself, might be and is used for an indefinite number of other objects; as when I say, *this stone*: "this" and "stone" being, each of them, names that may be used of many other objects besides the particular one meant, although the only object of which they can both be used at the given moment, consistently with their signification, may be the one of which I wish to speak.

Were this the sole purpose for which names, that are common to more things than one, could be employed; if they only served, by mutually limiting each other, to afford a designation for such individual objects as have no names of their own; they could only be ranked among contrivances for economizing the use of language. But it is evident that this is not their sole function. It is by their means that we are enabled to assert *general* propositions; to affirm or deny any predicate of an indefinite number of things at once. The distinction, therefore, between *general* names, and *individual* or *singular* names, is fundamental; and may be considered as the first grand division of names.

A general name is familiarly defined, a name which is capable of being truly affirmed, in the same sense, of each of an indefinite number of things. An individual or singular name is a name which is only capable of being truly affirmed, in the same sense, of one thing.

Thus, **man** is capable of being truly affirmed of John, Peter, George, Mary, and other persons without assignable limit: and it is affirmed of all of them in the same sense; for the word man expresses certain qualities, and when we predicate it of those persons, we assert that they all possess those qualities. But **John** is only capable of being truly affirmed of one single person, at least in the same sense. For although there are many persons who bear that name, it is not conferred upon them to indicate any qualities, or anything which belongs to them in common; and cannot be said to be affirmed of them in any **sense** at all, consequently not in the same sense. "The present queen of England" is also an individual name. For, that there never can be more than one person at a time of whom it can be truly affirmed, is implied in the meaning of the words.

It is not unusual, by way of explaining what is meant by a general name, to say that it is the name of a **class**. But this, though a convenient mode of expression for some purposes, is objectionable as a definition, since it explains the clearer of two things by the more obscure. It would be more logical to reverse the proposition, and turn it into a definition of the word **class**: "A class is the indefinite multitude of individuals denoted by a general name."

It is necessary to distinguish **general** from **collective** names. A general name is one which can be predicated of **each** individual of a multitude; a collective name cannot be predicated of each separately, but only of all taken together. "The 76th regiment of foot," which is a collective name, is not a general but an individual name; for although it can be predicated of a multitude of individual soldiers taken jointly, it cannot be predicated of them severally. We may say, Jones is a soldier, and Thompson is a soldier, and Smith is a soldier, but we cannot say, Jones is the 76th regiment, and Thompson is the 76th regiment, and Smith is the 76th regiment. We can only say, Jones, and Thompson, and Smith, and Brown, and so forth, (enumerating all the soldiers,) are the 76th regiment.

"The 76th regiment" is a collective name, but not a general one: "a regiment" is both a collective and a general name. General with respect to all individual regiments, of each of which separately it can be affirmed; collective with respect to the individual soldiers, of whom any regiment is composed.

§ 4. The second general division of names is into **concrete** and **abstract**. A concrete name is a name which stands for a thing; an abstract name is a name which stands for an attribute of a thing. Thus, *John*, *the sea*, *this table*, are names of things. *White*, also, is a name of a thing, or rather of things. Whiteness, again, is the name of a quality or attribute of those things. Man is a name of many things; humanity is a name of an attribute of those things. *Old* is a name of things; *old age* is a name of one of their attributes.

I have used the words concrete and abstract in the sense annexed to them by the schoolmen, who, notwithstanding the imperfections of their philosophy, were unrivalled in the construction of technical language, and whose definitions, in logic at least, though they never went more than a little way into the subject, have seldom, I think, been altered but to be spoiled. A practice, however, has grown up in more modern times, which, if not introduced by Locke, has gained currency chiefly from his example, of applying the expression "abstract name" to all names which are the result of abstraction or generalization, and consequently to all general names, instead of confining it to the names of attributes. The metaphysicians of the Condillac school,--whose admiration of Locke, passing over the profoundest speculations of that truly original genius, usually fastens with peculiar eagerness upon his weakest points,--have gone on imitating him in this abuse of language, until there is now some difficulty in restoring the word to its original signification. A more wanton alteration in the meaning of a word is rarely to be met with; for the expression **general name**, the exact equivalent of which exists in all languages I am acquainted with, was already available for the purpose to which **abstract** has been misappropriated, while the misappropriation leaves that important class of words, the names of attributes, without any compact distinctive appellation. The old acceptation, however, has not gone so completely out of use, as to deprive those who still adhere to it of all chance of being understood. By **abstract**, then, I shall always mean the opposite of **concrete**: by an abstract name, the name of an attribute; by a concrete name, the name of an object.

Do abstract names belong to the class of general, or to that of singular names? Some of them are certainly general. I mean those which are names not of one single and definite attribute, but of a class of attributes. Such is the word **colour**, which is a name common to whiteness, redness, &c. Such is even the word whiteness, in respect of the different shades of whiteness to which it is applied in common; the word magnitude, in respect of the various degrees of magnitude and the various dimensions of space; the word weight, in respect of the various degrees of weight. Such also is the word *attribute* itself, the common name of all particular attributes. But when only one attribute, neither variable in degree nor in kind, is designated by the name; as visibleness; tangibleness; equality; squareness; milkwhiteness; then the name can hardly be considered general; for though it denotes an attribute of many different objects, the attribute itself is always conceived as one, not many. The question is, however, of no moment, and perhaps the best way of deciding it would be to consider these names as neither general nor individual, but to place them in a class apart.

It may be objected to our definition of an abstract name, that not only the names which we have called abstract, but adjectives, which we have placed in the concrete class, are names of attributes; that *white*, for example, is as much the name of the colour, as *whiteness* is. But (as before remarked) a word ought to be considered as the name of that which we intend to be understood by it when we put it to its principal use, that is, when we employ it in predication. When we say snow is white, milk is white, linen is white, we do not mean it to be understood that snow, or linen, or milk, is a colour. We mean that they are things having the colour. The reverse is the case with the word whiteness; what we affirm to *be* whiteness is not snow but the colour of snow. Whiteness, therefore, is the name of the colour exclusively: white is a name of all things whatever having the colour; a name, not of the quality whiteness, but of every white object. It is true, this name was given to all those various objects on account of the quality; and we may therefore say, without impropriety, that the quality forms part of its signification; but a name can only be said to stand for, or to be a name of, the things of which it can be predicated. We shall presently see that all names which can be said to have any signification, all names by applying which to an individual we give any information respecting that individual, may be said to *imply* an attribute of some sort; but they are not names of the attribute; it has its own proper abstract name.

§ 5. This leads to the consideration of a third great division of names, into *connotative* and *non-connotative*, the latter sometimes, but improperly, called *absolute*. This is one of the most important distinctions which we shall have occasion to point out, and one of those which go deepest into the nature of language.

A non-connotative term is one which signifies a subject only, or an attribute only. A connotative term is one which denotes a subject, and implies an attribute. By a subject is here meant anything which possesses attributes. Thus John, or London, or England, are names which signify a subject only. Whiteness, length, virtue, signify an attribute only. None of these names, therefore, are connotative. But *white*, *long*, *virtuous*, are connotative. The word white, denotes all white things, as snow, paper, the foam of the sea, &c., and implies, or as it was termed by the schoolmen, *connotes*,(7) the attribute *whiteness*. The word white is not predicated of the attribute, but of the subjects, snow, &c.; but when we predicate it of them, we imply, or connote, that the attribute whiteness belongs to them. The same may be said of the other words above cited. Virtuous, for example, is the name of a class, which includes Socrates, Howard, the man of Ross, and an undefined number of other individuals, past, present, and to come. These individuals, collectively and severally, can alone be said with propriety to be denoted by the word: of them alone can it properly be said to be a name. But it is a name applied to all of them in consequence of an attribute which they are supposed to possess in common, the attribute which has received the name of virtue. It is applied to all beings that are considered to possess this attribute; and to none which are not so considered.

All concrete general names are connotative. The word *man*, for example, denotes Peter, Jane, John, and an indefinite number of other individuals, of whom, taken as a class, it is the name. But it is applied to them, because they possess, and to signify that they possess, certain attributes. These seem to be, corporeity, animal life, rationality, and a certain external form, which for distinction we call the human. Every existing thing, which possessed all these attributes, would be called a man; and anything which possessed none of them, or only one, or two, or even three of them without the fourth, would not be so called. For example, if in the interior of Africa there were to be discovered a race of animals possessing reason equal to that of human beings, but with the form of an elephant, they would not be called men. Swift's Houyhnhms were not so called. Or if such newly-discovered beings possessed the form of man without any vestige of reason, it is probable that some other name than that of man would be found for them. How it happens that there can be any doubt about the matter, will appear hereafter. The word *man*, therefore, signifies all these attributes, and all subjects which possess these attributes. But it can be predicated only of the subjects. What we call men, are the subjects, the individual Stiles and Nokes; not the qualities by which their humanity is constituted. The name, therefore, is said to signify the subjects *directly*, the attributes *indirectly*; it *denotes* the subjects, and implies, or involves, or indicates, or as we shall say henceforth, *connotes*, the attributes. It is a connotative name.

Connotative names have hence been also called *denominative*, because the subject which they denote is denominated by, or receives a name from, the attribute which they connote. Snow, and other objects, receive the name white, because they possess the attribute which is called whiteness; James, Mary, and others receive the name man, because they possess the attributes which are considered to constitute humanity. The attribute, or attributes, may therefore be said to denominate those objects, or to give them a common name.(8)

It has been seen that all concrete general names are connotative. Even abstract names, though the names only of attributes, may in some instances be justly considered as connotative; for attributes themselves may have attributes ascribed to them; and a word which denotes attributes may connote an attribute of those attributes. It is thus, for example, with such a word as *fault*; equivalent to *bad* or *hurtful quality*. This word is a name common to many attributes, and connotes hurtfulness, an attribute of those various attributes. When, for example, we say that slowness, in a horse, is a fault, we do not mean that the slow movement, the actual change of place of the slow horse, is a thing to be avoided, but that the property or peculiarity of the horse, from which it derives that name, the quality of being a slow mover, is an undesirable peculiarity.

In regard to those concrete names which are not general but individual, a distinction must be made.

Proper names are not connotative: they denote the individuals who are called by them; but they do not indicate or imply any attributes as belonging to those individuals. When we name a child by the name Paul, or a dog by the name Caesar, these names are simply marks used to enable those individuals to be made subjects of discourse. It may be said, indeed, that we must have had some reason for giving them those names rather than any others: and this is true; but the name, once given, becomes independent of the reason. A man may have been named John, because that was the name of his father; a town may have been named Dartmouth, because it is situated at the mouth of the Dart. But is no part of the signification of the word John, that the father of the person so called bore the same name; nor even of the word Dartmouth, to be situated at the mouth of the Dart. If sand should choke up the mouth of the river, or an earthquake change its course, and remove it to a distance from the town, the name of the town would not necessarily be changed. That fact, therefore, can form no part of the signification of the word; for otherwise, when the fact confessedly ceased to be true, no one would any longer think of applying the name. Proper names are attached to the objects themselves, and are not dependent on the continuance of any attribute of the object.

But there is another kind of names, which although they are individual names, that is, predicable only of one object, are really connotative. For, although we may give to an individual a name utterly unmeaning, which we call a proper name,--a word which answers the purpose of showing what thing it is we are talking about, but not of telling anything about it; yet a name peculiar to an individual is not necessarily of this description. It may be significant of some attribute, or some union of attributes, which being possessed by no object but one, determines the name exclusively to that individual. "The sun" is a name of this description; "God," when used by a monotheist, is another. These, however, are scarcely examples of what we are now attempting to illustrate, being, in strictness of language, general, and not individual names: for, however they may be *in fact* predicable only of one object, there is nothing in the meaning of the words themselves which implies this: and, accordingly, when we are imagining and not affirming, we may speak of many suns; and the majority of mankind have believed, and still believe, that there are many gods. But it is easy to produce words which are real instances of connotative individual names. It may be part of the meaning of the connotative name itself, that there exists but one individual possessing the attribute which it connotes; as, for instance, "the *only* son of John Stiles;" "the *first* emperor of Rome." Or the attribute connoted may be a connexion with some determinate event, and the connexion may be of such a kind as only one individual could have; or may at least be such as only one individual actually had; and this may be implied in the form of the expression. "The father of Socrates," is an example of the one kind (since Socrates could not have had two fathers); "the author of the Iliad," "the murderer of Henri

Quatre," of the second. For, although it is conceivable that more persons than one might have participated in the authorship of the Iliad, or in the murder of Henri Quatre, the employment of the article *the* implies that, in fact, this was not the case. What is here done by the word *the*, is done in other cases by the context: thus, "Caesar's army" is an individual name, if it appears from the context that the army meant is that which Caesar commanded in a particular battle. The still more general expressions, "the Roman army," or "the Christian army," may be individualized in a similar manner. Another case of frequent occurrence has already been noticed; it is the following. The name, being a many-worded one, may consist, in the first place, of a *general* name, capable therefore in itself of being affirmed of more things than one, but which is, in the second place, so limited by other words joined with it, that the entire expression can only be predicated of one object, consistently with the meaning of the general term. This is exemplified in such an instance as the following: "the present prime minister of England." Prime Minister of England is a general name; the attributes which it connotes may be possessed by an indefinite number of persons: in succession however, not simultaneously; since the meaning of the word itself imports (among other things) that there can be only one such person at a time. This being the case, and the application of the name being afterwards limited by the word *present*, to such individuals as possess the attributes at one indivisible point of time, it becomes applicable only to one individual. And as this appears from the meaning of the name, without any extrinsic proof, it is strictly an individual name.

From the preceding observations it will easily be collected, that whenever the names given to objects convey any information, that is, whenever they have properly any meaning, the meaning resides not in what they *denote*, but in what they *connote*. The only names of objects which connote nothing are *proper* names; and these have, strictly speaking, no signification.

If, like the robber in the Arabian Nights, we make a mark with chalk on a house to enable us to know it again, the mark has a purpose, but it has not properly any meaning. The chalk does not declare anything about the house; it does not mean, This is such a person's house, or This is a house which contains booty. The object of making the mark is merely distinction. I say to myself, All these houses are so nearly alike, that if I lose sight of them I shall not again be able to distinguish that which I am now looking at, from any of the others; I must therefore contrive to make the appearance of this one house unlike that of the others, that I may hereafter know, when I see the mark--not indeed any attribute of the house--but simply that it is the same house which I am now looking at. Morgiana chalked all the other houses in a similar manner, and defeated the scheme: how? simply by obliterating the difference of appearance between that house and the others. The chalk was still there, but it no longer served the purpose of a distinctive mark.

When we impose a proper name, we perform an operation in some degree analogous to what the robber intended in chalking the house. We put a mark, not indeed upon the object itself, but, so to speak, upon the idea of the object. A proper name is but an unmeaning mark which we connect in our minds with the idea of the object, in order that whenever the mark meets our eyes or occurs to our thoughts, we may think of that individual object. Not being attached to the thing itself, it does not, like the chalk, enable us to distinguish the object when we see it; but it enables us to distinguish it when it is spoken of, either in the records of our own experience, or in the discourse of others; to know that what we find asserted in any proposition of which it is the subject, is asserted of the individual thing with which we were previously acquainted.

When we predicate of anything its proper name; when we say, pointing to a man, this is Brown or Smith, or pointing to a city, that it is York, we do not, merely by so doing, convey to the hearer any information about them, except that those are their names. By enabling him to identify the individuals, we may connect them with information previously possessed by him; by saying, This is York, we may tell him that it contains the Minster. But this is in virtue of what he has previously heard concerning York; not by anything implied in the name. It is otherwise when objects are spoken of by connotative names. When we say, The town is built of marble, we give the hearer what may be entirely new information, and this merely by the signification of the many-worded connotative name, "built of marble." Such names are not signs of the mere objects, invented because we have occasion to think and speak of those objects individually; but signs which accompany an attribute: a kind of livery in which the attribute clothes all objects which are recognized as possessing it. They are not mere marks, but more, that is to say, significant marks; and the connotation is what constitutes their significance.

As a proper name is said to be the name of the one individual which it is predicated of, so (as well from the importance of adhering to analogy, as for the other reasons formerly assigned) a connotative name ought to be considered a name of all the various individuals which it is predicable of, or in other words ***denotes***, and not of what it connotes. But by learning what things it is a name of, we do not learn the meaning of the name: for to the same thing we may, with equal propriety, apply many names, not equivalent in meaning. Thus, I call a certain man by the name Sophroniscus: I call him by another name, The father of Socrates. Both these are names of the same individual, but their meaning is altogether different; they are applied to that individual for two different purposes; the one, merely to distinguish him from other persons who are spoken of; the other to indicate a fact relating to him, the fact that Socrates was his son. I further apply to him these other expressions: a man, a Greek, an Athenian, a sculptor, an old man, an honest man, a brave man. All these are names of Sophroniscus, not indeed of him alone, but of him and each of an indefinite number of other human beings. Each of these names is applied to Sophroniscus for a different reason, and by each whoever understands its meaning is apprised of a distinct fact or number of facts concerning him; but those who knew nothing about the names except that they were applicable to Sophroniscus, would be altogether ignorant of their meaning. It is even conceivable that I might know every single individual of whom a given name could be with truth affirmed, and yet could not be said to know the meaning of the name. A child knows who are its brothers and sisters, long before it has any definite conception of the nature of the facts which are involved in the signification of those words.

In some cases it is not easy to decide precisely how much a particular word does or does not connote; that is, we do not exactly know (the case not having arisen) what degree of difference in the object would occasion a difference in the name. Thus, it is clear that the word ***man***, besides animal life and rationality, connotes also a certain external form; but it would be impossible to say precisely what form; that is, to decide how great a deviation from the form ordinarily found in the beings whom we are accustomed to call men, would suffice in a newly-discovered race to make us refuse them the name of man. Rationality, also, being a quality which admits of degrees, it has never been settled what is the lowest degree of that quality which would entitle any creature to be considered a human being. In all such cases, the meaning of the general name is so far unsettled, and vague; mankind have not come to any positive agreement about the matter. When we come to treat of classification, we shall have occasion to show under what conditions this vagueness may exist without practical inconvenience; and cases will appear, in which the ends of language are better promoted by it than by complete precision; in order that, in natural history for instance, individuals or species of no very marked character may be ranged with those more strongly characterized individuals or species to which, in all their properties taken together, they bear the nearest resemblance.

But this partial uncertainty in the connotation of names can only be free from mischief when guarded by strict precautions. One of the chief sources, indeed, of lax habits of thought, is the custom of using connotative terms without a distinctly ascertained connotation, and with no more precise notion of their meaning than can be loosely collected from observing what objects they are used to denote. It is in this manner that we all acquire, and inevitably so, our first knowledge of our vernacular language. A child learns the meaning of the words *man*, or *white*, by hearing them applied to a variety of individual objects, and finding out, by a process of generalization and analysis of which he is but imperfectly conscious, what those different objects have in common. In the case of these two words the process is so easy as to require no assistance from culture; the objects called human beings, and the objects called white, differing from all others by qualities of a peculiarly definite and obvious character. But in many other cases, objects bear a general resemblance to one another, which leads to their being familiarly classed together under a common name, while, without more analytic habits than the generality of mankind possess, it is not immediately apparent what are the particular attributes, upon the possession of which in common by them all, their general resemblance depends. When this is the case, people use the name without any recognized connotation, that is, without any precise meaning; they talk, and consequently think, vaguely, and remain contented to attach only the same degree of significance to their own words, which a child three years old attaches to the words brother and sister. The child at least is seldom puzzled by the starting up of new individuals, on whom he is ignorant whether or not to confer the title; because there is usually an authority close at hand competent to solve all doubts. But a similar resource does not exist in the generality of cases; and new objects are continually presenting themselves to men, women, and children, which they are called upon to class *proprio motu*. They, accordingly, do this on no other principle than that of superficial similarity, giving to each new object the name of that familiar object, the idea of which it most readily recalls, or which, on a cursory inspection, it seems to them most to resemble: as an unknown substance found in the ground will be called, according to its texture, earth, sand, or a stone. In this manner, names creep on from subject to subject, until all traces of a common meaning sometimes disappear, and the word comes to denote a number of things not only independently of any common attribute, but which have actually no attribute in common; or none but what is shared by other things to which the name is capriciously refused.(9) Even scientific writers have aided in this perversion of general language from its purpose; sometimes because, like the vulgar, they knew no better; and sometimes in deference to that aversion to admit new words, which induces mankind, on all subjects not considered technical, to attempt to make the original small stock of names serve with but little augmentation to express a constantly increasing number of objects and distinctions, and, consequently, to express them in a manner progressively more and more imperfect.

To what degree this loose mode of classing and denominating objects has rendered the vocabulary of mental and moral philosophy unfit for the purposes of accurate thinking, is best known to whoever has most reflected on the present condition of those branches of knowledge. Since, however, the introduction of a new technical language as the vehicle of speculations on subjects belonging to the domain of daily discussion, is extremely difficult to effect, and would not be free from inconvenience even if effected, the problem for the philosopher, and one of the most difficult which he has to resolve, is, in retaining the existing phraseology, how best to alleviate its imperfections. This can only be accomplished by giving to every general concrete name which there is frequent occasion to predicate, a definite and fixed connotation; in order that it may be known what attributes, when we call an object by that name, we really mean to predicate of the object. And the question of most nicety is, how to give this fixed connotation to a name, with the least possible change in the objects which the name is habitually employed to denote; with the least possible disarrangement, either by adding or subtraction, of the group of objects which, in however imperfect a manner, it serves to circumscribe and hold together; and with the least vitiation of the truth of any propositions which are commonly received as true.

This desirable purpose, of giving a fixed connotation where it is wanting, is the end aimed at whenever any one attempts to give a definition of a general name already in use; every definition of a connotative name being an attempt either merely to declare, or to declare and analyse, the connotation of the name. And the fact, that no questions which have arisen in the moral sciences have been subjects of keener controversy than the definitions of almost all the leading expressions, is a proof how great an extent the evil to which we have adverted has attained.

Names with indeterminate connotation are not to be confounded with names which have more than one connotation, that is to say, ambiguous words. A word may have several meanings, but all of them fixed and recognised ones; as the word *post*, for example, or the word *box*, the various senses of which it would be endless to enumerate. And the paucity of existing names, in comparison with the demand for them, may often render it advisable and even necessary to retain a name in this multiplicity of acceptations, distinguishing these so clearly as to prevent their being confounded with one another. Such a word may be considered as two or more names, accidentally written and spoken alike.(10)

§ 6. The fourth principal division of names, is into *positive* and *negative*. Positive, as *man*, *tree*, *good*; negative, as *not-many*, *not-tree*, *not-good*. To every positive concrete name, a corresponding negative one might be framed. After giving a name to any one thing, or to any plurality of things, we might create a second name which should be a name of all things whatever except that particular thing or things. These negative names are employed whenever we have occasion to speak collectively of all things other than some thing or class of things. When the positive name is connotative, the corresponding negative name is connotative likewise; but in a peculiar way, connoting not the presence but the absence of an attribute. Thus, *not-white* denotes all things whatever except white things; and connotes the attribute of not possessing whiteness. For the non-possession of any given attribute is also an attribute, and may receive a name as such; and thus negative concrete names may obtain negative abstract names to correspond to them.

Names which are positive in form are often negative in reality, and others are really positive though their form is negative. The word *inconvenient*, for example, does not express the mere absence of convenience; it expresses a positive attribute, that of being the cause of discomfort or annoyance. So the word ***unpleasant***, notwithstanding its negative form, does not connote the mere absence of pleasantness, but a less degree of what is signified by the word ***painful***, which, it is hardly necessary to say, is positive. ***Idle***, on the other hand, is a word which, though positive in form, expresses nothing but what would be signified either by the phrase ***not working***, or by the phrase ***not disposed to work***; and ***sober***, either by ***not drunk*** or by ***not drunken***.

There is a class of names called ***privative***. A privative name is equivalent in its signification to a positive and a negative name taken together; being the name of something which has once had a particular attribute, or for some other reason might have been expected to have it, but which has it not. Such is the word ***blind***, which is not equivalent to ***not seeing***, or to ***not capable of seeing***, for it would not, except by a poetical or rhetorical figure, be applied to stocks and stones. A thing is not usually said to be blind, unless the class to which it is most familiarly referred, or to which it is referred on the particular occasion, be chiefly composed of things which can see, as in the case of a blind man, or a blind horse; or unless it is supposed for any reason that it ought to see; as in saying of a man, that he rushed blindly into an abyss, or of philosophers or the clergy that the greater part of them are blind guides. The names called privative, therefore, connote two things: the absence of certain attributes, and the presence of others, from which the presence also of the former might naturally have been expected.

§ 7. The fifth leading division of names is into ***relative*** and ***absolute***, or let us rather say, ***relative*** and ***non-relative***; for the word absolute is put upon much too hard duty in metaphysics, not to be willingly spared when its services can be dispensed with. It resembles the word ***civil*** in the language of jurisprudence, which stands for the opposite of criminal, the opposite of ecclesiastical, the opposite of military, the opposite of political, in short, the opposite of any positive word which wants a negative.

Relative names are such as father, son; ruler, subject; like; equal; unlike; unequal; longer, shorter; cause, effect. Their characteristic property is, that they are always given in pairs. Every relative name which is predicated of an object, supposes another object (or objects), of which we may predicate either that same name or another relative name which is said to be the ***correlative*** of the former. Thus, when we call any person a son, we suppose other persons who must be called parents. When we call any event a cause, we suppose another event which is an effect. When we say of any distance that it is longer, we suppose another distance which is shorter. When we say of any object that it is like, we mean that it is like some other object, which is also said to be like the first. In this last case, both objects receive the same name; the relative term is its own correlative.

It is evident that these words, when concrete, are, like other concrete general names, connotative; they denote a subject, and connote an attribute: and each of them has or might have a corresponding abstract name, to denote the attribute connoted by the concrete. Thus the concrete ***like*** has its abstract ***likeness***; the concretes, father and son, have, or might have, the abstracts, paternity, and filiety, or filiation. The concrete name connotes an attribute, and the abstract name which answers to it denotes that attribute. But of what nature is the attribute? Wherein consists the peculiarity in the connotation of a relative name?

The attribute signified by a relative name, say some, is a relation; and this they give, if not as a sufficient explanation, at least as the only one attainable. If they are asked, What then is a relation? they do not profess to be able to tell. It is generally regarded as something peculiarly recondite and mysterious. I cannot, however, perceive in what respect it is more so than any other attribute; indeed, it appears to me to be so in a somewhat less degree. I conceive, rather, that it is by examining into the signification of relative names, or in other words, into the nature of the attribute which they connote, that a clear insight may best be obtained into the nature of all attributes; of all that is meant by an attribute.

It is obvious, in fact, that if we take any two correlative names, ***father*** and ***son***, for instance, although the objects ***de***noted by the names are different, they both, in a certain sense, connote the same thing. They cannot, indeed, be said to connote the same ***attribute***; to be a father, is not the same thing as to be a son. But when we call one man a father, another his son, what we mean to affirm is a set of facts, which are exactly the same in both cases. To predicate of A that he is the father of B, and of B that he is the son of A, is to assert one and the same fact in different words. The two propositions are exactly equivalent: neither of them asserts more or asserts less than the other. The paternity of A and the filiety of B are not two facts, but two modes of expressing the same fact. That fact, when analysed, consists of a series of physical events or phenomena, in which both A and B are parties concerned, and from which they both derive names. What those names really connote, is this series of events: that is the meaning, and the whole meaning, which either of them is intended to convey. The series of events may be said to **constitute** the relation; the schoolmen called it the foundation of the relation, ***fundamentum relationis***.

In this manner any fact, or series of facts, in which two different objects are implicated, and which is therefore predicable of both of them, may be either considered as constituting an attribute of the one, or an attribute of the other. According as we consider it in the former, or in the latter aspect, it is connoted by the one or the other of the two correlative names. **Father** connotes the fact, regarded as constituting an attribute of A: **son** connotes the same fact, as constituting an attribute of B. It may evidently be regarded with equal propriety in either light. And all that appears necessary to account for the existence of relative names, is, that whenever there is a fact in which two individuals are concerned, an attribute grounded on that fact may be ascribed to either of these individuals.

A name, therefore, is said to be relative, when, over and above the object which it denotes, it implies in its signification the existence of another object, also deriving a denomination from the same fact which is the ground of the first name. Or (to express the same meaning in other words) a name is relative, when, being the name of one thing, its signification cannot be explained but by mentioning another. Or we may state it thus--when the name cannot be employed in discourse, so as to have a meaning, unless the name of some other thing than what it is itself the name of, be either expressed or understood. These definitions are all, at bottom, equivalent, being modes of variously expressing this one distinctive circumstance--that every other attribute of an object might, without any contradiction, be conceived still to exist if all objects besides that one were annihilated;(11) but those of its attributes which are expressed by relative names, would on that supposition be swept away.

§ 8. Names have been further distinguished into **univocal** and **aequivocal**: these, however, are not two kinds of names, but two different modes of employing names. A name is univocal, or applied univocally, with respect to all things of which it can be predicated **in the same sense**; but it is aequivocal, or applied aequivocally, as respects those things of which it is predicated in different senses. It is scarcely necessary to give instances of a fact so familiar as the double meaning of a word. In reality, as has been already observed, an aequivocal or ambiguous word is not one name, but two names, accidentally coinciding in sound. *File* standing for an iron instrument, and *file* standing for a line of soldiers, have no more title to be considered one word, because written alike, than **grease** and **Greece** have, because they are pronounced alike. They are one sound, appropriated to form two different words.

An intermediate case is that of a name used ***analogically*** or metaphorically; that is, a name which is predicated of two things, not univocally, or exactly in the same signification, but in significations somewhat similar, and which being derived one from the other, one of them may be considered the primary, and the other a secondary signification. As when we speak of a brilliant light, and a brilliant achievement. The word is not applied in the same sense to the light and to the achievement; but having been applied to the light in its original sense, that of brightness to the eye, it is transferred to the achievement in a derivative signification, supposed to be somewhat like the primitive one. The word, however, is just as properly two names instead of one, in this case, as in that of the most perfect ambiguity. And one of the commonest forms of fallacious reasoning arising from ambiguity, is that of arguing from a metaphorical expression as if it were literal; that is, as if a word, when applied metaphorically, were the same name as when taken in its original sense: which will be seen more particularly in its place.

CHAPTER III. OF THE THINGS DENOTED BY NAMES.

§ 1. Looking back now to the commencement of our inquiry, let us attempt to measure how far it has advanced. Logic, we found, is the Theory of Proof. But proof supposes something provable, which must be a Proposition or Assertion; since nothing but a Proposition can be an object of belief, or therefore of proof. A Proposition is, discourse which affirms or denies something of some other thing. This is one step:

there must, it seems, be two things concerned in every act of belief. But what are these Things? They can be no other than those signified by the two names, which being joined together by a copula constitute the Proposition. If, therefore, we knew what all Names signify, we should know everything which is capable either of being made a subject of affirmation or denial, or of being itself affirmed or denied of a subject. We have accordingly, in the preceding chapter, reviewed the various kinds of Names, in order to ascertain what is signified by each of them. And we have now carried this survey far enough to be able to take an account of its results, and to exhibit an enumeration of all the kinds of Things which are capable of being made predicates, or of having anything predicated of them: after which to determine the import of Predication, that is, of Propositions, can be no arduous task.

The necessity of an enumeration of Existences, as the basis of Logic, did not escape the attention of the schoolmen, and of their master, Aristotle, the most comprehensive, if not the most sagacious, of the ancient philosophers. The Categories, or Predicaments--the former a Greek word, the latter its literal translation in the Latin language--were intended by him and his followers as an enumeration of all things capable of being named; an enumeration by the ***summa genera***, ***i.e.*** the most extensive classes into which things could be distributed; which, therefore, were so many highest Predicates, one or other of which was supposed capable of being affirmed with truth of every nameable thing whatsoever. The following are the classes into which, according to this school of philosophy, Things in general might be reduced:--

Oὐσία, Substantia.
Ποσόν, Quantitas.
Ποιόν, Qualitas.
Πρός τι, Relatio.
Ποιεῖν, Actio.
Πάσχειν, Passio.
Ποῦ, Ubi.
Πότε, Quando.
Κεῖσθαι, Situs.
Εχειν, Habitus.

The imperfections of this classification are too obvious to require, and its merits are not sufficient to reward, a minute examination. It is a mere catalogue of the distinctions rudely marked out by the language of familiar life, with little or no attempt to penetrate, by philosophic analysis, to the **rationale** even of those common distinctions. Such an analysis, however superficially conducted, would have shown the enumeration to be both redundant and defective. Some objects are omitted, and others repeated several times under different heads. It is like a division of animals into men, quadrupeds, horses, asses, and ponies. That, for instance, could not be a very comprehensive view of the nature of Relation which could exclude action, passivity, and local situation from that category. The same observation applies to the categories Quando (or position in time), and Ubi (or position in space); while the distinction between the latter and Situs is merely verbal. The incongruity of erecting into a **summum genus** the class which forms the tenth category is manifest. On the other hand, the enumeration takes no notice of anything besides substances and attributes. In what category are we to place sensations, or any other feelings, and states of mind; as hope, joy, fear; sound, smell, taste; pain, pleasure; thought, judgment, conception, and the like? Probably all these would have been placed by the Aristotelian school in the categories of **actio** and **passio**; and the relation of such of them as are active, to their objects, and of such of them as are passive, to their causes, would rightly be so placed; but the things themselves, the feelings or states of mind, wrongly. Feelings, or states of consciousness, are assuredly to be counted among realities, but they cannot be reckoned either among substances or attributes.

§ 2. Before recommencing, under better auspices, the attempt made with such imperfect success by the great founder of the science of logic, we must take notice of an unfortunate ambiguity in all the concrete names which correspond to the most general of all abstract terms, the word Existence. When we have occasion for a name which shall be capable of denoting whatever exists, as contradistinguished from non-entity or Nothing, there is hardly a word applicable to the purpose which is not also, and even more familiarly, taken in a sense in which it denotes only substances. But substances are not all that exist; attributes, if such things are to be spoken of, must be said to exist; feelings also exist. Yet when we speak of an **object**, or of a **thing**, we are almost always supposed to mean a substance. There seems a kind of contradiction in using such an expression as that one *thing* is merely an attribute of another thing. And the announcement of a Classification of Things would, I believe, prepare most readers for an enumeration like those in natural history, beginning with the great divisions of animal, vegetable, and mineral, and subdividing them into classes and orders. If, rejecting the word Thing, we endeavour to find another of a more general import, or at least more exclusively confined to that general import, a word denoting all that exists, and connoting only simple existence; no word might be presumed fitter for such a purpose than *being*: originally the present participle of a verb which in one of its meanings is exactly equivalent to the verb *exist*; and therefore suitable, even by its grammatical formation, to be the concrete of the abstract *existence*. But this word, strange as the fact may appear, is still more completely spoiled for the purpose which it seemed expressly made for, than the word Thing. *Being* is, by custom, exactly synonymous with substance; except that it is free from a slight taint of a second ambiguity; being applied impartially to matter and to mind, while substance, though originally and in strictness applicable to both, is apt to suggest in preference the idea of matter. Attributes are never called Beings; nor are Feelings. A Being is that which excites feelings, and which possesses attributes. The soul is called a Being; God and angels are called Beings; but if we were to say, extension, colour, wisdom, virtue are beings, we should perhaps be suspected of thinking with some of the ancients, that the cardinal virtues are animals; or, at the least, of holding with the Platonic school the doctrine of self-existent Ideas, or with the followers of Epicurus that of Sensible Forms, which detach themselves in every direction from bodies, and by coming in contact with our organs, cause our perceptions. We should be supposed, in short, to believe that Attributes are Substances.

In consequence of this perversion of the word Being, philosophers looking about for something to supply its place, laid their hands upon the word Entity, a piece of barbarous Latin, invented by the schoolmen to be used as an abstract name, in which class its grammatical form would seem to place it; but being seized by logicians in distress to stop a leak in their terminology, it has ever since been used as a concrete name. The kindred word *essence*, born at the same time and of the same parents, scarcely underwent a more complete transformation when, from being the abstract of the verb *to be*, it came to denote something sufficiently concrete to be enclosed in a glass bottle. The word Entity, since it settled down into a concrete name, has retained its universality of signification somewhat less impaired than any of the names before mentioned. Yet the same gradual decay to which, after a certain age, all the language of psychology seems liable, has been at work even here. If you call virtue an *entity*, you are indeed somewhat less strongly suspected of believing it to be a substance than if you called it a *being*; but you are by no means free from the suspicion. Every word which was originally intended to connote mere existence, seems, after a time, to enlarge its connotation to *separate* existence, or existence freed from the condition of belonging to a substance; which condition being precisely what constitutes an attribute, attributes are gradually shut out; and along with them feelings, which in ninety-nine cases out of a hundred have no other name than that of the attribute which is grounded on them. Strange that when the greatest embarrassment felt by all who have any considerable number of thoughts to express, is to find a sufficient variety of precise words fitted to express them, there should be no practice to which even scientific thinkers are more addicted than that of taking valuable words to express ideas which are sufficiently expressed by other words already appropriated to them.

When it is impossible to obtain good tools, the next best thing is to understand thoroughly the defects of those we have. I have therefore warned the reader of the ambiguity of the very names which, for want of better, I am necessitated to employ. It must now be the writer's endeavour so to employ them as in no case to leave the meaning doubtful or obscure. No one of the above terms being altogether unambiguous, I shall not confine myself to any one, but shall employ on each occasion the word which seems least likely in the particular case to lead to misunderstanding; nor do I pretend to use either these or any other words with a rigorous adherence to one single sense. To do so would often leave us without a word to express what is signified by a known word in some one or other of its senses: unless authors had an unlimited licence to coin new words, together with (what it would be more difficult to assume) unlimited power of making their readers adopt them. Nor would it be wise in a writer, on a subject involving so much of abstraction, to deny himself the advantage derived from even an improper use of a term, when, by means of it, some familiar association is called up which brings the meaning home to the mind, as it were by a flash.

The difficulty both to the writer and reader, of the attempt which must be made to use vague words so as to convey a precise meaning, is not wholly a matter of regret. It is not unfitting that logical treatises should afford an example of that, to facilitate which is among the most important uses of logic. Philosophical language will for a long time, and popular language still longer, retain so much of vagueness and ambiguity, that logic would be of little value if it did not, among its other advantages, exercise the understanding in doing its work neatly and correctly with these imperfect tools.

After this preamble it is time to proceed to our enumeration. We shall commence with Feelings, the simplest class of nameable things; the term Feeling being of course understood in its most enlarged sense.

I. Feelings, or States of Consciousness.

§ 3. A Feeling and a State of Consciousness are, in the language of philosophy, equivalent expressions: everything is a feeling of which the mind is conscious; everything which it *feels*, or, in other words, which forms a part of its own sentient existence. In popular language Feeling is not always synonymous with State of Consciousness; being often taken more peculiarly for those states which are conceived as belonging to the sensitive, or to the emotional, phasis of our nature, and sometimes, with a still narrower restriction, to the emotional alone: as distinguished from what are conceived as belonging to the percipient or to the intellectual phasis. But this is an admitted departure from correctness of language; just as, by a popular perversion the exact converse of this, the word Mind is withdrawn from its rightful generality of signification, and restricted to the intellect. The still greater perversion by which Feeling is sometimes confined not only to bodily sensations, but to the sensations of a single sense, that of touch, needs not be more particularly adverted to.

Feeling, in the proper sense of the term, is a genus, of which Sensation, Emotion, and Thought, are subordinate species. Under the word Thought is here to be included whatever we are internally conscious of when we are said to think; from the consciousness we have when we think of a red colour without having it before our eyes, to the most recondite thoughts of a philosopher or poet. Be it remembered, however, that by a thought is to be understood what passes in the mind itself, and not any object external to the mind, which the person is commonly said to be thinking of. He may be thinking of the sun, or of God, but the sun and God are not thoughts; his mental image, however, of the sun, and his idea of God, are thoughts; states of his mind, not of the objects themselves: and so also is his belief of the existence of the sun, or of God; or his disbelief, if the case be so. Even imaginary objects, (which are said to exist only in our ideas,) are to be distinguished from our ideas of them. I may think of a hobgoblin, as I may think of the loaf which was eaten yesterday, or of the flower which will bloom to-morrow. But the hobgoblin which never existed is not the same thing with my idea of a hobgoblin, any more than the loaf which once existed is the same thing with my idea of a loaf, or the flower which does not yet exist, but which will exist, is the same with my idea of a flower. They are all, not thoughts, but objects of thought; though at the present time all the objects are alike non-existent.

In like manner, a Sensation is to be carefully distinguished from the object which causes the sensation; our sensation of white from a white object; nor is it less to be distinguished from the attribute whiteness, which we ascribe to the object in consequence of its exciting the sensation. Unfortunately for clearness and due discrimination in considering these subjects, our sensations seldom receive separate names. We have a name for the objects which produce in us a certain sensation; the word *white*. We have a name for the quality in those objects, to which we ascribe the sensation; the name *whiteness*. But when we speak of the sensation itself, (as we have not occasion to do this often except in our scientific speculations,) language, which adapts itself for the most part only to the common uses of life, has provided us with no single-worded or immediate designation; we must employ a circumlocution, and say, The sensation of white, or The sensation of whiteness; we must denominate the sensation either from the object, or from the attribute, by which it is excited. Yet the sensation, though it never *does*, might very well be *conceived* to exist, without anything whatever to excite it. We can conceive it as arising spontaneously in the mind. But if it so arose, we should have no name to denote it which would not be a misnomer. In the case of our sensations of hearing we are better provided; we have the word Sound, and a whole vocabulary of words to denote the various kinds of sounds. For as we are often conscious of these sensations in the absence of any *perceptible* object, we can more easily conceive having them in the absence of any object whatever. We need only shut our eyes and listen to music, to have a conception of an universe with nothing in it except sounds, and ourselves hearing them: and what is easily conceived separately, easily obtains a separate name. But in general our names of sensations denote indiscriminately the sensation and the attribute. Thus, **colour** stands for the sensations of white, red, &c., but also for the quality in the coloured object. We talk of the colours of things as among their **properties**.

§ 4. In the case of sensations, another distinction has also to be kept in view, which is often confounded, and never without mischievous consequences. This is, the distinction between the sensation itself, and the state of the bodily organs which precedes the sensation, and which constitutes the physical agency by which it is produced. One of the sources of confusion on this subject is the division commonly made of feelings into Bodily and Mental. Philosophically speaking, there is no foundation at all for this distinction: even sensations are states of the sentient mind, not states of the body, as distinguished from it. What I am conscious of when I see the colour blue, is a feeling of blue colour, which is one thing; the picture on my retina, or the phenomenon of hitherto mysterious nature which takes place in my optic nerve or in my brain, is another thing, of which I am not at all conscious, and which scientific investigation alone could have apprised me of. These are states of my body; but the sensation of blue, which is the consequence of these states of body, is not a state of body: that which perceives and is conscious is called Mind. When sensations are called bodily feelings, it is only as being the class of feelings which are immediately occasioned by bodily states; whereas the other kinds of feelings, thoughts, for instance, or emotions, are immediately excited not by anything acting upon the bodily organs, but by sensations, or by previous thoughts. This, however, is a distinction not in our feelings, but in the agency which produces our feelings: all of them when actually produced are states of mind.

Besides the affection of our bodily organs from without, and the sensation thereby produced in our minds, many writers admit a third link in the chain of phenomena, which they call a Perception, and which consists in the recognition of an external object as the exciting cause of the sensation. This perception, they say, is an **act** of the mind, proceeding from its own spontaneous activity; while in sensation the mind is passive, being merely acted upon by the outward object. And according to some metaphysicians it is by an act of the mind, similar to perception, except in not being preceded by any sensation, that the existence of God, the soul, and other hyperphysical objects is recognised.

These acts of what is termed perception, whatever be the conclusion ultimately come to respecting their nature, must, I conceive, take their place among the varieties of feelings or states of mind. In so classing them, I have not the smallest intention of declaring or insinuating any theory as to the law of mind in which these mental processes may be supposed to originate, or the conditions under which they may be legitimate or the reverse. Far less do I mean (as Dr. Whewell seems to suppose must be meant in an analogous case(12)) to indicate that as they are "*merely* states of mind," it is superfluous to inquire into their distinguishing peculiarities. I abstain from the inquiry as irrelevant to the science of logic. In these so-called perceptions, or direct recognitions by the mind, of objects, whether physical or spiritual, which are external to itself, I can see only cases of belief; but of belief which claims to be intuitive, or independent of external evidence. When a stone lies before me, I am conscious of certain sensations which I receive from it; but when I say that these sensations come to me from an external object which I *perceive*, the meaning of these words is, that receiving the sensations, I intuitively *believe* that an external cause of those sensations exists. The laws of intuitive belief, and the conditions under which it is legitimate, are a subject which, as we have already so often remarked, belongs not to logic, but to the science of the ultimate laws of the human mind.

To the same region of speculation belongs all that can be said respecting the distinction which the German metaphysicians and their French and English followers so elaborately draw between the *acts* of the mind and its merely passive *states*; between what it receives from, and what it gives to, the crude materials of its experience. I am aware that with reference to the view which those writers take of the primary elements of thought and knowledge, this distinction is fundamental. But for the present purpose, which is to examine, not the original groundwork of our knowledge, but how we come by that portion of it which is not original; the difference between active and passive states of mind is of secondary importance. For us, they all are states of mind, they all are feelings; by which, let it be said once more, I mean to imply nothing of passivity, but simply that they are psychological facts, facts which take place in the mind, and are to be carefully distinguished from the external or physical facts with which they may be connected, either as effects or as causes.

§ 5. Among active states of mind, there is however one species which merits particular attention, because it forms a principal part of the connotation of some important classes of names. I mean ***volitions***, or acts of the will. When we speak of sentient beings by relative names, a large portion of the connotation of the name usually consists of the ***actions*** of those beings; actions past, present, and possible or probable future. Take, for instance, the words Sovereign and Subject. What meaning do these words convey, but that of innumerable actions, done or to be done by the sovereign and the subjects, to or in regard to one another reciprocally? So with the words physician and patient, leader and follower, tutor and pupil. In many cases the words also connote actions which would be done under certain contingencies by persons other than those denoted: as the words mortgagor and mortgagee, obligor and obligee, and many other words expressive of legal relation, which connote what a court of justice would do to enforce the legal obligation if not fulfilled. There are also words which connote actions previously done by persons other than those denoted either by the name itself or by its correlative; as the word brother. From these instances, it may be seen how large a portion of the connotation of names consists of actions. Now what is an action? Not one thing, but a series of two things: the state of mind called a volition, followed by an effect. The volition or intention to produce the effect, is one thing; the effect produced in consequence of the intention, is another thing; the two together constitute the action. I form the purpose of instantly moving my arm; that is a state of my mind: my arm (not being tied or paralytic) moves in obedience to my purpose; that is a physical fact, consequent on a state of mind. The intention, followed by the fact, or, (if we prefer the expression,) the fact when preceded and caused by the intention, is called the action of moving my arm.

§ 6. Of the first leading division of nameable things, viz. Feelings or States of Consciousness, we began by recognising three sub-divisions; Sensations, Thoughts, and Emotions. The first two of these we have illustrated at considerable length; the third, Emotions, not being perplexed by similar ambiguities, does not require similar exemplification. And, finally, we have found it necessary to add to these three a fourth species, commonly known by the name Volitions. Without seeking to prejudge the metaphysical question whether any mental state or phenomenon can be found which is not included in one or other of these four species, it appears to me that the amount of illustration bestowed upon these may, so far as we are concerned, suffice for the whole genus. We shall, therefore, proceed to the two remaining classes of nameable things; all things which are external to the mind being considered as belonging either to the class of Substances or to that of Attributes.

II. Substances.

Logicians have endeavoured to define Substance and Attribute; but their definitions are not so much attempts to draw a distinction between the things themselves, as instructions what difference it is customary to make in the grammatical structure of the sentence, according as we are speaking of substances or of attributes. Such definitions are rather lessons of English, or of Greek, Latin, or German, than of mental philosophy. An attribute, say the school logicians, must be the attribute *of* something: colour, for example, must be the colour *of* something; goodness must be the goodness *of* something: and if this something should cease to exist, or should cease to be connected with the attribute, the existence of the attribute would be at an end. A substance, on the contrary, is self-existent; in speaking about it, we need not put *of* after its name. A stone is not the stone *of* anything; the moon is not the moon *of* anything, but simply the moon. Unless, indeed, the name which we choose to give to the substance be a relative name; if so, it must be followed either by *of* or by some other particle, implying, as that preposition does, a reference to something else: but then the other characteristic peculiarity of an attribute would fail; the ***something*** might be destroyed, and the substance might still subsist. Thus, a father must be the father *of* something, and so far resembles an attribute, in being referred to something besides himself: if there were no child, there would be no father: but this, when we look into the matter, only means that we should not call him father. The man called father might still exist though there were no child, as he existed before there was a child: and there would be no contradiction in supposing him to exist, although the whole universe except himself were destroyed. But destroy all white substances, and where would be the attribute whiteness? Whiteness, without any white thing, is a contradiction in terms.

This is the nearest approach to a solution of the difficulty, that will be found in the common treatises on logic. It will scarcely be thought to be a satisfactory one. If an attribute is distinguished from a substance by being the attribute *of* something, it seems highly necessary to understand what is meant by *of*: a particle which needs explanation too much itself to be placed in front of the explanation of anything else. And as for the self-existence of substances, it is very true that a substance may be conceived to exist without any other substance, but so also may an attribute without any other attribute: and we can no more imagine a substance without attributes than we can imagine attributes without a substance.

Metaphysicians, however, have probed the question deeper, and given an account of Substance considerably more satisfactory than this. Substances are usually distinguished as Bodies or Minds. Of each of these, philosophers have at length provided us with a definition which seems unexceptionable.

§ 7. A Body, according to the received doctrine of modern metaphysicians, may be defined the external cause to which we ascribe our sensations. When I see and touch a piece of gold, I am conscious of a sensation of yellow colour, and sensations of hardness and weight; and by varying the mode of handling, I may add to these sensations many others completely distinct from them. The sensations are all of which I am directly conscious; but I consider them as produced by something not only existing independently of my will, but external to my bodily organs and to my mind. This external something I call a body.

It may be asked, how come we to ascribe our sensations to any external cause? And is there sufficient ground for so ascribing them? It is known, that there are metaphysicians who have raised a controversy on the point; maintaining that we are not warranted in referring our sensations to a cause, such as we understand by the word Body, or to any cause whatever, unless, indeed, a First Cause. Though we have no concern here with this controversy, nor with the metaphysical niceties on which it turns, one of the best ways of showing what is meant by Substance is, to consider what position it is necessary to take up, in order to maintain its existence against opponents.

It is certain, then, that a part of our notion of a body consists of the notion of a number of sensations of our own, or of other sentient beings, habitually occurring simultaneously. My conception of the table at which I am writing is compounded of its visible form and size, which are complex sensations of sight; its tangible form and size, which are complex sensations of our organs of touch and of our muscles; its weight, which is also a sensation of touch and of the muscles; its colour, which is a sensation of sight; its hardness, which is a sensation of the muscles; its composition, which is another word for all the varieties of sensation which we receive under various circumstances from the wood of which it is made; and so forth. All or most of these various sensations frequently are, and, as we learn by experience, always might be, experienced simultaneously, or in many different orders of succession, at our own choice: and hence the thought of any one of them makes us think of the others, and the whole becomes mentally amalgamated into one mixed state of consciousness, which, in the language of the school of Locke and Hartley, is termed a Complex Idea.

Now, there are philosophers who have argued as follows. If we take an orange, and conceive it to be divested of its natural colour without acquiring any new one; to lose its softness without becoming hard, its roundness without becoming square or pentagonal, or of any other regular or irregular figure whatever; to be deprived of size, of weight, of taste, of smell; to lose all its mechanical and all its chemical properties, and acquire no new ones; to become, in short, invisible, intangible, imperceptible not only by all our senses, but by the senses of all other sentient beings, real or possible; nothing, say these thinkers, would remain. For of what nature, they ask, could be the residuum? and by what token could it manifest its presence? To the unreflecting its existence seems to rest on the evidence of the senses. But to the senses nothing is apparent except the sensations. We know, indeed, that these sensations are bound together by some law; they do not come together at random, but according to a systematic order, which is part of the order established in the universe. When we experience one of these sensations, we usually experience the others also, or know that we have it in our power to experience them. But a fixed law of connexion, making the sensations occur together, does not, say these philosophers, necessarily require what is called a substratum to support them. The conception of a substratum is but one of many possible forms in which that connexion presents itself to our imagination; a mode of, as it were, realizing the idea. If there be such a substratum, suppose it this instant miraculously annihilated, and let the sensations continue to occur in the same order, and how would the substratum be missed? By what signs should we be able to discover that its existence had terminated? should we not have as much reason to believe that it still existed as we now have? and if we should not then be warranted in believing it, how can we be so now? A body, therefore, according to these metaphysicians, is not anything intrinsically different from the sensations which the body is said to produce in us; it is, in short, a set of sensations joined together according to a fixed law.

The controversies to which these speculations have given rise, and the doctrines which have been developed in the attempt to find a conclusive answer to them, have been fruitful of important consequences to the Science of Mind. The sensations (it was answered) which we are conscious of, and which we receive not at random, but joined together in a certain uniform manner, imply not only a law or laws of connexion, but a cause external to our mind, which cause, by its own laws, determines the laws according to which the sensations are connected and experienced. The schoolmen used to call this external cause by the name we have already employed, a ***substratum***; and its attributes (as they expressed themselves) ***inhered***, literally ***stuck***, in it. To this substratum the name Matter is usually given in philosophical discussions. It was soon, however, acknowledged by all who reflected on the subject, that the existence of matter could not be proved by extrinsic evidence. The answer, therefore, now usually made to Berkeley and his followers, is, that the belief is intuitive; that mankind, in all ages, have felt themselves compelled, by a necessity of their nature, to refer their sensations to an external cause: that even those who deny it in theory, yield to the necessity in practice, and both in speech, thought, and feeling, do, equally with the vulgar, acknowledge their sensations to be the effects of something external to them: this knowledge, therefore, it is affirmed, is as evidently intuitive as our knowledge of our sensations themselves is intuitive. And here the question merges in the fundamental problem of metaphysics properly so called; to which science we leave it.

But although the extreme doctrine of the Idealist metaphysicians, that objects are nothing but our sensations and the laws which connect them, has not been generally adopted by subsequent thinkers; the point of most real importance is one on which those metaphysicians are now very generally considered to have made out their case: viz., that ***all we know*** of objects is the sensations which they give us, and the order of the occurrence of those sensations. Kant himself, on this point, is as explicit as Berkeley or Locke. However firmly convinced that there exists an universe of "Things in themselves," totally distinct from the universe of phenomena, or of things as they appear to our senses; and even when bringing into use a technical expression (***Noumenon***) to denote what the thing is in itself, as contrasted with the ***representation*** of it in our minds; he allows that this representation (the matter of which, he says, consists of our sensations, though the form is given by the laws of the mind itself) is all we know of the object: and that the real nature of the Thing is, and by the constitution of our faculties ever must remain, at least in the present state of existence, an impenetrable mystery to us.(13) There is not the slightest reason for believing that what we call the sensible qualities of the object are a type of anything inherent in itself, or bear any affinity to its own nature. A cause does not, as such, resemble its effects; an east wind is not like the feeling of cold, nor heat like the steam of boiling water: why then should matter resemble our sensations? why should the inmost nature of fire or water resemble the impressions made by these objects upon our senses?(14) And if not on the principle of resemblance, on what other principle can the manner in which objects affect us through our senses afford us any insight into the inherent nature of those objects? It may therefore safely be laid down as a truth both obvious in itself, and admitted by all whom it is at present necessary to take into consideration, that, of the outward world, we know and can know absolutely nothing, except the sensations which we experience from it. Those, however, who still look upon Ontology as a possible science, and think, not only that bodies have an essential constitution of their own, lying deeper than our perceptions, but that this essence or nature is accessible to human investigation, cannot expect to find their refutation here. The question depends on the nature and laws of Intuitive Knowledge, and is not within the province of logic.

§ 8. Body having now been defined the external cause, and (according to the more reasonable opinion) the ***hidden*** external cause, to which we refer our sensations; it remains to frame a definition of Mind. Nor, after the preceding observations, will this be difficult. For, as our conception of a body is that of an unknown exciting cause of sensations, so our conception of a mind is that of an unknown recipient, or percipient, of them; and not of them alone, but of all our other feelings. As body is the mysterious something which excites the mind to feel, so mind is the mysterious something which feels, and thinks. It is unnecessary to give in the case of mind, as we gave in the case of matter, a particular statement of the sceptical system by which its existence as a Thing in itself, distinct from the series of what are denominated its states, is called in question. But it is necessary to remark, that on the inmost nature of the thinking principle, as well as on the inmost nature of matter, we are, and with our faculties must always remain, entirely in the dark. All which we are aware of, even in our own minds, is (in the words of Mr. Mill) a certain "thread of consciousness;" a series of feelings, that is, of sensations, thoughts, emotions, and volitions, more or less numerous and complicated. There is a something I call Myself, or, by another form of expression, my mind, which I consider as distinct from these sensations, thoughts, &c.; a something which I conceive to be not the thoughts, but the being that has the thoughts, and which I can conceive as existing for ever in a state of quiescence, without any thoughts at all. But what this being is, although it is myself, I have no knowledge, other than the series of its states of consciousness. As bodies manifest themselves to me only through the sensations of which I regard them as the causes, so the thinking principle, or mind, in my own nature, makes itself known to me only by the feelings of which it is conscious. I know nothing about myself, save my capacities of feeling or being conscious (including, of course, thinking and willing): and were I to learn anything new concerning my own nature, I cannot with my present faculties conceive this new information to be anything else, than that I have some additional capacities, as yet unknown to me, of feeling, thinking, or willing.

Thus, then, as body is the unsentient cause to which we are naturally prompted to refer a certain portion of our feelings, so mind may be described as the sentient **subject** (in the German sense of the term) of all feelings; that which has or feels them. But of the nature of either body or mind, further than the feelings which the former excites, and which the latter experiences, we do not, according to the best existing doctrine, know anything; and if anything, logic has nothing to do with it, or with the manner in which the knowledge is acquired. With this result we may conclude this portion of our subject, and pass to the third and only remaining class or division of Nameable Things.

III. Attributes: and, first, Qualities.

§ 9. From what has already been said of Substance, what is to be said of Attribute is easily deducible. For if we know not, and cannot know, anything of bodies but the sensations which they excite in us or others, those sensations must be all that we can, at bottom, mean by their attributes; and the distinction which we verbally make between the properties of things and the sensations we receive from them, must originate in the convenience of discourse rather than in the nature of what is denoted by the terms.

Attributes are usually distributed under the three heads of Quality, Quantity, and Relation. We shall come to the two latter presently: in the first place we shall confine ourselves to the former.

Let us take, then, as our example, one of what are termed the sensible qualities of objects, and let that example be whiteness. When we ascribe whiteness to any substance, as, for instance, snow; when we say that snow has the quality whiteness, what do we really assert? Simply, that when snow is present to our organs, we have a particular sensation, which we are accustomed to call the sensation of white. But how do I know that snow is present? Obviously by the sensations which I derive from it, and not otherwise. I infer that the object is present, because it gives me a certain assemblage or series of sensations. And when I ascribe to it the attribute whiteness, my meaning is only, that, of the sensations composing this group or series, that which I call the sensation of white colour is one.

This is one view which may be taken of the subject. But there is also another, and a different view. It may be said, that it is true we *know* nothing of sensible objects, except the sensations they excite in us; that the fact of our receiving from snow the particular sensation which is called a sensation of white, is the *ground* on which we ascribe to that substance the quality whiteness; the sole proof of its possessing that quality. But because one thing may be the sole evidence of the existence of another thing, it does not follow that the two are one and the same. The attribute whiteness (it may be said) is not the fact of our receiving the sensation, but something in the object itself; a *power* inherent in it; something *in virtue* of which the object produces the sensation. And when we affirm that snow possesses the attribute whiteness, we do not merely assert that the presence of snow produces in us that sensation, but that it does so through, and by reason of, that power or quality.

For the purposes of logic it is not of material importance which of these opinions we adopt. The full discussion of the subject belongs to the other department of scientific inquiry, so often alluded to under the name of metaphysics; but it may be said here, that for the doctrine of the existence of a peculiar species of entities called qualities, I can see no foundation except in a tendency of the human mind which is the cause of many delusions. I mean, the disposition, wherever we meet with two names which are not precisely synonymous, to suppose that they must be the names of two different things; whereas in reality they may be names of the same thing viewed in two different lights, which is as much as to say under different suppositions as to surrounding circumstances. Because *quality* and *sensation* cannot be put indiscriminately one for the other, it is supposed that they cannot both signify the same thing, namely, the impression or feeling with which we are affected through our senses by the presence of an object; although there is at least no absurdity in supposing that this identical impression or feeling may be called a sensation when considered merely in itself, and a quality when regarded as emanating from any one of the numerous objects, the presence of which to our organs excites in our minds that among various other sensations or feelings. And if this be admissible as a supposition, it rests with those who contend for an entity *per se* called a quality, to show that their opinion is preferable, or is anything in fact but a lingering remnant of the scholastic doctrine of occult causes; the very absurdity which Moliere so happily ridiculed when he made one of his pedantic physicians account for the fact that "l'opium endormit," by the maxim "parcequ'il a une vertu soporifique."

It is evident that when the physician stated that opium had "une vertu soporifique," he did not account for, but merely asserted over again, the fact that it *endormit*. In like manner, when we say that snow is white because it has the quality of whiteness, we are only re-asserting in more technical language the fact that it excites in us the sensation of white. If it be said that the sensation must have some cause, I answer, its cause is the presence of the assemblage of phenomena which is termed the object. When we have asserted that as often as the object is present, and our organs in their normal state, the sensation takes place, we have stated all that we know about the matter. There is no need, after assigning a certain and intelligible cause, to suppose an occult cause besides, for the purpose of enabling the real cause to produce its effect. If I am asked, why does the presence of the object cause this sensation in me, I cannot tell: I can only say that such is my nature, and the nature of the object; that the fact forms a part of the constitution of things. And to this we must at last come, even after interpolating the imaginary entity. Whatever number of links the chain of causes and effects may consist of, how any one link produces the one which is next to it remains equally inexplicable to us. It is as easy to comprehend that the object should produce the sensation directly and at once, as that it should produce the same sensation by the aid of something else called the *power* of producing it.

But as the difficulties which may be felt in adopting this view of the subject cannot be removed without discussions transcending the bounds of our science, I content myself with a passing indication, and shall, for the purposes of logic, adopt a language compatible with either view of the nature of qualities. I shall say,--what at least admits of no dispute,--that the quality of whiteness ascribed to the object snow, is **grounded** on its exciting in us the sensation of white; and adopting the language already used by the school logicians in the case of the kind of attributes called Relations, I shall term the sensation of white the **foundation** of the quality whiteness. For logical purposes the sensation is the only essential part of what is meant by the word; the only part which we ever can be concerned in proving. When that is proved, the quality is proved; if an object excites a sensation it has, of course, the power of exciting it.

IV. Relations.

§ 10. The **qualities** of a body, we have said, are the attributes grounded on the sensations which the presence of that particular body to our organs excites in our minds. But when we ascribe to any object the kind of attribute called a Relation, the foundation of the attribute must be something in which other objects are concerned besides itself and the percipient.

As there may with propriety be said to be a relation between any two things to which two correlative names are or may be given; we may expect to discover what constitutes a relation in general, if we enumerate the principal cases in which mankind have imposed correlative names, and observe what these cases have in common.

What, then, is the character which is possessed in common by states of circumstances so heterogeneous and discordant as these: one thing *like* another; one thing *unlike* another; one thing *near* another; one thing *far from* another; one thing *before*, *after*, *along with* another; one thing *greater*, *equal*, *less*, than another; one thing the *cause* of another, the *effect* of another; one person the *master*, *servant*, *child*, *parent*, *debtor*, *creditor*, *sovereign*, *subject*, *attorney*, *client*, of another, and so on?

Omitting, for the present, the case of Resemblance, (a relation which requires to be considered separately,) there seems to be one thing common to all these cases, and only one; that in each of them there exists or occurs, or has existed or occurred, or may be expected to exist or occur, some *fact* or phenomenon, into which the two things which are said to be related to each other, both enter as parties concerned. This fact, or phenomenon, is what the Aristotelian logicians called the *fundamentum relationis*. Thus in the relation of greater and less between two magnitudes, the *fundamentum relationis* is the fact that one of the two magnitudes could, under certain conditions, be included in, without entirely filling, the space occupied by the other magnitude. In the relation of master and servant, the *fundamentum relationis* is the fact that the one has undertaken, or is compelled, to perform certain services for the benefit, and at the bidding of the other. Examples might be indefinitely multiplied; but it is already obvious that whenever two things are said to be related, there is some fact, or series of facts, into which they both enter; and that whenever any two things are involved in some one fact, or series of facts, we may ascribe to those two things a mutual relation grounded on the fact. Even if they have nothing in common but what is common to all things, that they are members of the universe, we call that a relation, and denominate them fellow-creatures, fellow-beings, or fellow-denizens of the universe. But in proportion as the fact into which the two objects enter as parts is of a more special and peculiar, or of a more complicated nature, so also is the relation grounded upon it. And there are as many conceivable relations as there are conceivable kinds of fact in which two things can be jointly concerned.

In the same manner, therefore, as a quality is an attribute grounded on the fact that a certain sensation or sensations are produced in us by the object, so an attribute grounded on some fact into which the object enters jointly with another object, is a relation between it and that other object. But the fact in the latter case consists of the very same kind of elements as the fact in the former: namely, states of consciousness. In the case, for example, of any legal relation, as debtor and creditor, principal and agent, guardian and ward, the *fundamentum relationis* consists entirely of thoughts, feelings, and volitions (actual or contingent), either of the persons themselves or of other persons concerned in the same series of transactions; as, for instance, the intentions which would be formed by a judge in case a complaint were made to his tribunal of the infringement of any of the legal obligations imposed by the relation; and the acts which the judge would perform in consequence; acts being (as we have already seen) another word for intentions followed by an effect, and that effect being but another word for sensations, or some other feelings, occasioned either to oneself or to somebody else. There is no part of what the names expressive of the relation imply, that is not resolvable into states of consciousness; outward objects being, no doubt, supposed throughout as the causes by which some of those states of consciousness are excited, and minds as the subjects by which all of them are experienced, but neither the external objects nor the minds making their existence known otherwise than by the states of consciousness.

Cases of relation are not always so complicated as those to which we last alluded. The simplest of all cases of relation are those expressed by the words antecedent and consequent, and by the word simultaneous. If we say, for instance, that dawn preceded sunrise, the fact in which the two things, dawn and sunrise, were jointly concerned, consisted only of the two things themselves; no third thing entered into the fact or phenomenon at all; unless, indeed, we choose to call the succession of the two objects a third thing; but their succession is not something added to the things themselves; it is something involved in them. Dawn and sunrise announce themselves to our consciousness by two successive sensations; our consciousness of the succession of these sensations is not a third sensation or feeling added to them; we have not first the two feelings, and then a feeling of their succession. To have two feelings at all, implies having them either successively, or else simultaneously. Sensations, or other feelings, being given, succession and simultaneousness are the two conditions, to the alternative of which they are subjected by the nature of our faculties; and no one has been able, or needs expect, to analyse the matter any farther.

§ 11. In a somewhat similar position are two other sorts of relation, Likeness and Unlikeness. I have two sensations; we will suppose them to be simple ones; two sensations of white, or one sensation of white and another of black. I call the first two sensations *like*; the last two *unlike*. What is the fact or phenomenon constituting the *fundamentum* of this relation? The two sensations first, and then what we call a feeling of resemblance, or of want of resemblance. Let us confine ourselves to the former case. Resemblance is evidently a feeling; a state of the consciousness of the observer. Whether the feeling of the resemblance of the two colours be a third state of consciousness, which I have **after** having the two sensations of colour, or whether (like the feeling of their succession) it is involved in the sensations themselves, may be a matter of discussion. But in either case, these feelings of resemblance, and of its opposite, dissimilarity, are parts of our nature; and parts so far from being capable of analysis, that they are presupposed in every attempt to analyse any of our other feelings. Likeness and unlikeness, therefore, as well as antecedence, sequence, and simultaneousness, must stand apart among relations, as things **sui generis**. They are attributes grounded on facts, that is, on states of consciousness, but on states which are peculiar, unresolvable, and inexplicable.

But, although likeness or unlikeness cannot be resolved into anything else, complex cases of likeness or unlikeness can be resolved into simpler ones. When we say of two things which consist of parts, that they are like one another, the likeness of the wholes does admit of analysis; it is compounded of likenesses between the various parts respectively. Of how vast a variety of resemblances of parts must that resemblance be composed, which induces us to say that a portrait, or a landscape, is like its original. If one person mimics another with any success, of how many simple likenesses must the general or complex likeness be compounded: likeness in a succession of bodily postures; likeness in voice, or in the accents and intonations of the voice; likeness in the choice of words, and in the thoughts or sentiments expressed, whether by word, countenance, or gesture.

All likeness and unlikeness of which we have any cognizance, resolve themselves into likeness and unlikeness between states of our own, or some other, mind. When we say that one body is like another, (since we know nothing of bodies but the sensations which they excite,) we mean really that there is a resemblance between the sensations excited by the two bodies, or between some portion at least of these sensations. If we say that two attributes are like one another, (since we know nothing of attributes except the sensations or states of feeling on which they are grounded,) we mean really that those sensations, or states of feeling, resemble each other. We may also say that two relations are alike. The fact of resemblance between relations is sometimes called **analogy**, forming one of the numerous meanings of that word. The relation in which Priam stood to Hector, namely, that of father and son, resembles the relation in which Philip stood to Alexander; resembles it so closely that they are called the same relation. The relation in which Cromwell stood to England resembles the relation in which Napoleon stood to France, though not so closely as to be called the same relation. The meaning in both these instances must be, that a resemblance existed between the facts which constituted the *fundamentum relationis*.

This resemblance may exist in all conceivable gradations, from perfect undistinguishableness to something extremely slight. When we say, that a thought suggested to the mind of a person of genius is like a seed cast into the ground, because the former produces a multitude of other thoughts, and the latter a multitude of other seeds, this is saying that between the relation of an inventive mind to a thought contained in it, and the relation of a fertile soil to a seed contained in it, there exists a resemblance: the real resemblance being in the two *fundamenta relationis*, in each of which there occurs a germ, producing by its development a multitude of other things similar to itself. And as, whenever two objects are jointly concerned in a phenomenon, this constitutes a relation between those objects, so, if we suppose a second pair of objects concerned in a second phenomenon, the slightest resemblance between the two phenomena is sufficient to admit of its being said that the two relations resemble; provided, of course, the points of resemblance are found in those portions of the two phenomena respectively which are connoted by the relative names.

While speaking of resemblance, it is necessary to take notice of an ambiguity of language, against which scarcely any one is sufficiently on his guard. Resemblance, when it exists in the highest degree of all, amounting to undistinguishableness, is often called identity, and the two similar things are said to be the same. I say often, not always; for we do not say that two visible objects, two persons for instance, are the same, because they are so much alike that one might be mistaken for the other: but we constantly use this mode of expression when speaking of feelings; as when I say that the sight of any object gives me the *same* sensation or emotion to-day that it did yesterday, or the *same* which it gives to some other person. This is evidently an incorrect application of the word *same*; for the feeling which I had yesterday is gone, never to return; what I have to-day is another feeling, exactly like the former perhaps, but distinct from it; and it is evident that two different persons cannot be experiencing the same feeling, in the sense in which we say that they are both sitting at the same table. By a similar ambiguity we say, that two persons are ill of the *same* disease; that two persons hold the *same* office; not in the sense in which we say that they are engaged in the same adventure, or sailing in the same ship, but in the sense that they fill offices exactly similar, though, perhaps, in distant places. Great confusion of ideas is often produced, and many fallacies engendered, in otherwise enlightened understandings, by not being sufficiently alive to the fact (in itself not always to be avoided,) that they use the same name to express ideas so different as those of identity and undistinguishable resemblance. Among modern writers, Archbishop Whately stands almost alone in having drawn attention to this distinction, and to the ambiguity connected with it.

Several relations, generally called by other names, are really cases of resemblance. As, for example, equality; which is but another word for the exact resemblance commonly called identity, considered as subsisting between things in respect of their *quantity*. And this example forms a suitable transition to the third and last of the three heads, under which, as already remarked, Attributes are commonly arranged.

V. Quantity.

§ 12. Let us imagine two things, between which there is no difference (that is, no dissimilarity), except in quantity alone: for instance, a gallon of water, and more than a gallon of water. A gallon of water, like any other external object, makes its presence known to us by a set of sensations which it excites. Ten gallons of water are also an external object, making its presence known to us in a similar manner; and as we do not mistake ten gallons of water for a gallon of water, it is plain that the set of sensations is more or less different in the two cases. In like manner, a gallon of water, and a gallon of wine, are two external objects, making their presence known by two sets of sensations, which sensations are different from each other. In the first case, however, we say that the difference is in quantity; in the last there is a difference in quality, while the quantity of the water and of the wine is the same. What is the real distinction between the two cases? It is not the province of Logic to analyse it; nor to decide whether it is susceptible of analysis or not. For us the following considerations are sufficient. It is evident that the sensations I receive from the gallon of water, and those I receive from the gallon of wine, are not the same, that is, not precisely alike; neither are they altogether unlike: they are partly similar, partly dissimilar; and that in which they resemble is precisely that in which alone the gallon of water and the ten gallons do not resemble. That in which the gallon of water and the gallon of wine are like each other, and in which the gallon and the ten gallons of water are unlike each other, is called their quantity. This likeness and unlikeness I do not pretend to explain, no more than any other kind of likeness or unlikeness. But my object is to show, that when we say of two things that they differ in quantity, just as when we say that they differ in quality, the assertion is always grounded on a difference in the sensations which they excite. Nobody, I presume, will say, that to see, or to lift, or to drink, ten gallons of water, does not include in itself a different set of sensations from those of seeing, lifting, or drinking one gallon; or that to see or handle a foot rule, and to see or handle a yard-measure made exactly like it, are the same sensations. I do not undertake to say what the difference in the sensations is. Everybody knows, and nobody can tell; no more than any one could tell what white is, to a person who had never had the sensation. But the difference, so far as cognizable by our faculties, lies in the sensations. Whatever difference we say there is in the things themselves, is, in this as in all other cases, grounded, and grounded exclusively, on a difference in the sensations excited by them.

VI. Attributes Concluded.

§ 13. Thus, then, all the attributes of bodies which are classed under Quality or Quantity, are grounded on the sensations which we receive from those bodies, and may be defined, the powers which the bodies have of exciting those sensations. And the same general explanation has been found to apply to most of the attributes usually classed under the head of Relation. They, too, are grounded on some fact or phenomenon into which the related objects enter as parts; that fact or phenomenon having no meaning and no existence to us, except the series of sensations or other states of consciousness by which it makes itself known: and the relation being simply the power or capacity which the object possesses, of taking part along with the correlated object in the production of that series of sensations or states of consciousness. We have been obliged, indeed, to recognise a somewhat different character in certain peculiar relations, those of succession and simultaneity, of likeness and unlikeness. These, not being grounded on any fact or phenomenon distinct from the related objects themselves, do not admit of the same kind of analysis. But these relations, though not, like other relations, grounded on states of consciousness, are themselves states of consciousness: resemblance is nothing but our feeling of resemblance; succession is nothing but our feeling of succession. Or, if this be disputed, (and we cannot, without transgressing the bounds of our science, discuss it here,) at least our knowledge of these relations, and even our possibility of knowledge, is confined to those which subsist between sensations, or other states of consciousness; for, though we ascribe resemblance, or succession, or simultaneity, to objects and to attributes, it is always in virtue of resemblance or succession or simultaneity in the sensations or states of consciousness which those objects excite, and on which those attributes are grounded.

§ 14. In the preceding investigation we have, for the sake of simplicity, considered bodies only, and omitted minds. But what we have said, is applicable, ***mutatis mutandis***, to the latter. The attributes of minds, as well as those of bodies, are grounded on states of feeling or consciousness. But in the case of a mind, we have to consider its own states, as well as those which it produces in other minds. Every attribute of a mind consists either in being itself affected in a certain way, or affecting other minds in a certain way. Considered in itself, we can predicate nothing of it but the series of its own feelings. When we say of any mind, that it is devout, or superstitious, or meditative, or cheerful, we mean that the ideas, emotions, or volitions implied in those words, form a frequently recurring part of the series of feelings, or states of consciousness, which fill up the sentient existence of that mind.

In addition, however, to those attributes of a mind which are grounded on its own states of feeling, attributes may also be ascribed to it, in the same manner as to a body, grounded on the feelings which it excites in other minds. A mind does not, indeed, like a body, excite sensations, but it may excite thoughts or emotions. The most important example of attributes ascribed on this ground, is the employment of terms expressive of approbation or blame. When, for example, we say of any character, or (in other words) of any mind, that it is admirable, we mean that the contemplation of it excites the sentiment of admiration; and indeed somewhat more, for the word implies that we not only feel admiration, but approve that sentiment in ourselves. In some cases, under the semblance of a single attribute, two are really predicated: one of them, a state of the mind itself; the other, a state with which other minds are affected by thinking of it. As when we say of any one that he is generous. The word generosity expresses a certain state of mind, but being a term of praise, it also expresses that this state of mind excites in us another mental state, called approbation. The assertion made, therefore, is twofold, and of the following purport: Certain feelings form habitually a part of this person's sentient existence; and the idea of those feelings of his, excites the sentiment of approbation in ourselves or others.

As we thus ascribe attributes to minds on the ground of ideas and emotions, so may we to bodies on similar grounds, and not solely on the ground of sensations: as in speaking of the beauty of a statue; since this attribute is grounded on the peculiar feeling of pleasure which the statue produces in our minds; which is not a sensation, but an emotion.

VII. General Results.

§ 15. Our survey of the varieties of Things which have been, or which are capable of being, named--which have been, or are capable of being, either predicated of other Things, or made themselves the subject of predications--is now concluded.

Our enumeration commenced with Feelings. These we scrupulously distinguished from the objects which excite them, and from the organs by which they are, or may be supposed to be, conveyed. Feelings are of four sorts: Sensations, Thoughts, Emotions, and Volitions. What are called perceptions are merely a particular case of Belief, and belief is a kind of thought. Actions are merely volitions followed by an effect. If there be any other kind of mental state not included under these subdivisions, we did not think it necessary or proper in this place to discuss its existence, or the rank which ought to be assigned to it.

After Feelings we proceeded to Substances. These are either Bodies or Minds. Without entering into the grounds of the metaphysical doubts which have been raised concerning the existence of Matter and Mind as objective realities, we stated as sufficient for us the conclusion in which the best thinkers are now very generally agreed, that all we can know of Matter is the sensations which it gives us, and the order of occurrence of those sensations; and that while the substance Body is the unknown cause of our sensations, the substance Mind is the unknown recipient.

The only remaining class of Nameable Things is Attributes; and these are of three kinds, Quality, Relation, and Quantity. Qualities, like substances, are known to us no otherwise than by the sensations or other states of consciousness which they excite: and while, in compliance with common usage, we have continued to speak of them as a distinct class of Things, we showed that in predicating them no one means to predicate anything but those sensations or states of consciousness, on which they may be said to be grounded, and by which alone they can be defined or described. Relations, except the simple cases of likeness and unlikeness, succession and simultaneity, are similarly grounded on some fact or phenomenon, that is, on some series of sensations or states of consciousness, more or less complicated. The third species of attribute, Quantity, is also manifestly grounded on something in our sensations or states of feeling, since there is an indubitable difference in the sensations excited by a larger and a smaller bulk, or by a greater or a less degree of intensity, in any object of sense or of consciousness. All attributes, therefore, are to us nothing but either our sensations and other states of feeling, or something inextricably involved therein; and to this even the peculiar and simple relations just adverted to are not exceptions. Those peculiar relations, however, are so important, and, even if they might in strictness be classed among states of consciousness, are so fundamentally distinct from any other of those states, that it would be a vain subtlety to confound them under that common head, and it is necessary that they should be classed apart.

As the result, therefore, of our analysis, we obtain the following as an enumeration and classification of all Nameable Things:--

1st. Feelings, or States of Consciousness.

2nd. The Minds which experience those feelings.

3rd. The Bodies, or external objects, which excite certain of those feelings, together with the powers or properties whereby they excite them; these being included rather in compliance with common opinion, and because their existence is taken for granted in the common language from which I cannot prudently deviate, than because the recognition of such powers or properties as real existences appears to me warranted by a sound philosophy.

4th, and last. The Successions and Co-existences, the Likenesses and Unlikenesses, between feelings or states of consciousness. Those relations, when considered as subsisting between other things, exist in reality only between the states of consciousness which those things, if bodies, excite, if minds, either excite or experience.

This, until a better can be suggested, may serve as a substitute for the abortive

Classification of Existences, termed the Categories of Aristotle. The practical application of it will appear when we commence the inquiry into the Import of Propositions; in other words, when we inquire what it is which the mind actually believes, when it gives what is called its assent to a proposition.

These four classes comprising, if the classification be correct, all Nameable Things, these or some of them must of course compose the signification of all names; and of these, or some of them, is made up whatever we call a fact.

For distinction's sake, every fact which is solely composed of feelings or states of consciousness considered as such, is often called a Psychological or Subjective fact; while every fact which is composed, either wholly or in part, of something different from these, that is, of substances and attributes, is called an Objective fact. We may say, then, that every objective fact is grounded on a corresponding subjective one; and has no meaning to us, (apart from the subjective fact which corresponds to it,) except as a name for the unknown and inscrutable process by which that subjective or psychological fact is brought to pass.

CHAPTER IV. OF PROPOSITIONS.

§ 1. In treating of Propositions, as already in treating of Names, some considerations of a comparatively elementary nature respecting their form and varieties must be premised, before entering upon that analysis of the import conveyed by them, which is the real subject and purpose of this preliminary book.

A proposition, we have before said, is a portion of discourse in which a predicate is affirmed or denied of a subject. A predicate and a subject are all that is necessarily required to make up a proposition: but as we cannot conclude from merely seeing two names put together, that they are a predicate and a subject, that is, that one of them is intended to be affirmed or denied of the other, it is necessary that there should be some mode or form of indicating that such is the intention; some sign to distinguish a predication from any other kind of discourse. This is sometimes done by a slight alteration of one of the words, called an *inflection*; as when we say, Fire burns; the change of the second word from *burn* to *burns* showing that we mean to affirm the predicate burn of the subject fire. But this function is more commonly fulfilled by the word *is*, when an affirmation is intended, *is not*, when a negation; or by some other part of the verb *to be*. The word which thus serves the purpose of a sign of predication is called, as we formerly observed, the *copula*. It is important that there should be no indistinctness in our conception of the nature and office of the copula; for confused notions respecting it are among the causes which have spread mysticism over the field of logic, and perverted its speculations into logomachies.

It is apt to be supposed that the copula is something more than a mere sign of predication; that it also signifies *existence*. In the proposition, Socrates is just, it may seem to be implied not only that the quality *just* can be affirmed of Socrates, but moreover that Socrates *is*, that is to say, exists. This, however, only shows that there is an ambiguity in the word *is*; a word which not only performs the function of the copula in affirmations, but has also a meaning of its own, in virtue of which it may itself be made the predicate of a proposition. That the employment of it as a copula does not necessarily include the affirmation of existence, appears from such a proposition as this, A centaur is a fiction of the poets; where it cannot possibly be implied that a centaur exists, since the proposition itself expressly asserts that the thing has no real existence.

Many volumes might be filled with the frivolous speculations concerning the nature of Being, (το ὄν, οὐσία, Ens, Entitas, Essentia, and the like,) which have arisen from overlooking this double meaning of the words *to be*; from supposing that when it signifies *to exist*, and when it signifies to *be* some specified thing, as to *be* a man, to *be* Socrates, to *be* seen or spoken of, to *be* a phantom, even to *be* a non-entity, it must still, at bottom, answer to the same idea; and that a meaning must be found for it which shall suit all these cases. The fog which rose from this narrow spot diffused itself at an early period over the whole surface of metaphysics. Yet it becomes us not to triumph over the great intellects of Plato and Aristotle because we are now able to preserve ourselves from many errors into which they, perhaps inevitably, fell. The fire-teazer of a modern steam-engine produces by his exertions far greater effects than Milo of Crotona could, but he is not therefore a stronger man. The Greeks seldom knew any language but their own. This rendered it far more difficult for them than it is for us, to acquire a readiness in detecting ambiguities. One of the advantages of having accurately studied a plurality of languages, especially of those languages which eminent thinkers have used as the vehicle of their thoughts, is the practical lesson we learn respecting the ambiguities of words, by finding that the same word in one language corresponds, on different occasions, to different words in another. When not thus exercised, even the strongest understandings find it difficult to believe that things which have a common name, have not in some respect or other a common nature; and often expend much labour not only unprofitably but mischievously, (as was frequently done by the two philosophers just mentioned,) on vain attempts to discover in what this common nature consists. But, the habit once formed, intellects much inferior are capable of detecting even ambiguities which are common to many languages: and it is surprising that the one now under consideration, though it exists in the modern languages as well as in the ancient, should have been overlooked by almost all authors. The quantity of futile speculation which had been caused by a misapprehension of the nature of the copula, was hinted at by Hobbes; but Mr. Mill(15) was, I believe, the first who distinctly characterized the ambiguity, and pointed out how many errors in the received systems of philosophy it has had to answer for. It has indeed misled the moderns scarcely less than the ancients, though their mistakes, because our understandings are not yet so completely emancipated from their influence, do not appear equally irrational.

We shall now briefly review the principal distinctions which exist among propositions, and the technical terms most commonly in use to express those distinctions.

§ 2. A proposition being a portion of discourse in which something is affirmed or denied of something, the first division of propositions is into affirmative and negative. An affirmative proposition is that in which the predicate is *affirmed* of the subject; as, Caesar is dead. A negative proposition is that in which the predicate is *denied* of the subject; as, Caesar is not dead. The copula, in this last species of proposition, consists of the words *is not*, which are the sign of negation; *is* being the sign of affirmation.

Some logicians, among whom may be mentioned Hobbes, state this distinction differently; they recognise only one form of copula, *is*, and attach the negative sign to the predicate. "Caesar is dead," and "Caesar is not dead," according to these writers, are propositions agreeing not in the subject and predicate, but in the subject only. They do not consider "dead," but "not dead," to be the predicate of the second proposition, and they accordingly define a negative proposition to be one in which the predicate is a negative name. The point, though not of much practical moment, deserves notice as an example (not unfrequent in logic) where by means of an apparent simplification, but which is merely verbal, matters are made more complex than before. The notion of these writers was, that they could get rid of the distinction between affirming and denying, by treating every case of denying as the affirming of a negative name. But what is meant by a negative name? A name expressive of the ***absence*** of an attribute. So that when we affirm a negative name, what we are really predicating is absence and not presence; we are asserting not that anything ***is***, but that something is ***not***; to express which operation no word seems so proper as the word denying. The fundamental distinction is between a fact and the non-existence of that fact; between seeing something and not seeing it, between Caesar's being dead and his not being dead; and if this were a merely verbal distinction, the generalization which brings both within the same form of assertion would be a real simplification: the distinction, however, being real, and in the facts, it is the generalization confounding the distinction that is merely verbal; and tends to obscure the subject, by treating the difference between two kinds of truth as if it were only a difference between two kinds of words. To put things together, and to put them or keep them asunder, will remain different operations, whatever tricks we may play with language.

A remark of a similar nature may be applied to most of those distinctions among propositions which are said to have reference to their ***modality***; as, difference of tense or time; the sun ***did*** rise, the sun ***is*** rising, the sun ***will*** rise. These differences, like that between affirmation and negation, might be glossed over by considering the incident of time as a mere modification of the predicate: thus, The sun is ***an object having risen***, The sun is ***an object now rising***, The sun is ***an object to rise hereafter***. But the simplification would be merely verbal. Past, present, and future, do not constitute so many different kinds of rising; they are the designations belonging to the event asserted, to the ***sun's*** rising to-day. They affect, not the predicate, but the applicability of the predicate to the particular subject. That which we affirm to be past, present, or future, is not what the subject signifies, nor what the predicate signifies, but specifically and expressly what the predication signifies;

what is expressed only by the proposition as such, and not by either or both of the terms. Therefore the circumstance of time is properly considered as attaching to the copula, which is the sign of predication, and not to the predicate. If the same cannot be said of such modifications as these, Caesar *may* be dead; Caesar is *perhaps* dead; it is *possible* that Caesar is dead; it is only because these fall altogether under another head, being properly assertions not of anything relating to the fact itself, but of the state of our own mind in regard to it; namely, our absence of disbelief of it. Thus "Caesar may be dead" means "I am not sure that Caesar is alive."

§ 3. The next division of propositions is into Simple and Complex. A simple proposition is that in which one predicate is affirmed or denied of one subject. A complex proposition is that in which there is more than one predicate, or more than one subject, or both.

At first sight this division has the air of an absurdity; a solemn distinction of things into one and more than one; as if we were to divide horses into single horses and teams of horses. And it is true that what is called a complex proposition is often not a proposition at all, but several propositions, held together by a conjunction. Such, for example, is this: Caesar is dead, and Brutus is alive: or even this, Caesar is dead, *but* Brutus is alive. There are here two distinct assertions; and we might as well call a street a complex house, as these two propositions a complex proposition. It is true that the syncategorematic words *and* and *but* have a meaning; but that meaning is so far from making the two propositions one, that it adds a third proposition to them. All particles are abbreviations, and generally abbreviations of propositions; a kind of short-hand, whereby that which, to be expressed fully, would have required a proposition or a series of propositions, is suggested to the mind at once. Thus the words, Caesar is dead and Brutus is alive, are equivalent to these: Caesar is dead; Brutus is alive; it is desired that the two preceding propositions should be thought of together. If the words were, Caesar is dead *but* Brutus is alive, the sense would be equivalent to the same three propositions together with a fourth; "between the two preceding propositions there exists a contrast:" viz., either between the two facts themselves, or between the feelings with which it is desired that they should be regarded.

In the instances cited, the two propositions are kept visibly distinct, each subject having its separate predicate, and each predicate its separate subject. For brevity, however, and to avoid repetition, the propositions are often blended together: as in this, "Peter and James preached at Jerusalem and in Galilee," which contains four propositions: Peter preached at Jerusalem, Peter preached in Galilee, James preached at Jerusalem, James preached in Galilee.

We have seen that when the two or more propositions comprised in what is called a complex proposition, are stated absolutely, and not under any condition or proviso, it is not a proposition at all, but a plurality of propositions; since what it expresses is not a single assertion, but several assertions, which, if true when joined, are true also when separated. But there is a kind of proposition which, though it contains a plurality of subjects and of predicates, and may be said in one sense of the word to consist of several propositions, contains but one assertion; and its truth does not at all imply that of the simple propositions which compose it. An example of this is, when the simple propositions are connected by the particle *or*; as, Either A is B *or* C is D; or by the particle *if*; as, A is B *if* C is D. In the former case, the proposition is called *disjunctive*, in the latter *conditional*: the name *hypothetical* was originally common to both. As has been well remarked by Archbishop Whately and others, the disjunctive form is resolvable into the conditional; every disjunctive proposition being equivalent to two or more conditional ones. "Either A is B or C is D," means, "if A is not B, C is D; and if C is not D, A is B." All hypothetical propositions, therefore, though disjunctive in form, are conditional in meaning; and the words hypothetical and conditional may be, as indeed they generally are, used synonymously. Propositions in which the assertion is not dependent on a condition, are said, in the language of logicians, to be *categorical*.

An hypothetical proposition is not, like the pretended complex propositions which we previously considered, a mere aggregation of simple propositions. The simple propositions which form part of the words in which it is couched, form no part of the assertion which it conveys. When we say, If the Koran comes from God, Mahomet is the prophet of God, we do not intend to affirm either that the Koran does come from God, or that Mahomet is really his prophet. Neither of these simple propositions may be true, and yet the truth of the hypothetical proposition may be indisputable. What is asserted is not the truth of either of the propositions, but the inferribility of the one from the other. What, then, is the subject, and what the predicate, of the hypothetical proposition? "The Koran" is not the subject of it, nor is "Mahomet:" for nothing is affirmed or denied either of the Koran or of Mahomet. The real subject of the predication is the entire proposition, "Mahomet is the prophet of God;" and the affirmation is, that this is a legitimate inference from the proposition, "The Koran comes from God." The subject and predicate, therefore, of an hypothetical proposition are names of propositions. The subject is some one proposition. The predicate is a general relative name applicable to propositions; of this form--"an inference from so and so." A fresh instance is here afforded of the remark, that all particles are abbreviations; since "*If* A is B, C is D," is found to be an abbreviation of the following: "The proposition C is D, is a legitimate inference from the proposition A is B."

The distinction, therefore, between hypothetical and categorical propositions, is not so great as it at first appears. In the conditional, as well as in the categorical form, one predicate is affirmed of one subject, and no more: but a conditional proposition is a proposition concerning a proposition; the subject of the assertion is itself an assertion. Nor is this a property peculiar to hypothetical propositions. There are other classes of assertions concerning propositions. Like other things, a proposition has attributes which may be predicated of it. The attribute predicated of it in an hypothetical proposition, is that of being an inference from a certain other proposition. But this is only one of many attributes that might be predicated. We may say, That the whole is greater than its part, is an axiom in mathematics: That the Holy Ghost proceeds from the Father alone, is a tenet of the Greek Church: The doctrine of the divine right of kings was renounced by Parliament at the Revolution: The infallibility of the Pope has no countenance from Scripture. In all these cases the subject of the predication is an entire proposition. That which these different predicates are affirmed of, is *the proposition*, "the whole is greater than its part;" *the proposition*, "the Holy Ghost proceeds from the Father alone;" *the proposition*, "kings have a divine right;" *the proposition*, "the Pope is infallible."

Seeing, then, that there is much less difference between hypothetical propositions and any others, than one might be led to imagine from their form, we should be at a loss to account for the conspicuous position which they have been selected to fill in treatises on Logic, if we did not remember that what they predicate of a proposition, namely, its being an inference from something else, is precisely that one of its attributes with which most of all a logician is concerned.

§ 4. The next of the common divisions of Propositions is into Universal, Particular, Indefinite, and Singular: a distinction founded on the degree of generality in which the name, which is the subject of the proposition, is to be understood. The following are examples:

All men are mortal--
>> Universal. *Some men* are mortal--
> Particular. *Man* is mortal--
>> Indefinite. *Julius Caesar* is mortal--
> Singular.

The proposition is Singular, when the subject is an individual name. The individual name needs not be a proper name. "The Founder of Christianity was crucified," is as much a singular proposition as "Christ was crucified."

When the name which is the subject of the proposition is a general name, we may intend to affirm or deny the predicate, either of *all* the things that the subject denotes, or only of some. When the predicate is affirmed or denied of all and each of the things denoted by the subject, the proposition is universal; when of some non-assignable portion of them only, it is particular. Thus, All men are mortal; Every man is mortal; are universal propositions. No man is immortal, is also an universal proposition, since the predicate, immortal, is denied of each and every individual denoted by the term man; the negative proposition being exactly equivalent to the following, Every man is not-immortal. But "some men are wise," "some men are not wise," are particular propositions; the predicate *wise* being in the one case affirmed and in the other denied not of each and every individual denoted by the term man, but only of each and every one of some portion of those individuals, without specifying what portion; for if this were specified, the proposition would be changed either into a singular proposition, or into an universal proposition with a different subject; as, for instance, "all *properly instructed* men are wise." There are other forms of particular propositions: as, "*Most* men are imperfectly educated:" it being immaterial how large a portion of the subject the predicate is asserted of, as long as it is left uncertain how that portion is to be distinguished from the rest.

When the form of the expression does not clearly show whether the general name which is the subject of the proposition is meant to stand for all the individuals denoted by it, or only for some of them, the proposition is commonly called Indefinite; but this, as Archbishop Whately observes, is a solecism, of the same nature as that committed by some grammarians when in their list of genders they enumerate the *doubtful* gender. The speaker must mean to assert the proposition either as an universal or as a particular proposition, though he has failed to declare which: and it often happens that though the words do not show which of the two he intends, the context, or the custom of speech, supplies the deficiency. Thus, when it is affirmed that "Man is mortal," nobody doubts that the assertion is intended of all human beings, and the word indicative of universality is commonly omitted, only because the meaning is evident without it. In the proposition, "Wine is good," it is understood with equal readiness, though for somewhat different reasons, that the assertion is not intended to be universal, but particular.

When a general name stands for each and every individual which it is a name of, or in other words, which it denotes, it is said by logicians to be *distributed*, or taken distributively. Thus, in the proposition, All men are mortal, the subject, Man, is distributed, because mortality is affirmed of each and every man. The predicate, Mortal, is not distributed, because the only mortals who are spoken of in the proposition are those who happen to be men; while the word may, for aught that appears, (and in fact does,) comprehend within it an indefinite number of objects besides men. In the proposition, Some men are mortal, both the predicate and the subject are undistributed. In the following, No men have wings, both the predicate and the subject are distributed. Not only is the attribute of having wings denied of the entire class Man, but that class is severed and cast out from the whole of the class Winged, and not merely from some part of that class.

This phraseology, which is of great service in stating and demonstrating the rules of the syllogism, enables us to express very concisely the definitions of an universal and a particular proposition. An universal proposition is that of which the subject is distributed; a particular proposition is that of which the subject is undistributed.

There are many more distinctions among propositions than those we have here stated, some of them of considerable importance. But, for explaining and illustrating these, more suitable opportunities will occur in the sequel.

CHAPTER V. OF THE IMPORT OF PROPOSITIONS.

§ 1. An inquiry into the nature of propositions must have one of two objects: to analyse the state of mind called Belief, or to analyse what is believed. All language recognises a difference between a doctrine or opinion, and the act of entertaining the opinion; between assent, and what is assented to.

Logic, according to the conception here formed of it, has no concern with the nature of the act of judging or believing; the consideration of that act, as a phenomenon of the mind, belongs to another science. Philosophers, however, from Descartes downwards, and especially from the era of Leibnitz and Locke, have by no means observed this distinction; and would have treated with great disrespect any attempt to analyse the import of Propositions, unless founded on an analysis of the act of Judgment. A proposition, they would have said, is but the expression in words of a Judgment. The thing expressed, not the mere verbal expression, is the important matter. When the mind assents to a proposition, it judges. Let us find out what the mind does when it judges, and we shall know what propositions mean, and not otherwise.

Conformably to these views, almost all the writers on Logic in the last two centuries, whether English, German, or French, have made their theory of Propositions, from one end to the other, a theory of Judgments. They considered a Proposition, or a Judgment, for they used the two words indiscriminately, to consist in affirming or denying one *idea* of another. To judge, was to put two ideas together, or to bring one idea under another, or to compare two ideas, or to perceive the agreement or disagreement between two ideas: and the whole doctrine of Propositions, together with the theory of Reasoning, (always necessarily founded on the theory of Propositions,) was stated as if Ideas, or Conceptions, or whatever other term the writer preferred as a name for mental representations generally, constituted essentially the subject matter and substance of those operations.

It is, of course, true, that in any case of judgment, as for instance when we judge that gold is yellow, a process takes place in our minds, of which some one or other of these theories is a partially correct account. We must have the idea of gold and the idea of yellow, and these two ideas must be brought together in our mind. But in the first place, it is evident that this is only a part of what takes place; for we may put two ideas together without any act of belief; as when we merely imagine something, such as a golden mountain; or when we actually disbelieve: for in order even to disbelieve that Mahomet was an apostle of God, we must put the idea of Mahomet and that of an apostle of God together. To determine what it is that happens in the case of assent or dissent besides putting two ideas together, is one of the most intricate of metaphysical problems. But whatever the solution may be, we may venture to assert that it can have nothing whatever to do with the import of propositions; for this reason, that propositions (except where the mind itself is the subject treated of) are not assertions respecting our ideas of things, but assertions respecting the things themselves. In order to believe that gold is yellow, I must, indeed, have the idea of gold, and the idea of yellow, and something having reference to those ideas must take place in my mind; but my belief has not reference to the ideas, it has reference to the things. What I believe is a fact relating to the outward thing, gold, and to the impression made by that outward thing upon the human organs; not a fact relating to my conception of gold, which would be a fact in my mental history, not a fact of external nature. It is true, that in order to believe this fact in external nature, another fact must take place in my mind, a process must be performed upon my ideas; but so it must in everything else that I do. I cannot dig the ground unless I have the idea of the ground, and of a spade, and of all the other things I am operating upon, and unless I put those ideas together.(16) But it would be a very ridiculous description of digging the ground to say that it is putting one idea into another. Digging is an operation which is performed upon the things themselves, although it cannot be performed unless I have in my mind the ideas of them. And so, in like manner, believing is an act which has for its subject the facts themselves, although a previous mental conception of the facts is an indispensable condition. When I say that fire causes heat, do I mean that my idea of fire causes my idea of heat? No: I mean that the natural phenomenon, fire, causes the natural phenomenon, heat. When I mean to assert anything respecting the ideas, I give them their proper name, I call them ideas: as when I say, that a child's idea of a battle is unlike the reality, or that the ideas entertained of the Deity have a great effect on the characters of mankind.

The notion that what is of primary importance to the logician in a proposition, is the relation between the two ***ideas*** corresponding to the subject and predicate, (instead of the relation between the two ***phenomena*** which they respectively express,) seems to me one of the most fatal errors ever introduced into the philosophy of Logic; and the principal cause why the theory of the science has made such inconsiderable progress during the last two centuries. The treatises on Logic, and on the branches of Mental Philosophy connected with Logic, which have been produced since the intrusion of this cardinal error, though sometimes written by men of extraordinary abilities and attainments, almost always tacitly imply a theory that the investigation of truth consists in contemplating and handling our ideas, or conceptions of things, instead of the things themselves: a doctrine tantamount to the assertion, that the only mode of acquiring knowledge of nature is to study it at second hand, as represented in our own minds. Meanwhile, inquiries into every kind of natural phenomena were incessantly establishing great and fruitful truths on the most important subjects, by processes upon which these views of the nature of Judgment and Reasoning threw no light, and in which they afforded no assistance whatever. No wonder that those who knew by practical experience how truths are come at, should deem a science futile, which consisted chiefly of such speculations. What has been done for the advancement of Logic since these doctrines came into vogue, has been done not by professed logicians, but by discoverers in the other sciences; in whose methods of investigation many principles of logic, not previously thought of, have successively come forth into light, but who have generally committed the error of supposing that nothing whatever was known of the art of philosophizing by the old logicians, because their modern interpreters have written to so little purpose respecting it.

We have to inquire, then, on the present occasion, not into Judgment, but judgments; not into the act of believing, but into the thing believed. What is the immediate object of belief in a Proposition? What is the matter of fact signified by it? What is it to which, when I assert the proposition, I give my assent, and call upon others to give theirs? What is that which is expressed by the form of discourse called a Proposition, and the conformity of which to fact constitutes the truth of the proposition?

§ 2. One of the clearest and most consecutive thinkers whom this country or the world has produced, I mean Hobbes, has given the following answer to this question. In every proposition (says he) what is signified is, the belief of the speaker that the predicate is a name of the same thing of which the subject is a name; and if it really is so, the proposition is true. Thus the proposition, All men are living beings (he would say) is true, because ***living being*** is a name of everything of which ***man*** is a name. All men are six feet high, is not true, because ***six feet high*** is not a name of everything (though it is of some things) of which ***man*** is a name.

What is stated in this theory as the definition of a true proposition, must be allowed to be a property which all true propositions possess. The subject and predicate being both of them names of things, if they were names of quite different things the one name could not, consistently with its signification, be predicated of the other. If it be true that some men are copper-coloured, it must be true--and the proposition does really assert--that among the individuals denoted by the name man, there are some who are also among those denoted by the name copper-coloured. If it be true that all oxen ruminate, it must be true that all the individuals denoted by the name ox are also among those denoted by the name ruminating; and whoever asserts that all oxen ruminate, undoubtedly does assert that this relation subsists between the two names.

The assertion, therefore, which, according to Hobbes, is the only one made in any proposition, really is made in every proposition: and his analysis has consequently one of the requisites for being the true one. We may go a step farther; it is the only analysis that is rigorously true of all propositions without exception. What he gives as the meaning of propositions, is part of the meaning of all propositions, and the whole meaning of some. This, however, only shows what an extremely minute fragment of meaning it is quite possible to include within the logical formula of a proposition. It does not show that no proposition means more. To warrant us in putting together two words with a copula between them, it is really enough that the thing or things denoted by one of the names should be capable, without violation of usage, of being called by the other name also. If, then, this be all the meaning necessarily implied in the form of discourse called a Proposition, why do I object to it as the scientific definition of what a proposition means? Because, though the mere collocation which makes the proposition a proposition, conveys no more than this scanty amount of meaning, that same collocation combined with other circumstances, that *form* combined with other *matter*, does convey more, and much more.

The only propositions of which Hobbes' principle is a sufficient account, are that limited and unimportant class in which both the predicate and the subject are proper names. For, as has already been remarked, proper names have strictly no meaning; they are mere marks for individual objects: and when a proper name is predicated of another proper name, all the signification conveyed is, that both the names are marks for the same object. But this is precisely what Hobbes produces as a theory of predication in general. His doctrine is a full explanation of such predications as these: Hyde was Clarendon, or, Tully is Cicero. It exhausts the meaning of those propositions. But it is a sadly inadequate theory of any others. That it should ever have been thought of as such, can be accounted for only by the fact, that Hobbes, in common with the other Nominalists, bestowed little or no attention upon the *connotation* of words; and sought for their meaning exclusively in what they *denote*: as if all names had been (what none but proper names really are) marks put upon individuals; and as if there were no difference between a proper and a general name, except that the first denotes only one individual, and the last a greater number.

It has been seen, however, that the meaning of all names, except proper names and that portion of the class of abstract names which are not connotative, resides in the connotation. When, therefore, we are analysing the meaning of any proposition in which the predicate and the subject, or either of them, are connotative names, it is to the connotation of those terms that we must exclusively look, and not to what they *denote*, or in the language of Hobbes, (language so far correct,) are names of.

In asserting that the truth of a proposition depends on the conformity of import between its terms, as, for instance, that the proposition, Socrates is wise, is a true proposition, because Socrates and wise are names applicable to, or, as he expresses it, names of, the same person; it is very remarkable that so powerful a thinker should not have asked himself the question, But how came they to be names of the same person? Surely not because such was the intention of those who invented the words. When mankind fixed the meaning of the word wise, they were not thinking of Socrates, nor, when his parents gave him the name Socrates, were they thinking of wisdom. The names *happen* to fit the same person because of a certain *fact*, which fact was not known, nor in being, when the names were invented. If we want to know what the fact is, we shall find the clue to it in the **connotation** of the names.

A bird, or a stone, a man, or a wise man, means simply, an object having such and such attributes. The real meaning of the word man, is those attributes, and not John, Jane, and the remainder of the individuals. The word *mortal*, in like manner connotes a certain attribute or attributes; and when we say, All men are mortal, the meaning of the proposition is, that all beings which possess the one set of attributes, possess also the other. If, in our experience, the attributes connoted by *man* are always accompanied by the attribute connoted by *mortal*, it will follow as a consequence, that the class *man* will be wholly included in the class *mortal*, and that *mortal* will be a name of all things of which *man* is a name: but why? Those objects are brought under the name, by possessing the attributes connoted by it: but their possession of the attributes is the real condition on which the truth of the proposition depends; not their being called by the name. Connotative names do not precede, but follow, the attributes which they connote. If one attribute happens to be always found in conjunction with another attribute, the concrete names which answer to those attributes will of course be predicable of the same subjects, and may be said, in Hobbes' language, (in the propriety of which on this occasion I fully concur,) to be two names for the same things. But the possibility of a concurrent application of the two names, is a mere consequence of the conjunction between the two attributes, and was, in most cases, never thought of when the names were invented and their signification fixed. That the diamond is combustible, was a proposition certainly not dreamt of when the words Diamond and Combustible first received their meaning; and could not have been discovered by the most ingenious and refined analysis of the signification of those words. It was found out by a very different process, namely, by exerting the senses, and learning from them, that the attribute of combustibility existed in all those diamonds upon which the experiment was tried; the number and character of the experiments being such, that what was true of those individuals might be concluded to be true of all substances "called by the name," that is, of all substances possessing the attributes which the name connotes. The assertion, therefore, when analysed, is, that wherever we find certain attributes, there will be found a certain other attribute: which is not a question of the signification of names, but of laws of nature; the order existing among phenomena.

§ 3. Although Hobbes' theory of Predication has not, in the terms in which he stated it, met with a very favourable reception from subsequent thinkers, a theory virtually identical with it, and not by any means so perspicuously expressed, may almost be said to have taken the rank of an established opinion. The most generally received notion of Predication decidedly is that it consists in referring something to a *class*, *i.e.*, either placing an individual under a class, or placing one class under another class. Thus, the proposition, Man is mortal, asserts, according to this view of it, that the class man is included in the class mortal. "Plato is a philosopher," asserts that the individual Plato is one of those who compose the class philosopher. If the proposition is negative, then instead of placing something in a class, it is said to exclude something from a class. Thus, if the following be the proposition, The elephant is not carnivorous; what is asserted (according to this theory) is, that the elephant is excluded from the class carnivorous, or is not numbered among the things comprising that class. There is no real difference, except in language, between this theory of Predication and the theory of Hobbes. For a class *is* absolutely nothing but an indefinite number of individuals denoted by a general name. The name given to them in common, is what makes them a class. To refer anything to a class, therefore, is to look upon it as one of the things which are to be called by that common name. To exclude it from a class, is to say that the common name is not applicable to it.

How widely these views of predication have prevailed, is evident from this, that they are the basis of the celebrated ***dictum de omni et nullo***. When the syllogism is resolved, by all who treat of it, into an inference that what is true of a class is true of all things whatever that belong to the class; and when this is laid down by almost all professed logicians as the ultimate principle to which all reasoning owes its validity; it is clear that in the general estimation of logicians, the propositions of which reasonings are composed can be the expression of nothing but the process of dividing things into classes, and referring everything to its proper class.

This theory appears to me a signal example of a logical error very often committed in logic, that of ὕστερον πρότερον, or explaining a thing by something which presupposes it. When I say that snow is white, I may and ought to be thinking of snow as a class, because I am asserting a proposition as true of all snow: but I am certainly not thinking of white objects as a class; I am thinking of no white object whatever except snow, but only of that, and of the sensation of white which it gives me. When, indeed, I have judged, or assented to the propositions, that snow is white, and that several other things also are white, I gradually begin to think of white objects as a class, including snow and those other things. But this is a conception which followed, not preceded, those judgments, and therefore cannot be given as an explanation of them. Instead of explaining the effect by the cause, this doctrine explains the cause by the effect, and is, I conceive, founded on a latent misconception of the nature of classification.

There is a sort of language very generally prevalent in these discussions, which seems to suppose that classification is an arrangement and grouping of definite and known individuals: that when names were imposed, mankind took into consideration all the individual objects in the universe, made them up into parcels or lists, and gave to the objects of each list a common name, repeating this operation ***toties quoties*** until they had invented all the general names of which language consists; which having been once done, if a question subsequently arises whether a certain general name can be truly predicated of a certain particular object, we have only (as it were) to read the roll of the objects upon which that name was conferred, and see whether the object about which the question arises, is to be found among them. The framers of language (it would seem to be supposed) have predetermined all the objects that are to compose each class, and we have only to refer to the record of an antecedent decision.

So absurd a doctrine will be owned by nobody when thus nakedly stated; but if the commonly received explanations of classification and naming do not imply this theory, it requires to be shown how they admit of being reconciled with any other.

General names are not marks put upon definite objects; classes are not made by drawing a line round a given number of assignable individuals. The objects which compose any given class are perpetually fluctuating. We may frame a class without knowing the individuals, or even any of the individuals, of which it will be composed; we may do so while believing that no such individuals exist. If by the ***meaning*** of a general name are to be understood the things which it is the name of, no general name, except by accident, has a fixed meaning at all, or ever long retains the same meaning. The only mode in which any general name has a definite meaning, is by being a name of an indefinite variety of things; namely, of all things, known or unknown, past, present, or future, which possess certain definite attributes. When, by studying not the meaning of words, but the phenomena of nature, we discover that these attributes are possessed by some object not previously known to possess them, (as when chemists found that the diamond was combustible,) we include this new object in the class; but it did not already belong to the class. We place the individual in the class because the proposition is true; the proposition is not true because the object is placed in the class.

It will appear hereafter in treating of reasoning, how much the theory of that intellectual process has been vitiated by the influence of these erroneous notions, and by the habit which they exemplify of assimilating all the operations of the human understanding which have truth for their object, to processes of mere classification and naming. Unfortunately, the minds which have been entangled in this net are precisely those which have escaped the other cardinal error commented upon in the beginning of the present chapter. Since the revolution which dislodged Aristotle from the schools, logicians may almost be divided into those who have looked upon reasoning as essentially an affair of Ideas, and those who have looked upon it as essentially an affair of Names.

Although, however, Hobbes' theory of Predication, according to the well-known remark of Leibnitz, and the avowal of Hobbes himself,(17) renders truth and falsity completely arbitrary, with no standard but the will of men, it must not be concluded that either Hobbes, or any of the other thinkers who have in the main agreed with him, did in fact consider the distinction between truth and error as less real, or attached less importance to it, than other people. To suppose that they did so would argue total unacquaintance with their other speculations. But this shows how little hold their doctrine possessed over their own minds. No person at bottom ever imagined that there was nothing more in truth than propriety of expression; than using language in conformity to a previous convention. When the inquiry was brought down from generals to a particular case, it has always been acknowledged that there is a distinction between verbal and real questions; that some false propositions are uttered from ignorance of the meaning of words, but that in others the source of the error is a misapprehension of things; that a person who has not the use of language at all may form propositions mentally, and that they may be untrue, that is, he may believe as matters of fact what are not really so. This last admission cannot be made in stronger terms than it is by Hobbes himself;(18) though he will not allow such erroneous belief to be called falsity, but only error. And he has himself laid down, in other places, doctrines in which the true theory of predication is by implication contained. He distinctly says that general names are given to things on account of their attributes, and that abstract names are the names of those attributes. "Abstract is that which in any subject denotes the cause of the concrete name.... And these causes of names are the same with the causes of our conceptions, namely, some power of action, or affection, of the thing conceived, which some call the manner by which anything works upon our senses, but by most men they are called *accidents*."(19) It is strange that having gone so far, he should not have gone one step farther, and seen that what he calls the cause of the concrete name, is in reality the meaning of it; and that when we predicate of any subject a name which is given *because* of an attribute, (or, as he calls it, an accident,) our object is not to affirm the name, but, by means of the name, to affirm the attribute.

§ 4. Let the predicate be, as we have said, a connotative term; and to take the simplest case first, let the subject be a proper name: "The summit of Chimborazo is white." The word white connotes an attribute which is possessed by the individual object designated by the words, "summit of Chimborazo," which attribute consists in the physical fact, of its exciting in human beings the sensation which we call a sensation of white. It will be admitted that, by asserting the proposition, we wish to communicate information of that physical fact, and are not thinking of the names, except as the necessary means of making that communication. The meaning of the proposition, therefore, is, that the individual thing denoted by the subject, has the attributes connoted by the predicate.

If we now suppose the subject also to be a connotative name, the meaning expressed by the proposition has advanced a step farther in complication. Let us first suppose the proposition to be universal, as well as affirmative: "All men are mortal." In this case, as in the last, what the proposition asserts, (or expresses a belief of,) is, of course, that the objects denoted by the subject (man) possess the attributes connoted by the predicate (mortal). But the characteristic of this case is, that the objects are no longer ***individually*** designated. They are pointed out only by some of their attributes: they are the objects called men, that is, possessing the attributes connoted by the name man; and the only thing known of them may be those attributes: indeed, as the proposition is general, and the objects denoted by the subject are therefore indefinite in number, most of them are not known individually at all. The assertion, therefore, is not, as before, that the attributes which the predicate connotes are possessed by any given individual, or by any number of individuals previously known as John, Thomas, &c., but that those attributes are possessed by each and every individual possessing certain other attributes; that whatever has the attributes connoted by the subject, has also those connoted by the predicate; that the latter set of attributes ***constantly accompany*** the former set. Whatever has the attributes of man has the attribute of mortality; mortality constantly accompanies the attributes of man.

If it be remembered that every attribute is ***grounded*** on some fact or phenomenon, either of outward sense or of inward consciousness, and that to ***possess*** an attribute is another phrase for being the cause of, or forming part of, the fact or phenomenon upon which the attribute is grounded; we may add one more step to complete the analysis. The proposition which asserts that one attribute always accompanies another attribute, really asserts thereby no other thing than this, that one phenomenon always accompanies another phenomenon; insomuch that where we find the one, we have assurance of the existence of the other. Thus, in the proposition, All men are mortal, the word man connotes the attributes which we ascribe to a certain kind of living creatures, on the ground of certain phenomena which they exhibit, and which are partly physical phenomena, namely the impressions made on our senses by their bodily form and structure, and partly mental phenomena, namely the sentient and intellectual life which they have of their own. All this is understood when we utter the word man, by any one to whom the meaning of the word is known. Now, when we say, Man is mortal, we mean that wherever these various physical and mental phenomena are all found, there we have assurance that the other physical and mental phenomenon, called death, will not fail to take place. The proposition does not affirm ***when***; for the connotation of the word ***mortal*** goes no farther than to the occurrence of the phenomenon at some time or other, leaving the precise time undecided.

§ 5. We have already proceeded far enough not only to demonstrate the error of Hobbes, but to ascertain the real import of by far the most numerous class of propositions. The object of belief in a proposition, when it asserts anything more than the meaning of words, is generally, as in the cases which we have examined, either the coexistence or the sequence of two phenomena. At the very commencement of our inquiry, we found that every act of belief implied two Things; we have now ascertained what, in the most frequent case, these two things are, namely two Phenomena, in other words, two states of consciousness; and what it is which the proposition affirms (or denies) to subsist between them, namely either succession, or coexistence. And this case includes innumerable instances which no one, previous to reflection, would think of referring to it. Take the following example: A generous person is worthy of honour. Who would expect to recognize here a case of coexistence between phenomena? But so it is. The attribute which causes a person to be termed generous, is ascribed to him on the ground of states of his mind, and particulars of his conduct: both are phenomena; the former are facts of internal consciousness, the latter, so far as distinct from the former, are physical facts, or perceptions of the senses. Worthy of honour, admits of a similar analysis. Honour, as here used, means a state of approving and admiring emotion, followed on occasion by corresponding outward acts. "Worthy of honour" connotes all this, together with our approval of the act of showing honour. All these are phenomena; states of internal consciousness, accompanied or followed by physical facts. When we say, A generous person is worthy of honour, we affirm coexistence between the two complicated phenomena connoted by the two terms respectively. We affirm, that wherever and whenever the inward feelings and outward facts implied in the word generosity, have place, then and there the existence and manifestation of an inward feeling, honour, would be followed in our minds by another inward feeling, approval.

After the analysis in a former chapter of the import of names, many examples are not needed to illustrate the import of propositions. When there is any obscurity or difficulty, it does not lie in the meaning of the proposition, but in the meaning of the names which compose it; in the very complicated connotation of many words; the immense multitude and prolonged series of facts which often constitute the phenomenon connoted by a name. But where it is seen what the phenomenon is, there is seldom any difficulty in seeing that the assertion conveyed by the proposition is, the coexistence of one such phenomenon with another; or the succession of one such phenomenon to another: their ***conjunction***, in short, so that where the one is found, we may calculate on finding both.

This, however, though the most common, is not the only meaning which propositions are ever intended to convey. In the first place, sequences and coexistences are not only asserted respecting Phenomena; we make propositions also respecting those hidden causes of phenomena, which are named substances and attributes. A substance, however, being to us nothing but either that which causes, or that which is conscious of, phenomena; and the same being true, ***mutatis mutandis***, of attributes; no assertion can be made, at least with a meaning, concerning these unknown and unknowable entities, except in virtue of the Phenomena by which alone they manifest themselves to our faculties. When we say, Socrates was cotemporary with the Peloponnesian war, the foundation of this assertion, as of all assertions concerning substances, is an assertion concerning the phenomena which they exhibit,--namely, that the series of facts by which Socrates manifested himself to mankind, and the series of mental states which constituted his sentient existence, went on simultaneously with the series of facts known by the name of the Peloponnesian war. Still, the proposition does not assert that alone; it asserts that the Thing in itself, the ***noumenon*** Socrates, was existing, and doing or experiencing those various facts, during the same time. Coexistence and sequence, therefore, may be affirmed or denied not only between phenomena, but between noumena, or between a noumenon and phenomena. And both of noumena and of phenomena we may affirm simple existence. But what is a noumenon? An unknown cause. In affirming, therefore, the existence of a noumenon, we affirm causation. Here, therefore, are two additional kinds of fact, capable of being asserted in a proposition. Besides the propositions which assert Sequence or Coexistence, there are some which assert simple Existence; and others assert Causation, which, subject to the explanations which will follow in the Third Book, must be considered provisionally as a distinct and peculiar kind of assertion.

§ 6. To these four kinds of matter-of-fact or assertion, must be added a fifth, Resemblance. This was a species of attribute which we found it impossible to analyse; for which no ***fundamentum***, distinct from the objects themselves, could be assigned. Besides propositions which assert a sequence or coexistence between two phenomena, there are therefore also propositions which assert resemblance between them: as, This colour is like that colour;--The heat of to-day is *equal* to the heat of yesterday. It is true that such an assertion might with some plausibility be brought within the description of an affirmation of sequence, by considering it as an assertion that the simultaneous contemplation of the two colours is *followed* by a specific feeling termed the feeling of resemblance. But there would be nothing gained by encumbering ourselves, especially in this place, with a generalization which may be looked upon as strained. Logic does not undertake to analyse mental facts into their ultimate elements. Resemblance between two phenomena is more intelligible in itself than any explanation could make it, and under any classification must remain specifically distinct from the ordinary cases of sequence and coexistence.

It is sometimes said that all propositions whatever, of which the predicate is a general name, do, in point of fact, affirm or deny resemblance. All such propositions affirm that a thing belongs to a class; but things being classed together according to their resemblance, everything is of course classed with the things which it is supposed to resemble most; and thence, it may be said, when we affirm that Gold is a metal, or that Socrates is a man, the affirmation intended is, that gold resembles other metals, and Socrates other men, more nearly than they resemble the objects contained in any other of the classes co-ordinate with these.

There is some slight degree of foundation for this remark, but no more than a slight degree. The arrangement of things into classes, such as the class *metal*, or the class *man*, is grounded indeed on a resemblance among the things which are placed in the same class, but not on a mere general resemblance: the resemblance it is grounded on consists in the possession by all those things, of certain common peculiarities; and those peculiarities it is which the terms connote, and which the propositions consequently assert; not the resemblance: for though when I say, Gold is a metal, I say by implication that if there be any other metals it must resemble them, yet if there were no other metals I might still assert the proposition with the same meaning as at present, namely, that gold has the various properties implied in the word metal; just as it might be said, Christians are men, even if there were no men who were not Christians. Propositions, therefore, in which objects are referred to a class because they possess the attributes constituting the class, are so far from asserting nothing but resemblance, that they do not, properly speaking, assert resemblance at all.

But we remarked some time ago, (and the reasons of the remark will be more fully entered into in a subsequent Book,(20)) that there is sometimes a convenience in extending the boundaries of a class so as to include things which possess in a very inferior degree, if in any, some of the characteristic properties of the class,-- provided they resemble that class more than any other, insomuch that the general propositions which are true of the class will be nearer to being true of those things than any other equally general propositions. As, for instance, there are substances called metals which have very few of the properties by which metals are commonly recognised; and almost every great family of plants or animals has a few anomalous genera or species on its borders, which are admitted into it by a sort of courtesy, and concerning which it has been matter of discussion to what family they properly belonged. Now when the class-name is predicated of any object of this description, we do, by so predicating it, affirm resemblance and nothing more. And in order to be scrupulously correct it ought to be said, that in every case in which we predicate a general name, we affirm, not absolutely that the object possesses the properties designated by the name, but that it *either* possesses those properties, or if it does not, at any rate resembles the things which do so, more than it resembles any other things. In most cases, however, it is unnecessary to suppose any such alternative, the latter of the two grounds being very seldom that on which the assertion is made: and when it is, there is generally some slight difference in the form of the expression, as, This species (or genus) is *considered*, or *may be ranked*, as belonging to such and such a family: we should hardly say positively that it does belong to it, unless it possessed unequivocally the properties of which the class-name is scientifically significant.

There is still another exceptional case, in which, though the predicate is a name of a class, yet in predicating it we affirm nothing but resemblance, the class being founded not on resemblance in any given particular, but on general unanalysable resemblance. The classes in question are those into which our simple sensations, or other simple feelings, are divided. Sensations of white, for instance, are classed together, not because we can take them to pieces, and say they are alike in this, and not alike in that, but because we feel them to be alike altogether, though in different degrees. When, therefore, I say, The colour I saw yesterday was a white colour, or, The sensation I feel is one of tightness, in both cases the attribute I affirm of the colour or of the other sensation is mere resemblance,--simple *likeness* to sensations which I have had before, and which have had those names bestowed upon them. The names of feelings, like other concrete general names, are connotative; but they connote a mere resemblance. When predicated of any individual feeling, the information they convey is that of its likeness to the other feelings which we have been accustomed to call by the same name. Thus much may suffice in illustration of the kind of Propositions in which the matter-of-fact asserted (or denied) is simple Resemblance.

Existence, Coexistence, Sequence, Causation, Resemblance: one or other of these is asserted (or denied) in every proposition without exception. This five-fold division is an exhaustive classification of matters-of-fact; of all things that can be believed or tendered for belief; of all questions that can be propounded, and all answers that can be returned to them. Instead of Coexistence and Sequence, we shall sometimes say, for greater particularity, Order in Place, and Order in Time: Order in Place being one of the modes of coexistence, not necessary to be more particularly analysed here; while the mere fact of coexistence, or simultaneousness, may be classed, together with Sequence, under the head of Order in Time.

§ 7. In the foregoing inquiry into the import of Propositions, we have thought it necessary to analyse *directly* those alone, in which the terms of the proposition (or the predicate at least) are concrete terms. But, in doing so, we have indirectly analysed those in which the terms are abstract. The distinction between an abstract term and its corresponding concrete, does not turn upon any difference in what they are appointed to signify; for the real signification of a concrete general name is, as we have so often said, its connotation; and what the concrete term connotes, forms the entire meaning of the abstract name. Since there is nothing in the import of an abstract name which is not in the import of the corresponding concrete, it is natural to suppose that neither can there be anything in the import of a proposition of which the terms are abstract, but what there is in some proposition which can be framed of concrete terms.

And this presumption a closer examination will confirm. An abstract name is the name of an attribute, or combination of attributes. The corresponding concrete is a name given to things, because of, and in order to express, their possessing that attribute, or that combination of attributes. When, therefore, we predicate of anything a concrete name, the attribute is what we in reality predicate of it. But it has now been shown that in all propositions of which the predicate is a concrete name, what is really predicated is one of five things: Existence, Coexistence, Causation, Sequence, or Resemblance. An attribute, therefore, is necessarily either an existence, a coexistence, a causation, a sequence, or a resemblance. When a proposition consists of a subject and predicate which are abstract terms, it consists of terms which must necessarily signify one or other of these things. When we predicate of anything an abstract name, we affirm of the thing that it is one or other of these five things; that it is a case of Existence, or of Coexistence, or of Causation, or of Sequence, or of Resemblance.

It is impossible to imagine any proposition expressed in abstract terms, which cannot be transformed into a precisely equivalent proposition in which the terms are concrete, namely, either the concrete names which connote the attributes themselves, or the names of the ***fundamenta*** of those attributes, the facts or phenomena on which they are grounded. To illustrate the latter case, let us take this proposition, of which the subject only is an abstract name,--"Thoughtlessness is dangerous." Thoughtlessness is an attribute grounded on the facts which we call thoughtless actions; and the proposition is equivalent to this, Thoughtless actions are dangerous. In the next example the predicate as well as the subject are abstract names: "Whiteness is a colour;" or "The colour of snow is a whiteness." These attributes being grounded on sensations, the equivalent propositions in the concrete would be, The sensation of white is one of the sensations called those of colour,--The sensation of sight, caused by looking at snow, is one of the sensations called sensations of white. In these propositions, as we have before seen, the matter-of-fact asserted is a Resemblance. In the following examples, the concrete terms are those which directly correspond to the abstract names; connoting the attribute which these denote. "Prudence is a virtue:" this may be rendered, "All prudent persons, ***in so far as*** prudent, are virtuous:" "Courage is deserving of honour," thus, "All courageous persons are deserving of honour ***in so far*** as they are courageous;" which is equivalent to this--"All courageous persons deserve an addition to the honour, or a diminution of the disgrace, which would attach to them on other grounds."

In order to throw still further light upon the import of propositions of which the terms are abstract, we will subject one of the examples given above to a minuter analysis. The proposition we shall select is the following:--"Prudence is a virtue." Let us substitute for the word virtue an equivalent but more definite expression, such as "a mental quality beneficial to society," or "a mental quality pleasing to God," or whatever else we adopt as the definition of virtue. What the proposition asserts is a sequence, accompanied with causation, namely, that benefit to society, or that the approval of God, is consequent on, and caused by, prudence. Here is a sequence; but between what? We understand the consequent of the sequence, but we have yet to analyse the antecedent. Prudence is an attribute; and, in connexion with it, two things besides itself are to be considered; prudent persons, who are the *subjects* of the attribute, and prudential conduct, which may be called the *foundation* of it. Now is either of these the antecedent? and, first, is it meant, that the approval of God, or benefit to society, is attendant upon all prudent *persons*? No; except *in so far* as they are prudent; for prudent persons who are scoundrels can seldom on the whole be beneficial to society, nor acceptable to any good being. Is it upon prudential *conduct*, then, that divine approbation and benefit to mankind are supposed to be invariably consequent? Neither is this the assertion meant when it is said that prudence is a virtue; except with the same reservation as before, and for the same reason, namely, that prudential conduct, although in *so far as* it is prudential it is beneficial to society, may yet, by reason of some other of its qualities, be productive of an injury outweighing the benefit, and deserve a displeasure exceeding the approbation which would be due to the prudence. Neither the substance, therefore, (viz., the person,) nor the phenomenon, (the conduct,) is an antecedent on which the other term of the sequence is universally consequent. But the proposition, "Prudence is a virtue," is an universal proposition. What is it, then, upon which the proposition affirms the effects in question to be universally consequent? Upon that *in* the person, and in the conduct, which causes them to be called prudent, and which is equally in them when the action, though prudent, is wicked; namely, a correct foresight of consequences, a just estimation of their importance to the object in view, and repression of any unreflecting impulse at variance with the deliberate purpose. These, which are states of the person's mind, are the real antecedent in the sequence, the real cause in the causation, asserted by the proposition. But these are also the real ground, or foundation, of the attribute Prudence; since wherever these states of mind exist we may predicate prudence, even before we know whether any conduct has followed. And in this manner every assertion respecting an attribute may be transformed into an assertion exactly equivalent respecting the fact or phenomenon which is the ground of the attribute. And no case can be assigned, where that which is predicated of the fact or phenomenon, does not belong to one or other of the five species formerly enumerated: it is either simple Existence, or it is some Sequence, Coexistence, Causation, or Resemblance.

And as these five are the only things which can be affirmed, so are they the only things which can be denied. "No horses are web-footed" denies that the attributes of a horse ever coexist with web-feet. It is scarcely necessary to apply the same analysis to Particular affirmations and negations. "Some birds are web-footed," affirms that, with the attributes connoted by *bird*, the phenomenon web-feet is sometimes coexistent: "Some birds are not web-footed," asserts that there are other instances in which this coexistence does not have place. Any further explanation of a thing which, if the previous exposition has been assented to, is so obvious, may here be spared.

CHAPTER VI. OF PROPOSITIONS MERELY VERBAL.

§ 1. As a preparation for the inquiry which is the proper object of Logic, namely, in what manner propositions are to be proved, we have found it necessary to inquire what they contain which requires, or is susceptible of, proof; or (which is the same thing) what they assert. In the course of this preliminary investigation into the import of Propositions, we examined the opinion of the Conceptualists, that a proposition is the expression of a relation between two ideas; and the doctrine of the Nominalists, that it is the expression of an agreement or disagreement between the meanings of two names. We decided that, as general theories, both of these are erroneous; and that, although propositions may be made both respecting names and respecting ideas, neither the one nor the other are the subject-matter of Propositions considered generally. We then examined the different kinds of Propositions, and found that, with the exception of those which are merely verbal, they assert five different kinds of matters of fact, namely, Existence, Order in Place, Order in Time, Causation, and Resemblance; that in every proposition one of these five is either affirmed, or denied, of some fact or phenomenon, or of some object the unknown source of a fact or phenomenon.

In distinguishing, however, the different kinds of matters of fact asserted in propositions, we reserved one class of propositions, which do not relate to any matter of fact, in the proper sense of the term, at all, but to the meaning of names. Since names and their signification are entirely arbitrary, such propositions are not, strictly speaking, susceptible of truth or falsity, but only of conformity or disconformity to usage or convention; and all the proof they are capable of, is proof of usage; proof that the words have been employed by others in the acceptation in which the speaker or writer desires to use them. These propositions occupy, however, a conspicuous place in philosophy; and their nature and characteristics are of as much importance in logic, as those of any of the other classes of propositions previously adverted to.

If all propositions respecting the signification of words were as simple and unimportant as those which served us for examples when examining Hobbes' theory of predication, viz. those of which the subject and predicate are proper names, and which assert only that those names have, or that they have not, been conventionally assigned to the same individual; there would be little to attract to such propositions the attention of philosophers. But the class of merely verbal propositions embraces not only much more than these, but much more than any propositions which at first sight present themselves as verbal; comprehending a kind of assertions which have been regarded not only as relating to things, but as having actually a more intimate relation with them than any other propositions whatever. The student in philosophy will perceive that I allude to the distinction on which so much stress was laid by the schoolmen, and which has been retained either under the same or under other names by most metaphysicians to the present day, viz. between what were called ***essential***, and what were called ***accidental***, propositions, and between essential and accidental properties or attributes.

§ 2. Almost all metaphysicians prior to Locke, as well as many since his time, have made a great mystery of Essential Predication, and of predicates which were said to be of the *essence* of the subject. The essence of a thing, they said, was that without which the thing could neither be, nor be conceived to be. Thus, rationality was of the essence of man, because without rationality, man could not be conceived to exist. The different attributes which made up the essence of the thing, were called its essential properties; and a proposition in which any of these were predicated of it, was called an Essential Proposition, and was considered to go deeper into the nature of the thing, and to convey more important information respecting it, than any other proposition could do. All properties, not of the essence of the thing, were called its accidents; were supposed to have nothing at all, or nothing comparatively, to do with its inmost nature; and the propositions in which any of these were predicated of it were called Accidental Propositions. A connexion may be traced between this distinction, which originated with the schoolmen, and the well known dogmas of *substantiae secundae* or general substances, and *substantial forms*, doctrines which under varieties of language pervaded alike the Aristotelian and the Platonic schools, and of which more of the spirit has come down to modern times than might be conjectured from the disuse of the phraseology. The false views of the nature of classification and generalization which prevailed among the schoolmen, and of which these dogmas were the technical expression, afford the only explanation which can be given of their having misunderstood the real nature of those Essences which held so conspicuous a place in their philosophy. They said, truly, that *man* cannot be conceived without rationality. But though *man* cannot, a being may be conceived exactly like a man in all points except that one quality, and those others which are the conditions or consequences of it. All therefore which is really true in the assertion that man cannot be conceived without rationality, is only, that if he had not rationality, he would not be reputed a man. There is no impossibility in conceiving the *thing*, nor, for aught we know, in its existing: the impossibility is in the conventions of language, which will not allow the thing, even if it exist, to be called by the name which is reserved for rational beings. Rationality, in short, is involved in the meaning of the word man; is one of the attributes connoted by the name. The essence of man, simply means the whole of the attributes connoted by the word; and any one of those attributes taken singly, is an essential property of man.

The doctrines which prevented the real meaning of Essences from being understood, not having assumed so settled a shape in the time of Aristotle and his immediate followers as was afterwards given to them by the Realists of the middle ages, we find a nearer approach to a rational view of the subject in the writings of the ancient Aristotelians than in their more modern followers. Porphyry, in his *Isagoge*, approached so near to the true conception of essences, that only one step remained to be taken, but this step, so easy in appearance, was reserved for the Nominalists of modern times. By altering any property, not of the essence of the thing, you merely, according to Porphyry, made a difference in it; you made it Ἀλλοῖον : but by altering any property which was of its essence, you made it *another thing*, Ἀλλο.(21) To a modern it is obvious that between the change which only makes a thing different, and the change which makes it *another thing*, the only distinction is that in the one case, though changed, it is still called by the same name. Thus, pound ice in a mortar, and being still called ice, it is only made Ἀλλο , another thing, namely, water. Now it is really the same thing, *i.e.* the same particles of matter, in both cases; and you cannot so change anything that it shall cease to be the same thing in this sense. The identity which it can be deprived of is merely that of the name: when the thing ceases to be called ice, it becomes *another thing*; its essence, what constituted it ice, is gone; while, as long as it continues to be so called, nothing is gone except some of its accidents. But these reflections, so easy to us, would have been difficult to persons who thought, as most of the Aristotelians did, that objects were made what they were called, that ice (for instance) was made ice, not by the possession of certain properties to which mankind have chosen to attach that name, but by participation in the nature of a certain *general substance*, called *Ice in general*, which substance, together with all the properties that belonged to it, *inhered* in every individual piece of ice. As they did not consider these universal substances to be attached to all general names, but only to some, they thought that an object borrowed only a part of its properties from an universal substance, and that the rest belonged to it individually: the former they called its essence, and the latter its accidents. The scholastic doctrine of essences long survived the theory on which it rested, that of the existence of real entities corresponding to general terms; and it was reserved for Locke, at the end of the seventeenth century, to convince philosophers that the supposed essences of classes were merely the signification of their names; nor, among the signal services which his writings rendered to philosophy, was there one more needful or more valuable.(22)

Now, as the most familiar of the general names by which an object is designated usually connotes not one only, but several attributes of the object, each of which attributes separately forms also the bond of union of some class, and the meaning of some general name; we may predicate of a name which connotes a variety of attributes, another name which connotes only one of these attributes, or some smaller number of them than all. In such cases, the universal affirmative proposition will be true; since whatever possesses the whole of any set of attributes, must possess any part of that same set. A proposition of this sort, however, conveys no information to any one who previously understood the whole meaning of the terms. The propositions, Every man is a corporeal being, Every man is a living creature, Every man is rational, convey no knowledge to any one who was already aware of the entire meaning of the word *man*, for the meaning of the word includes all this: and, that every *man* has the attributes connoted by all these predicates, is already asserted when he is called a man. Now, of this nature are all the propositions which have been called essential; they are, in fact, identical propositions.

It is true that a proposition which predicates any attribute, even though it be one implied in the name, is in most cases understood to involve a tacit assertion that there *exists* a thing corresponding to the name, and possessing the attributes connoted by it; and this implied assertion may convey information, even to those who understood the meaning of the name. But all information of this sort, conveyed by all the essential propositions of which man can be made the subject, is included in the assertion, Men exist. And this assumption of real existence is after all only the result of an imperfection of language. It arises from the ambiguity of the copula, which, in addition to its proper office of a mark to show that an assertion is made, is also, as we have formerly remarked, a concrete word connoting existence. The actual existence of the subject of the proposition is therefore only apparently, not really, implied in the predication, if an essential one: we may say, A ghost is a disembodied spirit, without believing in ghosts. But an accidental, or non-essential, affirmation, does imply the real existence of the subject, because in the case of a nonexistent subject there is nothing for the proposition to assert. Such a proposition as, The ghost of a murdered person haunts the couch of the murderer, can only have a meaning if understood as implying a belief in ghosts; for since the signification of the word ghost implies nothing of the kind, the speaker either means nothing, or means to assert a thing which he wishes to be believed to have really taken place.

It will be hereafter seen that when any important consequences seem to follow, as in mathematics, from an essential proposition, or, in other words, from a proposition involved in the meaning of a name, what they really flow from is the tacit assumption of the real existence of the object so named. Apart from this assumption of real existence, the class of propositions in which the predicate is of the essence of the subject (that is, in which the predicate connotes the whole or part of what the subject connotes, but nothing besides) answer no purpose but that of unfolding the whole or some part of the meaning of the name, to those who did not previously know it. Accordingly, the most useful, and in strictness the only useful kind of essential propositions, are Definitions: which, to be complete, should unfold the whole of what is involved in the meaning of the word defined; that is, (when it is a connotative word,) the whole of what it connotes. In defining a name, however, it is not usual to specify its entire connotation, but so much only as is sufficient to mark out the objects usually denoted by it from all other known objects. And sometimes a merely accidental property, not involved in the meaning of the name, answers this purpose equally well. The various kinds of definition which these distinctions give rise to, and the purposes to which they are respectively subservient, will be minutely considered in the proper place.

§ 3. According to the above view of essential propositions, no proposition can be reckoned such which relates to an individual by name, that is, in which the subject is a proper name. Individuals have no essences. When the schoolmen talked of the essence of an individual, they did not mean the properties implied in its name, for the names of individuals imply no properties. They regarded as of the essence of an individual whatever was of the essence of the species in which they were accustomed to place that individual; *i.e.* of the class to which it was most familiarly referred, and to which, therefore, they conceived that it by nature belonged. Thus, because the proposition, Man is a rational being, was an essential proposition, they affirmed the same thing of the proposition, Julius Caesar is a rational being. This followed very naturally if genera and species were to be considered as entities, distinct from, but *inhering* in, the individuals composing them. If *man* was a substance inhering in each individual man, the *essence* of man (whatever that might mean) was naturally supposed to accompany it; to inhere in John Thompson, and to form the *common essence* of Thompson and Julius Caesar. It might then be fairly said, that rationality, being of the essence of Man, was of the essence also of Thompson. But if Man altogether be only the individual men and a name bestowed upon them in consequence of certain common properties, what becomes of John Thompson's essence?

A fundamental error is seldom expelled from philosophy by a single victory. It retreats slowly, defends every inch of ground, and often retains a footing in some remote fastness after it has been driven from the open country. The essences of individuals were an unmeaning figment arising from a misapprehension of the essences of classes, yet even Locke, when he extirpated the parent error, could not shake himself free from that which was its fruit. He distinguished two sorts of essences, Real and Nominal. His nominal essences were the essences of classes, explained nearly as we have now explained them. Nor is anything wanting to render the third book of Locke's Essay a nearly unexceptionable treatise on the connotation of names, except to free its language from the assumption of what are called Abstract Ideas, which unfortunately is involved in the phraseology, although not necessarily connected with the thoughts, contained in that immortal Third Book. (23) But, besides nominal essences, he admitted real essences, or essences of individual objects, which he supposed to be the causes of the sensible properties of those objects. We know not (said he) what these are; (and this acknowledgment rendered the fiction comparatively innocuous;) but if we did, we could, from them alone, demonstrate the sensible properties of the object, as the properties of the triangle are demonstrated from the definition of the triangle. I shall have occasion to revert to this theory in treating of Demonstration, and of the conditions under which one property of a thing admits of being demonstrated from another property. It is enough here to remark that according to this definition, the real essence of an object has, in the progress of physics, come to be conceived as nearly equivalent, in the case of bodies, to their corpuscular structure: what it is now supposed to mean in the case of any other entities, I would not take upon myself to define.

§ 4. An essential proposition, then, is one which is purely verbal; which asserts of a thing under a particular name, only what is asserted of it in the fact of calling it by that name; and which therefore either gives no information, or gives it respecting the name, not the thing. Non-essential, or accidental propositions, on the contrary, may be called Real Propositions, in opposition to Verbal. They predicate of a thing, some fact not involved in the signification of the name by which the proposition speaks of it; some attribute not connoted by that name. Such are all propositions concerning things individually designated, and all general or particular propositions in which the predicate connotes any attribute not connoted by the subject. All these, if true, add to our knowledge: they convey information, not already involved in the names employed. When I am told that all, or even that some objects, which have certain qualities, or which stand in certain relations, have also certain other qualities, or stand in certain other relations, I learn from this proposition a new fact; a fact not included in my knowledge of the meaning of the words, nor even of the existence of Things answering to the signification of those words. It is this class of propositions only which are in themselves instructive, or from which any instructive propositions can be inferred.

Nothing has probably contributed more to the opinion so commonly prevalent of the futility of the school logic, than the circumstance that almost all the examples used in the common school books to illustrate the doctrine of predication and of the syllogism, consist of essential propositions. They were usually taken either from the branches or from the main trunk of the Predicamental Tree, which included nothing but what was of the *essence* of the species: *Omne corpus est substantia*, *Omne animal est corpus*, *Omnis homo est corpus*, *Omnis homo est animal*, *Omnis homo est rationalis*, and so forth. It is far from wonderful that the syllogistic art should have been thought to be of no use in assisting correct reasoning, when almost the only propositions which, in the hands of its professed teachers, it was employed to prove, were such as every one assented to without proof the moment he comprehended the meaning of the words; and stood exactly on a level, in point of evidence, with the premises from which they were drawn. I have, therefore, throughout this work, avoided the employment of essential propositions as examples, except where the nature of the principle to be illustrated specifically required them.

§ 5. With respect to propositions which do convey information--which assert something of a Thing, under a name that does not already presuppose what is about to be asserted; there are two different aspects in which these, or rather such of them as are general propositions, may be considered: we may either look at them as portions of speculative truth, or as memoranda for practical use. According as we consider propositions in one or the other of these lights, their import may be conveniently expressed in one or in the other of two formulas.

According to the formula which we have hitherto employed, and which is best adapted to express the import of the proposition as a portion of our theoretical knowledge, All men are mortal, means that the attributes of man are always accompanied by the attribute mortality: No men are gods, means that the attributes of man are never accompanied by the attributes, or at least never by all the attributes, signified by the word god. But when the proposition is considered as a memorandum for practical use, we shall find a different mode of expressing the same meaning better adapted to indicate the office which the proposition performs. The practical use of a proposition is, to apprise or remind us what we have to expect, in any individual case which comes within the assertion contained in the proposition. In reference to this purpose, the proposition, All men are mortal, means that the attributes of man are ***evidence of***, are a ***mark*** of, mortality; an indication by which the presence of that attribute is made manifest. No men are gods, means that the attributes of man are a mark or evidence that some or all of the attributes supposed to belong to a god are not there; that where the former are, we need not expect to find the latter.

These two forms of expression are at bottom equivalent; but the one points the attention more directly to what a proposition means, the latter to the manner in which it is to be used.

Now it is to be observed that Reasoning (the subject to which we are next to proceed) is a process into which propositions enter not as ultimate results, but as means to the establishment of other propositions. We may expect, therefore, that the mode of exhibiting the import of a general proposition which shows it in its application to practical use, will best express the function which propositions perform in Reasoning. And accordingly, in the theory of Reasoning, the mode of viewing the subject which considers a Proposition as asserting that one fact or phenomenon is a ***mark*** or ***evidence*** of another fact or phenomenon, will be found almost indispensable. For the purposes of that Theory, the best mode of defining the import of a proposition is not the mode which shows most clearly what it is in itself, but that which most distinctly suggests the manner in which it may be made available for advancing from it to other propositions.

CHAPTER VII. OF THE NATURE OF CLASSIFICATION, AND THE FIVE PREDICABLES.

§ 1. In examining into the nature of general propositions, we have adverted much less than is usual with Logicians, to the ideas of a Class, and Classification; ideas which, since the Realist doctrine of General Substances went out of vogue, have formed the basis of almost every attempt at a philosophical theory of general terms and general propositions. We have considered general names as having a meaning, quite independently of their being the names of classes. That circumstance is in truth accidental, it being wholly immaterial to the signification of the name whether there are many objects or only one to which it happens to be applicable, or whether there be any at all. God is as much a general term to the Christian or the Jew as to the Polytheist; and dragon, hippogriff, chimera, mermaid, ghost, are as much so as if real objects existed, corresponding to those names. Every name the signification of which is constituted by attributes, is potentially a name of an indefinite number of objects; but it needs not be actually the name of any; and if of any, it may be the name of only one. As soon as we employ a name to connote attributes, the things, be they more or fewer, which happen to possess those attributes, are constituted, *ipso facto*, a class. But in predicating the name we predicate only the attributes; and the fact of belonging to a class does not, in ordinary cases, come into view at all.

Although, however, Predication does not presuppose Classification, and although the theory of Names and of Propositions is not cleared up, but only encumbered, by intruding the idea of classification into it, there is nevertheless a close connexion between Classification and the employment of General Names. By every general name which we introduce, we create a class, if there be any things, real or imaginary, to compose it; that is, any Things corresponding to the signification of the name. Classes, therefore, mostly owe their existence to general language. But general language, also, though that is not the most common case, sometimes owes its existence to classes. A general, which is as much as to say a significant, name, is indeed mostly introduced because we have a signification to express by it; because we need a word by means of which to predicate the attributes which it connotes. But it is also true that a name is sometimes introduced because we have found it convenient to create a class; because we have thought it useful for the regulation of our mental operations, that a certain group of objects should be thought of together. A naturalist, for purposes connected with his particular science, sees reason to distribute the animal or vegetable creation into certain groups rather than into any others, and he requires a name to bind, as it were, each of his groups together. It must not however be supposed that such names, when introduced, differ in any respect, as to their mode of signification, from other connotative names. The classes which they denote are, as much as any other classes, constituted by certain common attributes, and their names are significant of those attributes, and of nothing else. The names of Cuvier's classes and orders, ***Plantigrades***, ***Digitigrades***, &c., are as much the expression of attributes as if those names had preceded, instead of growing out of, his classification of animals. The only peculiarity of the case is, that the convenience of classification was here the primary motive for introducing the names; while in other cases the name is introduced as a means of predication, and the formation of a class denoted by it is only an indirect consequence.

The principles which ought to regulate Classification as a logical process subservient to the investigation of truth, cannot be discussed to any purpose until a much later stage of our inquiry. But, of classification as resulting from, and implied in, the fact of employing general language, we cannot forbear to treat here, without leaving the theory of general names, and of their employment in predication, mutilated and formless.

§ 2. This portion of the theory of general language is the subject of what is termed the doctrine of the Predicables; a set of distinctions handed down from Aristotle, and his follower Porphyry, many of which have taken a firm root in scientific, and some of them even in popular, phraseology. The predicables are a five-fold division of General Names, not grounded as usual on a difference in their meaning, that is, in the attribute which they connote, but on a difference in the kind of class which they denote. We may predicate of a thing five different varieties of class-name:--

A genus of the thing (γⵏνος).
A species (εⵏδος).
A differentia (διαφορⵏ).
A proprium (ⵏδιⵏν).
An accidens (συμβεβηκⵏς).

It is to be remarked of these distinctions, that they express, not what the predicate is in its own meaning, but what relation it bears to the subject of which it happens on the particular occasion to be predicated. There are not some names which are exclusively genera, and others which are exclusively species, or differentiae; but the same name is referred to one or another Predicable, according to the subject of which it is predicated on the particular occasion. *Animal*, for instance, is a genus with respect to man, or John; a species with respect to Substance, or Being. *Rectangular* is one of the Differentiae of a geometrical square; it is merely one of the Accidentia of the table at which I am writing. The words genus, species, &c., are therefore relative terms; they are names applied to certain predicates, to express the relation between them and some given subject: a relation grounded, as we shall see, not on what the predicate connotes, but on the class which it *de*notes, and on the place which, in some given classification, that class occupies relatively to the particular subject.

§ 3. Of these five names, two, Genus and Species, are not only used by naturalists in a technical acceptation not precisely agreeing with their philosophical meaning, but have also acquired a popular acceptation, much more general than either. In this popular sense any two classes, one of which includes the whole of the other and more, may be called a Genus and a Species. Such, for instance, are Animal and Man; Man and Mathematician. Animal is a genus; Man and Brute are its two species; or we may divide it into a greater number of species, as man, horse, dog, &c. *Biped*, or *two-footed animal*, may also be considered a genus, of which man and bird are two species. *Taste* is a genus, of which sweet taste, sour taste, salt taste, &c. are species. *Virtue* is a genus; justice, prudence, courage, fortitude, generosity, &c. are its species.

The same class which is a genus with reference to the sub-classes or species included in it, may be itself a species with reference to a more comprehensive, or, as it is often called, a superior, genus. Man is a species with reference to animal, but a genus with reference to the species mathematician. Animal is a genus, divided into two species, man and brute; but animal is also a species, which, with another species, vegetable, makes up the genus, organized being. Biped is a genus with reference to man and bird, but a species with respect to the superior genus, animal. Taste is a genus divided into species, but also a species of the genus sensation. Virtue, a genus with reference to justice, temperance, &c., is one of the species of the genus, mental quality.

In this popular sense the words Genus and Species have passed into common discourse. And it should be observed that, in ordinary parlance, not the name of the class, but the class itself, is said to be the genus or species; not, of course, the class in the sense of each individual of that class, but the individuals collectively, considered as an aggregate whole; the name by which the class is designated being then called not the genus or species, but the generic or specific name. And this is an admissible form of expression; nor is it of any importance which of the two modes of speaking we adopt, provided the rest of our language is consistent with it; but if we call the class itself the genus, we must not talk of predicating the genus. We predicate of man the *name* mortal; and by predicating the name, we may be said, in an intelligible sense, to predicate what the name expresses, the *attribute* mortality; but in no allowable sense of the word predication do we predicate of man the *class* mortal. We predicate of him the fact of *belonging* to the class.

By the Aristotelian logicians, the terms genus and species were used in a more restricted sense. They did not admit every class which could be divided into other classes to be a genus, or every class which could be included in a larger class to be a species. Animal was by them considered a genus; and man and brute co-ordinate species under that genus: *biped* would not have been admitted to be a genus with reference to man, but a *proprium* or *accidens* only. It was requisite, according to their theory, that genus and species should be of the *essence* of the subject. *Animal* was of the essence of man; *biped* was not. And in every classification they considered some one class as the lowest or *infima* species. Man, for instance, was a lowest species. Any further divisions into which the class might be capable of being broken down, as man into white, black, and red man, or into priest and layman, they did not admit to be species.

It has been seen, however, in the preceding chapter, that the distinction between the essence of a class, and the attributes or properties which are not of its essence--a distinction which has given occasion to so much abstruse speculation, and to which so mysterious a character was formerly, and by many writers is still, attached,--amounts to nothing more than the difference between those attributes of the class which are, and those which are not, involved in the signification of the class-name. As applied to individuals, the word Essence, we found, has no meaning, except in connexion with the exploded tenets of the Realists; and what the schoolmen chose to call the essence of an individual, was simply the essence of the class to which that individual was most familiarly referred.

Is there no difference, then, save this merely verbal one, between the classes which the schoolmen admitted to be genera or species, and those to which they refused the title? Is it an error to regard some of the differences which exist among objects as differences *in kind* (*genere* or *specie*), and others only as differences in the accidents? Were the schoolmen right or wrong in giving to some of the classes into which things may be divided, the name of *kinds*, and considering others as secondary divisions, grounded on differences of a comparatively superficial nature? Examination will show that the Aristotelians did mean something by this distinction, and something important; but which, being but indistinctly conceived, was inadequately expressed by the phraseology of essences, and by the various other modes of speech to which they had recourse.

§ 4. It is a fundamental principle in logic, that the power of framing classes is unlimited, as long as there is any (even the smallest) difference to found a distinction upon. Take any attribute whatever, and if some things have it, and others have not, we may ground on the attribute a division of all things into two classes; and we actually do so, the moment we create a name which connotes the attribute. The number of possible classes, therefore, is boundless; and there are as many actual classes (either of real or of imaginary things) as there are of general names, positive and negative together.

But if we contemplate any one of the classes so formed, such as the class animal or plant, or the class sulphur or phosphorus, or the class white or red, and consider in what particulars the individuals included in the class differ from those which do not come within it, we find a very remarkable diversity in this respect between some classes and others. There are some classes, the things contained in which differ from other things only in certain particulars which may be numbered; while others differ in more than can be numbered, more even than we need ever expect to know. Some classes have little or nothing in common to characterise them by, except precisely what is connoted by the name: white things, for example, are not distinguished by any common properties, except whiteness; or if they are, it is only by such as are in some way dependent on, or connected with, whiteness. But a hundred generations have not exhausted the common properties of animals or of plants, of sulphur or of phosphorus; nor do we suppose them to be exhaustible, but proceed to new observations and experiments, in the full confidence of discovering new properties which were by no means implied in those we previously knew. While, if any one were to propose for investigation the common properties of all things which are of the same colour, the same shape, or the same specific gravity, the absurdity would be palpable. We have no ground to believe that any such common properties exist, except such as may be shown to be involved in the supposition itself, or to be derivable from it by some law of causation. It appears, therefore, that the properties, on which we ground our classes, sometimes exhaust all that the class has in common, or contain it all by some mode of implication; but in other instances we make a selection of a few properties from among not only a greater number, but a number inexhaustible by us, and to which as we know no bounds, they may, so far as we are concerned, be regarded as infinite.

There is no impropriety in saying that of these two classifications, the one answers to a much more radical distinction in the things themselves, than the other does. And if any one even chooses to say that the one classification is made by nature, the other by us for our convenience, he will be right; provided he means no more than this: Where a certain apparent difference between things (although perhaps in itself of little moment) answers to we know not what number of other differences, pervading not only their known properties but properties yet undiscovered, it is not optional but imperative to recognise this difference as the foundation of a specific distinction: while, on the contrary, differences that are merely finite and determinate, like those designated by the words white, black, or red, may be disregarded if the purpose for which the classification is made does not require attention to those particular properties. The differences, however, are made by nature, in both cases; while the recognition of those differences as grounds of classification and of naming, is, equally in both cases, the act of man: only in the one case, the ends of language and of classification would be subverted if no notice were taken of the difference, while in the other case, the necessity of taking notice of it depends on the importance or unimportance of the particular qualities in which the difference happens to consist.

Now, these classes, distinguished by unknown multitudes of properties, and not solely by a few determinate ones, are the only classes which, by the Aristotelian logicians, were considered as genera or species. Differences which extended only to a certain property or properties, and there terminated, they considered as differences only in the *accidents* of things; but where any class differed from other things by an infinite series of differences, known and unknown, they considered the distinction as one of *kind*, and spoke of it as being an *essential* difference, which is also one of the usual meanings of that vague expression at the present day.

Conceiving the schoolmen to have been justified in drawing a broad line of separation between these two kinds of classes and of class-distinctions, I shall not only retain the division itself, but continue to express it in their language. According to that language, the proximate (or lowest) Kind to which any individual is referrible, is called its species. Conformably to this, Sir Isaac Newton would be said to be of the species man. There are indeed numerous sub-classes included in the class man, to which Newton also belongs; as, for example, Christian, and Englishman, and Mathematician. But these, though distinct classes, are not, in our sense of the term, distinct Kinds of men. A Christian, for example, differs from other human beings; but he differs only in the attribute which the word expresses, namely, belief in Christianity, and whatever else that implies, either as involved in the fact itself, or connected with it through some law of cause and effect. We should never think of inquiring what properties, unconnected with Christianity either as cause or effect, are common to all Christians and peculiar to them; while in regard to all Men, physiologists are perpetually carrying on such an inquiry; nor is the answer ever likely to be completed. Man, therefore, we may call a species; Christian, or Mathematician, we cannot.

Note here, that it is by no means intended to imply that there may not be different Kinds, or logical species, of man. The various races and temperaments, the two sexes, and even the various ages, maybe differences of kind, within our meaning of the term. I do not say that they are so. For in the progress of physiology it may almost be said to be made out, that the differences which really exist between different races, sexes, &c., follow as consequences, under laws of nature, from a small number of primary differences which can be precisely determined, and which, as the phrase is, *account for* all the rest. If this be so, these are not distinctions in kind; no more than Christian, Jew, Mussulman, and Pagan, a difference which also carries many consequences along with it. And in this way classes are often mistaken for real kinds, which are afterwards proved not to be so. But if it turned out, that the differences were not capable of being thus accounted for, then Caucasian, Mongolian, Negro, &c., would be really different Kinds of human beings, and entitled to be ranked as species by the logician; though not by the naturalist. For (as already noticed) the word species is used in a very different signification in logic and in natural history. By the naturalist, organized beings are never said to be of different species, if it is supposed that they could possibly have descended from the same stock. That, however, is a sense artificially given to the word, for the technical purposes of a particular science. To the logician, if a negro and a white man differ in the same manner (however less in degree) as a horse and a camel do, that is, if their differences are inexhaustible, and not referrible to any common cause, they are different species, whether they are descended from common ancestors or not. But if their differences can all be traced to climate and habits, or to some one special difference in structure, they are not, in the logician's view, specifically distinct.

When the *infima species*, or proximate Kind, to which an individual belongs, has been ascertained, the properties common to that Kind include necessarily the whole of the common properties of every other real Kind to which the individual can be referrible. Let the individual, for example, be Socrates, and the proximate Kind, man. Animal, or living creature, is also a real Kind, and includes Socrates; but since it likewise includes man, or in other words, since all men are animals, the properties common to animals form a portion of the common properties of the subclass, man: and if there be any class which includes Socrates without including man, that class is not a real Kind. Let the class, for example, be *flat-nosed*; that being a class which includes Socrates, without including all men. To determine whether it is a real Kind, we must ask ourselves this question: Have all flat-nosed animals, in addition to whatever is implied in their flat noses, any common properties, other than those which are common to all animals whatever? If they had; if a flat nose were a mark or index to an indefinite number of other peculiarities, not deducible from the former by any ascertainable law; then out of the class man we might cut another class, flat-nosed man, which, according to our definition, would be a Kind. But if we could do this, man would not be, as it was assumed to be, the proximate Kind. Therefore, the properties of the proximate Kind do comprehend those (whether known or unknown) of all other Kinds to which the individual belongs; which was the point we undertook to prove. And hence, every other Kind which is predicable of the individual, will be to the proximate Kind in the relation of a genus, according to even the popular acceptation of the terms genus and species; that is, it will be a larger class, including it and more.

We are now able to fix the logical meaning of these terms. Every class which is a real Kind, that is, which is distinguished from all other classes by an indeterminate multitude of properties not derivable from one another, is either a genus or a species. A Kind which is not divisible into other Kinds, cannot be a genus, because it has no species under it; but it is itself a species, both with reference to the individuals below and to the genera above, (Species Praedicabilis and Species Subjicibilis.) But every Kind which admits of division into real Kinds (as animal into quadruped, bird, &c., or quadruped into various species of quadrupeds) is a genus to all below it, a species to all genera in which it is itself included. And here we may close this part of the discussion, and pass to the three remaining predicables, Differentia, Proprium, and Accidens.

§ 5. To begin with Differentia. This word is correlative with the words genus and species, and as all admit, it signifies the attribute which distinguishes a given species from every other species of the same genus. This is so far clear: but we may still ask, which of the distinguishing attributes it signifies. For we have seen that every Kind (and a species must be a Kind) is distinguished from other Kinds not by any one attribute, but by an indefinite number. Man, for instance, is a species of the genus animal; Rational (or rationality, for it is of no consequence whether we use the concrete or the abstract form) is generally assigned by logicians as the Differentia; and doubtless this attribute serves the purpose of distinction: but it has also been remarked of man, that he is a cooking animal; the only animal that dresses its food. This, therefore, is another of the attributes by which the species man is distinguished from other species of the same genus: would this attribute serve equally well for a differentia? The Aristotelians say No; having laid it down that the differentia must, like the genus and species, be of the ***essence*** of the subject.

And here we lose even that vestige of a meaning grounded in the nature of the things themselves, which may be supposed to be attached to the word essence when it is said that genus and species must be of the essence of the thing. There can be no doubt that when the schoolmen talked of the essences of things as opposed to their accidents, they had confusedly in view the distinction between differences of kind, and the differences which are not of kind; they meant to intimate that genera and species must be Kinds. Their notion of the essence of a thing was a vague notion of a something which makes it what it is, ***i.e.***, which makes it the Kind of thing that it is--which causes it to have all that variety of properties which distinguish its Kind. But when the matter came to be looked at more closely, nobody could discover what caused the thing to have all those properties, nor even that there was anything which caused it to have them. Logicians, however, not liking to admit this, and being unable to detect what made the thing to be what it was, satisfied themselves with what made it to be what it was called. Of the innumerable properties, known and unknown, that are common to the class man, a portion only, and of course a very small portion, are connoted by its name; these few, however, will naturally have been thus distinguished from the rest either for their greater obviousness, or for greater supposed importance. These properties, then, which were connoted by the name, logicians seized upon, and called them the essence of the species; and not stopping there, they affirmed them, in the case of the ***infima species***, to be the essence of the individual too; for it was their maxim, that the species contained the "whole essence" of the thing. Metaphysics, that fertile field of delusion propagated by language, does not afford a more signal instance of such delusion. On this account it was that rationality, being connoted by the name man, was allowed to be a differentia of the class; but the peculiarity of cooking their food, not being connoted, was relegated to the class of accidental properties.

The distinction, therefore, between Differentia, Proprium, and Accidens, is not founded in the nature of things, but in the connotation of names; and we must seek it there, if we wish to find what it is.

From the fact that the genus includes the species, in other words *de*notes more than the species, or is predicable of a greater number of individuals, it follows that the species must connote more than the genus. It must connote all the attributes which the genus connotes, or there would be nothing to prevent it from denoting individuals not included in the genus. And it must connote something besides, otherwise it would include the whole genus. Animal denotes all the individuals denoted by man, and many more. Man, therefore, must connote all that animal connotes, otherwise there might be men who are not animals; and it must connote something more than animal connotes, otherwise all animals would be men. This surplus of connotation--this which the species connotes over and above the connotation of the genus--is the Differentia, or specific difference; or, to state the same proposition in other words, the Differentia is that which must be added to the connotation of the genus, to complete the connotation of the species.

The word man, for instance, exclusively of what it connotes in common with animal, also connotes rationality, and at least some approximation to that external form, which we all know, but which, as we have no name for it considered in itself, we are content to call the human. The differentia, or specific difference, therefore, of man, as referred to the genus animal, is that outward form and the possession of reason. The Aristotelians said, the possession of reason, without the outward form. But if they adhered to this, they would have been obliged to call the Houyhnhms men. The question never arose, and they were never called upon to decide how such a case would have affected their notion of essentiality. However this may be, they were satisfied with taking such a portion of the differentia as sufficed to distinguish the species from all other *existing* things, although by so doing they might not exhaust the connotation of the name.

§ 6. And here, to prevent the notion of differentia from being restricted within too narrow limits, it is necessary to remark, that a species, even as referred to the same genus, will not always have the same differentia, but a different one, according to the principle and purpose which preside over the particular classification. For example, a naturalist surveys the various kinds of animals, and looks out for the classification of them most in accordance with the order in which, for zoological purposes, he thinks it desirable that our ideas should arrange themselves.

With this view he finds it advisable that one of his fundamental divisions should be into warm-blooded and cold-blooded animals; or into animals which breathe with lungs and those which breathe with gills; or into carnivorous, and frugivorous or graminivorous; or into those which walk on the flat part and those which walk on the extremity of the foot, a distinction on which some of Cuvier's families are founded. In doing this, the naturalist creates so many new classes, which are by no means those to which the individual animal is familiarly and spontaneously referred; nor should we ever think of assigning to them so prominent a position in our arrangement of the animal kingdom, unless for a preconceived purpose of scientific convenience. And to the liberty of doing this there is no limit. In the examples we have given, most of the classes are real Kinds, since each of the peculiarities is an index to a multitude of properties, belonging to the class which it characterizes: but even if the case were otherwise--if the other properties of those classes could all be derived, by any process known to us, from the one peculiarity on which the class is founded--even then, if those derivative properties were of primary importance for the purposes of the naturalist, he would be warranted in founding his primary divisions on them.

If, however, practical convenience is a sufficient warrant for making the main demarcations in our arrangement of objects run in lines not coinciding with any distinction of Kind, and so creating genera and species in the popular sense which are not genera or species in the rigorous sense at all; *a fortiori* must we be warranted, when our genera and species *are* real genera and species, in marking the distinction between them by those of their properties which considerations of practical convenience most strongly recommend. If we cut a species out of a given genus--the species man, for instance, out of the genus animal--with an intention on our part that the peculiarity by which we are to be guided in the application of the name man should be rationality, then rationality is the differentia of the species man. Suppose, however, that, being naturalists, we, for the purposes of our particular study, cut out of the genus animal the same species man, but with an intention that the distinction between man and all other species of animal should be, not rationality, but the possession of "four incisors in each jaw, tusks solitary, and erect posture." It is evident that the word man, when used by us as naturalists, no longer connotes rationality, but connotes the three other properties specified;

for that which we have expressly in view when we impose a name, assuredly forms part of the meaning of that name. We may, therefore, lay it down as a maxim, that wherever there is a Genus, and a Species marked out from that genus by an assignable differentia, the name of the species must be connotative, and must connote the differentia; but the connotation may be special--not involved in the signification of the term as ordinarily used, but given to it when employed as a term of art or science. The word Man, in common use, connotes rationality and a certain form, but does not connote the number or character of the teeth: in the Linnaean system it connotes the number of incisor and canine teeth, but does not connote rationality nor any particular form. The word **man** has, therefore, two different meanings; although not commonly considered as ambiguous, because it happens in both cases to **de**note the same individual objects. But a case is conceivable in which the ambiguity would become evident: we have only to imagine that some new kind of animal were discovered, having Linnaeus's three characteristics of humanity, but not rational, or not of the human form. In ordinary parlance these animals would not be called men; but in natural history they must still be called so by those, if any there be, who adhere to the Linnaean classification; and the question would arise, whether the word should continue to be used in two senses, or the classification be given up, and the technical sense of the term be abandoned along with it.

Words not otherwise connotative may, in the mode just adverted to, acquire a special or technical connotation. Thus the word whiteness, as we have so often remarked, connotes nothing; it merely denotes the attribute corresponding to a certain sensation: but if we are making a classification of colours, and desire to justify, or even merely to point out, the particular place assigned to whiteness in our arrangement, we may define it "the colour produced by the mixture of all the simple rays;" and this fact, though by no means implied in the meaning of the word whiteness as ordinarily used, but only known by subsequent scientific investigation, is part of its meaning in the particular essay or treatise, and becomes the differentia of the species.(24)

The differentia, therefore, of a species, may be defined to be, that part of the connotation of the specific name, whether ordinary, or special and technical, which distinguishes the species in question from all other species of the genus to which on the particular occasion we are referring it.

§ 7. Having disposed of Genus, Species, and Differentia, we shall not find much difficulty in attaining a clear conception of the distinction between the other two predicables, as well as between them and the first three.

In the Aristotelian phraseology, Genus and Differentia are of the **essence** of the subject; by which, as we have seen, is really meant that the properties signified by the genus and those signified by the differentia, form part of the connotation of the name denoting the species. Proprium and Accidens, on the other hand, form no part of the essence, but are predicated of the species only **accidentally**. Both are Accidents, in the wider sense in which the accidents of a thing are opposed to its essence; though, in the doctrine of the Predicables, Accidens is used for one sort of accident only, Proprium being another sort. Proprium, continue the schoolmen, is predicated **accidentally**, indeed, but **necessarily**; or, as they further explain it, signifies an attribute which is not indeed part of the essence, but which flows from, or is a consequence of, the essence, and is, therefore, inseparably attached to the species; *e.g.* the various properties of a triangle, which, though no part of its definition, must necessarily be possessed by whatever comes under that definition. Accidens, on the contrary, has no connexion whatever with the essence, but may come and go, and the species still remain what it was before. If a species could exist without its Propria, it must be capable of existing without that on which its Propria are necessarily consequent, and therefore without its essence, without that which constitutes it a species. But an Accidens, whether separable or inseparable from the species in actual experience, may be supposed separated, without the necessity of supposing any other alteration; or at least, without supposing any of the essential properties of the species to be altered, since with them an Accidens has no connexion.

A Proprium, therefore, of the species, may be defined, any attribute which belongs to all the individuals included in the species, and which, although not connoted by the specific name, (either ordinarily if the classification we are considering be for ordinary purposes, or specially if it be for a special purpose,) yet follows from some attribute which the name either ordinarily or specially connotes.

One attribute may follow from another in two ways; and there are consequently two kinds of Proprium. It may follow as a conclusion follows premises, or it may follow as an effect follows a cause. Thus, the attribute of having the opposite sides equal, which is not one of those connoted by the word Parallelogram, nevertheless follows from those connoted by it, namely, from having the opposite sides straight lines and parallel, and the number of sides four. The attribute, therefore, of having the opposite sides equal, is a Proprium of the class parallelogram; and a Proprium of the first kind, which follows from the connoted attributes by way of ***demonstration***. The attribute of being capable of understanding language, is a Proprium of the species man, since, without being connoted by the word, it follows from an attribute which the word does connote, viz. from the attribute of rationality. But this is a Proprium of the second kind, which follows by way of ***causation***. How it is that one property of a thing follows, or can be inferred, from another; under what conditions this is possible, and what is the exact meaning of the phrase; are among the questions which will occupy us in the two succeeding Books. At present it needs only be said, that whether a Proprium follows by demonstration or by causation, it follows ***necessarily***; that is to say, it ***cannot but*** follow, consistently with some law which we regard as a part of the constitution either of our thinking faculty or of the universe.

§ 8. Under the remaining predicable, Accidens, are included all attributes of a thing which are neither involved in the signification of the name, (whether ordinarily or as a term of art,) nor have, so far as we know, any necessary connexion with attributes which are so involved. They are commonly divided into Separable and Inseparable Accidents. Inseparable accidents are those which--although we know of no connexion between them and the attributes constitutive of the species, and although, therefore, so far as we are aware, they might be absent without making the name inapplicable and the species a different species--are yet never in fact known to be absent. A concise mode of expressing the same meaning is, that inseparable accidents are properties which are universal to the species, but not necessary to it. Thus, blackness is an attribute of a crow, and, as far as we know, a universal one. But if we were to discover a race of white birds, in other respects resembling crows, we should not say, These are not crows; we should say, These are white crows. Crow, therefore, does not connote blackness; nor, from any of the attributes which it does connote, whether as a word in popular use or as a term of art, could blackness be inferred. Not only, therefore, can we conceive a white crow, but we know of no reason why such an animal should not exist. Since, however, none but black crows are known to exist, blackness, in the present state of our knowledge, ranks as an accident, but an inseparable accident, of the species crow.

Separable Accidents are those which are found, in point of fact, to be sometimes absent from the species; which are not only not necessary, but not even universal. They are such as do not belong to every individual of the species, but only to some individuals; or if to all, not at all times. Thus the colour of an European is one of the separable accidents of the species man, because it is not an attribute of all human creatures. Being born, is also (speaking in the logical sense) a separable accident of the species man, because, although an attribute of all human beings, it is so only at one particular time. *A fortiori* those attributes which are not constant even in the same individual, as, to be in one or in another place, to be hot or cold, sitting or walking, must be ranked as separable accidents.

CHAPTER VIII. OF DEFINITION.

§ 1. One necessary part of the theory of Names and of Propositions remains to be treated of in this place: the theory of Definitions. As being the most important of the class of propositions which we have characterized as purely verbal, they have already received some notice in the chapter preceding the last. But their fuller treatment was at that time postponed, because definition is so closely connected with classification, that, until the nature of the latter process is in some measure understood, the former cannot be discussed to much purpose.

The simplest and most correct notion of a Definition is, a proposition declaratory of the meaning of a word; namely, either the meaning which it bears in common acceptation, or that which the speaker or writer, for the particular purposes of his discourse, intends to annex to it.

The definition of a word being the proposition which enunciates its meaning, words which have no meaning are unsusceptible of definition. Proper names, therefore, cannot be defined. A proper name being a mere mark put upon an individual, and of which it is the characteristic property to be destitute of meaning, its meaning cannot of course be declared; though we may indicate by language, as we might indicate still more conveniently by pointing with the finger, upon what individual that particular mark has been, or is intended to be, put. It is no definition of "John Thomson" to say he is "the son of General Thomson;" for the name John Thomson does not express this. Neither is it any definition of "John Thomson" to say he is "the man now crossing the street." These propositions may serve to make known who is the particular man to whom the name belongs; but that may be done still more unambiguously by pointing to him, which, however, has not usually been esteemed one of the modes of definition.

In the case of connotative names, the meaning, as has been so often observed, is the connotation; and the definition of a connotative name, is the proposition which declares its connotation. This may be done either directly or indirectly. The direct mode would be by a proposition in this form: "Man" (or whatsover the word may be) "is a name connoting such and such attributes," or "is a name which, when predicated of anything, signifies the possession of such and such attributes by that thing." Or thus: Man is everything which possesses such and such attributes: Man is everything which possesses corporeity, organization, life, rationality, and certain peculiarities of external form.

This form of definition is the most precise and least equivocal of any; but it is not brief enough, and is besides too technical and pedantic for common discourse. The more usual mode of declaring the connotation of a name, is to predicate of it another name or names of known signification, which connote the same aggregation of attributes. This may be done either by predicating of the name intended to be defined, another connotative name exactly synonymous, as, "Man is a human being," which is not commonly accounted a definition at all; or by predicating two or more connotative names, which make up among them the whole connotation of the name to be defined. In this last case, again, we may either compose our definition of as many connotative names as there are attributes, each attribute being connoted by one; as, Man is a corporeal, organized, animated, rational being, shaped so and so; or we may employ names which connote several of the attributes at once, as, Man is a rational ***animal***, shaped so and so.

The definition of a name, according to this view of it, is the sum total of all the ***essential*** propositions which can be framed with that name for their subject. All propositions the truth of which is implied in the name, all those which we are made aware of by merely hearing the name, are included in the definition, if complete, and may be evolved from it without the aid of any other premisses; whether the definition expresses them in two or three words, or in a larger number. It is, therefore, not without reason that Condillac and other writers have affirmed a definition to be an *analysis*. To resolve any complex whole into the elements of which it is compounded, is the meaning of analysis; and this we do when we replace one word which connotes a set of attributes collectively, by two or more which connote the same attributes singly, or in smaller groups.

§ 2. From this, however, the question naturally arises, in what manner are we to define a name which connotes only a single attribute? for instance, "white," which connotes nothing but whiteness; "rational," which connotes nothing but the possession of reason. It might seem that the meaning of such names could only be declared in two ways; by a synonymous term, if any such can be found; or in the direct way already alluded to: "White is a name connoting the attribute whiteness." Let us see, however, whether the analysis of the meaning of the name, that is, the breaking down of that meaning into several parts, admits of being carried farther. Without at present deciding this question as to the word *white*, it is obvious that in the case of *rational* some further explanation may be given of its meaning than is contained in the proposition, "Rational is that which possesses the attribute of reason;" since the attribute reason itself admits of being defined. And here we must turn our attention to the definitions of attributes, or rather of the names of attributes, that is, of abstract names.

In regard to such names of attributes as are connotative, and express attributes of those attributes, there is no difficulty: like other connotative names, they are defined by declaring their connotation. Thus, the word *fault* may be defined, "a quality productive of evil or inconvenience." Sometimes, again, the attribute to be defined is not one attribute, but an union of several: we have only, therefore, to put together the names of all the attributes taken separately, and we obtain the definition of the name which belongs to them all taken together; a definition which will correspond exactly to that of the corresponding concrete name. For, as we define a concrete name by enumerating the attributes which it connotes, and as the attributes connoted by a concrete name form the entire signification of the corresponding abstract one, the same enumeration will serve for the definition of both. Thus, if the definition of *a human being* be this, "a being, corporeal, animated, rational, and shaped so and so," the definition of *humanity* will be, corporeity and animal life, combined with rationality, and with such and such a shape.

When, on the other hand, the abstract name does not express a complication of attributes, but a single attribute, we must remember that every attribute is grounded on some fact or phenomenon, from which, and which alone, it derives its meaning. To that fact or phenomenon, called in a former chapter the foundation of the attribute, we must, therefore, have recourse for its definition. Now, the foundation of the attribute may be a phenomenon of any degree of complexity, consisting of many different parts, either coexistent or in succession. To obtain a definition of the attribute, we must analyse the phenomenon into these parts. Eloquence, for example, is the name of one attribute only; but this attribute is grounded on external effects of a complicated nature, flowing from acts of the person to whom we ascribe the attribute; and by resolving this phenomenon of causation into its two parts, the cause and the effect, we obtain a definition of eloquence, viz., the power of influencing the feelings by speech or writing.

A name, therefore, whether concrete or abstract, admits of definition, provided we are able to analyse, that is, to distinguish into parts, the attribute or set of attributes which constitute the meaning both of the concrete name and of the corresponding abstract: if a set of attributes, by enumerating them; if a single attribute, by dissecting the fact or phenomenon (whether of perception or of internal consciousness) which is the foundation of the attribute. But, further, even when the fact is one of our simple feelings or states of consciousness, and therefore unsusceptible of analysis, the names both of the object and of the attribute still admit of definition; or, rather, would do so if all our simple feelings had names. Whiteness may be defined, the property or power of exciting the sensation of white. A white object may be defined an object which excites the sensation of white. The only names which are unsusceptible of definition, because their meaning is unsusceptible of analysis, are the names of the simple feelings themselves. These are in the same condition as proper names. They are not indeed, like proper names, unmeaning; for the words ***sensation of white*** signify, that the sensation which I so denominate resembles other sensations which I remember to have had before, and to have called by that name. But as we have no words by which to recall those former sensations, except the very word which we seek to define, or some other which, being exactly synonymous with it, requires definition as much, words cannot unfold the signification of this class of names; and we are obliged to make a direct appeal to the personal experience of the individual whom we address.

§ 3. Having stated what seems to be the true idea of a Definition, we proceed to examine some opinions of philosophers, and some popular conceptions on the subject, which conflict more or less with that idea.

The only adequate definition of a name is, as already remarked, one which declares the facts, and the whole of the facts, which the name involves in its signification. But with most persons the object of a definition does not embrace so much; they look for nothing more, in a definition, than a guide to the correct use of the term--a protection against applying it in a manner inconsistent with custom and convention. Anything, therefore, is to them a sufficient definition of a term, which will serve as a correct index to what the term *de*notes; although not embracing the whole, and sometimes, perhaps, not even any part, of what it connotes. This gives rise to two sorts of imperfect, or unscientific definition; namely, Essential but incomplete Definitions, and Accidental Definitions, or Descriptions. In the former, a connotative name is defined by a part only of its connotation; in the latter, by something which forms no part of the connotation at all.

An example of the first kind of imperfect definitions is the following:--Man is a rational animal. It is impossible to consider this as a complete definition of the word Man, since (as before remarked) if we adhered to it we should be obliged to call the Houyhnhms men; but as there happen to be no Houyhnhms, this imperfect definition is sufficient to mark out and distinguish from all other things, the objects at present denoted by "man;" all the beings actually known to exist, of whom the name is predicable. Though the word is defined by some only among the attributes which it connotes, not by all, it happens that all known objects which possess the enumerated attributes, possess also those which are omitted; so that the field of predication which the word covers, and the employment of it which is conformable to usage, are as well indicated by the inadequate definition as by an adequate one. Such definitions, however, are always liable to be overthrown by the discovery of new objects in nature.

Definitions of this kind are what logicians have had in view, when they laid down the rule, that the definition of a species should be *per genus et differentiam*. Differentia being seldom taken to mean the whole of the peculiarities constitutive of the species, but some one of those peculiarities only, a complete definition would be *per genus et differentias*, rather than *differentiam*. It would include, with the name of the superior genus, not merely *some* attribute which distinguishes the species intended to be defined from all other species of the same genus, but *all* the attributes implied in the name of the species, which the name of the superior genus has not already implied. The assertion, however, that a definition must of necessity consist of a genus and differentiae, is not tenable. It was early remarked by logicians, that the *summum genus* in any classification, having no genus superior to itself, could not be defined in this manner. Yet we have seen that all names, except those of our elementary feelings, are susceptible of definition in the strictest sense; by setting forth in words the constituent parts of the fact or phenomenon, of which the connotation of every word is ultimately composed.

§ 4. Although the first kind of imperfect definition, (which defines a connotative term by a part only of what it connotes, but a part sufficient to mark out correctly the boundaries of its denotation,) has been considered by the ancients, and by logicians in general, as a complete definition; it has always been deemed necessary that the attributes employed should really form part of the connotation; for the rule was that the definition must be drawn from the *essence* of the class; and this would not have been the case if it had been in any degree made up of attributes not connoted by the name. The second kind of imperfect definition, therefore, in which the name of a class is defined by any of its accidents,--that is, by attributes which are not included in its connotation,--has been rejected from the rank of genuine Definition by all logicians, and has been termed Description.

This kind of imperfect definition, however, takes its rise from the same cause as the other, namely, the willingness to accept as a definition anything which, whether it expounds the meaning of the name or not, enables us to discriminate the things denoted by the name from all other things, and consequently to employ the term in predication without deviating from established usage. This purpose is duly answered by stating any (no matter what) of the attributes which are common to the whole of the class, and peculiar to it; or any combination of attributes which may happen to be peculiar to it, though separately each of those attributes may be common to it with some other things. It is only necessary that the definition (or description) thus formed, should be *convertible* with the name which it professes to define; that is, should be exactly co-extensive with it, being predicable of everything of which it is predicable, and of nothing of which it is not predicable; although the attributes specified may have no connexion with those which mankind had in view when they formed or recognised the class, and gave it a name. The following are correct definitions of Man, according to this test: Man is a mammiferous animal, having (by nature) two hands (for the human species answers to this description, and no other animal does): Man is an animal who cooks his food: Man is a featherless biped.

What would otherwise be a mere description, may be raised to the rank of a real definition by the peculiar purpose which the speaker or writer has in view. As was seen in the preceding chapter, it may, for the ends of a particular art or science, or for the more convenient statement of an author's particular doctrines, be advisable to give to some general name, without altering its denotation, a special connotation, different from its ordinary one. When this is done, a definition of the name by means of the attributes which make up the special connotation, though in general a mere accidental definition or description, becomes on the particular occasion and for the particular purpose a complete and genuine definition. This actually occurs with respect to one of the preceding examples, "Man is a mammiferous animal having two hands," which is the scientific definition of man considered as one of the species in Cuvier's distribution of the animal kingdom.

In cases of this sort, although the definition is still a declaration of the meaning which in the particular instance the name is appointed to convey, it cannot be said that to state the meaning of the word is the purpose of the definition. The purpose is not to expound a name, but to help to expound a classification. The special meaning which Cuvier assigned to the word Man, (quite foreign to its ordinary meaning, though involving no change in the denotation of the word,) was incidental to a plan of arranging animals into classes on a certain principle, that is, according to a certain set of distinctions. And since the definition of Man according to the ordinary connotation of the word, though it would have answered every other purpose of a definition, would not have pointed out the place which the species ought to occupy in that particular classification; he gave the word a special connotation, that he might be able to define it by the kind of attributes on which, for reasons of scientific convenience, he had resolved to found his division of animated nature.

Scientific definitions, whether they are definitions of scientific terms or of common terms used in a scientific sense, are almost always of the kind last spoken of: their main purpose is to serve as the landmarks of scientific classification. And since the classifications in any science are continually modified as scientific knowledge advances, the definitions in the sciences are also constantly varying. A striking instance is afforded by the words Acid and Alkali, especially the former. As experimental discovery advanced, the substances classed with acids have been constantly multiplying, and by a natural consequence the attributes connoted by the word have receded and become fewer. At first it connoted the attributes, of combining with an alkali to form a neutral substance (called a salt); being compounded of a base and oxygen; causticity to the taste and touch; fluidity, &c. The true analysis of muriatic acid, into chlorine and hydrogen, caused the second property, composition from a base and oxygen, to be excluded from the connotation. The same discovery fixed the attention of chemists upon hydrogen as an important element in acids; and more recent discoveries having led to the recognition of its presence in sulphuric, nitric, and many other acids, where its existence was not previously suspected, there is now a tendency to include the presence of this element in the connotation of the word. But carbonic acid, silica, sulphurous acid, have no hydrogen in their composition; that property cannot therefore be connoted by the term, unless those substances are no longer to be considered acids. Causticity, and fluidity, have long since been excluded from the characteristics of the class, by the inclusion of silica and many other substances in it; and the formation of neutral bodies by combination with alkalis, together with such electro-chemical peculiarities as this is supposed to imply, are now the only *differentiae* which form the fixed connotation of the word Acid, as a term of chemical science.

Scientific men are still seeking, and may be long ere they find, a suitable definition of one of the earliest words in the vocabulary of the human race, and one of those of which the popular sense is plainest and best understood. The word I mean is Heat; and the source of the difficulty is the imperfect state of our scientific knowledge, which has shown to us multitudes of phenomena certainly connected with the same power which causes what our senses recognise as heat, but has not yet taught us the laws of those phenomena with sufficient accuracy to admit of our determining under what characteristics the whole of those phenomena shall ultimately be embodied as a class: which characteristics would of course be so many differentiae for the definition of the power itself. We have advanced far enough to know that one of the attributes connoted must be that of operating as a repulsive force; but this is certainly not all which must ultimately be included in the scientific definition of heat.

What is true of the definition of any term of science, is of course true of the definition of a science itself: and accordingly, (as observed in the Introductory Chapter of this work,) the definition of a science must necessarily be progressive and provisional. Any extension of knowledge or alteration in the current opinions respecting the subject matter, may lead to a change more or less extensive in the particulars included in the science; and its composition being thus altered, it may easily happen that a different set of characteristics will be found better adapted as differentiae for defining its name.

In the same manner in which a special or technical definition has for its object to expound the artificial classification out of which it grows; the Aristotelian logicians seem to have imagined that it was also the business of ordinary definition to expound the ordinary, and what they deemed the natural, classification of things, namely, the division of them into Kinds; and to show the place which each Kind occupies, as superior, collateral, or subordinate among other Kinds. This notion would account for the rule that all definition must necessarily be ***per genus et differentiam***, and would also explain why any one differentia was deemed sufficient. But to expound, or express in words, a distinction of Kind, has already been shown to be an impossibility: the very meaning of a Kind is, that the properties which distinguish it do not grow out of one another, and cannot therefore be set forth in words, even by implication, otherwise than by enumerating them all: and all are not known, nor ever will be so. It is idle, therefore, to look to this as one of the purposes of a definition: while, if it be only required that the definition of a Kind should indicate what Kinds include it or are included by it, any definitions which expound the connotation of the names will do this: for the name of each class must necessarily connote enough of its properties to fix the boundaries of the class. If the definition, therefore, be a full statement of the connotation, it is all that a definition can be required to be.

§ 5. Of the two incomplete or unscientific modes of definition, and in what they differ from the complete or scientific mode, enough has now been said. We shall next examine an ancient doctrine, once generally prevalent and still by no means exploded, which I regard as the source of a great part of the obscurity hanging over some of the most important processes of the understanding in the pursuit of truth. According to this, the definitions of which we have now treated are only one of two sorts into which definitions may be divided, viz. definitions of names, and definitions of things. The former are intended to explain the meaning of a term; the latter, the nature of a thing; the last being incomparably the most important.

This opinion was held by the ancient philosophers, and by their followers, with the exception of the Nominalists; but as the spirit of modern metaphysics, until a recent period, has been on the whole a Nominalist spirit, the notion of definitions of things has been to a certain extent in abeyance, still continuing, however, to breed confusion in logic, by its consequences indeed rather than by itself. Yet the doctrine in its own proper form now and then breaks out, and has appeared (among other places) where it was scarcely to be expected, in a deservedly popular work, Archbishop Whately's *Logic*.(25) In a review of that work published by me in the **Westminster Review** for January 1828, and containing some opinions which I no longer entertain, I find the following observations on the question now before us; observations with which my present view of that question is still sufficiently in accordance.

"The distinction between nominal and real definitions, between definitions of words and what are called definitions of things, though conformable to the ideas of most of the Aristotelian logicians, cannot, as it appears to us, be maintained. We apprehend that no definition is ever intended to 'explain and unfold the nature of the thing.' It is some confirmation of our opinion, that none of those writers who have thought that there were definitions of things, have ever succeeded in discovering any criterion by which the definition of a thing can be distinguished from any other proposition relating to the thing. The definition, they say, unfolds the nature of the thing: but no definition can unfold its whole nature; and every proposition in which any quality whatever is predicated of the thing, unfolds some part of its nature. The true state of the case we take to be this. All definitions are of names, and of names only; but, in some definitions, it is clearly apparent, that nothing is intended except to explain the meaning of the word; while in others, besides explaining the meaning of the word, it is intended to be implied that there exists a thing, corresponding to the word. Whether this be or be not implied in any given case, cannot be collected from the mere form of the expression. 'A centaur is an animal with the upper parts of a man and the lower parts of a horse,' and 'A triangle is a rectilineal figure with three sides,' are, in form, expressions precisely similar; although in the former it is not implied that any ***thing***, conformable to the term, really exists, while in the latter it is; as may be seen by substituting, in both definitions, the word ***means*** for ***is***. In the first expression, 'A centaur means an animal,' &c., the sense would remain unchanged: in the second 'A triangle means,' &c., the meaning would be altered, since it would be obviously impossible to deduce any of the truths of geometry from a proposition expressive only of the manner in which we intend to employ a particular sign.

"There are, therefore, expressions, commonly passing for definitions, which include in themselves more than the mere explanation of the meaning of a term. But it is not correct to call an expression of this sort a peculiar kind of definition. Its difference from the other kind consists in this, that it is not a definition, but a definition and something more. The definition above given of a triangle, obviously comprises not one, but two propositions, perfectly distinguishable. The one is, 'There may exist a figure, bounded by three straight lines:' the other, 'And this figure may be termed a triangle.' The former of these propositions is not a definition at all: the latter is a mere nominal definition, or explanation of the use and application of a term. The first is susceptible of truth or falsehood, and may therefore be made the foundation of a train of reasoning. The latter can neither be true nor false; the only character it is susceptible of is that of conformity or disconformity to the ordinary usage of language."

There is a real distinction, then, between definitions of names, and what are erroneously called definitions of things; but it is, that the latter, along with the meaning of a name, covertly asserts a matter of fact. This covert assertion is not a definition, but a postulate. The definition is a mere identical proposition, which gives information only about the use of language, and from which no conclusions affecting matters of fact can possibly be drawn. The accompanying postulate, on the other hand, affirms a fact, which may lead to consequences of every degree of importance. It affirms the real existence of Things possessing the combination of attributes set forth in the definition; and this, if true, may be foundation sufficient on which to build a whole fabric of scientific truth.

We have already made, and shall often have to repeat, the remark, that the philosophers who overthrew Realism by no means got rid of the consequences of Realism, but retained long afterwards, in their own philosophy, numerous propositions which could only have a rational meaning as part of a Realistic system. It had been handed down from Aristotle, and probably from earlier times, as an obvious truth, that the science of Geometry is deduced from definitions. This, so long as a definition was considered to be a proposition "unfolding the nature of the thing," did well enough. But Hobbes followed, and rejected utterly the notion that a definition declares the nature of the thing, or does anything but state the meaning of a name; yet he continued to affirm as broadly as any of his predecessors, that the ᾽αρχαί, *principia*, or original premises of mathematics, and even of all science, are definitions; producing the singular paradox, that systems of scientific truth, nay, all truths whatever at which we arrive by reasoning, are deduced from the arbitrary conventions of mankind concerning the signification of words.

To save the credit of the doctrine that definitions are the premises of scientific knowledge, the proviso is sometimes added, that they are so only under a certain condition, namely, that they be framed conformably to the phenomena of nature; that is, that they ascribe such meanings to terms as shall suit objects actually existing. But this is only an instance of the attempt so often made, to escape from the necessity of abandoning old language after the ideas which it expresses have been exchanged for contrary ones. From the meaning of a name (we are told) it is possible to infer physical facts, provided the name has corresponding to it an existing thing. But if this proviso be necessary, from which of the two is the inference really drawn? from the existence of a thing having the properties? or from the existence of a name meaning them?

Take, for instance, any of the definitions laid down as premises in Euclid's Elements; the definition, let us say, of a circle. This, being analysed, consists of two propositions; the one an assumption with respect to a matter of fact, the other a genuine definition. "A figure may exist, having all the points in the line which bounds it equally distant from a single point within it:" "Any figure possessing this property is called a circle." Let us look at one of the demonstrations which are said to depend on this definition, and observe to which of the two propositions contained in it the demonstration really appeals. "About the centre A, describe the circle BCD." Here is an assumption, that a figure, such as the definition expresses, *may* be described; which is no other than the postulate, or covert assumption, involved in the so-called definition. But whether that figure be called a circle or not is quite immaterial. The purpose would be as well answered, in all respects except brevity, were we to say, "Through the point B, draw a line returning into itself, of which every point shall be at an equal distance from the point A." By this the definition of a circle would be got rid of, and rendered needless; but not the postulate implied in it; without that the demonstration could not stand. The circle being now described, let us proceed to the consequence. "Since B C D is a circle, the radius B A is equal to the radius C A." B A is equal to C A, not because B C D is a circle, but because B C D is a figure with the radii equal. Our warrant for assuming that such a figure about the centre A, with the radius B A, may be made to exist, is the postulate. Whether the admissibility of these postulates rests on intuition, or on proof, may be a matter of dispute; but in either case they are the premises on which the theorems depend; and while these are retained it would make no difference in the certainty of geometrical truths, though every definition in Euclid, and every technical term therein defined, were laid aside.

It is, perhaps, superfluous to dwell at so much length on what is so nearly self-evident; but when a distinction, obvious as it may appear, has been confounded, and by powerful intellects, it is better to say too much than too little for the purpose of rendering such mistakes impossible in future. I will, therefore, detain the reader while I point out one of the absurd consequences flowing from the supposition that definitions, as such, are the premises in any of our reasonings, except such as relate to words only. If this supposition were true, we might argue correctly from true premises, and arrive at a false conclusion. We should only have to assume as a premiss the definition of a nonentity; or rather of a name which has no entity corresponding to it. Let this, for instance, be our definition:

A dragon is a serpent breathing flame.

This proposition, considered only as a definition, is indisputably correct. A dragon *is* a serpent breathing flame: the word *means* that. The tacit assumption, indeed, (if there were any such understood assertion,) of the existence of an object with properties corresponding to the definition, would, in the present instance, be false. Out of this definition we may carve the premisses of the following syllogism:

A dragon is a thing which breathes flame: A dragon is a serpent:

From which the conclusion is,

Therefore some serpent or serpents breathe flame:--

an unexceptionable syllogism in the first mode of the third figure, in which both premisses are true and yet the conclusion false; which every logician knows to be an absurdity. The conclusion being false and the syllogism correct, the premisses cannot be true. But the premisses, considered as parts of a definition, are true. Therefore, the premisses considered as parts of a definition cannot be the real ones. The real premisses must be--

A dragon is a *really existing* thing which breathes flame: A dragon is a *really existing* serpent:

which implied premisses being false, the falsity of the conclusion presents no absurdity.

If we would determine what conclusion follows from the same ostensible premisses when the tacit assumption of real existence is left out, let us, according to the recommendation in the Westminster Review, substitute *means* for *is*. We then have--

Dragon is *a word meaning* a thing which breathes flame: Dragon is *a word meaning* a serpent:

From which the conclusion is,

Some *word or words which mean* a serpent, also mean a thing which breathes flame:

where the conclusion (as well as the premisses) is true, and is the only kind of conclusion which can ever follow from a definition, namely, a proposition relating to the meaning of words.

There is still another shape into which we may transform this syllogism. We may suppose the middle term to be the designation neither of a thing nor of a name, but of an idea. We then have--

The *idea of* a dragon is *an idea of* a thing which breathes flame: The *idea of* a dragon is *an idea of* a serpent:

Therefore, there is *an idea of* a serpent, which is *an idea of* a thing breathing flame.

Here the conclusion is true, and also the premisses; but the premisses are not definitions. They are propositions affirming that an idea existing in the mind, includes certain ideal elements. The truth of the conclusion follows from the existence of the psychological phenomenon called the idea of a dragon; and therefore still from the tacit assumption of a matter of fact.(26)

When, as in this last syllogism, the conclusion is a proposition respecting an idea, the assumption on which it depends may be merely that of the existence of an idea. But when the conclusion is a proposition concerning a Thing, the postulate involved in the definition which stands as the apparent premiss, is the existence of a Thing conformable to the definition, and not merely of an idea conformable to it. This assumption of real existence we always convey the impression that we intend to make, when we profess to define any name which is already known to be a name of really existing objects. On this account it is, that the assumption was not necessarily implied in the definition of a dragon, while there was no doubt of its being included in the definition of a circle.

§ 6. One of the circumstances which have contributed to keep up the notion, that demonstrative truths follow from definitions rather than from the postulates implied in those definitions, is, that the postulates, even in those sciences which are considered to surpass all others in demonstrative certainty, are not always exactly true. It is not true that a circle exists, or can be described, which has all its radii *exactly* equal. Such accuracy is ideal only; it is not found in nature, still less can it be realised by art. People had a difficulty, therefore, in conceiving that the most certain of all conclusions could rest on premisses which, instead of being certainly true, are certainly not true to the full extent asserted. This apparent paradox will be examined when we come to treat of Demonstration; where we shall be able to show that as much of the postulate is true, as is required to support as much as is true of the conclusion. Philosophers however to whom this view had not occurred, or whom it did not satisfy, have thought it indispensable that there should be found in definitions something *more* certain, or at least more accurately true, than the implied postulate of the real existence of a corresponding object. And this something they flattered themselves they had found, when they laid it down that a definition is a statement and analysis not of the mere meaning of a word, nor yet of the nature of a thing, but of an idea. Thus, the proposition, "A circle is a plane figure bounded by a line all the points of which are at an equal distance from a given point within it," was considered by them, not as an assertion that any real circle has that property, (which would not be exactly true,) but that we **conceive** a circle as having it; that our abstract idea of a circle is an idea of a figure with its radii exactly equal.

Conformably to this it is said, that the subject matter of mathematics, and of every other demonstrative science, is not things as they really exist, but abstractions of the mind. A geometrical line is a line without breadth; but no such line exists in nature; it is a notion made up by the mind, out of the materials in nature. The definition (it is said) is a definition of this mental line, not of any actual line: and it is only of the mental line, not of any line existing in nature, that the theorems of geometry are accurately true.

Allowing this doctrine respecting the nature of demonstrative truth to be correct, (which, in a subsequent place, I shall endeavour to prove that it is not;) even on that supposition, the conclusions which seem to follow from a definition, do not follow from the definition as such, but from an implied postulate. Even if it be true that there is no object in nature answering to the definition of a line, and that the geometrical properties of lines are not true of any lines in nature, but only of the idea of a line; the definition, at all events, postulates the real existence of such an idea: it assumes that the mind can frame, or rather has framed, the notion of length without breadth, and without any other sensible property whatever. To me, indeed, it appears that the mind cannot form any such notion; it cannot conceive length without breadth; it can only, in contemplating objects, **attend** to their length, exclusively of their other sensible qualities, and so determine what properties may be predicated of them in virtue of their length alone. If this be true, the postulate involved in the geometrical definition of a line, is the real existence, not of length without breadth, but merely of length, that is, of long objects. This is quite enough to support all the truths of geometry, since every property of a geometrical line is really a property of all physical objects possessing length. But even what I hold to be the false doctrine on the subject, leaves the conclusion that our reasonings are grounded on the matters of fact postulated in definitions, and not on the definitions themselves, entirely unaffected; and accordingly this conclusion is one which I have in common with Dr. Whewell, in his **Philosophy of the Inductive Sciences**: although, on the nature of demonstrative truth, Dr. Whewell's opinions are greatly at variance with mine. And here, as in many other instances, I gladly acknowledge that his writings are eminently serviceable in clearing from confusion the initial steps in the analysis of the mental processes, even where his views respecting the ultimate analysis are such as (though with unfeigned respect) I cannot but regard as fundamentally erroneous.

§ 7. Although, according to the opinion here presented, Definitions are properly of names only, and not of things, it does not follow from this that definitions are arbitrary. How to define a name, may not only be an inquiry of considerable difficulty and intricacy, but may involve considerations going deep into the nature of the things which are denoted by the name. Such, for instance, are the inquiries which form the subjects of the most important of Plato's Dialogues; as, "What is rhetoric?" the topic of the Gorgias, or "What is justice?" that of the Republic. Such, also, is the question scornfully asked by Pilate, "What is truth?" and the fundamental question with speculative moralists in all ages, "What is virtue?"

It would be a mistake to represent these difficult and noble inquiries as having nothing in view beyond ascertaining the conventional meaning of a name. They are inquiries not so much to determine what is, as what should be, the meaning of a name; which, like other practical questions of terminology, requires for its solution that we should enter, and sometimes enter very deeply, into the properties not merely of names but of the things named.

Although the meaning of every concrete general name resides in the attributes which it connotes, the objects were named before the attributes; as appears from the fact that in all languages, abstract names are mostly compounds or other derivatives of the concrete names which correspond to them. Connotative names, therefore, were, after proper names, the first which were used: and in the simpler cases, no doubt, a distinct connotation was present to the minds of those who first used the name, and was distinctly intended by them to be conveyed by it. The first person who used the word *white*, as applied to snow or to any other object, knew, no doubt, very well what quality he intended to predicate, and had a perfectly distinct conception in his mind of the attribute signified by the name.

But where the resemblances and differences on which our classifications are founded are not of this palpable and easily determinable kind; especially where they consist not in any one quality but in a number of qualities, the effects of which being blended together are not very easily discriminated, and referred each to its true source; it often happens that names are applied to nameable objects, with no distinct connotation present to the minds of those who apply them. They are only influenced by a general resemblance between the new object and all or some of the old familiar objects which they have been accustomed to call by that name. This, as we have seen, is the law which even the mind of the philosopher must follow, in giving names to the simple elementary feelings of our nature: but, where the things to be named are complex wholes, a philosopher is not content with noticing a general resemblance; he examines what the resemblance consists in: and he only gives the same name to things which resemble one another in the same definite particulars. The philosopher, therefore, habitually employs his general names with a definite connotation. But language was not made, and can only in some small degree be mended, by philosophers. In the minds of the real arbiters of language, general names, especially where the classes they denote cannot be brought before the tribunal of the outward senses to be identified and discriminated, connote little more than a vague gross resemblance to the things which they were earliest, or have been most, accustomed to call by those names. When, for instance, ordinary persons predicate the words *just* or *unjust* of any action, *noble* or *mean* of any sentiment, expression, or demeanour, *statesman* or *charlatan* of any personage figuring in politics, do they mean to affirm of those various subjects any determinate attributes, of whatever kind? No: they merely recognise, as they think, some likeness, more or less vague and loose, between these and some other things which they have been accustomed to denominate or to hear denominated by those appellations.

Language, as Sir James Mackintosh used to say of governments, "is not made, but grows." A name is not imposed at once and by previous purpose upon a *class* of objects, but is first applied to one thing, and then extended by a series of transitions to another and another. By this process (as has been remarked by several writers, and illustrated with great force and clearness by Dugald Stewart, in his Philosophical Essays,) a name not unfrequently passes by successive links of resemblance from one object to another, until it becomes applied to things having nothing in common with the first things to which the name was given; which, however, do not, for that reason, drop the name; so that it at last denotes a confused huddle of objects, having nothing whatever in common; and connotes nothing, not even a vague and general resemblance. When a name has fallen into this state, in which by predicating it of any object we assert literally nothing about the object, it has become unfit for the purposes either of thought or of the communication of thought; and can only be made serviceable by stripping it of some part of its multifarious denotation, and confining it to objects possessed of some attributes in common, which it may be made to connote. Such are the inconveniences of a language which "is not made, but grows." Like the governments which are in a similar case, it may be compared to a road which is not made but has made itself: it requires continual mending in order to be passable.

From this it is already evident, why the question respecting the definition of an abstract name is often one of so much difficulty. The question, What is justice? is, in other words, What is the attribute which mankind mean to predicate when they call an action just? To which the first answer is, that having come to no precise agreement on the point, they do not mean to predicate distinctly any attribute at all. Nevertheless, all believe that there is some common attribute belonging to all the actions which they are in the habit of calling just. The question then must be, whether there is any such common attribute? and, in the first place, whether mankind agree sufficiently with one another as to the particular actions which they do or do not call just, to render the inquiry, what quality those actions have in common, a possible one: if so, whether the actions really have any quality in common; and if they have, what it is. Of these three, the first alone is an inquiry into usage and convention; the other two are inquiries into matters of fact. And if the second question (whether the actions form a class at all) has been answered negatively, there remains a fourth, often more arduous than all the rest, namely, how best to form a class artificially, which the name may denote.

And here it is fitting to remark, that the study of the spontaneous growth of languages is of the utmost importance to those who would logically remodel them. The classifications rudely made by established language, when retouched, as they almost always require to be, by the hands of the logician, are often in themselves excellently suited to his purposes. When compared with the classifications of a philosopher, they are like the customary law of a country, which has grown up as it were spontaneously, compared with laws methodized and digested into a code: the former are a far less perfect instrument than the latter; but being the result of a long, though unscientific, course of experience, they contain a mass of materials which may be made very usefully available in the formation of the systematic body of written law. In like manner, the established grouping of objects under a common name, though it may be founded only on a gross and general resemblance, is evidence, in the first place, that the resemblance is obvious, and therefore considerable; and, in the next place, that it is a resemblance which has struck great numbers of persons during a series of years and ages. Even when a name, by successive extensions, has come to be applied to things among which there does not exist this gross resemblance common to them all, still at every step in its progress we shall find such a resemblance. And these transitions of the meaning of words are often an index to real connexions between the things denoted by them, which might otherwise escape the notice of thinkers; of those at least who, from using a different language, or from any difference in their habitual associations, have fixed their attention in preference on some other aspect of the things. The history of philosophy abounds in examples of such oversights, committed for want of perceiving the hidden link that connected together the seemingly disparate meanings of some ambiguous word.(27)

Whenever the inquiry into the definition of the name of any real object consists of anything else than a mere comparison of authorities, we tacitly assume that a meaning must be found for the name, compatible with its continuing to denote, if possible all, but at any rate the greater or the more important part, of the things of which it is commonly predicated. The inquiry, therefore, into the definition, is an inquiry into the resemblances and differences among those things: whether there be any resemblance running through them all; if not, through what portion of them such a general resemblance can be traced: and finally, what are the common attributes, the possession of which gives to them all, or to that portion of them, the character of resemblance which has led to their being classed together. When these common attributes have been ascertained and specified, the name which belongs in common to the resembling objects acquires a distinct instead of a vague connotation; and by possessing this distinct connotation, becomes susceptible of definition.

In giving a distinct connotation to the general name, the philosopher will endeavour to fix upon such attributes as, while they are common to all the things usually denoted by the name, are also of greatest importance in themselves; either directly, or from the number, the conspicuousness, or the interesting character, of the consequences to which they lead. He will select, as far as possible, such ***differentiae*** as lead to the greatest number of interesting ***propria***. For these, rather than the more obscure and recondite qualities on which they often depend, give that general character and aspect to a set of objects, which determine the groups into which they naturally fall. But to penetrate to the more hidden agreement on which these obvious and superficial agreements depend, is often one of the most difficult of scientific problems. As it is among the most difficult, so it seldom fails to be among the most important. And since upon the result of this inquiry respecting the causes of the properties of a class of things, there incidentally depends the question what shall be the meaning of a word; some of the most profound and most valuable investigations which philosophy presents to us, have been introduced by, and have offered themselves under the guise of, inquiries into the definition of a name.

BOOK II. OF REASONING.

Διωρισμένων δε τούτων, λέγωμεν ἤδη, διὰ τίνων, καὶ πότε, καὶ πῶς γίνεται πᾶς συλλογισμός· ὕστερον δὲ λεκτέον περὶ ἀποδείξεως. Πρότερον γὰρ περὶ συλλογισμοῦ λεκτέον, ἢ περὶ ἀποδείξεως, διὰ τὸ καθόλου μᾶλλον εἶναί τὸν συλλογισμόν. Ἡ μὲν γὰρ ἀπόδειξις, συλλογισμός τις· ὁ συλλογισμὸς δὲ οὐ πᾶς, ἀπόδειξις.

Arist. Analyt. Prior. 1. i. cap. 4.

CHAPTER I. OF INFERENCE,
OR REASONING, IN GENERAL.

§ 1. In the preceding Book, we have been occupied not with the nature of Proof, but with the nature of Assertion: the import conveyed by a Proposition, whether that Proposition be true or false; not the means by which to discriminate true from false Propositions. The proper subject, however, of Logic is Proof. Before we could understand what Proof is, it was necessary to understand what that is to which proof is applicable; what that is which can be a subject of belief or disbelief, of affirmation or denial; what, in short, the different kinds of Propositions assert.

This preliminary inquiry we have prosecuted to a definite result. Assertion, in the first place, relates either to the meaning of words, or to some property of the things which words signify. Assertions respecting the meaning of words, among which definitions are the most important, hold a place, and an indispensable one, in philosophy; but as the meaning of words is essentially arbitrary, this class of assertions are not susceptible of truth or falsity, nor therefore of proof or disproof. Assertions respecting Things, or what may be called Real Propositions in contradistinction to verbal ones, are of various sorts. We have analysed the import of each sort, and have ascertained the nature of the things they relate to, and the nature of what they severally assert respecting those things. We found that whatever be the form of the proposition, and whatever its nominal subject or predicate, the real subject of every proposition is some one or more facts or phenomena of consciousness, or some one or more of the hidden causes or powers to which we ascribe those facts; and that what is predicated or asserted, either in the affirmative or negative, of those phenomena or those powers, is always either Existence, Order in Place, Order in Time, Causation, or Resemblance. This, then, is the theory of the Import of Propositions, reduced to its ultimate elements: but there is another and a less abstruse expression for it, which, though stopping short in an earlier stage of the analysis, is sufficiently scientific for many of the purposes for which such a general expression is required. This expression recognises the commonly received distinction between Subject and Attribute, and gives the following as the analysis of the meaning of propositions:--Every Proposition asserts, that some given subject does or does not possess some attribute; or that some attribute is or is not (either in all or in some portion of the subjects in which it is met with) conjoined with some other attribute.

We shall now for the present take our leave of this portion of our inquiry, and proceed to the peculiar problem of the Science of Logic, namely, how the assertions, of which we have analysed the import, are proved, or disproved: such of them, at least, as, not being amenable to direct consciousness or intuition, are appropriate subjects of proof.

We say of a fact or statement, that it is proved, when we believe its truth by reason of some other fact or statement from which it is said to *follow*. Most of the propositions, whether affirmative or negative, universal, particular, or singular, which we believe, are not believed on their own evidence, but on the ground of something previously assented to, and from which they are said to be *inferred*. To infer a proposition from a previous proposition or propositions; to give credence to it, or claim credence for it, as a conclusion from something else; is to *reason*, in the most extensive sense of the term. There is a narrower sense, in which the name reasoning is confined to the form of inference which is termed ratiocination, and of which the syllogism is the general type. The reasons for not conforming to this restricted use of the term were stated in an early stage of our inquiry, and additional motives will be suggested by the considerations on which we are now about to enter.

§ 2. In proceeding to take into consideration the cases in which inferences can legitimately be drawn, we shall first mention some cases in which the inference is apparent, not real; and which require notice chiefly that they may not be confounded with cases of inference properly so called. This occurs when the proposition ostensibly inferred from another, appears on analysis to be merely a repetition of the same, or part of the same, assertion, which was contained in the first. All the cases mentioned in books of Logic as examples of aequipollency or equivalence of propositions, are of this nature. Thus, if we were to argue, No man is incapable of reason, for every man is rational; or, All men are mortal, for no man is exempt from death; it would be plain that we were not proving the proposition, but only appealing to another mode of wording it, which may or may not be more readily comprehensible by the hearer, or better adapted to suggest the real proof, but which contains in itself no shadow of proof.

Another case is where, from an universal proposition, we affect to infer another which differs from it only in being particular: as, All A is B, therefore Some A is B: No A is B, therefore Some A is not B. This, too, is not to conclude one proposition from another, but to repeat a second time something which had been asserted at first; with the difference, that we do not here repeat the whole of the previous assertion, but only an indefinite part of it.

A third case is where, the antecedent having affirmed a predicate of a given subject, the consequent affirms of the same subject something already connoted by the former predicate: as, Socrates is a man, therefore Socrates is a living creature; where all that is connoted by living creature was affirmed of Socrates when he was asserted to be a man. If the propositions are negative, we must invert their order, thus: Socrates is not a living creature, therefore he is not a man; for if we deny the less, the greater, which includes it, is already denied by implication. These, therefore, are not really cases of inference; and yet the trivial examples by which, in manuals of Logic, the rules of the syllogism are illustrated, are often of this ill-chosen kind; demonstrations in form, of conclusions to which whoever understands the terms used in the statement of the data, has already, and consciously, assented.

The most complex case of this sort of apparent inference is what is called the Conversion of Propositions; which consists in turning the predicate into a subject, and the subject into a predicate, and framing out of the same terms thus reversed, another proposition, which must be true if the former is true. Thus, from the particular affirmative proposition, Some A is B, we may infer that Some B is A. From the universal negative, No A is B, we may conclude that No B is A. From the universal affirmative proposition, All A is B, it cannot be inferred that All B is A; though all water is liquid, it is not implied that all liquid is water; but it is implied that some liquid is so; and hence the proposition, All A is B, is legitimately convertible into Some B is A. This process, which converts an universal proposition into a particular, is termed conversion *per accidens*. From the proposition, Some A is not B, we cannot even infer that some B is not A; though some men are not Englishmen, it does not follow that some Englishmen are not men. The only legitimate conversion, if such it can be called, of a particular negative proposition, is in the form, Some A is not B, therefore, something which is not B is A; and this is termed conversion by contraposition. In this case, however, the predicate and subject are not merely reversed, but one of them is altered. Instead of [A] and [B], the terms of the new proposition are [a thing which is not B], and [A]. The original proposition, Some A *is not* B, is first changed into a proposition aequipollent with it, Some A *is* "a thing which is not B"; and the proposition, being now no longer a particular negative, but a particular affirmative, admits of conversion in the first mode, or, as it is called, *simple* conversion.

In all these cases there is not really any inference; there is in the conclusion no new truth, nothing but what was already asserted in the premises, and obvious to whoever apprehends them. The fact asserted in the conclusion is either the very same fact, or part of the fact, asserted in the original proposition. This follows from our previous analysis of the Import of Propositions. When we say, for example, that some lawful sovereigns are tyrants, what is the meaning of the assertion? That the attributes connoted by the term "lawful sovereign," and the attributes connoted by the term "tyrant," sometimes coexist in the same individual. Now this is also precisely what we mean, when we say that some tyrants are lawful sovereigns; which, therefore, is not a second proposition inferred from the first, any more than the English translation of Euclid's Elements is a collection of theorems different from, and consequences of, those contained in the Greek original. Again, if we assert that no great general is a rash man, we mean that the attributes connoted by "great general," and those connoted by "rash," never coexist in the same subject; which is also the exact meaning which would be expressed by saying, that no rash man is a great general. When we say, that all quadrupeds are warm-blooded, we assert, not only that the attributes connoted by "quadruped" and those connoted by "warm-blooded" sometimes coexist, but that the former never exist without the latter: now the proposition, Some warm-blooded creatures are quadrupeds, expresses the first half of this meaning, dropping the latter half; and, therefore, has been already affirmed in the antecedent proposition, All quadrupeds are warm-blooded. But that ***all*** warm-blooded creatures are quadrupeds, or, in other words, that the attributes connoted by "warm-blooded" never exist without those connoted by "quadruped," has not been asserted, and cannot be inferred. In order to reassert, in an inverted form, the whole of what was affirmed in the proposition, All quadrupeds are warm-blooded, we must convert it by contraposition, thus, Nothing which is not warm-blooded is a quadruped. This proposition, and the one from which it is derived, are exactly equivalent, and either of them may be substituted for the other; for, to say that when the attributes of a quadruped are present, those of a warm-blooded creature are present, is to say that when the latter are absent the former are absent.

In a manual for young students, it would be proper to dwell at greater length on the conversion and aequipollency of propositions. For, although that cannot be called reasoning or inference which is a mere reassertion in different words of what had been asserted before, there is no more important intellectual habit, nor any the cultivation of which falls more strictly within the province of the art of logic, than that of discerning rapidly and surely the identity of an assertion when disguised under diversity of language. That important chapter in logical treatises which relates to the Opposition of Propositions, and the excellent technical language which logic provides for distinguishing the different kinds or modes of opposition, are of use chiefly for this purpose. Such considerations as these, that contrary propositions may both be false, but cannot both be true; that sub-contrary propositions may both be true, but cannot both be false; that of two contradictory propositions one must be true and the other false; that of two subalternate propositions the truth of the universal proves the truth of the particular, and the falsity of the particular proves the falsity of the universal, but not *vice versa*(28); are apt to appear, at first sight, very technical and mysterious, but when explained, seem almost too obvious to require so formal a statement, since the same amount of explanation which is necessary to make the principles intelligible, would enable the truths which they convey to be apprehended in any particular case which can occur. In this respect, however, these axioms of logic are on a level with those of mathematics. That things which are equal to the same thing are equal to one another, is as obvious in any particular case as it is in the general statement: and if no such general maxim had ever been laid down, the demonstrations in Euclid would never have halted for any difficulty in stepping across the gap which this axiom at present serves to bridge over. Yet no one has ever censured writers on geometry, for placing a list of these elementary generalizations at the head of their treatises, as a first exercise to the learner of the faculty which will be required in him at every step, that of apprehending a *general* truth. And the student of logic, in the discussion even of such truths as we have cited above, acquires habits of circumspect interpretation of words, and of exactly measuring the length and breadth of his assertions, which are among the most indispensable conditions of any considerable mental attainment, and which it is one of the primary objects of logical discipline to cultivate.

§ 3. Having noticed, in order to exclude from the province of Reasoning or Inference properly so called, the cases in which the progression from one truth to another is only apparent, the logical consequent being a mere repetition of the logical antecedent; we now pass to those which are cases of inference in the proper acceptation of the term, those in which we set out from known truths, to arrive at others really distinct from them.

Reasoning, in the extended sense in which I use the term, and in which it is synonymous with Inference, is popularly said to be of two kinds: reasoning from particulars to generals, and reasoning from generals to particulars; the former being called Induction, the latter Ratiocination or Syllogism. It will presently be shown that there is a third species of reasoning, which falls under neither of these descriptions, and which, nevertheless, is not only valid, but is the foundation of both the others.

It is necessary to observe, that the expressions, reasoning from particulars to generals, and reasoning from generals to particulars, are recommended by brevity rather than by precision, and do not adequately mark, without the aid of a commentary, the distinction between Induction (in the sense now adverted to) and Ratiocination. The meaning intended by these expressions is, that Induction is inferring a proposition from propositions *less general* than itself, and Ratiocination is inferring a proposition from propositions *equally* or *more* general. When, from the observation of a number of individual instances, we ascend to a general proposition, or when, by combining a number of general propositions, we conclude from them another proposition still more general, the process, which is substantially the same in both instances, is called Induction. When from a general proposition, not alone (for from a single proposition nothing can be concluded which is not involved in the terms,) but by combining it with other propositions, we infer a proposition of the same degree of generality with itself, or a less general proposition, or a proposition merely individual, the process is Ratiocination. When, in short, the conclusion is more general than the largest of the premisses, the argument is commonly called Induction; when less general, or equally general, it is Ratiocination.

As all experience begins with individual cases, and proceeds from them to generals, it might seem most conformable to the natural order of thought that Induction should be treated of before we touch upon Ratiocination. It will, however, be advantageous, in a science which aims at tracing our acquired knowledge to its sources, that the inquirer should commence with the latter rather than with the earlier stages of the process of constructing our knowledge; and should trace derivative truths backward to the truths from which they are deduced, and on which they depend for their evidence, before attempting to point out the original spring from which both ultimately take their rise. The advantages of this order of proceeding in the present instance will manifest themselves as we advance, in a manner superseding the necessity of any further justification or explanation.

Of Induction, therefore, we shall say no more at present, than that it at least is, without doubt, a process of real inference. The conclusion in an induction embraces more than is contained in the premisses. The principle or law collected from particular instances, the general proposition in which we embody the result of our experience, covers a much larger extent of ground than the individual experiments which are said to form its basis. A principle ascertained by experience, is more than a mere summing up of what has been specifically observed in the individual cases which have been examined; it is a generalization grounded on those cases, and expressive of our belief, that what we there found true is true in an indefinite number of cases which we have not examined, and are never likely to examine. The nature and grounds of this inference, and the conditions necessary to make it legitimate, will be the subject of discussion in the Third Book: but that such inference really takes place is not susceptible of question. In every induction we proceed from truths which we knew, to truths which we did not know; from facts certified by observation, to facts which we have not observed, and even to facts not capable of being now observed; future facts, for example; but which we do not hesitate to believe on the sole evidence of the induction itself.

Induction, then, is a real process of Reasoning or Inference. Whether, and in what sense, so much can be said of the Syllogism, remains to be determined by the examination into which we are about to enter.

CHAPTER II. OF RATIOCINATION, OR SYLLOGISM.

§ 1. The analysis of the Syllogism has been so accurately and fully performed in the common manuals of Logic, that in the present work, which is not designed as a manual, it is sufficient to recapitulate, *memoriae causa*, the leading results of that analysis, as a foundation for the remarks to be afterwards made on the functions of the syllogism, and the place which it holds in science.

To a legitimate syllogism it is essential that there should be three, and no more than three, propositions, namely, the conclusion, or proposition to be proved, and two other propositions which together prove it, and which are called the premisses. It is essential that there should be three, and no more than three, terms, namely, the subject and predicate of the conclusion, and another called the middleterm, which must be found in both premisses, since it is by means of it that the other two terms are to be connected together. The predicate of the conclusion is called the major term of the syllogism; the subject of the conclusion is called the minor term.

As there can be but three terms, the major and minor terms must each be found in one, and only one, of the premisses, together with the middleterm which is in them both. The premiss which contains the middleterm and the major term is called the major premiss; that which contains the middle term and the minor term is called the minor premiss.

Syllogisms are divided by some logicians into three *figures*, by others into four, according to the position of the middleterm, which may either be the subject in both premisses, the predicate in both, or the subject in one and the predicate in the other. The most common case is that in which the middleterm is the subject of the major premiss and the predicate of the minor. This is reckoned as the first figure. When the middleterm is the predicate in both premisses, the syllogism belongs to the second figure; when it is the subject in both, to the third. In the fourth figure the middleterm is the subject of the minor premiss and the predicate of the major. Those writers who reckon no more than three figures, include this case in the first.

Each figure is divided into *modes*, according to what are called the *quantity* and *quality* of the propositions, that is, according as they are universal or particular, affirmative or negative. The following are examples of all the legitimate modes, that is, all those in which the conclusion correctly follows from the premisses. A is the minor term, C the major, B the middleterm.

First Figure.

All B is C	No B is C	All B is C	No B is C
All A is B	All A is B	Some A is B	Some A is B
therefore	therefore	therefore	therefore
All A is C	No A is C	Some A is C	Some A is not C

Second Figure.

No C is B	All C is B	No C is B	All C is B
All A is B	No A is B	Some A is B	Some A is not B
therefore	therefore	therefore	therefore
No A is C	No A is C	Some A is not C	Some A is not C

Third Figure.

All B is C	No B is C	Some B is C	All B is C	Some B is not C	No B is C
All B is A	All B is A	All B is A	Some B is A	All B is A	Some B is A
therefore	therefore	therefore	therefore	therefore	therefore
Some A is C	Some A is not C	Some A is C	Some A is C	Some A is not C	Some A is not C

Fourth Figure.

All C is B	All C is B	Some C is B	No C is B	No C is B
All B is A	No B is A	All B is A	All B is A	Some B is A
therefore	therefore	therefore	therefore	therefore
Some A is C	Some A is not C	Some A is C	Some A is not C	Some A is not C

In these exemplars, or blank forms of making syllogisms, no place is assigned to *singular* propositions; not, of course, because such propositions are not used in ratiocination, but because, their predicate being affirmed or denied of the whole of the subject, they are ranked, for the purposes of the syllogism, with universal propositions. Thus, these two syllogisms--

> All men are mortal,
>> All men are mortal, All kings are men,
>> Socrates is a man, therefore
>>> therefore All kings are mortal,   Socrates is mortal,

are arguments precisely similar, and are both ranked in the first mode of the first figure.

The reasons why syllogisms in any of the above forms are legitimate, that is, why, if the premises be true, the conclusion must necessarily be so, and why this is not the case in any other possible *mode*, (that is, in any other combination of universal and particular, affirmative and negative propositions,) any person taking interest in these inquiries may be presumed to have either learnt from the common school books of the syllogistic logic, or to be capable of divining for himself. The reader may, however, be referred, for every needful explanation, to Archbishop Whately's *Elements of Logic*, where he will find stated with philosophical preci-sion, and explained with remarkable perspicuity, the whole of the common doctrine of the syllogism.

All valid ratiocination; all reasoning by which, from general propositions previously admitted, other propositions equally or less general are inferred; may be exhibited in some of the above forms. The whole of Euclid, for example, might be thrown without difficulty into a series of syllogisms, regular in mode and figure.

Although a syllogism framed according to any of these formulae is a valid argument, all correct ratiocination admits of being stated in syllogisms of the first figure alone. The rules for throwing an argument in any of the other figures into the first figure, are called rules for the ***reduction*** of syllogisms. It is done by the ***conversion*** of one or other, or both, of the premisses. Thus an argument in the first mode of the second figure, as--

No C is B All A is B therefore No A is C,

may be reduced as follows. The proposition, No C is B, being an universal negative, admits of simple conversion, and may be changed into No B is C, which, as we showed, is the very same assertion in other words--the same fact differently expressed. This transformation having been effected, the argument assumes the following form:--

No B is C All A is B therefore No A is C,

which is a good syllogism in the second mode of the first figure. Again, an argument in the first mode of the third figure must resemble the following:--

All B is C All B is A therefore Some A is C,

where the minor premiss, All B is A, conformably to what was laid down in the last chapter respecting universal affirmatives, does not admit of simple conversion, but may be converted ***per accidens***, thus, Some A is B; which, though it does not express the whole of what is asserted in the proposition All B is A, expresses, as was formerly shown, part of it, and must therefore be true if the whole is true. We have, then, as the result of the reduction, the following syllogism in the third mode of the first figure:--

All B is C Some A is B, from which it obviously follows, that Some A is C.

In the same manner, or in a manner on which after these examples it is not necessary to enlarge, every mode of the second, third, and fourth figures may be reduced to some one of the four modes of the first. In other words, every conclusion which can be proved in any of the last three figures, may be proved in the first figure from the same premisses, with a slight alteration in the mere manner of expressing them. Every valid ratiocination, therefore, may be stated in the first figure, that is, in one of the following forms:--

Every B is C No B is C All A is B,   All A is B, Some A is B,   Some A is B,
therefore   therefore
 All A is C.   No A is C. Some A is C.   Some A is not C.

Or if more significant symbols are preferred:--

To prove an affirmative, the argument must admit of being stated in this form:--

All animals are mortal; All men/Some men/Socrates are animals; therefore All men/Some men/Socrates are mortal.

To prove a negative, the argument must be capable of being expressed in this form:--

No one who is capable of self-control is necessarily vicious; All negroes/Some negroes/Mr. A's negro are capable of self-control; therefore No negroes are/Some negroes are not/Mr. A's negro is not necessarily vicious.

Although all ratiocination admits of being thrown into one or the other of these forms, and sometimes gains considerably by the transformation, both in clearness and in the obviousness of its consequence; there are, no doubt, cases in which the argument falls more naturally into one of the other three figures, and in which its conclusiveness is more apparent at the first glance in those figures, than when reduced to the first. Thus, if the proposition were that pagans may be virtuous, and the evidence to prove it were the example of Aristides; a syllogism in the third figure,

Aristides was virtuous, Aristides was a pagan, therefore Some pagan was virtuous,

would be a more natural mode of stating the argument, and would carry conviction more instantly home, than the same ratiocination strained into the first figure, thus--

Aristides was virtuous, Some pagan was Aristides, therefore Some pagan was virtuous.

A German philosopher, Lambert, whose ***Neues Organon*** (published in the year 1764) contains among other things one of the most elaborate and complete expositions ever yet made of the syllogistic doctrine, has expressly examined what sorts of arguments fall most naturally and suitably into each of the four figures; and his solution is characterized by great ingenuity and clearness of thought.(29) The argument, however, is one and the same, in whichever figure it is expressed; since, as we have already seen, the premisses of a syllogism in the second, third, or fourth figure, and those of the syllogism in the first figure to which it may be reduced, are the same premisses in everything except language, or, at least, as much of them as contributes to the proof of the conclusion is the same. We are therefore at liberty, in conformity with the general opinion of logicians, to consider the two elementary forms of the first figure as the universal types of all correct ratiocination; the one, when the conclusion to be proved is affirmative, the other, when it is negative; even though certain arguments may have a tendency to clothe themselves in the forms of the second, third, and fourth figures; which, however, cannot possibly happen with the only class of arguments which are of first-rate scientific importance, those in which the conclusion is an universal affirmative, such conclusions being susceptible of proof in the first figure alone.

§ 2. On examining, then, these two general formulae, we find that in both of them, one premiss, the major, is an universal proposition; and according as this is affirmative or negative, the conclusion is so too. All ratiocination, therefore, starts from a **general** proposition, principle, or assumption: a proposition in which a predicate is affirmed or denied of an entire class; that is, in which some attribute, or the negation of some attribute, is asserted of an indefinite number of objects distinguished by a common characteristic, and designated, in consequence, by a common name.

The other premiss is always affirmative, and asserts that something (which may be either an individual, a class, or part of a class) belongs to, or is included in, the class respecting which something was affirmed or denied in the major premiss. It follows that the attribute affirmed or denied of the entire class may (if there was truth in that affirmation or denial) be affirmed or denied of the object or objects alleged to be included in the class: and this is precisely the assertion made in the conclusion.

Whether or not the foregoing is an adequate account of the constituent parts of the syllogism, will be presently considered; but as far as it goes it is a true account. It has accordingly been generalized, and erected into a logical maxim, on which all ratiocination is said to be founded, insomuch that to reason, and to apply the maxim, are supposed to be one and the same thing. The maxim is, That whatever can be affirmed (or denied) of a class, may be affirmed (or denied) of everything included in the class. This axiom, supposed to be the basis of the syllogistic theory, is termed by logicians the *dictum de omni et nullo*.

This maxim, however, when considered as a principle of reasoning, appears suited to a system of metaphysics once indeed generally received, but which for the last two centuries has been considered as finally abandoned, though there have not been wanting, in our own day, attempts at its revival. So long as what were termed Universals were regarded as a peculiar kind of substances, having an objective existence distinct from the individual objects classed under them, the *dictum de omni* conveyed an important meaning; because it expressed the intercommunity of nature, which it was necessary on that theory that we should suppose to exist between those general substances and the particular substances which were subordinated to them. That everything predicable of the universal was predicable of the various individuals contained under it, was then no identical proposition, but a statement of what was conceived as a fundamental law of the universe. The assertion that the entire nature and properties of the *substantia secunda* formed part of the properties of each of the individual substances called by the same name; that the properties of Man, for example, were properties of all men; was a proposition of real significance when man did not *mean* all men, but something inherent in men, and vastly superior to them in dignity. Now, however, when it is known that a class, an universal, a genus or species, is not an entity *per se*, but neither more nor less than the individual substances themselves which are placed in the class, and that there is nothing real in the matter except those objects, a common name given to them, and common attributes indicated by the name; what, I should be glad to know, do we learn by being told, that whatever can be affirmed of a class, may be affirmed of every object contained in the class? The class *is* nothing but the objects contained in it: and the *dictum de omni* merely amounts to the identical proposition, that whatever is true of certain objects, is true of each of those objects. If all ratiocination were no more than the application of this maxim to particular cases, the syllogism would indeed be, what it has so often been declared to be, solemn trifling. The ***dictum de omni*** is on a par with another truth, which in its time was also reckoned of great importance, "Whatever is, is;" and not to be compared in point of significance to the cognate aphorism, "It is impossible for the same thing to be and not to be;" since this is, at the lowest, equivalent to the logical axiom that contradictory propositions cannot both be true. To give any real meaning to the ***dictum de omni***, we must consider it not as an axiom, but as a definition; we must look upon it as intended to explain, in a circuitous and paraphrastic manner, the meaning of the word ***class***.

An error which seemed finally refuted and dislodged from thought, often needs only put on a new suit of phrases, to be welcomed back to its old quarters, and allowed to repose unquestioned for another cycle of ages. Modern philosophers have not been sparing in their contempt for the scholastic dogma that genera and species are a peculiar kind of substances, which general substances being the only permanent things, while the individual substances comprehended under them are in a perpetual flux, knowledge, which necessarily imports stability, can only have relation to those general substances or universals, and not to the facts or particulars included under them. Yet, though nominally rejected, this very doctrine, whether disguised under the Abstract Ideas of Locke (whose speculations, however, it has less vitiated than those of perhaps any other writer who has been infected with it), under the ultra-nominalism of Hobbes and Condillac, or the ontology of the later Kantians, has never ceased to poison philosophy. Once accustomed to consider scientific investigation as essentially consisting in the study of universals, men did not drop this habit of thought when they ceased to regard universals as possessing an independent existence: and even those who went the length of considering them as mere names, could not free themselves from the notion that the investigation of truth consisted entirely or partly in some kind of conjuration or juggle with those names. When a philosopher adopted fully the Nominalist view of the signification of general language, retaining along with it the ***dictum de omni*** as the foundation of all reasoning, two such premises fairly put together were likely, if he was a consistent thinker, to land him in rather startling conclusions. Accordingly it has been seriously held, by writers of deserved celebrity, that the process of arriving at new truths by reasoning consists in the mere substitution of one set of arbitrary signs for another; a doctrine which they supposed to derive irresistible confirmation from the example of algebra. If there were any process in sorcery or necromancy more preternatural than this, I should be much surprised. The culminating point of this philosophy is the noted aphorism of Condillac, that a science is nothing, or scarcely anything, but *une langue bien faite*: in other words, that the one sufficient rule for discovering the nature and properties of objects is to name them properly: as if the reverse were not the truth, that it is impossible to name them properly except in proportion as we are already acquainted with their nature and properties. Can it be necessary to say, that none, not even the most trivial knowledge with respect to Things, ever was or could be originally got at by any conceivable manipulation of mere names, as such; and that what can be learnt from names, is only what somebody who used the names, knew before? Philosophical analysis confirms the indication of common sense, that the function of names is but that of enabling us to **remember** and to **communicate** our thoughts. That they also strengthen, even to an incalculable extent, the power of thought itself, is most true: but they do this by no intrinsic and peculiar virtue; they do it by the power inherent in an artificial memory, an instrument of which few have adequately considered the immense potency. As an artificial memory, language truly is, what it has so often been called, an instrument of thought: but it is one thing to be the instrument, and another to be the exclusive subject upon which the instrument is exercised. We think, indeed, to a considerable extent, by means of names, but what we think of, are the things called by those names; and there cannot be a greater error than to imagine that thought can be carried on with nothing in our mind but names, or that we can make the names think for us.

§ 3. Those who considered the ***dictum de omni*** as the foundation of the syllogism, looked upon arguments in a manner corresponding to the erroneous view which Hobbes took of propositions. Because there are some propositions which are merely verbal, Hobbes, in order apparently that his definition might be rigorously universal, defined a proposition as if no propositions declared anything except the meaning of words. If Hobbes was right; if no further account than this could be given of the import of propositions; no theory could be given but the commonly received one, of the combination of propositions in a syllogism. If the minor premiss asserted nothing more than that something belongs to a class, and if the major premiss asserted nothing of that class except that it is included in another class, the conclusion would only be, that what was included in the lower class is included in the higher, and the result, therefore, nothing except that the classification is consistent with itself. But we have seen that it is no sufficient account of the meaning of a proposition, to say that it refers something to, or excludes something from, a class. Every proposition which conveys real information asserts a matter of fact, dependent on the laws of nature, and not on artificial classification. It asserts that a given object does or does not possess a given attribute; or it asserts that two attributes, or sets of attributes, do or do not (constantly or occasionally) coexist. Since such is the purport of all propositions which convey any real knowledge, and since ratiocination is a mode of acquiring real knowledge, any theory of ratiocination which does not recognise this import of propositions, cannot, we may be sure, be the true one.

Applying this view of propositions to the two premisses of a syllogism, we obtain the following results. The major premiss, which, as already remarked, is always universal, asserts, that all things which have a certain attribute (or attributes) have or have not along with it, a certain other attribute (or attributes). The minor premiss asserts that the thing or set of things which are the subject of that premiss, have the first-mentioned attribute; and the conclusion is, that they have (or that they have not) the second. Thus in our former example,

All men are mortal, Socrates is a man, therefore Socrates is mortal,

the subject and predicate of the major premiss are connotative terms, denoting objects and connoting attributes. The assertion in the major premiss is, that along with one of the two sets of attributes, we always find the other: that the attributes connoted by "man" never exist unless conjoined with the attribute called mortality. The assertion in the minor premiss is that the individual named Socrates possesses the former attributes; and it is concluded that he possesses also the attribute mortality. Or if both the premisses are general propositions, as

All men are mortal, All kings are men, therefore All kings are mortal,

the minor premiss asserts that the attributes denoted by kingship only exist in conjunction with those signified by the word man. The major asserts as before, that the last mentioned attributes are never found without the attribute of mortality. The conclusion is, that wherever the attributes of kingship are found, that of mortality is found also.

If the major premiss were negative, as, No men are omnipotent, it would assert, not that the attributes connoted by "man" never exist without, but that they never exist with, those connoted by "omnipotent:" from which, together with the minor premiss, it is concluded, that the same incompatibility exists between the attribute omnipotence and those constituting a king. In a similar manner we might analyse any other example of the syllogism.

If we generalize this process, and look out for the principle or law involved in every such inference, and presupposed in every syllogism the propositions of which are anything more than merely verbal; we find, not the unmeaning ***dictum de omni et nullo***, but a fundamental principle, or rather two principles, strikingly resembling the axioms of mathematics. The first, which is the principle of affirmative syllogisms, is, that things which coexist with the same thing, coexist with one another. The second is the principle of negative syllogisms, and is to this effect: that a thing which coexists with another thing, with which other a third thing does not coexist, is not coexistent with that third thing. These axioms manifestly relate to facts, and not to conventions; and one or other of them is the ground of the legitimacy of every argument in which facts and not conventions are the matter treated of.

§ 4. It remains to translate this exposition of the syllogism from the one into the other of the two languages in which we formerly remarked(30) that all propositions, and of course therefore all combinations of propositions, might be expressed. We observed that a proposition might be considered in two different lights; as a portion of our knowledge of nature, or as a memorandum for our guidance. Under the former, or speculative aspect, an affirmative general proposition is an assertion of a speculative truth, viz. that whatever has a certain attribute has a certain other attribute. Under the other aspect, it is to be regarded not as a part of our knowledge, but as an aid for our practical exigencies, by enabling us, when we see or learn that an object possesses one of the two attributes, to infer that it possesses the other; thus employing the first attribute as a mark or evidence of the second. Thus regarded, every syllogism comes within the following general formula:--

Attribute A is a mark of attribute B, A given object has the mark A, therefore The given object has the attribute B.

Referred to this type, the arguments which we have lately cited as specimens of the syllogism, will express themselves in the following manner:--

The attributes of man are a mark of the attribute mortality, Socrates has the attributes of man, therefore Socrates has the attribute mortality.

And again,

The attributes of man are a mark of the attribute mortality, The attributes of a king are a mark of the attributes of man, therefore The attributes of a king are a mark of the attribute mortality.

And lastly,

The attributes of man are a mark of the *absence* of the attribute omnipotence, The attributes of a king are a mark of the attributes of man, therefore The attributes of a king are a mark of the absence of the attribute signified by the word omnipotent, (or, are *evidence* of the absence of that attribute.)

To correspond with this alteration in the form of the syllogisms, the axioms on which the syllogistic process is founded must undergo a corresponding transformation. In this altered phraseology, both those axioms may be brought under one general expression; namely, that whatever possesses any mark, possesses that which it is a mark of. Or, when the minor premiss as well as the major is universal, we may state it thus: Whatever is a mark of any mark, is a mark of that which this last is a mark of. To trace the identity of these axioms with those previously laid down, may be left to the intelligent reader. We shall find, as we proceed, the great convenience of the phraseology into which we have last thrown them, and which is better adapted than any I am acquainted with, to express with precision and force what is aimed at, and actually accomplished, in every case of the ascertainment of a truth by ratiocination.

CHAPTER III. OF THE FUNCTIONS, AND LOGICAL VALUE, OF THE SYLLOGISM.

§ 1. We have shown what is the real nature of the truths with which the Syllogism is conversant, in contradistinction to the more superficial manner in which their import is conceived in the common theory; and what are the fundamental axioms on which its probative force or conclusiveness depends. We have now to inquire, whether the syllogistic process, that of reasoning from generals to particulars, is, or is not, a process of inference; a progress from the known to the unknown; a means of coming to a knowledge of something which we did not know before.

Logicians have been remarkably unanimous in their mode of answering this question. It is universally allowed that a syllogism is vicious if there be anything more in the conclusion than was assumed in the premisses. But this is, in fact, to say, that nothing ever was, or can be, proved by syllogism, which was not known, or assumed to be known, before. Is ratiocination, then, not a process of inference? And is the syllogism, to which the word reasoning has so often been represented to be exclusively appropriate, not really entitled to be called reasoning at all? This seems an inevitable consequence of the doctrine, admitted by all writers on the subject, that a syllogism can prove no more than is involved in the premisses. Yet the acknowledgment so explicitly made, has not prevented one set of writers from continuing to represent the syllogism as the correct analysis of what the mind actually performs in discovering and proving the larger half of the truths, whether of science or of daily life, which we believe; while those who have avoided this inconsistency, and followed out the general theorem respecting the logical value of the syllogism to its legitimate corollary, have been led to impute uselessness and frivolity to the syllogistic theory itself, on the ground of the ***petitio principii*** which they allege to be inherent in every syllogism. As I believe both these opinions to be fundamentally erroneous, I must request the attention of the reader to certain considerations, without which any just appreciation of the true character of the syllogism, and the functions it performs in philosophy, appears to me impossible; but which seem to have been either overlooked, or insufficiently adverted to, both by the defenders of the syllogistic theory and by its assailants.

§ 2. It must be granted that in every syllogism, considered as an argument to prove the conclusion, there is a ***petitio principii***. When we say,

All men are mortal Socrates is a man therefore Socrates is mortal;

it is unanswerably urged by the adversaries of the syllogistic theory, that the proposition, Socrates is mortal, is presupposed in the more general assumption, All men are mortal: that we cannot be assured of the mortality of all men, unless we are already certain of the mortality of every individual man: that if it be still doubtful whether Socrates, or any other individual you choose to name, be mortal or not, the same degree of uncertainty must hang over the assertion, All men are mortal: that the general principle, instead of being given as evidence of the particular case, cannot itself be taken for true without exception, until every shadow of doubt which could affect any case comprised with it, is dispelled by evidence *aliunde*; and then what remains for the syllogism to prove? That, in short, no reasoning from generals to particulars can, as such, prove anything: since from a general principle you cannot infer any particulars, but those which the principle itself assumes as known.

This doctrine appears to me irrefragable; and if logicians, though unable to dispute it, have usually exhibited a strong disposition to explain it away, this was not because they could discover any flaw in the argument itself, but because the contrary opinion seemed to rest on arguments equally indisputable. In the syllogism last referred to, for example, or in any of those which we previously constructed, is it not evident that the conclusion may, to the person to whom the syllogism is presented, be actually and *bona fide* a new truth? Is it not matter of daily experience that truths previously undreamt of, facts which have not been, and cannot be, directly observed, are arrived at by way of general reasoning? We believe that the Duke of Wellington is mortal. We do not know this by direct observation, since he is not dead. If we were asked how, this being the case, we know the duke to be mortal, we should probably answer, Because all men are so. Here, therefore, we arrive at the knowledge of a truth not (as yet) susceptible of observation, by a reasoning which admits of being exhibited in the following syllogism:--

All men are mortal The Duke of Wellington is a man therefore The Duke of Wellington is mortal.

And since a large portion of our knowledge is thus acquired, logicians have persisted in representing the syllogism as a process of inference or proof; although none of them has cleared up the difficulty which arises from the inconsistency between that assertion, and the principle, that if there be anything in the conclusion which was not already asserted in the premises, the argument is vicious. For it is impossible to attach any serious scientific value to such a mere salvo, as the distinction drawn between being involved *by implication* in the premises, and being directly asserted in them. When Archbishop Whately, for example, says,(31) that the object of reasoning is "merely to expand and unfold the assertions wrapt up, as it were, and implied in those with which we set out, and to bring a person to perceive and acknowledge the full force of that which he has admitted," he does not, I think, meet the real difficulty requiring to be explained, namely, how it happens that a science, like geometry, ***can*** be all "wrapt up" in a few definitions and axioms. Nor does this defence of the syllogism differ much from what its assailants urge against it as an accusation, when they charge it with being of no use except to those who seek to press the consequences of an admission into which a person has been entrapped without having considered and understood its full force. When you admitted the major premiss, you asserted the conclusion; but, says Archbishop Whately, you asserted it by implication merely: this, however, can here only mean that you asserted it unconsciously; that you did not know you were asserting it; but, if so, the difficulty revives in this shape--Ought you not to have known? Were you warranted in asserting the general proposition without having satisfied yourself of the truth of everything which it fairly includes? And if not, what then is the syllogistic art but a contrivance for catching you in a trap, and holding you fast in it?(32)

§ 3. From this difficulty there appears to be but one issue. The proposition that the Duke of Wellington is mortal, is evidently an inference; it is got at as a conclusion from something else; but do we, in reality, conclude it from the proposition, All men are mortal? I answer, no.

The error committed is, I conceive, that of overlooking the distinction between the two parts of the process of philosophizing, the inferring part, and the registering part; and ascribing to the latter the functions of the former. The mistake is that of referring a person to his own notes for the origin of his knowledge. If a person is asked a question, and is at the moment unable to answer it, he may refresh his memory by turning to a memorandum which he carries about with him. But if he were asked, how the fact came to his knowledge, he would scarcely answer, because it was set down in his note-book: unless the book was written, like the Koran, with a quill from the wing of the angel Gabriel.

Assuming that the proposition, The Duke of Wellington is mortal, is immediately an inference from the proposition, All men are mortal; whence do we derive our knowledge of that general truth? Of course from observation. Now, all which man can observe are individual cases. From these all general truths must be drawn, and into these they may be again resolved: for a general truth is but an aggregate of particular truths; a comprehensive expression, by which an indefinite number of individual facts are affirmed or denied at once. But a general proposition is not merely a compendious form for recording and preserving in the memory a number of particular facts, all of which have been observed. Generalization is not a process of mere naming, it is also a process of inference. From instances which we have observed, we feel warranted in concluding, that what we found true in those instances, holds in all similar ones, past, present, and future, however numerous they may be. We then, by that valuable contrivance of language which enables us to speak of many as if they were one, record all that we have observed, together with all that we infer from our observations, in one concise expression; and have thus only one proposition, instead of an endless number, to remember or to communicate. The results of many observations and inferences, and instructions for making innumerable inferences in unforeseen cases, are compressed into one short sentence.

When, therefore, we conclude from the death of John and Thomas, and every other person we ever heard of in whose case the experiment had been fairly tried, that the Duke of Wellington is mortal like the rest; we may, indeed, pass through the generalization, All men are mortal, as an intermediate stage; but it is not in the latter half of the process, the descent from all men to the Duke of Wellington, that the *inference* resides. The inference is finished when we have asserted that all men are mortal. What remains to be performed afterwards is merely decyphering our own notes.

Archbishop Whately has contended that syllogising, or reasoning from generals to particulars, is not, agreeably to the vulgar idea, a peculiar *mode* of reasoning, but the philosophical analysis of *the* mode in which all men reason, and must do so if they reason at all. With the deference due to so high an authority, I cannot help thinking that the vulgar notion is, in this case, the more correct. If, from our experience of John, Thomas, &c., who once were living, but are now dead, we are entitled to conclude that all human beings are mortal, we might surely without any logical inconsequence have concluded at once from those instances, that the Duke of Wellington is mortal. The mortality of John, Thomas, and company is, after all, the whole evidence we have for the mortality of the Duke of Wellington. Not one iota is added to the proof by interpolating a general proposition. Since the individual cases are all the evidence we can possess, evidence which no logical form into which we choose to throw it can make greater than it is; and since that evidence is either sufficient in itself, or, if insufficient for the one purpose, cannot be sufficient for the other; I am unable to see why we should be forbidden to take the shortest cut from these sufficient premises to the conclusion, and constrained to travel the "high priori road," by the arbitrary fiat of logicians. I cannot perceive why it should be impossible to journey from one place to another unless we "march up a hill, and then march down again." It may be the safest road, and there may be a resting place at the top of the hill, affording a commanding view of the surrounding country; but for the mere purpose of arriving at our journey's end, our taking that road is perfectly optional; it is a question of time, trouble, and danger.

Not only *may* we reason from particulars to particulars without passing through generals, but we perpetually do so reason. All our earliest inferences are of this nature. From the first dawn of intelligence we draw inferences, but years elapse before we learn the use of general language. The child, who, having burnt his fingers, avoids to thrust them again into the fire, has reasoned or inferred, though he has never thought of the general maxim, Fire burns. He knows from memory that he has been burnt, and on this evidence believes, when he sees a candle, that if he puts his finger into the flame of it, he will be burnt again. He believes this in every case which happens to arise; but without looking, in each instance, beyond the present case. He is not generalizing; he is inferring a particular from particulars. In the same way, also, brutes reason. There is no ground for attributing to any of the lower animals the use of signs, of such a nature as to render general propositions possible. But those animals profit by experience, and avoid what they have found to cause them pain, in the same manner, though not always with the same skill, as a human creature. Not only the burnt child, but the burnt dog, dreads the fire.

I believe that, in point of fact, when drawing inferences from our personal experience, and not from maxims handed down to us by books or tradition, we much oftener conclude from particulars to particulars directly, than through the intermediate agency of any general proposition. We are constantly reasoning from ourselves to other people, or from one person to another, without giving ourselves the trouble to erect our observations into general maxims of human or external nature. When we conclude that some person will, on some given occasion, feel or act so and so, we sometimes judge from an enlarged consideration of the manner in which human beings in general, or persons of some particular character, are accustomed to feel and act; but much oftener from having known the feelings and conduct of the same person in some previous instance, or from considering how we should feel or act ourselves. It is not only the village matron who, when called to a consultation upon the case of a neighbour's child, pronounces on the evil and its remedy simply on the recollection and authority of what she accounts the similar case of her Lucy. We all, where we have no definite maxims to steer by, guide ourselves in the same way; and if we have an extensive experience, and retain its impressions strongly, we may acquire in this manner a very considerable power of accurate judgment, which we may be utterly incapable of justifying or of communicating to others. Among the higher order of practical intellects, there have been many of whom it was remarked how admirably they suited their means to their ends, without being able to give any sufficient reasons for what they did; and applied, or seemed to apply, recondite principles which they were wholly unable to state. This is a natural consequence of having a mind stored with appropriate particulars, and having been long accustomed to reason at once from these to fresh particulars, without practising the habit of stating to oneself or to others the corresponding general propositions. An old warrior, on a rapid glance at the outlines of the ground, is able at once to give the necessary orders for a skilful arrangement of his troops; though if he has received little theoretical instruction, and has seldom been called upon to answer to other people for his conduct, he may never have had in his mind a single general theorem respecting the relation between ground and array. But his experience of encampments, in circumstances more or less similar, has left a number of vivid, unexpressed, ungeneralized analogies in his mind, the most appropriate of which, instantly suggesting itself, determines him to a judicious arrangement.

The skill of an uneducated person in the use of weapons, or of tools, is of a precisely similar nature. The savage who executes unerringly the exact throw which brings down his game, or his enemy, in the manner most suited to his purpose, under the operation of all the conditions necessarily involved, the weight and form of the weapon, the direction and distance of the object, the action of the wind, &c., owes this power to a long series of previous experiments, the results of which he certainly never framed into any verbal theorems or rules. The same thing may generally be said of any other extraordinary manual dexterity. Not long ago a Scotch manufacturer procured from England, at a high rate of wages, a working dyer, famous for producing very fine colours, with the view of teaching to his other workmen the same skill. The workman came; but his mode of proportioning the ingredients, in which lay the secret of the effects he produced, was by taking them up in handfuls, while the common method was to weigh them. The manufacturer sought to make him turn his handling system into an equivalent weighing system, that the general principle of his peculiar mode of proceeding might be ascertained. This, however, the man found himself quite unable to do, and therefore could impart his skill to nobody. He had, from the individual cases of his own experience, established a connexion in his mind between fine effects of colour, and tactual perceptions in handling his dyeing materials; and from these perceptions he could, in any particular case, infer the means to be employed, and the effects which would be produced, but could not put others in possession of the grounds on which he proceeded, from having never generalized them in his own mind, or expressed them in language.

Almost every one knows Lord Mansfield's advice to a man of practical good sense, who, being appointed governor of a colony, had to preside in its court of justice, without previous judicial practice or legal education. The advice was to give his decision boldly, for it would probably be right; but never to venture on assigning reasons, for they would almost infallibly be wrong. In cases like this, which are of no uncommon occurrence, it would be absurd to suppose that the bad reason was the source of the good decision. Lord Mansfield knew that if any reason were assigned it would be necessarily an afterthought, the judge being *in fact* guided by impressions from past experience, without the circuitous process of framing general principles from them, and that if he attempted to frame any such he would assuredly fail. Lord Mansfield, however, would not have doubted that a man of equal experience, who had also a mind stored with general propositions derived by legitimate induction from that experience, would have been greatly preferable as a judge, to one, however sagacious, who could not be trusted with the explanation and justification of his own judgments. The cases of men of talent performing wonderful things they know not how, are examples of the rudest and most spontaneous form of the operations of superior minds; it is a defect in them, and often a source of errors, not to have generalized as they went on; but generalization, though a help, the most important indeed of all helps, is not an essential.

Even the scientifically instructed, who possess, in the form of general propositions, a systematic record of the results of the experience of mankind, need not always revert to those general propositions in order to apply that experience to a new case. It is justly remarked by Dugald Stewart, that though our reasonings in mathematics depend entirely on the axioms, it is by no means necessary to our seeing the conclusiveness of the proof, that the axioms should be expressly adverted to. When it is inferred that A B is equal to C D because each of them is equal to E F, the most uncultivated understanding, as soon as the propositions were understood, would assent to the inference, without having ever heard of the general truth that "things which are equal to the same thing are equal to one another." This remark of Stewart, consistently followed out, goes to the root, as I conceive, of the philosophy of ratiocination; and it is to be regretted that he himself stopt short at a much more limited application of it. He saw that the general propositions on which a reasoning is said to depend, may, in certain cases, be altogether omitted, without impairing its probative force. But he imagined this to be a peculiarity belonging to axioms; and argued from it, that axioms are not the foundations or first principles of geometry, from which all the other truths of the science are synthetically deduced (as the laws of motion and of the composition of forces in dynamics, the equal mobility of fluids in hydrostatics, the laws of reflection and refraction in optics, are the first principles of those sciences); but are merely necessary assumptions, self-evident indeed, and the denial of which would annihilate all demonstration, but from which, as premisses, nothing can be demonstrated. In the present, as in many other instances, this thoughtful and elegant writer has perceived an important truth, but only by halves. Finding, in the case of geometrical axioms, that general names have not any talismanic virtue for conjuring new truths out of the pit of darkness, and not seeing that this is equally true in every other case of generalization, he contended that axioms are in their nature barren of consequences, and that the really fruitful truths, the real first principles of geometry, are the definitions; that the definition, for example, of the circle is to the properties of the circle, what the laws of equilibrium and of the pressure of the atmosphere are to the rise of the mercury in the Torricellian tube. Yet all that he had asserted respecting the function to which the axioms are confined in the demonstrations of geometry, holds equally true of the definitions. Every demonstration in Euclid might be carried on without them. This is apparent from the ordinary process of proving a proposition of geometry by means of a diagram. What assumption, in fact, do we set out from, to demonstrate by a diagram any of the properties of the circle? Not that in all circles the radii are equal, but only that they are so in the circle ABC. As our warrant for assuming this, we appeal, it is true, to the definition of a circle in general; but it is only necessary that the assumption be granted in the case of the particular circle supposed. From this, which is not a general but a singular proposition, combined with other propositions of a similar kind, some of which ***when generalized*** are called definitions, and others axioms, we prove that a certain conclusion is true, not of all circles, but of the particular circle ABC; or at least would be so, if the facts precisely accorded with our assumptions. The enunciation, as it is called, that is, the general theorem which stands at the head of the demonstration, is not the proposition actually demonstrated. One instance only is demonstrated: but the process by which this is done, is a process which, when we consider its nature, we perceive might be exactly copied in an indefinite number of other instances; in every instance which conforms to certain conditions. The contrivance of general language furnishing us with terms which connote these conditions, we are able to assert this indefinite multitude of truths in a single expression, and this expression is the general theorem. By dropping the use of diagrams, and substituting, in the demonstrations, general phrases for the letters of the alphabet, we might prove the general theorem directly, that is, we might demonstrate all the cases at once; and to do this we must, of course, employ as our premises, the axioms and definitions in their general form. But this only means, that if we can prove an individual conclusion by assuming an individual fact, then in whatever case we are warranted in making an exactly similar assumption, we may draw an exactly similar conclusion. The definition is a sort of notice to ourselves and others, what assumptions we think ourselves entitled to make. And so in all cases, the general propositions, whether called definitions, axioms, or laws of nature, which we lay down at the beginning of our reasonings, are merely abridged statements, in a kind of short-hand, of the particular facts, which, as occasion arises, we either think we may proceed on as proved, or intend to assume. In any one demonstration it is enough if we assume for a particular case suitably selected, what by the statement of the definition or principle we announce that we intend to assume in all cases which may arise. The definition of the circle, therefore, is to one of Euclid's demonstrations, exactly what, according to Stewart, the axioms are; that is, the demonstration does not depend on it, but yet if we deny it the demonstration fails. The proof does not rest on the general assumption, but on a similar assumption confined to the particular case: that case, however, being chosen as a specimen or paradigm of the whole class of cases included in the theorem, there can be no ground for making the assumption in that case which does not exist in every other; and if you deny the assumption as a general truth, you deny the right to make it in the particular instance.

There are, undoubtedly, the most ample reasons for stating both the principles and the theorems in their general form, and these will be explained presently, so far as explanation is requisite. But, that unpractised learners, even in making use of one theorem to demonstrate another, reason rather from particular to particular than from the general proposition, is manifest from the difficulty they find in applying a theorem to a case in which the configuration of the diagram is extremely unlike that of the diagram by which the original theorem was demonstrated. A difficulty which, except in cases of unusual mental power, long practice can alone remove, and removes chiefly by rendering us familiar with all the configurations consistent with the general conditions of the theorem.

§ 4. From the considerations now adduced, the following conclusions seem to be established. All inference is from particulars to particulars: General propositions are merely registers of such inferences already made, and short formulae for making more: The major premiss of a syllogism, consequently, is a formula of this description: and the conclusion is not an inference drawn ***from*** the formula, but an inference drawn ***according*** to the formula: the real logical antecedent, or premisses, being the particular facts from which the general proposition was collected by induction. Those facts, and the individual instances which supplied them, may have been forgotten; but a record remains, not indeed descriptive of the facts themselves, but showing how those cases may be distinguished respecting which the facts, when known, were considered to warrant a given inference. According to the indications of this record we draw our conclusion; which is, to all intents and purposes, a conclusion from the forgotten facts. For this it is essential that we should read the record correctly: and the rules of the syllogism are a set of precautions to ensure our doing so.

This view of the functions of the syllogism is confirmed by the consideration of precisely those cases which might be expected to be least favourable to it, namely, those in which ratiocination is independent of any previous induction. We have already observed that the syllogism, in the ordinary course of our reasoning, is only the latter half of the process of travelling from premises to a conclusion. There are, however, some peculiar cases in which it is the whole process. Particulars alone are capable of being subjected to observation; and all knowledge which is derived from observation, begins, therefore, of necessity, in particulars; but our knowledge may, in cases of a certain description, be conceived as coming to us from other sources than observation. It may present itself as coming from testimony, which, on the occasion and for the purpose in hand, is accepted as of an authoritative character: and the information thus communicated, may be conceived to comprise not only particular facts but general propositions, as when a scientific doctrine is accepted without examination on the authority of writers. Or the generalization may not be, in the ordinary sense, an assertion at all, but a command; a law, not in the philosophical, but in the moral and political sense of the term: an expression of the desire of a superior, that we, or any number of other persons, shall conform our conduct to certain general instructions. So far as this asserts a fact, namely, a volition of the legislator, that fact is an individual fact, and the proposition, therefore, is not a general proposition. But the description therein contained of the conduct which it is the will of the legislator that his subjects should observe, is general. The proposition asserts, not that all men *are* anything, but that all men *shall* do something.

In both these cases the generalities are the original data, and the particulars are elicited from them by a process which correctly resolves itself into a series of syllogisms. The real nature, however, of the supposed deductive process, is evident enough. The only point to be determined is, whether the authority which declared the general proposition, intended to include this case in it; and whether the legislator intended his command to apply to the present case among others, or not. This is ascertained by examining whether the case possesses the marks by which, as those authorities have signified, the cases which they meant to certify or to influence may be known. The object of the inquiry is to make out the witness's or the legislator's intention, through the indication given by their words. This is a question, as the Germans express it, of hermeneutics. The operation is not a process of inference, but a process of interpretation.

In this last phrase we have obtained an expression which appears to me to characterize, more aptly than any other, the functions of the syllogism in all cases. When the premises are given by authority, the function of Reasoning is to ascertain the testimony of a witness, or the will of a legislator, by interpreting the signs in which the one has intimated his assertion and the other his command. In like manner, when the premises are derived from observation, the function of Reasoning is to ascertain what we (or our predecessors) formerly thought might be inferred from the observed facts, and to do this by interpreting a memorandum of ours, or of theirs. The memorandum reminds us, that from evidence, more or less carefully weighed, it formerly appeared that a certain attribute might be inferred wherever we perceive a certain mark. The proposition, All men are mortal, (for instance) shows that we have had experience from which we thought it followed that the attributes connoted by the term man, are a mark of mortality. But when we conclude that the Duke of Wellington is mortal, we do not infer this from the memorandum, but from the former experience. All that we infer from the memorandum, is our own previous belief, (or that of those who transmitted to us the proposition,) concerning the inferences which that former experience would warrant.

This view of the nature of the syllogism renders consistent and intelligible what otherwise remains obscure and confused in the theory of Archbishop Whately and other enlightened defenders of the syllogistic doctrine, respecting the limits to which its functions are confined. They affirm in as explicit terms as can be used, that the sole office of general reasoning is to prevent inconsistency in our opinions; to prevent us from assenting to anything, the truth of which would contradict something to which we had previously on good grounds given our assent. And they tell us, that the sole ground which a syllogism affords for assenting to the conclusion, is that the supposition of its being false, combined with the supposition that the premises are true, would lead to a contradiction in terms. Now this would be but a lame account of the real grounds which we have for believing the facts which we learn from reasoning, in contradistinction to observation. The true reason why we believe that the Duke of Wellington will die, is that his fathers, and our fathers, and all other persons who were cotemporary with them, have died. Those facts are the real premises of the reasoning. But we are not led to infer the conclusion from those premises, by the necessity of avoiding any verbal inconsistency. There is no contradiction in supposing that all those persons have died, and that the Duke of Wellington may, notwithstanding, live for ever. But there would be a contradiction if we first, on the ground of those same premises, made a general assertion including and covering the case of the Duke of Wellington, and then refused to stand to it in the individual case. There is an inconsistency to be avoided between the memorandum we make of the inferences which may be justly drawn in future cases, and the inferences we actually draw in those cases when they arise. With this view we interpret our own formula, precisely as a judge interprets a law: in order that we may avoid drawing any inferences not conformable to our former intention, as a judge avoids giving any decision not conformable to the legislator's intention. The rules for this interpretation are the rules of the syllogism: and its sole purpose is to maintain consistency between the conclusions we draw in every particular case, and the previous general directions for drawing them; whether those general directions were framed by ourselves as the result of induction, or were received by us from an authority competent to give them.

§ 5. In the above observations it has, I think, been clearly shown, that, although there is always a process of reasoning or inference where a syllogism is used, the syllogism is not a correct analysis of that process of reasoning or inference; which is, on the contrary, (when not a mere inference from testimony,) an inference from particulars to particulars; authorized by a previous inference from particulars to generals, and substantially the same with it; of the nature, therefore, of Induction. But, while these conclusions appear to me undeniable, I must yet enter a protest, as strong as that of Archbishop Whately himself; against the doctrine that the syllogistic art is useless for the purposes of reasoning. The reasoning lies in the act of generalization, not in interpreting the record of that act; but the syllogistic form is an indispensable collateral security for the correctness of the generalization itself.

It has already been seen, that if we have a collection of particulars sufficient for grounding an induction, we need not frame a general proposition; we may reason at once from those particulars to other particulars. But it is to be remarked withal, that whenever, from a set of particular cases, we can legitimately draw any inference, we may legitimately make our inference a general one. If, from observation and experiment, we can conclude to one new case, so may we to an indefinite number. If that which has held true in our past experience will therefore hold in time to come, it will hold not merely in some individual case, but in all cases of a given description. Every induction, therefore, which suffices to prove one fact, proves an indefinite multitude of facts: the experience which justifies a single prediction must be such as will suffice to bear out a general theorem. This theorem it is extremely important to ascertain and declare, in its broadest form of generality; and thus to place before our minds, in its full extent, the whole of what our evidence must prove if it proves anything.

This throwing of the whole body of possible inferences from a given set of particulars, into one general expression, operates as a security for their being just inferences, in more ways than one. First, the general principle presents a larger object to the imagination than any of the singular propositions which it contains. A process of thought which leads to a comprehensive generality, is felt as of greater importance than one which terminates in an insulated fact; and the mind is, even unconsciously, led to bestow greater attention upon the process, and to weigh more carefully the sufficiency of the experience appealed to, for supporting the inference grounded upon it. There is another, and a more important, advantage. In reasoning from a course of individual observations to some new and unobserved case, which we are but imperfectly acquainted with (or we should not be inquiring into it), and in which, since we are inquiring into it, we probably feel a peculiar interest; there is very little to prevent us from giving way to negligence, or to any bias which may affect our wishes or our imagination, and, under that influence, accepting insufficient evidence as sufficient. But if, instead of concluding straight to the particular case, we place before ourselves an entire class of facts--the whole contents of a general proposition, every tittle of which is legitimately inferrible from our premises, if that one particular conclusion is so; there is then a considerable likelihood that if the premises are insufficient, and the general inference, therefore, groundless, it will comprise within it some fact or facts the reverse of which we already know to be true; and we shall thus discover the error in our generalization by what the schoolmen termed a *reductio ad impossibile*.

Thus if, during the reign of Marcus Aurelius, a subject of the Roman empire, under the bias naturally given to the imagination and expectations by the lives and characters of the Antonines, had been disposed to conclude that Commodus would be a just ruler; supposing him to stop there, he might only have been undeceived by sad experience. But if he reflected that this conclusion could not be justifiable unless from the same evidence he was also warranted in concluding some general proposition, as, for instance, that all Roman emperors are just rulers; he would immediately have thought of Nero, Domitian, and other instances, which, showing the falsity of the general conclusion, and therefore the insufficiency of the premises, would have warned him that those premises could not prove in the instance of Commodus, what they were inadequate to prove in any collection of cases in which his was included.

The advantage, in judging whether any controverted inference is legitimate, of referring to a parallel case, is universally acknowledged. But by ascending to the general proposition, we bring under our view not one parallel case only, but all possible parallel cases at once; all cases to which the same set of evidentiary considerations are applicable.

When, therefore, we argue from a number of known cases to another case supposed to be analogous, it is always possible, and generally advantageous, to divert our argument into the circuitous channel of an induction from those known cases to a general proposition, and a subsequent application of that general proposition to the unknown case. This second part of the operation, which, as before observed, is essentially a process of interpretation, will be resolvable into a syllogism or a series of syllogisms, the majors of which will be general propositions embracing whole classes of cases; every one of which propositions must be true in all its extent, if the argument is maintainable. If, therefore, any fact fairly coming within the range of one of these general propositions, and consequently asserted by it, is known or suspected to be other than the proposition asserts it to be, this mode of stating the argument causes us to know or to suspect that the original observations, which are the real grounds of our conclusion, are not sufficient to support it. And in proportion to the greater chance of our detecting the inconclusiveness of our evidence, will be the increased reliance we are entitled to place in it if no such evidence of defect shall appear.

The value, therefore, of the syllogistic form, and of the rules for using it correctly, does not consist in their being the form and the rules according to which our reasonings are necessarily, or even usually, made; but in their furnishing us with a mode in which those reasonings may always be represented, and which is admirably calculated, if they are inconclusive, to bring their inconclusiveness to light. An induction from particulars to generals, followed by a syllogistic process from those generals to other particulars, is a form in which we may always state our reasonings if we please. It is not a form in which we **must** reason, but it is a form in which we **may** reason, and into which it is indispensable to throw our reasoning, when there is any doubt of its validity: though when the case is familiar and little complicated, and there is no suspicion of error, we may, and do, reason at once from the known particular cases to unknown ones.

These are the uses of syllogism, as a mode of verifying any given argument. Its ulterior uses, as respects the general course of our intellectual operations, hardly require illustration, being in fact the acknowledged uses of general language. They amount substantially to this, that the inductions may be made once for all: a single careful interrogation of experience may suffice, and the result may be registered in the form of a general proposition, which is committed to memory or to writing, and from which afterwards we have only to syllogize. The particulars of our experiments may then be dismissed from the memory, in which it would be impossible to retain so great a multitude of details; while the knowledge which those details afforded for future use, and which would otherwise be lost as soon as the observations were forgotten, or as their record became too bulky for reference, is retained in a commodious and immediately available shape by means of general language.

Against this advantage is to be set the countervailing inconvenience, that inferences originally made on insufficient evidence, become consecrated, and, as it were, hardened into general maxims; and the mind cleaves to them from habit, after it has outgrown any liability to be misled by similar fallacious appearances if they were now for the first time presented; but having forgotten the particulars, it does not think of revising its own former decision. An inevitable drawback, which, however considerable in itself, forms evidently but a small deduction from the immense advantages of general language.

The use of the syllogism is in truth no other than the use of general propositions in reasoning. We **can** reason without them; in simple and obvious cases we habitually do so; minds of great sagacity can do it in cases not simple and obvious, provided their experience supplies them with instances essentially similar to every combination of circumstances likely to arise. But other minds, or the same minds

without the same pre-eminent advantages of personal experience, are quite help-
less without the aid of general propositions, wherever the case presents the smallest
complication; and if we made no general propositions, few persons would get much
beyond those simple inferences which are drawn by the more intelligent of the
brutes. Though not necessary to reasoning, general propositions are necessary to
any considerable progress in reasoning. It is, therefore, natural and indispensable to
separate the process of investigation into two parts; and obtain general formulae for
determining what inferences may be drawn, before the occasion arises for drawing
the inferences. The work of drawing them is then that of applying the formulae;
and the rules of syllogism are a system of securities for the correctness of the application.

§ 6. To complete the series of considerations connected with the philosophical
character of the syllogism, it is requisite to consider, since the syllogism is not the
universal type of the reasoning process, what is the real type. This resolves itself
into the question, what is the nature of the minor premiss, and in what manner it
contributes to establish the conclusion: for as to the major, we now fully understand, that the place which it nominally occupies in our reasonings, properly belongs to the individual facts or observations of which it expresses the general result;
the major itself being no real part of the argument, but an intermediate halting
place for the mind, interposed by an artifice of language between the real premisses
and the conclusion, by way of a security, which it is in a most material degree, for
the correctness of the process. The minor, however, being an indispensable part of
the syllogistic expression of an argument, without doubt either is, or corresponds
to, an equally indispensable part of the argument itself, and we have only to inquire
what part.

It is perhaps worth while to notice here a speculation of one of the philosophers to whom mental science is most indebted, but who, though a very penetrating, was a very hasty thinker, and whose want of due circumspection rendered
him fully as remarkable for what he did not see, as for what he saw. I allude to Dr.
Thomas Brown, whose theory of ratiocination is peculiar. He saw the *petitio principii* which is inherent in every syllogism, if we consider the major to be itself the
evidence by which the conclusion is proved, instead of being, what in fact it is, an
assertion of the existence of evidence sufficient to prove any conclusion of a given

description. Seeing this, Dr. Brown not only failed to see the immense advantage, in point of security for correctness, which is gained by interposing this step between the real evidence and the conclusion; but he thought it incumbent on him to strike out the major altogether from the reasoning process, without substituting anything else, and maintained that our reasonings consist only of the minor premiss and the conclusion, Socrates is a man, therefore Socrates is mortal: thus actually suppressing, as an unnecessary step in the argument, the appeal to former experience. The absurdity of this was disguised from him by the opinion he adopted, that reasoning is merely analysing our own general notions, or abstract ideas; and that the proposition, Socrates is mortal, is evolved from the proposition, Socrates is a man, simply by recognising the notion of mortality as already contained in the notion we form of a man.

After the explanations so fully entered into on the subject of propositions, much further discussion cannot be necessary to make the radical error of this view of ratiocination apparent. If the word man connoted mortality; if the meaning of "mortal" were involved in the meaning of "man;" we might, undoubtedly, evolve the conclusion from the minor alone, because the minor would have distinctly asserted it. But if, as is in fact the case, the word man does not connote mortality, how does it appear that in the mind of every person who admits Socrates to be a man, the idea of man must include the idea of mortality? Dr. Brown could not help seeing this difficulty, and in order to avoid it, was led, contrary to his intention, to re-establish, under another name, that step in the argument which corresponds to the major, by affirming the necessity of *previously perceiving* the relation between the idea of man and the idea of mortal. If the reasoner has not previously perceived this relation, he will not, says Dr. Brown, infer because Socrates is a man, that Socrates is mortal. But even this admission, though amounting to a surrender of the doctrine that an argument consists of the minor and the conclusion alone, will not save the remainder of Dr. Brown's theory. The failure of assent to the argument does not take place merely because the reasoner, for want of due analysis, does not perceive that his idea of man includes the idea of mortality; it takes place, much more commonly, because in his mind that relation between the two ideas has never existed. And in truth it never does exist, except as the result of experience. Consenting, for the sake of the argument, to discuss the question on a supposition of which we have recognised the radical incorrectness, namely, that the meaning of a proposition relates to the ideas of the things spoken of, and not to the things themselves; I must yet observe, that the idea of man, as an universal idea, the common property of all rational creatures, cannot involve anything but what is strictly implied in the name. If any one includes in his own private idea of man, as no doubt is almost always the case, some other attributes, such for instance as mortality, he does so only as the consequence of experience, after having satisfied himself that all men possess that attribute: so that whatever the idea contains, in any person's mind, beyond what is included in the conventional signification of the word, has been added to it as the result of assent to a proposition; while Dr. Brown's theory requires us to suppose, on the contrary, that assent to the proposition is produced by evolving, through an analytic process, this very element out of the idea. This theory, therefore, may be considered as sufficiently refuted; and the minor premiss must be regarded as totally insufficient to prove the conclusion, except with the assistance of the major, or of that which the major represents, namely, the various singular propositions expressive of the series of observations, of which the generalization called the major premiss is the result.

In the argument, then, which proves that Socrates is mortal, one indispensable part of the premisses will be as follows: "My father, and my father's father, A, B, C, and an indefinite number of other persons, were mortal;" which is only an expression in different words of the observed fact that they have died. This is the major premiss, divested of the ***petitio principii***, and cut down to as much as is really known by direct evidence.

In order to connect this proposition with the conclusion, Socrates is mortal, the additional link necessary is such a proposition as the following: "Socrates resembles my father, and my father's father, and the other individuals specified." This proposition we assert when we say that Socrates is a man. By saying so we likewise assert in what respect he resembles them, namely, in the attributes connoted by the word man. And from this we conclude that he further resembles them in the attribute mortality.

§ 7. We have thus obtained what we were seeking, an universal type of the reasoning process. We find it resolvable in all cases into the following elements: Certain individuals have a given attribute; an individual or individuals resemble the former in certain other attributes; therefore they resemble them also in the given attribute. This type of ratiocination does not claim, like the syllogism, to be conclusive from the mere form of the expression; nor can it possibly be so. That one proposition does or does not assert the very fact which was already asserted in another, may appear from the form of the expression, that is, from a comparison of the language; but when the two propositions assert facts which are *bona fide* different, whether the one fact proves the other or not can never appear from the language, but must depend on other considerations. Whether, from the attributes in which Socrates resembles those men who have heretofore died, it is allowable to infer that he resembles them also in being mortal, is a question of Induction; and is to be decided by the principles or canons which we shall hereafter recognise as tests of the correct performance of that great mental operation.

Meanwhile, however, it is certain, as before remarked, that if this inference can be drawn as to Socrates, it can be drawn as to all others who resemble the observed individuals in the same attributes in which he resembles them; that is (to express the thing concisely), of all mankind. If, therefore, the argument be conclusive in the case of Socrates, we are at liberty, once for all, to treat the possession of the attributes of man as a mark, or satisfactory evidence, of the attribute of mortality. This we do by laying down the universal proposition, All men are mortal, and interpreting this, as occasion arises, in its application to Socrates and others. By this means we establish a very convenient division of the entire logical operation into two steps; first, that of ascertaining what attributes are marks of mortality; and, secondly, whether any given individuals possess those marks. And it will generally be advisable, in our speculations on the reasoning process, to consider this double operation as in fact taking place, and all reasoning as carried on in the form into which it must necessarily be thrown to enable us to apply to it any test of its correct performance.

Although, therefore, all processes of thought in which the ultimate premisses are particulars, whether we conclude from particulars to a general formula, or from particulars to other particulars according to that formula, are equally Induction; we shall yet, conformably to usage, consider the name Induction as more peculiarly belonging to the process of establishing the general proposition, and the remaining operation, which is substantially that of interpreting the general proposition, we shall call by its usual name, Deduction. And we shall consider every process by which anything is inferred respecting an unobserved case, as consisting of an Induction followed by a Deduction; because, although the process needs not necessarily be carried on in this form, it is always susceptible of the form, and must be thrown into it when assurance of scientific accuracy is needed and desired.

NOTE SUPPLEMENTARY TO THE PRECEDING CHAPTER.

This theory of the syllogism, (which has received the important adhesion of Dr. Whewell,(33)) has been controverted by a writer in the "British Quarterly Review."(34) The doctrine being new, discussion respecting it is extremely desirable, to ensure that nothing essential to the question escapes observation; and I shall, therefore, reply to this writer's objections with somewhat more minuteness than their strength may seem to require.

The reviewer denies that there is a ***petitio principii*** in the syllogism, or that the proposition, All men are mortal, asserts or assumes that Socrates is mortal. In support of this denial, he argues that we may, and in fact do, admit the general proposition that all men are mortal, without having particularly examined the case of Socrates, and even without knowing whether the individual so named is a man or not. But this of course was never denied. That we can and do draw conclusions concerning cases specifically unknown to us, is the datum from which all who discuss this subject must set out. The question is, in what terms the evidence, or ground, on which we draw these conclusions, may best be designated--whether it is most correct to say, that the unknown case is proved by known cases, or that it is proved by a general proposition, including both sets of cases, the unknown and the known? I contend for the former mode of expression. I hold it an abuse of language to say, that the proof that Socrates is mortal, is that all men are mortal. Turn it in what way we will, this seems to me to be asserting that a thing is the proof of itself. Whoever pronounces the words, All men are mortal, has affirmed that Socrates is mortal, though he may never have heard of Socrates; for since Socrates, whether known to be so or not, really is a man, he is included in the words, All men, and in every assertion of which they are the subject. If the reviewer does not see that there is a difficulty here, I can only advise him to reconsider the subject until he does: after which he will be a more competent judge of the success or failure of an attempt to remove the difficulty.(35) That he had reflected very little on the point when he wrote his remarks, is shown by his oversight respecting the *dictum de omni et nullo*. He acknowledges that this maxim as commonly expressed,--"Whatever is true of a class, is true of everything included in the class," is a mere identical proposition, since the class *is* nothing but the things included in it. But he thinks this defect would be cured by wording the maxim thus,--"Whatever is true of a class, is true of everything which *can be shown* to be a member of the class:" as if a thing could "be shown" to be a member of the class without being one. If a class means the sum of all the things included in the class, the things which "can be shown" to be included in it are a part of these; it is the sum of them too, and the *dictum* is as much an identical proposition with respect to them as to the rest. One would almost imagine that, in the reviewer's opinion, things are not members of a class until they are called up publicly to take their place in it--that so long, in fact, as Socrates is not known to be a man, he *is not* a man, and any assertion which can be made concerning men does not at all regard him, nor is affected as to its truth or falsity by anything in which he is concerned.

The reviewer says that if the major premiss included the conclusion, "we should be able to affirm the conclusion without the intervention of the minor premiss; but every one sees that that is impossible." It does not follow, because the major premiss contains the conclusion, that the words themselves must show all the conclusions which it contains, and which, or evidence of which, it presupposes. The minor is equally required on both theories. It is respecting the functions of the major premiss that the theories differ; whether that premiss merely affirms the existence of proof, or is itself part of the proof--whether the conclusion follows from the minor and major, or from the minor and the particular instances which are the foundation of the major. On either supposition, it is necessary that the new case should be perceived to be one coming within the description of those to which the previous experience is applicable; which is the purport of the minor premiss. When we say that all men are mortal, we make an assertion reaching beyond the sphere of our knowledge of individual cases; and when a new individual, Socrates, is brought within the field of our knowledge by means of the minor premiss, we learn that we have already made an assertion respecting Socrates without knowing it: our own general formula is, to that extent, for the first time *interpreted* to us. But according to the reviewer's theory, it is our having *made* the assertion which proves the assertion: while I contend that the proof is not the assertion, but the grounds (of experience) on which the assertion was made, and by which it must be justified.

The reviewer comes much nearer to the gist of the question, when he objects that the formula in which the major is left out--"A, B, C, &c., were mortal, therefore the Duke of Wellington is mortal," does not express all the steps of the mental process, but omits one of the most essential, that which consists in recognising the cases A, B, C, as **sufficient evidence** of what is true of the Duke of Wellington. This recognition of the sufficiency of the induction he calls an "inference," and says, that its result must be interpolated between the cases A, B, C, and the case of the Duke of Wellington; and that "our final conclusion is from what is thus interpolated, and not directly from the individual facts that A, B, C, &c. were mortal." On this it may first be observed, that the formula does express all that takes place in ordinary unscientific reasoning. Mankind in general conclude at once from experience of death in past cases, to the expectation of it in future, without testing the experience by any principles of induction, or passing through any general proposition. This is not safe reasoning, but it is reasoning; and the syllogism, therefore, is not the universal type of reasoning, but only a form in which it is **desirable** that we should reason. But, in the second place, suppose that the enquirer does logically satisfy himself that the conditions of legitimate induction are realized in the cases A, B, C. It is still obvious, that if he knows the Duke of Wellington to be a man, he is as much justified in concluding at once that the Duke of Wellington is mortal, as in concluding that all men are mortal. The general conclusion is not legitimate, unless the particular one would be so too; and in no sense, intelligible to me, can the particular conclusion be said to be drawn **from** the general one.(36) That the process of testing the sufficiency of an inductive inference is an operation of a general character, I readily concede to the reviewer; I had myself said as much, by laying down as a fundamental law, that whenever there is ground for drawing any conclusion at all from particular instances, there is ground for a **general** conclusion. But that this general conclusion should be actually drawn, however useful, cannot be an indispensable condition of the validity of the inference in the particular case. A man gives away sixpence by the same power by which he disposes of his whole fortune; but it is not necessary to the lawfulness of his doing the one, that he should formally assert, even to himself, his right to do the other.

The reviewer has recourse for an example, to syllogisms in the second figure (though all are, by a mere verbal transformation, reducible to the first), and asks, where is the petitio principii in this syllogism, "Every poet is a man of genius, A B is not a man of genius, therefore A B is not a poet." It is true that in a syllogism of this particular type, the petitio principii is disguised. A B is not included in the terms, every poet. But the proposition, "every poet is a man of genius" (a very questionable proposition, by the way), cannot have been inductively proved, unless the negative branch of the enquiry has been attended to as well as the positive; unless it has been fully considered whether among persons who are not "men of genius," there are not some who ought to be termed poets, and unless this has been determined in the negative. Therefore, the case of A B has been decided by implication, as much as the case of Socrates in the first example. The proposition, Every poet is a man of genius, is confessedly aequipollent with "No one who is not a man of genius is a poet," and in this the ***petitio principii***, as regards A B, is no longer implied, but express, as in an ordinary syllogism of the first figure.

Another critic has endeavoured to get rid of the petitio principii in the syllogism by substituting for the common form of expression, the following form--All ***known*** men were mortal, Socrates is a man, therefore Socrates is mortal. To this, however, there is the fatal objection, that the syllogism, thus transformed, does not prove the conclusion; it wants not the form

only, but the substance of proof. It is not merely because a thing
is true in all **known** instances that it can be inferred to be
true in any new instance: many things may be true of all known men
which would not be true of all men; while, on the other hand, a
thing may be superabundantly proved true of all men, without
having been ascertained by actual experience to be true of all
known men, or even of the hundredth part of them.

CHAPTER IV. OF TRAINS OF REASONING, AND DEDUCTIVE SCIENCES.

§ 1. In our analysis of the syllogism it appeared that the minor premiss always affirms a resemblance between a new case, and some cases previously known; while the major premiss asserts something which, having been found true of those known cases, we consider ourselves warranted in holding true of any other case resembling the former in certain given particulars.

If all ratiocinations resembled, as to the minor premiss, the examples which were exclusively employed in the preceding chapter; if the resemblance, which that premiss asserts, were obvious to the senses, as in the proposition "Socrates is a man," or were at once ascertainable by direct observation; there would be no necessity for trains of reasoning, and Deductive or Ratiocinative Sciences would not exist. Trains of reasoning exist only for the sake of extending an induction, founded, as all inductions must be, on observed cases, to other cases in which we not only cannot directly observe what is to be proved, but cannot directly observe even the mark which is to prove it.

§ 2. Suppose the syllogism to be, All cows ruminate, the animal which is before me is a cow, therefore it ruminates. The minor, if true at all, is obviously so: the only premiss the establishment of which requires any anterior process of inquiry, is the major; and provided the induction of which that premiss is the expression was correctly performed, the conclusion respecting the animal now present will be instantly drawn; because, as soon as she is compared with the formula, she will be identified as being included in it. But suppose the syllogism to be the following:--All arsenic is poisonous, the substance which is before me is arsenic, therefore it is poisonous. The truth of the minor may not here be obvious at first sight; it may not be intuitively evident, but may itself be known only by inference. It may be the conclusion of another argument, which, thrown into the syllogistic form, would stand thus:--Whatever forms a compound with hydrogen, which yields a black precipitate with nitrate of silver, is arsenic; the substance before me conforms to this condition; therefore it is arsenic. To establish, therefore, the ultimate conclusion, The substance before me is poisonous, requires a process, which, in order to be syllogistically expressed, stands in need of two syllogisms; and we have a Train of Reasoning.

When, however, we thus add syllogism to syllogism, we are really adding induction to induction. Two separate inductions must have taken place to render this chain of inference possible; inductions founded, probably, on different sets of individual instances, but which converge in their results, so that the instance which is the subject of inquiry comes within the range of them both. The record of these inductions is contained in the majors of the two syllogisms. First, we, or others for us, have examined various objects which yielded under the given circumstances the given precipitate, and found that they possessed the properties connoted by the word arsenic; they were metallic, volatile, their vapour had a smell of garlic, and so forth. Next, we, or others for us, have examined various specimens which possessed this metallic and volatile character, whose vapour had this smell, &c., and have invariably found that they were poisonous. The first observation we judge that we may extend to all substances whatever which yield the precipitate: the second, to all metallic and volatile substances resembling those we examined; and consequently, not to those only which are seen to be such, but to those which are concluded to be such by the prior induction. The substance before us is only seen to come within one of these inductions; but by means of this one, it is brought within the other. We are still, as before, concluding from particulars to particulars; but we are now concluding from particulars observed, to other particulars which are not, as in the simple case, **seen** to resemble them in the material points, but **inferred** to do so, because resembling them in something else, which we have been led by quite a different set of instances to consider as a mark of the former resemblance.

This first example of a train of reasoning is still extremely simple, the series consisting of only two syllogisms. The following is somewhat more complicated:-- No government, which earnestly seeks the good of its subjects, is likely to be overthrown; some particular government earnestly seeks the good of its subjects, therefore it is not likely to be overthrown. The major premiss in this argument we shall suppose not to be derived from considerations *a priori*, but to be a generalization from history, which, whether correct or erroneous, must have been founded on observation of governments concerning whose desire of the good of their subjects there was no doubt. It has been found, or thought to be found, that these were not likely to be overthrown, and it has been deemed that those instances warranted an extension of the same predicate to any and every government which resembles them in the attribute of desiring earnestly the good of its subjects. But *does* the government in question thus resemble them? This may be debated *pro* and *con* by many arguments, and must, in any case, be proved by another induction; for we cannot directly observe the sentiments and desires of the persons who carry on the government. To prove the minor, therefore, we require an argument in this form: Every government which acts in a certain manner, desires the good of its subjects; the supposed government acts in that particular manner, therefore it desires the good of its subjects. But is it true that the government acts in the manner supposed? This minor also may require proof; still another induction, as thus:--What is asserted by intelligent and disinterested witnesses, may be believed to be true; that the government acts in this manner, is asserted by such witnesses, therefore it may be believed to be true. The argument hence consists of three steps. Having the evidence of our senses that the case of the government under consideration resembles a number of former cases, in the circumstance of having something asserted respecting it by intelligent and disinterested witnesses, we infer, first, that, as in those former instances, so in this instance, the assertion is true. Secondly, what was asserted of the government being that it acts in a particular manner, and other governments or persons having been observed to act in the same manner, the government in question is brought into known resemblance with those other governments or persons; and since they were known to desire the good of the people, it is thereupon, by a second induction, inferred that the particular government spoken of, desires the good of the people. This brings that government into known resemblance with the other governments which were thought likely to escape revolution, and thence, by a third induction, it is predicted that this particular government is also likely to escape. This is still reasoning from particulars to particulars, but we now reason to the new instance from three distinct sets of former instances: to one only of those sets of instances do we directly perceive the new one to be similar; but from that similarity we inductively infer that it has the attribute by which it is assimilated to the next set, and brought within the corresponding induction; after which by a repetition of the same operation we infer it to be similar to the third set, and hence a third induction conducts us to the ultimate conclusion.

§ 3. Notwithstanding the superior complication of these examples, compared with those by which in the preceding chapter we illustrated the general theory of reasoning, every doctrine which we then laid down holds equally true in these more intricate cases. The successive general propositions are not steps in the reasoning, are not intermediate links in the chain of inference, between the particulars observed and those to which we apply the observation. If we had sufficiently capacious memories, and a sufficient power of maintaining order among a huge mass of details, the reasoning could go on without any general propositions; they are mere formulae for inferring particulars from particulars. The principle of general reasoning is, (as before explained,) that if from observation of certain known particulars, what was seen to be true of them can be inferred to be true of any others, it may be inferred of all others which are of a certain description. And in order that we may never fail to draw this conclusion in a new case when it can be drawn correctly, and may avoid drawing it when it cannot, we determine once for all what are the distinguishing marks by which such cases may be recognised. The subsequent process is merely that of identifying an object, and ascertaining it to have those marks; whether we identify it by the very marks themselves, or by others which we have ascertained (through another and a similar process) to be marks of those marks. The real inference is always from particulars to particulars, from the observed instances to an unobserved one: but in drawing this inference, we conform to a formula which we have adopted for our guidance in such operations, and which is a record of the criteria by which we thought we had ascertained that we might distinguish when the inference could, and when it could not, be drawn. The real premises are the individual observations, even though they may have been forgotten, or, being the observations of others and not of ourselves, may, to us, never have been known: but we have before us proof that we or others once thought them sufficient for an induction, and we have marks to show whether any new case is one of those to which, if then known, the induction would have been deemed to extend. These marks we either recognise at once, or by the aid of other marks, which by another previous induction we collected to be marks of *them*. Even these marks of marks may only be recognised through a third set of marks; and we may have a train of reasoning, of any length, to bring a new case within the scope of an induction grounded on particulars its similarity to which is only ascertained in this indirect manner.

Thus, in the preceding example, the ultimate inductive inference was, that a certain government was not likely to be overthrown: this inference was drawn according to a formula in which desire of the public good was set down as a mark of not being likely to be overthrown; a mark of this mark was, acting in a particular manner; and a mark of acting in that manner was, being asserted to do so by intelligent and disinterested witnesses: this mark, the government under discussion was recognised by the senses as possessing. Hence that government fell within the last induction, and by it was brought within all the others. The perceived resemblance of the case to one set of observed particular cases, brought it into known resemblance with another set, and that with a third.

In the more complex branches of knowledge, the deductions seldom consist, as in the examples hitherto exhibited, of a single chain, *a* a mark of *b*, *b* of *c*, *c* of *d*, therefore *a* a mark of *d*. They consist (to carry on the same metaphor) of several chains united at the extremity, as thus: *a* a mark of *d*, *b* of *e*, *c* of *f*, *d e f* of *n*, therefore *a b c* a mark of *n*. Suppose, for example, the following combination of circumstances: 1st, rays of light impinging on a reflecting surface; 2nd, that surface parabolic; 3rd, those rays parallel to each other and to the axis of the surface. It is to be proved that the concourse of these three circumstances is a mark that the reflected rays will pass through the focus of the parabolic surface. Now, each of the three circumstances is singly a mark of something material to the case. Rays of light impinging on a reflecting surface, are a mark that those rays will be reflected at an angle equal to the angle of incidence. The parabolic form of the surface is a mark that, from any point of it, a line drawn to the focus and a line parallel to the axis will make equal angles with the surface. And finally, the parallelism of the rays to the axis is a mark that their angle of incidence coincides with one of these equal angles. The three marks taken together are therefore a mark of all these three things united. But the three united are evidently a mark that the angle of reflexion must coincide with the other of the two equal angles, that formed by a line drawn to the focus; and this again, by the fundamental axiom concerning straight lines, is a mark that the reflected rays pass through the focus. Most chains of physical deduction are of this more complicated type; and even in mathematics such are abundant, as in all propositions where the hypothesis includes numerous conditions: "*If* a circle be taken, and *if* within that circle a point be taken, not the centre, and *if* straight lines be drawn from that point to the circumference, then," &c.

§ 4. The considerations now stated remove a serious difficulty from the view we have taken of reasoning; which view might otherwise have seemed not easily reconcilable with the fact that there are Deductive or Ratiocinative Sciences. It might seem to follow, if all reasoning be induction, that the difficulties of philosophical investigation must lie in the inductions exclusively, and that when these were easy, and susceptible of no doubt or hesitation, there could be no science, or, at least, no difficulties in science. The existence, for example, of an extensive Science of Mathematics, requiring the highest scientific genius in those who contributed to its creation, and calling for a most continued and vigorous exertion of intellect in order to appropriate it when created, may seem hard to be accounted for on the foregoing theory. But the considerations more recently adduced remove the mystery, by showing, that even when the inductions themselves are obvious, there may be much difficulty in finding whether the particular case which is the subject of inquiry comes within them; and ample room for scientific ingenuity in so combining various inductions, as, by means of one within which the case evidently falls, to bring it within others in which it cannot be directly seen to be included.

When the more obvious of the inductions which can be made in any science from direct observations, have been made, and general formulas have been framed, determining the limits within which these inductions are applicable; as often as a new case can be at once seen to come within one of the formulas, the induction is applied to the new case, and the business is ended. But new cases are continually arising, which do not obviously come within any formula whereby the question we want solved in respect of them could be answered. Let us take an instance from geometry; and as it is taken only for illustration, let the reader concede to us for the present, what we shall endeavour to prove in the next chapter, that the first principles of geometry are results of induction. Our example shall be the fifth proposition of the first book of Euclid. The inquiry is, Are the angles at the base of an isosceles triangle equal or unequal? The first thing to be considered is, what inductions we have, from which we can infer equality or inequality. For inferring equality we have the following formulae:--Things which being applied to each other coincide, are equals. Things which are equal to the same thing are equals. A whole and the sum of its parts are equals. The sums of equal things are equals. The differences of equal things are equals. There are no other formulae to prove equality. For inferring inequality we have the following:--A whole and its parts are unequals. The sums of equal things and unequal things are unequals. The differences of equal things and unequal things are unequals. In all, eight formulae. The angles at the base of an isosceles triangle do not obviously come within any of these. The formulae specify certain marks of equality and of inequality, but the angles cannot be perceived intuitively to have any of those marks. We can, however, examine whether they have properties which, in any other formulae, are set down as marks of those marks. On examination it appears that they have; and we ultimately succeed in bringing them within this formula, "The differences of equal things are equal." Whence comes the difficulty in recognising these angles as the differences of equal things? Because each of them is the difference not of one pair only, but of innumerable pairs of angles; and out of these we had to imagine and select two, which could either be intuitively perceived to be equals, or possessed some of the marks of equality set down in the various formulae. By an exercise of ingenuity, which, on the part of the first inventor, deserves to be regarded as considerable, two pairs of angles were hit upon, which united these requisites. First, it could be perceived intuitively that their differences were the angles at the base; and, secondly; they possessed one of the marks of equality, namely, coincidence when applied to one another. This coincidence, however, was not perceived intuitively, but inferred, in conformity to another formula.

For greater clearness, I subjoin an analysis of the demonstration. Euclid, it will be remembered, demonstrates his fifth proposition by means of the fourth. This it is not allowable for us to do, because we are undertaking to trace deductive truths not to prior deductions, but to their original inductive foundation. We must therefore use the premisses of the fourth proposition instead of its conclusion, and prove the fifth directly from first principles. To do so requires six formulas. (We presuppose an equilateral triangle, whose vertices are A, D, E, with point B on the side AD, and point C on the side AE, such that BC is parallel to DE. We must begin as in Euclid, by prolonging the equal sides AB, AC, to equal distances, and joining the extremities BE, DC.)

FIRST FORMULA. ***The sums of equals are equal.***

A D and A E are sums of equals by the supposition. Having that mark of equality, they are concluded by this formula to be equal.

SECOND FORMULA. ***Equal straight lines being applied to one another coincide***.

A C, A B, are within this formula by supposition; A D, A E, have been brought within it by the preceding step. Both these pairs of straight lines have the property of equality; which, according to the second formula, is a mark that, if applied to each other, they will coincide. Coinciding altogether means coinciding in every part, and of course at their extremities, D, E, and B, C.

THIRD FORMULA. ***Straight lines, having their extremities coincident, coincide***.

B E and C D have been brought within this formula by the preceding induction; they will, therefore, coincide.

FOURTH FORMULA. ***Angles, having their sides coincident, coincide***.

The third induction having shown that B E and C D coincide, and the second that A B, A C, coincide, the angles A B E and A C D are thereby brought within the fourth formula, and accordingly coincide.

FIFTH FORMULA. ***Things which coincide are equal***.

The angles A B E and A C D are brought within this formula by the induction immediately preceding. This train of reasoning being also applicable, ***mutatis mutandis***, to the angles E B C, D C B, these also are brought within the fifth formula. And, finally,

SIXTH FORMULA. ***The differences of equals are equal***.

The angle A B C being the difference of A B E, C B E, and the angle A C B being the difference of A C D, D C B; which have been proved to be equals; A B C and A C B are brought within the last formula by the whole of the previous process.

The difficulty here encountered is chiefly that of figuring to ourselves the two angles at the base of the triangle A B C, as remainders made by cutting one pair of angles out of another, while each pair shall be corresponding angles of triangles which have two sides and the intervening angle equal. It is by this happy contrivance that so many different inductions are brought to bear upon the same particular case. And this not being at all an obvious idea, it may be seen from an example so near the threshold of mathematics, how much scope there may well be for scientific dexterity in the higher branches of that and other sciences, in order so to combine a few simple inductions, as to bring within each of them innumerable cases which are not obviously included in it; and how long, and numerous, and complicated may be the processes necessary for bringing the inductions together, even when each induction may itself be very easy and simple. All the inductions involved in all geometry are comprised in those simple ones, the formulae of which are the Axioms, and a few of the so-called Definitions. The remainder of the science is made up of the processes employed for bringing unforeseen cases within these inductions; or (in syllogistic language) for proving the minors necessary to complete the syllogisms; the majors being the definitions and axioms. In those definitions and axioms are laid down the whole of the marks, by an artful combination of which it has been found possible to discover and prove all that is proved in geometry. The marks being so few, and the inductions which furnish them being so obvious and familiar; the connecting of several of them together, which constitutes Deductions, or Trains of Reasoning, forms the whole difficulty of the science, and, with a trifling exception, its whole bulk; and hence Geometry is a Deductive Science.

§ 5. It will be seen hereafter that there are weighty scientific reasons for giving to every science as much of the character of a Deductive Science as possible; for endeavouring to construct the science from the fewest and the simplest possible inductions, and to make these, by any combinations however complicated, suffice for proving even such truths, relating to complex cases, as could be proved, if we chose, by inductions from specific experience. Every branch of natural philosophy was originally experimental; each generalization rested on a special induction, and was derived from its own distinct set of observations and experiments. From being sciences of pure experiment, as the phrase is, or, to speak more correctly, sciences in which the reasonings mostly consist of no more than one step, and are expressed by single syllogisms, all these sciences have become to some extent, and some of them in nearly the whole of their extent, sciences of pure reasoning; whereby multitudes of truths, already known by induction from as many different sets of experiments, have come to be exhibited as deductions or corollaries from inductive propositions of a simpler and more universal character. Thus mechanics, hydrostatics, optics, acoustics, and thermology, have successively been rendered mathematical; and astronomy was brought by Newton within the laws of general mechanics. Why it is that the substitution of this circuitous mode of proceeding for a process apparently much easier and more natural, is held, and justly, to be the greatest triumph of the investigation of nature, we are not, in this stage of our inquiry, prepared to examine. But it is necessary to remark, that although, by this progressive transformation, all sciences tend to become more and more Deductive, they are not therefore the less Inductive; every step in the Deduction is still an Induction. The opposition is not between the terms Deductive and Inductive, but between Deductive and Experimental. A science is experimental, in proportion as every new case, which presents any peculiar features, stands in need of a new set of observations and experiments, a fresh induction. It is Deductive, in proportion as it can draw conclusions, respecting cases of a new kind, by processes which bring those cases under old inductions; by ascertaining that cases which cannot be observed to have the requisite marks, have, however, marks of those marks.

We can now, therefore, perceive what is the generic distinction between sciences which can be made Deductive, and those which must as yet remain Experimental. The difference consists in our having been able, or not yet able, to discover marks of marks. If by our various inductions we have been able to proceed no further than to such propositions as these, a a mark of b, or a and b marks of one another, c a mark of d, or c and d marks of one another, without anything to connect a or b with c or d; we have a science of detached and mutually independent generalizations, such as these, that acids redden vegetable blues, and that alkalies colour them green; from neither of which propositions could we, directly or indirectly, infer the other: and a science, so far as it is composed of such propositions, is purely experimental. Chemistry, in the present state of our knowledge, has not yet thrown off this character. There are other sciences, however, of which the propositions are of this kind: *a* a mark of *b*, *b* a mark of *c*, *c* of *d*, *d* of *e*, &c. In these sciences we can mount the ladder from *a* to *e* by a process of ratiocination; we can conclude that *a* is a mark of *e*, and that every object which has the mark *a* has the property *e*, although, perhaps, we never were able to observe *a* and *e* together, and although even *d*, our only direct mark of *e*, may be not perceptible in those objects, but only inferrible. Or varying the first metaphor, we may be said to get from *a* to *e* underground: the marks *b*, *c*, *d*, which indicate the route, must all be possessed somewhere by the objects concerning which we are inquiring; but they are below the surface: *a* is the only mark that is visible, and by it we are able to trace in succession all the rest.

§ 6. We can now understand how an experimental may transform itself into a deductive science by the mere progress of experiment. In an experimental science, the inductions, as we have said, lie detached, as, *a* a mark of *b*, *c* a mark of *d*, *e* a mark of *f*, and so on: now, a new set of instances, and a consequent new induction, may at any time bridge over the interval between two of these unconnected arches; *b*, for example, may be ascertained to be a mark of *c*, which enables us thenceforth to prove deductively that *a* is a mark of *c*. Or, as sometimes happens, some comprehensive induction may raise an arch high in the air, which bridges over hosts of them at once: *b*, *d*, *f*, and all the rest, turning out to be marks of some one thing, or of things between which a connexion has already been traced. As when Newton discovered that the motions, whether regular or apparently anomalous, of all the bodies of the solar system, (each of which motions had been inferred by a separate logical operation, from separate marks,) were all marks of moving round a common centre, with a centripetal force varying directly as the mass, and inversely as the square of the distance from that centre. This is the greatest example which has yet occurred of the transformation, at one stroke, of a science which was still to a great degree merely experimental, into a deductive science.

Transformations of the same nature, but on a smaller scale, continually take place in the less advanced branches of physical knowledge, without enabling them to throw off the character of experimental sciences. Thus with regard to the two unconnected propositions before cited, namely, Acids redden vegetable blues, Alkalies make them green; it is remarked by Liebig, that all blue colouring matters which are reddened by acids (as well as, reciprocally, all red colouring matters which are rendered blue by alkalies) contain nitrogen: and it is quite possible that this circumstance may one day furnish a bond of connexion between the two propositions in question, by showing that the antagonist action of acids and alkalies in producing or destroying the colour blue, is the result of some one, more general, law. Although this connecting of detached generalizations is so much gain, it tends but little to give a deductive character to any science as a whole; because the new courses of observation and experiment, which thus enable us to connect together a few general truths, usually make known to us a still greater number of unconnected new ones. Hence chemistry, though similar extensions and simplifications of its generalizations are continually taking place, is still in the main an experimental science; and is likely so to continue, unless some comprehensive induction should be hereafter arrived at, which, like Newton's, shall connect a vast number of the smaller known inductions together, and change the whole method of the science at once. Chemistry has already one great generalization, which, though relating to one of the subordinate aspects of chemical phenomena, possesses within its limited sphere this comprehensive character; the principle of Dalton, called the atomic theory, or the doctrine of chemical equivalents: which by enabling us to a certain extent to foresee the proportions in which two substances will combine, before the experiment has been tried, constitutes undoubtedly a source of new chemical truths obtainable by deduction, as well as a connecting principle for all truths of the same description previously obtained by experiment.

§ 7. The discoveries which change the method of a science from experimental to deductive, mostly consist in establishing, either by deduction or by direct experiment, that the varieties of a particular phenomenon uniformly accompany the varieties of some other phenomenon better known. Thus the science of sound, which previously stood in the lowest rank of merely experimental science, became deductive when it was proved by experiment that every variety of sound was consequent on, and therefore a mark of, a distinct and definable variety of oscillatory motion among the particles of the transmitting medium. When this was ascertained, it followed that every relation of succession or coexistence which obtained between phenomena of the more known class, obtained also between the phenomena which corresponded to them in the other class. Every sound, being a mark of a particular oscillatory motion, became a mark of everything which, by the laws of dynamics, was known to be inferrible from that motion; and everything which by those same laws was a mark of any oscillatory motion among the particles of an elastic medium, became a mark of the corresponding sound. And thus many truths, not before suspected, concerning sound, become deducible from the known laws of the propagation of motion through an elastic medium; while facts already empirically known respecting sound, become an indication of corresponding properties of vibrating bodies, previously undiscovered.

But the grand agent for transforming experimental into deductive sciences, is the science of number. The properties of numbers, alone among all known phenomena, are, in the most rigorous sense, properties of all things whatever. All things are not coloured, or ponderable, or even extended; but all things are numerable. And if we consider this science in its whole extent, from common arithmetic up to the calculus of variations, the truths already ascertained seem all but infinite, and admit of indefinite extension.

These truths, though affirmable of all things whatever, of course apply to them only in respect of their quantity. But if it comes to be discovered that variations of quality in any class of phenomena, correspond regularly to variations of quantity either in those same or in some other phenomena; every formula of mathematics applicable to quantities which vary in that particular manner, becomes a mark of a corresponding general truth respecting the variations in quality which accompany them: and the science of quantity being (as far as any science can be) altogether deductive, the theory of that particular kind of qualities becomes, to this extent, deductive likewise.

The most striking instance in point which history affords (though not an example of an experimental science rendered deductive, but of an unparalleled extension given to the deductive process in a science which was deductive already,) is the revolution in geometry which originated with Descartes, and was completed by Clairaut. These great mathematicians pointed out the importance of the fact, that to every variety of position in points, direction in lines, or form in curves or surfaces, (all of which are Qualities,) there corresponds a peculiar relation of quantity between either two or three rectilineal co-ordinates; insomuch that if the law were known according to which those co-ordinates vary relatively to one another, every other geometrical property of the line or surface in question, whether relating to quantity or quality, would be capable of being inferred. Hence it followed that every geometrical question could be solved, if the corresponding algebraical one could; and geometry received an accession (actual or potential) of new truths, corresponding to every property of numbers which the progress of the calculus had brought, or might in future bring, to light. In the same general manner, mechanics, astronomy, and in a less degree, every branch of natural philosophy commonly so called, have been made algebraical. The varieties of physical phenomena with which those sciences are conversant, have been found to answer to determinable varieties in the quantity of some circumstance or other; or at least to varieties of form or position, for which corresponding equations of quantity had already been, or were susceptible of being, discovered by geometers.

In these various transformations, the propositions of the science of number do but fulfil the function proper to all propositions forming a train of reasoning, viz. that of enabling us to arrive in an indirect method, by marks of marks, at such of the properties of objects as we cannot directly ascertain (or not so conveniently) by experiment. We travel from a given visible or tangible fact, through the truths of numbers, to the fact sought. The given fact is a mark that a certain relation subsists between the quantities of some of the elements concerned; while the fact sought presupposes a certain relation between the quantities of some other elements: now, if these last quantities are dependent in some known manner upon the former, or *vice versa*, we can argue from the numerical relation between the one set of quantities, to determine that which subsists between the other set; the theorems of the calculus affording the intermediate links. And thus one of the two physical facts becomes a mark of the other, by being a mark of a mark of a mark of it.

CHAPTER V. OF DEMONSTRATION, AND NECES SARY TRUTHS.

§ 1. If, as laid down in the two preceding chapters, the foundation of all sciences, even deductive or demonstrative sciences, is Induction; if every step in the ratiocinations even of geometry is an act of induction; and if a train of reasoning is but bringing many inductions to bear upon the same subject of inquiry, and drawing a case within one induction by means of another; wherein lies the peculiar certainty always ascribed to the sciences which are entirely, or almost entirely, deductive? Why are they called the Exact Sciences? Why are mathematical certainty, and the evidence of demonstration, common phrases to express the very highest degree of assurance attainable by reason? Why are mathematics by almost all philosophers, and (by many) even those branches of natural philosophy which, through the medium of mathematics, have been converted into deductive sciences, considered to be independent of the evidence of experience and observation, and characterized as systems of Necessary Truth?

The answer I conceive to be, that this character of necessity, ascribed to the truths of mathematics, and even (with some reservations to be hereafter made) the peculiar certainty attributed to them, is an illusion; in order to sustain which, it is necessary to suppose that those truths relate to, and express the properties of, purely imaginary objects. It is acknowledged that the conclusions of geometry are deduced, partly at least, from the so-called Definitions, and that those definitions are assumed to be correct descriptions, as far as they go, of the objects with which geometry is conversant. Now we have pointed out that, from a definition as such, no proposition, unless it be one concerning the meaning of a word, can ever follow; and that what apparently follows from a definition, follows in reality from an implied assumption that there exists a real thing conformable thereto. This assumption, in the case of the definitions of geometry, is false: there exist no real things exactly conformable to the definitions. There exist no points without magnitude; no lines without breadth, nor perfectly straight; no circles with all their radii exactly equal, nor squares with all their angles perfectly right. It will perhaps be said that the assumption does not extend to the actual, but only to the possible, existence of such things. I answer that, according to any test we have of possibility, they are not even possible. Their existence, so far as we can form any judgment, would seem to be inconsistent with the physical constitution of our planet at least, if not of the universe. To get rid of this difficulty, and at the same time to save the credit of the supposed system of necessary truth, it is customary to say that the points, lines, circles, and squares which are the subject of geometry, exist in our conceptions merely, and are part of our minds; which minds, by working on their own materials, construct an *a priori* science, the evidence of which is purely mental, and has nothing whatever to do with outward experience. By howsoever high authorities this doctrine may have been sanctioned, it appears to me psychologically incorrect. The points, lines, circles, and squares, which any one has in his mind, are (I apprehend) simply copies of the points, lines, circles, and squares which he has known in his experience. Our idea of a point, I apprehend to be simply our idea of the *minimum visibile*, the smallest portion of surface which we can see. A line, as defined by geometers, is wholly inconceivable. We can reason about a line as if it had no breadth; because we have a power, which is the foundation of all the control we can exercise over the operations of our minds; the power, when a perception is present to our senses, or a conception to our intellects, of *attending* to a part only of that perception or conception, instead of the whole. But we cannot *conceive* a line without breadth; we can form no mental picture of such a line: all the lines which we have in our minds are lines possessing breadth. If any one doubts this, we may refer him to his own experience. I much question if any one who fancies that he can conceive what is called a mathematical line, thinks so from the evidence of his consciousness: I suspect it is rather because he supposes that unless such a conception were possible, mathematics could not exist as a science: a supposition which there will be no difficulty in showing to be entirely groundless.

Since, then, neither in nature, nor in the human mind, do there exist any objects exactly corresponding to the definitions of geometry, while yet that science cannot be supposed to be conversant about non-entities; nothing remains but to consider geometry as conversant with such lines, angles, and figures, as really exist; and the definitions, as they are called, must be regarded as some of our first and most obvious generalizations concerning those natural objects. The correctness of those generalizations, *as* generalizations, is without a flaw: the equality of all the radii of a circle is true of all circles, so far as it is true of any one: but it is not exactly true of any circle: it is only nearly true; so nearly that no error of any importance in practice will be incurred by feigning it to be exactly true. When we have occasion to extend these inductions, or their consequences, to cases in which the error would be appreciable--to lines of perceptible breadth or thickness, parallels which deviate sensibly from equidistance, and the like--we correct our conclusions, by combining with them a fresh set of propositions relating to the aberration; just as we also take in propositions relating to the physical or chemical properties of the material, if those properties happen to introduce any modification into the result; which they easily may, even with respect to figure and magnitude, as in the case, for instance, of expansion by heat. So long, however, as there exists no practical necessity for attending to any of the properties of the object except its geometrical properties, or to any of the natural irregularities in those, it is convenient to neglect the consideration of the other properties and of the irregularities, and to reason as if these did not exist: accordingly, we formally announce, in the definitions, that we intend to proceed on this plan. But it is an error to suppose, because we resolve to confine our attention to a certain number of the properties of an object, that we therefore conceive, or have an idea of the object, denuded of its other properties. We are thinking, all the time, of precisely such objects as we have seen and touched, and with all the properties which naturally belong to them; but for scientific convenience, we feign them to be divested of all properties, except those which are material to our purpose, and in regard to which we design to consider them.

The peculiar accuracy, supposed to be characteristic of the first principles of geometry, thus appears to be fictitious. The assertions on which the reasonings of the science are founded, do not, any more than in other sciences, exactly correspond with the fact; but we ***suppose*** that they do so, for the sake of tracing the consequences which follow from the supposition. The opinion of Dugald Stewart respecting the foundations of geometry, is, I conceive, substantially correct; that it is built on hypotheses; that it owes to this alone the peculiar certainty supposed to distinguish it; and that in any science whatever, by reasoning from a set of hypotheses, we may obtain a body of conclusions as certain as those of geometry, that is, as strictly in accordance with the hypotheses, and as irresistibly compelling assent, ***on condition*** that those hypotheses are true.

When, therefore, it is affirmed that the conclusions of geometry are necessary truths, the necessity consists in reality only in this, that they necessarily follow from the suppositions from which they are deduced. Those suppositions are so far from being necessary, that they are not even true; they purposely depart, more or less widely, from the truth. The only sense in which necessity can be ascribed to the conclusions of any scientific investigation, is that of necessarily following from some assumption, which, by the conditions of the inquiry, is not to be questioned. In this relation, of course, the derivative truths of every deductive science must stand to the inductions, or assumptions, on which the science is founded, and which, whether true or untrue, certain or doubtful in themselves, are always supposed certain for the purposes of the particular science. And therefore the conclusions of all deductive sciences were said by the ancients to be necessary propositions. We have observed already that to be predicated necessarily was characteristic of the predicable Proprium, and that a proprium was any property of a thing which could be deduced from its essence, that is, from the properties included in its definition.

§ 2. The important doctrine of Dugald Stewart, which I have endeavoured to enforce, has been contested by Dr. Whewell, both in the dissertation appended to his excellent **Mechanical Euclid**, and in his more recent elaborate work on the **Philosophy of the Inductive Sciences**; in which last he also replies to an article in the **Edinburgh Review**, (ascribed to a writer of great scientific eminence,) in which Stewart's opinion was defended against his former strictures. The supposed refutation of Stewart consists in proving against him (as has also been done in this work) that the premisses of geometry are not definitions, but assumptions of the real existence of things corresponding to those definitions. This, however, is doing little for Dr. Whewell's purpose; for it is these very assumptions which are asserted to be hypotheses, and which he, if he denies that geometry is founded on hypotheses, must show to be absolute truths. All he does, however, is to observe, that they at any rate are not **arbitrary** hypotheses; that we should not be at liberty to substitute other hypotheses for them; that not only "a definition, to be admissible, must necessarily refer to and agree with some conception which we can distinctly frame in our thoughts," but that the straight lines, for instance, which we define, must be "those by which angles are contained, those by which triangles are bounded, those of which parallelism may be predicated, and the like."(37) And this is true; but this has never been contradicted. Those who say that the premisses of geometry are hypotheses, are not bound to maintain them to be hypotheses which have no relation whatever to fact. Since an hypothesis framed for the purpose of scientific inquiry must relate to something which has real existence, (for there can be no science respecting non-entities,) it follows that any hypothesis we make respecting an object, to facilitate our study of it, must not involve anything which is distinctly false, and repugnant to its real nature: we must not ascribe to the thing any property which it has not; our liberty extends only to suppressing some of those which it has, under the indispensable obligation of restoring them whenever, and in as far as, their presence or absence would make any material difference in the truth of our conclusions. Of this nature, accordingly, are the first principles involved in the definitions of geometry. In their positive part they are observed facts; it is only in their negative part that they are hypothetical. That the hypotheses should be of this particular character, is however no further necessary, than inasmuch as no others could enable us to deduce conclusions which, with due corrections, would be true of real objects: and in fact, when our aim is only to illustrate truths, and not to investigate them, we are not under any such restriction. We might suppose an imaginary animal, and work out by deduction, from the known laws of physiology, its natural history; or an imaginary commonwealth, and from the elements composing it, might argue what would be its fate. And the conclusions which we might thus draw from purely arbitrary hypotheses, might form a highly useful intellectual exercise: but as they could only teach us what *would* be the properties of objects which do not really exist, they would not constitute any addition to our knowledge of nature: while on the contrary, if the hypothesis merely divests a real object of some portion of its properties, without clothing it in false ones, the conclusions will always express, under known liability to correction, actual truth.

§ 3. But although Dr. Whewell has not shaken Stewart's doctrine as to the hypothetical character of that portion of the first principles of geometry which are involved in the so-called definitions, he has, I conceive, greatly the advantage of Stewart on another important point in the theory of geometrical reasoning; the necessity of admitting, among those first principles, axioms as well as definitions. Some of the axioms of Euclid might, no doubt, be exhibited in the form of definitions, or might be deduced, by reasoning, from propositions similar to what are so called. Thus, if instead of the axiom, Magnitudes which can be made to coincide are equal, we introduce a definition, "Equal magnitudes are those which may be so applied to one another as to coincide;" the three axioms which follow, (Magnitudes which are equal to the same are equal to one another--If equals are added to equals the sums are equal--If equals are taken from equals the remainders are equal,) may be proved by an imaginary superposition, resembling that by which the fourth proposition of the first book of Euclid is demonstrated. But although these and several others may be struck out of the list of first principles, because, though not requiring demonstration, they are susceptible of it; there will be found in the list of axioms two or three fundamental truths, not capable of being demonstrated: among which must be reckoned the proposition that two straight lines cannot inclose a space, (or its equivalent, Straight lines which coincide in two points coincide altogether,) and some property of parallel lines, other than that which constitutes their definition: the most suitable, perhaps, being that selected by Professor Playfair: "Two straight lines which intersect each other cannot both of them be parallel to a third straight line."(38)

The axioms, as well those which are indemonstrable as those which admit of being demonstrated, differ from that other class of fundamental principles which are involved in the definitions, in this, that they are true without any mixture of hypothesis. That things which are equal to the same thing are equal to one another, is as true of the lines and figures in nature, as it would be of the imaginary ones assumed in the definitions. In this respect, however, mathematics are only on a par with most other sciences. In almost all sciences there are some general propositions which are exactly true, while the greater part are only more or less distant approximations to the truth. Thus in mechanics, the first law of motion (the continuance of a movement once impressed, until stopped or slackened by some resisting force) is true without qualification or error. The rotation of the earth in twenty-four hours, of the same length as in our time, has gone on since the first accurate observations, without the increase or diminution of one second in all that period. These are inductions which require no fiction to make them be received as accurately true: but along with them there are others, as for instance the propositions respecting the figure of the earth, which are but approximations to the truth; and in order to use them for the further advancement of our knowledge, we must feign that they are exactly true, though they really want something of being so.

§ 4. It remains to inquire, what is the ground of our belief in axioms--what is the evidence on which they rest? I answer, they are experimental truths; generalizations from observation. The proposition, Two straight lines cannot inclose a space--or in other words, Two straight lines which have once met, do not meet again, but continue to diverge--is an induction from the evidence of our senses.

This opinion runs counter to a scientific prejudice of long standing and great strength, and there is probably no one proposition enunciated in this work for which a more unfavourable reception is to be expected. It is, however, no new opinion; and even if it were so, would be entitled to be judged, not by its novelty, but by the strength of the arguments by which it can be supported. I consider it very fortunate that so eminent a champion of the contrary opinion as Dr. Whewell, has recently found occasion for a most elaborate treatment of the whole theory of axioms, in attempting to construct the philosophy of the mathematical and physical sciences on the basis of the doctrine against which I now contend. Whoever is anxious that a discussion should go to the bottom of the subject, must rejoice to see the opposite side of the question worthily represented. If what is said by Dr. Whewell, in support of an opinion which he has made the foundation of a systematic work, can be shown not to be conclusive, enough will have been done without going further to seek stronger arguments and a more powerful adversary.

It is not necessary to show that the truths which we call axioms are originally *suggested* by observation, and that we should never have known that two straight lines cannot inclose a space if we had never seen a straight line: thus much being admitted by Dr. Whewell, and by all, in recent times, who have taken his view of the subject. But they contend, that it is not experience which *proves* the axiom; but that its truth is perceived *a priori*, by the constitution of the mind itself, from the first moment when the meaning of the proposition is apprehended; and without any necessity for verifying it by repeated trials, as is requisite in the case of truths really ascertained by observation.

They cannot, however, but allow that the truth of the axiom, Two straight lines cannot inclose a space, even if evident independently of experience, is also evident from experience. Whether the axiom *needs* confirmation or not, it *receives* confirmation in almost every instant of our lives; since we cannot look at any two straight lines which intersect one another, without seeing that from that point they continue to diverge more and more. Experimental proof crowds in upon us in such endless profusion, and without one instance in which there can be even a suspicion of an exception to the rule, that we should soon have a stronger ground for believing the axiom, even as an experimental truth, than we have for almost any of the general truths which we confessedly learn from the evidence of our senses. Independently of *a priori* evidence, we should certainly believe it with an intensity of conviction far greater than we accord to any ordinary physical truth: and this too at a time of life much earlier than that from which we date almost any part of our acquired knowledge, and much too early to admit of our retaining any recollection of the history of our intellectual operations at that period. Where then is the necessity for assuming that our recognition of these truths has a different origin from the rest of our knowledge, when its existence is perfectly accounted for by supposing its origin to be the same? when the causes which produce belief in all other instances, exist in this instance, and in a degree of strength as much superior to what exists in other cases, as the intensity of the belief itself is superior? The burden of proof lies on the advocates of the contrary opinion: it is for them to point out some fact, inconsistent with the supposition that this part of our knowledge of nature is derived from the same sources as every other part.

This, for instance, they would be able to do, if they could prove chronologically that we had the conviction (at least practically) so early in infancy as to be anterior to those impressions on the senses, upon which, on the other theory, the conviction is founded. This, however, cannot be proved: the point being too far back to be within the reach of memory, and too obscure for external observation. The advocates of the *a priori* theory are obliged to have recourse to other arguments. These are reducible to two, which I shall endeavour to state as clearly and as forcibly as possible.

§ 5. In the first place it is said, that if our assent to the proposition that two straight lines cannot inclose a space, were derived from the senses, we could only be convinced of its truth by actual trial, that is, by seeing or feeling the straight lines; whereas in fact it is seen to be true by merely thinking of them. That a stone thrown into water goes to the bottom, may be perceived by our senses, but mere thinking of a stone thrown into the water would never have led us to that conclusion: not so, however, with the axioms relating to straight lines: if I could be made to conceive what a straight line is, without having seen one, I should at once recognise that two such lines cannot inclose a space. Intuition is "imaginary looking;"(39) but experience must be real looking: if we see a property of straight lines to be true by merely fancying ourselves to be looking at them, the ground of our belief cannot be the senses, or experience; it must be something mental.

To this argument it might be added in the case of this particular axiom, (for the assertion would not be true of all axioms,) that the evidence of it from actual ocular inspection, is not only unnecessary, but unattainable. What says the axiom? That two straight lines ***cannot*** inclose a space; that after having once intersected, if they are prolonged to infinity they do not meet, but continue to diverge from one another. How can this, in any single case, be proved by actual observation? We may follow the lines to any distance we please; but we cannot follow them to infinity: for aught our senses can testify, they may, immediately beyond the farthest point to which we have traced them, begin to approach, and at last meet. Unless, therefore, we had some other proof of the impossibility than observation affords us, we should have no ground for believing the axiom at all.

To these arguments, which I trust I cannot be accused of understating, a satisfactory answer will, I conceive, be found, if we advert to one of the characteristic properties of geometrical forms--their capacity of being painted in the imagination with a distinctness equal to reality: in other words, the exact resemblance of our ideas of form to the sensations which suggest them. This, in the first place, enables us to make (at least with a little practice) mental pictures of all possible combinations of lines and angles, which resemble the realities quite as well as any which we could make on paper; and in the next place, makes those pictures just as fit subjects of geometrical experimentation as the realities themselves; inasmuch as pictures, if sufficiently accurate, exhibit of course all the properties which would be manifested by the realities at one given instant, and on simple inspection: and in geometry we are concerned only with such properties, and not with that which pictures could not exhibit, the mutual action of bodies one upon another. The foundations of geometry would therefore be laid in direct experience, even if the experiments (which in this case consist merely in attentive contemplation) were practised solely upon what we call our ideas, that is, upon the diagrams in our minds, and not upon outward objects. For in all systems of experimentation we take some objects to serve as representatives of all which resemble them; and in the present case the conditions which qualify a real object to be the representative of its class, are completely fulfilled by an object existing only in our fancy. Without denying, therefore, the possibility of satisfying ourselves that two straight lines cannot inclose a space, by merely thinking of straight lines without actually looking at them; I contend, that we do not believe this truth on the ground of the imaginary intuition simply, but because we know that the imaginary lines exactly resemble real ones, and that we may conclude from them to real ones with quite as much certainty as we could conclude from one real line to another. The conclusion, therefore, is still an induction from observation. And we should not be authorized to substitute observation of the image in our mind, for observation of the reality, if we had not learnt by long-continued experience that the properties of the reality are faithfully represented in the image; just as we should be scientifically warranted in describing an animal which we had never seen, from a picture made of it with a daguerreotype; but not until we had learnt by ample experience, that observation of such a picture is precisely equivalent to observation of the original.

These considerations also remove the objection arising from the impossibility of ocularly following the lines in their prolongation to infinity, for though, in order actually to see that two given lines never meet, it would be necessary to follow them to infinity; yet without doing so we may know that if they ever do meet, or if, after diverging from one another, they begin again to approach, this must take place not at an infinite, but at a finite distance. Supposing, therefore, such to be the case, we can transport ourselves thither in imagination, and can frame a mental image of the appearance which one or both of the lines must present at that point, which we may rely on as being precisely similar to the reality. Now, whether we fix our contemplation upon this imaginary picture, or call to mind the generalizations we have had occasion to make from former ocular observation, we learn by the evidence of experience, that a line which, after diverging from another straight line, begins to approach to it, produces the impression on our senses which we describe by the expression, "a bent line," not by the expression, "a straight line."(40)

§ 6. The first of the two arguments in support of the theory that axioms are *a priori* truths, having, I think, been sufficiently answered; I proceed to the second, which is usually the most relied on. Axioms (it is asserted) are conceived by us not only as true, but as universally and necessarily true. Now, experience cannot possibly give to any proposition this character. I may have seen snow a hundred times, and may have seen that it was white, but this cannot give me entire assurance even that all snow is white; much less that snow *must* be white. "However many instances we may have observed of the truth of a proposition, there is nothing to assure us that the next case shall not be an exception to the rule. If it be strictly true that every ruminant animal yet known has cloven hoofs, we still cannot be sure that some creature will not hereafter be discovered which has the first of these attributes, without having the other.... Experience must always consist of a limited number of observations; and, however numerous these may be, they can show nothing with regard to the infinite number of cases in which the experiment has not been made." Besides, axioms are not only universal, they are also necessary. Now "experience cannot offer the smallest ground for the necessity of a proposition. She can observe and record what has happened; but she cannot find, in any case, or in any accumulation of cases, any reason for what *must* happen. She may see objects side by side; but she cannot see a reason why they must ever be side by side. She finds certain events to occur in succession; but the succession supplies, in its occurrence, no reason for its recurrence. She contemplates external objects; but she cannot detect any internal bond, which indissolubly connects the future with the past, the possible with the real. To learn a proposition by experience, and to see it to be necessarily true, are two altogether different processes of thought."(41) And Dr. Whewell adds, "If any one does not clearly comprehend this distinction of necessary and contingent truths, he will not be able to go along with us in our researches into the foundations of human knowledge; nor, indeed, to pursue with success any speculation on the subject."(42)

In the following passage, we are told what the distinction is, the non-recognition of which incurs this denunciation. "Necessary truths are those in which we not only learn that the proposition *is* true, but see that it *must be* true; in which the negation of the truth is not only false, but impossible; in which we cannot, even by an effort of imagination, or in a supposition, conceive the reverse of that which is asserted. That there are such truths cannot be doubted. We may take, for example, all relations of number. Three and Two, added together, make Five. We cannot conceive it to be otherwise. We cannot, by any freak of thought, imagine Three and Two to make Seven."(43)

Although Dr. Whewell has naturally and properly employed a variety of phrases to bring his meaning more forcibly home, he will, I presume, allow that they are all equivalent; and that what he means by a necessary truth, would be sufficiently defined, a proposition the negation of which is not only false but inconceivable. I am unable to find in any of his expressions, turn them what way you will, a meaning beyond this, and I do not believe he would contend that they mean anything more.

This, therefore, is the principle asserted: that propositions, the negation of which is inconceivable, or in other words, which we cannot figure to ourselves as being false, must rest on evidence of a higher and more cogent description than any which experience can afford. And we have next to consider whether there is any ground for this assertion.

Now I cannot but wonder that so much stress should be laid on the circumstance of inconceivableness, when there is such ample experience to show, that our capacity or incapacity of conceiving a thing has very little to do with the possibility of the thing in itself; but is in truth very much an affair of accident, and depends on the past history and habits of our own minds. There is no more generally acknowledged fact in human nature, than the extreme difficulty at first felt in conceiving anything as possible, which is in contradiction to long established and familiar experience; or even to old familiar habits of thought. And this difficulty is a necessary result of the fundamental laws of the human mind. When we have often seen and thought of two things together, and have never in any one instance either seen or thought of them separately, there is by the primary law of association an increasing difficulty, which may in the end become insuperable, of conceiving the two things apart. This is most of all conspicuous in uneducated persons, who are in general utterly unable to separate any two ideas which have once become firmly associated in their minds; and if persons of cultivated intellect have any advantage on the point, it is only because, having seen and heard and read more, and being more accustomed to exercise their imagination, they have experienced their sensations and thoughts in more varied combinations, and have been prevented from forming many of these inseparable associations. But this advantage has necessarily its limits. The most practised intellect is not exempt from the universal laws of our conceptive faculty. If daily habit presents to any one for a long period two facts in combination, and if he is not led during that period either by accident or by his voluntary mental operations to think of them apart, he will probably in time become incapable of doing so even by the strongest effort; and the supposition that the two facts can be separated in nature, will at last present itself to his mind with all the characters of an inconceivable phenomenon.(44) There are remarkable instances of this in the history of science: instances in which the most instructed men rejected as impossible, because inconceivable, things which their posterity, by earlier practice and longer perseverance in the attempt, found it quite easy to conceive, and which everybody now knows to be true. There was a time when men of the most culti-vated intellects, and the most emancipated from the dominion of early prejudice, could not credit the existence of antipodes; were unable to conceive, in opposition to old association, the force of gravity acting upwards instead of downwards. The Cartesians long rejected the Newtonian doctrine of the gravitation of all bodies towards one another, on the faith of a general proposition, the reverse of which seemed to them to be inconceivable--the proposition that a body cannot act where it is not. All the cumbrous machinery of imaginary vortices, assumed without the smallest particle of evidence, appeared to these philosophers a more rational mode of explaining the heavenly motions, than one which involved what seemed to them so great an absurdity.(45) And they no doubt found it as impossible to conceive that a body should act upon the earth, at the distance of the sun or moon, as we find it to conceive an end to space or time, or two straight lines inclosing a space. Newton himself had not been able to realize the conception, or we should not have had his hypothesis of a subtle ether, the occult cause of gravitation; and his writings prove, that although he deemed the particular nature of the intermediate agency a mat-ter of conjecture, the necessity of *some* such agency appeared to him indubitable. It would seem that even now the majority of scientific men have not completely got over this very difficulty; for though they have at last learnt to conceive the sun *attracting* the earth without any intervening fluid, they cannot yet conceive the sun *illuminating* the earth without some such medium.

If, then, it be so natural to the human mind, even in a high state of culture, to be incapable of conceiving, and on that ground to believe impossible, what is afterwards not only found to be conceivable but proved to be true; what wonder if in cases where the association is still older, more confirmed, and more familiar, and in which nothing ever occurs to shake our conviction, or even suggest to us any conception at variance with the association, the acquired incapacity should continue, and be mistaken for a natural incapacity? It is true, our experience of the varieties in nature enables us, within certain limits, to conceive other variet-ies analogous to them. We can conceive the sun or moon falling; for although we never saw them fall, nor ever perhaps imagined them falling, we have seen so many other things fall, that we have innumerable familiar analogies to assist the concep-tion; which, after all, we should probably have some difficulty in framing, were we not well accustomed to see the sun and moon move, (or appear to move,) so that we are only called upon to conceive a slight change in the direction of motion, a circumstance familiar to our experience. But when experience affords no model on which to shape the new conception, how is it possible for us to form it? How, for example, can we imagine an end to space or time? We never saw any object with-out something beyond it, nor experienced any feeling without something following it. When, therefore, we attempt to conceive the last point of space, we have the idea irresistibly raised of other points beyond it. When we try to imagine the last instant of time, we cannot help conceiving another instant after it. Nor is there any necessity to assume, as is done by a modern school of metaphysicians, a peculiar fundamental law of the mind to account for the feeling of infinity inherent in our conceptions of space and time; that apparent infinity is sufficiently accounted for by simpler and universally acknowledged laws.

Now, in the case of a geometrical axiom, such, for example, as that two straight lines cannot inclose a space,--a truth which is testified to us by our very earliest im-pressions of the external world,--how is it possible (whether those external impres-sions be or be not the ground of our belief) that the reverse of the proposition *could* be otherwise than inconceivable to us? What analogy have we, what similar order of facts in any other branch of our experience, to facilitate to us the conception of two straight lines inclosing a space? Nor is even this all. I have already called atten-tion to the peculiar property of our impressions of form, that the ideas or mental images exactly resemble their prototypes, and adequately represent them for the purposes of scientific observation. From this, and from the intuitive character of the observation, which in this case reduces itself to simple inspection, we cannot so much as call up in our imagination two straight lines, in order to attempt to conceive them inclosing a space, without by that very act repeating the scientific experiment which establishes the contrary. Will it really be contended that the inconceivableness of the thing, in such circumstances, proves anything against the experimental origin of the conviction? Is it not clear that in whichever mode our belief in the proposition may have originated, the impossibility of our conceiving the negative of it must, on either hypothesis, be the same? As, then, Dr. Whewell exhorts those who have any difficulty in recognising the distinction held by him between necessary and contingent truths, to study geometry,--a condition which I can assure him I have conscientiously fulfilled,--I, in return, with equal confidence, exhort those who agree with him, to study the elementary laws of association; being convinced that nothing more is requisite than a moderate familiarity with those laws, to dispel the illusion which ascribes a peculiar necessity to our earliest inductions from experience, and measures the possibility of things in themselves, by the human capacity of conceiving them.

I hope to be pardoned for adding, that Dr. Whewell himself has both confirmed by his testimony the effect of habitual association in giving to an experimental truth the appearance of a necessary one, and afforded a striking instance of that remarkable law in his own person. In his ***Philosophy of the Inductive Sciences*** he continually asserts, that propositions which not only are not self-evident, but which we know to have been discovered gradually, and by great efforts of genius and patience, have, when once established, appeared so self-evident that, but for historical proof, it would have been impossible to conceive that they had not been recognised from the first by all persons in a sound state of their faculties. "We now despise those who, in the Copernican controversy, could not conceive the apparent motion of the sun on the heliocentric hypothesis; or those who, in opposition to Galileo, thought that a uniform force might be that which generated a velocity proportional to the space; or those who held there was something absurd in Newton's doctrine of the different refrangibility of differently coloured rays; or those who imagined that when elements combine, their sensible qualities must be manifest in the compound; or those who were reluctant to give up the distinction of vegetables into herbs, shrubs, and trees. We cannot help thinking that men must have been singularly dull of comprehension to find a difficulty in admitting what is to us so plain and simple. We have a latent persuasion that we in their place should have been wiser and more clearsighted; that we should have taken the right side, and given our assent at once to the truth. Yet in reality such a persuasion is a mere delusion. The persons who, in such instances as the above, were on the losing side, were very far in most cases from being persons more prejudiced, or stupid, or narrow-minded, than the greater part of mankind now are; and the cause for which they fought was far from being a manifestly bad one, till it had been so decided by the result of the war.... So complete has been the victory of truth in most of these instances, that at present we can hardly imagine the struggle to have been necessary. ***The very essence of these triumphs is, that they lead us to regard the views we reject as not only false but inconceivable.***"(46)

This last proposition is precisely what I contend for; and I ask no more, in order to overthrow the whole theory of its author on the nature of the evidence of axioms. For what is that theory? That the truth of axioms cannot have been learnt from experience, because their falsity is inconceivable. But Dr. Whewell himself says, that we are continually led by the natural progress of thought, to regard as inconceivable what our forefathers not only conceived but believed, nay even (he might have added) were unable to conceive the contrary of. He cannot intend to justify this mode of thought: he cannot mean to say, that we can be ***right*** in regarding as inconceivable what others have conceived, and as self-evident what to others did not appear evident at all. After so complete an admission that inconceivableness is an accidental thing, not inherent in the phenomenon itself, but dependent on the mental history of the person who tries to conceive it, how can he ever call upon us to reject a proposition as impossible on no other ground than its inconceivableness? Yet he not only does so, but has unintentionally afforded some of the most remarkable examples which can be cited of the very illusion which he has himself so clearly pointed out. I select as specimens, his remarks on the evidence of the three laws of motion, and of the atomic theory.

With respect to the laws of motion, Dr. Whewell says: "No one can doubt that, in historical fact, these laws were collected from experience. That such is the case, is no matter of conjecture. We know the time, the persons, the circumstances, belonging to each step of each discovery."(47) After this testimony, to adduce evidence of the fact would be superfluous. And not only were these laws by no means intuitively evident, but some of them were originally paradoxes. The first law was especially so. That a body, once in motion, would continue for ever to move in the same direction with undiminished velocity unless acted upon by some new force, was a proposition which mankind found for a long time the greatest difficulty in crediting. It stood opposed to apparent experience of the most familiar kind, which taught that it was the nature of motion to abate gradually, and at last terminate of itself. Yet when once the contrary doctrine was firmly established, mathematicians, as Dr. Whewell observes, speedily began to believe that laws, thus contradictory to first appearances, and which, even after full proof had been obtained, it had required generations to render familiar to the minds of the scientific world, were under "a demonstrable necessity, compelling them to be such as they are and no other;" and he himself, though not venturing "absolutely to pronounce" that *all* these laws "can be rigorously traced to an absolute necessity in the nature of things,"(48) does actually think in that manner of the law just mentioned; of which he says: "Though the discovery of the first law of motion was made, historically speaking, by means of experiment, we have now attained a point of view in which we see that it might have been certainly known to be true, independently of experience."(49) Can there be a more striking exemplification than is here afforded, of the effect of association which we have described? Philosophers, for generations, have the most extraordinary difficulty in putting certain ideas together; they at last succeed in doing so; and after a sufficient repetition of the process, they first fancy a natural bond between the ideas, then experience a growing difficulty, which at last, by the continuation of the same progress, becomes an impossibility, of severing them from one another. If such be the progress of an experimental conviction of which the date is of yesterday, and which is in opposition to first appearances, how must it fare with those which are conformable to appearances familiar from the first dawn of intelligence, and of the conclusiveness of which, from the earliest records of human thought, no sceptic has suggested even a momentary doubt?

The other instance which I shall quote is a truly astonishing one, and may be called the ***reductio ad absurdum*** of the theory of inconceivableness. Speaking of the laws of chemical composition, Dr. Whewell says:(50) "That they could never have been clearly understood, and therefore never firmly established, without laborious and exact experiments, is certain; but yet we may venture to say, that being once known, they possess an evidence beyond that of mere experiment. *For how, in fact, can we conceive combinations, otherwise than as definite in kind and quality?* If we were to suppose each element ready to combine with any other indifferently, and indifferently in any quantity, we should have a world in which all would be confusion and indefiniteness. There would be no fixed kinds of bodies; salts, and stones, and ores, would approach to and graduate into each other by insensible degrees. Instead of this, we know that the world consists of bodies distinguishable from each other by definite differences, capable of being classified and named, and of having general propositions asserted concerning them. And as *we cannot conceive a world in which this should not be the case*, it would appear that we cannot conceive a state of things in which the laws of the combination of elements should not be of that definite and measured kind which we have above asserted."(51)

That a philosopher of Dr. Whewell's eminence should gravely assert that we cannot conceive a world in which the simple elements would combine in other than definite proportions; that by dint of meditating on a scientific truth, the original discoverer of which was still living, he should have rendered the association in his own mind between the idea of combination and that of constant proportions so familiar and intimate as to be unable to conceive the one fact without the other; is so signal an instance of the mental law for which I am contending, that one word more in illustration must be superfluous.(52)

CHAPTER VI. THE SAME SUBJECT CONTINUED.

§ 1. In the examination which formed the subject of the last chapter, into the nature of the evidence of those deductive sciences which are commonly represented to be systems of necessary truth, we have been led to the following conclusions. The results of those sciences are indeed necessary, in the sense of necessarily following from certain first principles, commonly called axioms and definitions; of being certainly true if those axioms and definitions are so. But their claim to the character of necessity in any sense beyond this, as implying an evidence independent of and superior to observation and experience, must depend on the previous establishment of such a claim in favour of the definitions and axioms themselves. With regard to axioms, we found that, considered as experimental truths, they rest on superabundant and obvious evidence. We inquired, whether, since this is the case, it be necessary to suppose any other evidence of those truths than experimental evidence, any other origin for our belief of them than an experimental origin. We decided, that the burden of proof lies with those who maintain the affirmative, and we examined, at considerable length, such arguments as they have produced. The examination having led to the rejection of those arguments, we have thought ourselves warranted in concluding that axioms are but a class, the highest class, of inductions from experience; the simplest and easiest cases of generalization from the facts furnished to us by our senses or by our internal consciousness.

While the axioms of demonstrative sciences thus appeared to be experimental truths, the definitions, as they are incorrectly called, in those sciences, were found by us to be generalizations from experience which are not even, accurately speaking, truths; being propositions in which, while we assert of some kind of object, some property or properties which observation shows to belong to it, we at the same time deny that it possesses any other properties, although in truth other properties do in every individual instance accompany, and in almost all instances modify, the property thus exclusively predicated. The denial, therefore, is a mere fiction, or supposition, made for the purpose of excluding the consideration of those modifying circumstances, when their influence is of too trifling amount to be worth considering, or adjourning it, when important, to a more convenient moment.

From these considerations it would appear that Deductive or Demonstrative Sciences are all, without exception, Inductive Sciences; that their evidence is that of experience; but that they are also, in virtue of the peculiar character of one indispensable portion of the general formulas according to which their inductions are made, Hypothetical Sciences. Their conclusions are only true on certain suppositions, which are, or ought to be, approximations to the truth, but are seldom, if ever, exactly true; and to this hypothetical character is to be ascribed the peculiar certainty, which is supposed to be inherent in demonstration.

What we have now asserted, however, cannot be received as universally true of Deductive or Demonstrative Sciences, until verified by being applied to the most remarkable of all those sciences, that of Numbers; the theory of the Calculus; Arithmetic and Algebra. It is harder to believe of the doctrines of this science than of any other, either that they are not truths *a priori*, but experimental truths, or that their peculiar certainty is owing to their being not absolute but only conditional truths. This, therefore, is a case which merits examination apart; and the more so, because on this subject we have a double set of doctrines to contend with; that of the *a priori* philosophers on one side; and on the other, a theory the most opposite to theirs, which was at one time very generally received, and is still far from being altogether exploded among metaphysicians.

§ 2. This theory attempts to solve the difficulty apparently inherent in the case, by representing the propositions of the science of numbers as merely verbal, and its processes as simple transformations of language, substitutions of one expression for another. The proposition, Two and one are equal to three, according to these writers, is not a truth, is not the assertion of a really existing fact, but a definition of the word three; a statement that mankind have agreed to use the name three as a sign exactly equivalent to two and one; to call by the former name whatever is called by the other more clumsy phrase. According to this doctrine, the longest process in algebra is but a succession of changes in terminology, by which equivalent expressions are substituted one for another; a series of translations of the same fact, from one into another language; though how, after such a series of translations, the fact itself comes out changed, (as when we demonstrate a new geometrical theorem by algebra,) they have not explained; and it is a difficulty which is fatal to their theory.

It must be acknowledged that there are peculiarities in the processes of arithmetic and algebra which render the theory in question very plausible, and have not unnaturally made those sciences the stronghold of Nominalism. The doctrine that we can discover facts, detect the hidden processes of nature, by an artful manipulation of language, is so contrary to common sense, that a person must have made some advances in philosophy to believe it; men fly to so paradoxical a belief to avoid, as they think, some even greater difficulty, which the vulgar do not see. What has led many to believe that reasoning is a mere verbal process, is, that no other theory seemed reconcileable with the nature of the Science of Numbers. For we do not carry any ideas along with us when we use the symbols of arithmetic or of algebra. In a geometrical demonstration we have a mental diagram, if not one on paper; AB, AC, are present to our imagination as lines, intersecting other lines, forming an angle with one another, and the like; but not so *a* and *b*. These may represent lines or any other magnitudes, but those magnitudes are never thought of; nothing is realized in our imagination but *a* and *b*. The ideas which, on the particular occasion, they happen to represent, are banished from the mind during every intermediate part of the process, between the beginning, when the premises are translated from things into signs, and the end, when the conclusion is translated back from signs into things. Nothing, then, being in the reasoner's mind but the symbols, what can seem more inadmissible than to contend that the reasoning process has to do with anything more? We seem to have come to one of Bacon's Prerogative Instances; an ***experimentum crucis*** on the nature of reasoning itself.

Nevertheless, it will appear on consideration, that this apparently so decisive instance is no instance at all; that there is in every step of an arithmetical or algebraical calculation a real induction, a real inference of facts from facts; and that what disguises the induction is simply its comprehensive nature, and the consequent extreme generality of the language. All numbers must be numbers of something: there are no such things as numbers in the abstract. ***Ten*** must mean ten bodies, or ten sounds, or ten beatings of the pulse. But though numbers must be numbers of something, they may be numbers of anything. Propositions, therefore, concerning numbers, have the remarkable peculiarity that they are propositions concerning all things whatever; all objects, all existences of every kind, known to our experience. All things possess quantity; consist of parts which can be numbered; and in that character possess all the properties which are called properties of numbers. That half of four is two, must be true whatever the word four represents, whether four men, four miles, or four pounds weight. We need only conceive a thing divided into four equal parts, (and all things may be conceived as so divided,) to be able to predicate of it every property of the number four, that is, every arithmetical proposition in which the number four stands on one side of the equation. Algebra extends the generalization still farther: every number represents that particular number of all things without distinction, but every algebraical symbol does more, it represents all numbers without distinction. As soon as we conceive a thing divided into equal parts, without knowing into what number of parts, we may call it a or x, and apply to it, without danger of error, every algebraical formula in the books. The proposition, $2(a + b) = 2a + 2b$, is a truth coextensive with all nature. Since then algebraical truths are true of all things whatever, and not, like those of geometry, true of lines only or angles only, it is no wonder that the symbols should not excite in our minds ideas of any things in particular. When we demonstrate the forty-seventh proposition of Euclid, it is not necessary that the words should raise in us an image of all right-angled triangles, but only of some one right-angled triangle: so in algebra we need not, under the symbol *a*, picture to ourselves all things whatever, but only some one thing; why not, then, the letter itself? The mere written characters, *a*, *b*, *x*, *y*, *z*, serve as well for representatives of Things in general, as any more complex and apparently more concrete conception. That we are conscious of them however in their character of things, and not of mere signs, is evident from the fact that our whole process of reasoning is carried on by predicating of them the properties of things. In resolving an algebraic equation, by what rules do we proceed? By applying at each step to *a*, *b*, and *x* the proposition that equals added to equals make equals; that equals taken from equals leave equals; and other propositions founded on these two. These are not properties of language, or of signs as such, but of magnitudes, which is as much as to say, of all things. The inferences, therefore, which are successively drawn, are inferences concerning things, not symbols; although as any Things whatever will serve the turn, there is no necessity for keeping the idea of the Thing at all distinct, and consequently the process of thought may, in this case, be allowed without danger to do what all processes of thought, when they have been performed often, will do if permitted, namely, to become entirely mechanical. Hence the general language of algebra comes to be used familiarly without exciting ideas, as all other general language is prone to do from mere habit, though in no other case than this can it be done with complete safety. But when we look back to see from whence the probative force of the process is derived, we find that at every single step, unless we suppose ourselves to be thinking and talking of the things, and not the mere symbols, the evidence fails.

There is another circumstance, which, still more than that which we have now mentioned, gives plausibility to the notion that the propositions of arithmetic and algebra are merely verbal. This is, that when considered as propositions respecting Things, they all have the appearance of being identical propositions. The assertion, Two and one are equal to three, considered as an assertion respecting objects, as for instance "Two pebbles and one pebble are equal to three pebbles," does not affirm equality between two collections of pebbles, but absolute identity. It affirms that if we put one pebble to two pebbles, those very pebbles are three. The objects, therefore, being the very same, and the mere assertion that "objects are themselves" being insignificant, it seems but natural to consider the proposition, Two and one are equal to three, as asserting mere identity of signification between the two names.

This, however, though it looks so plausible, will not bear examination. The expression "two pebbles and one pebble," and the expression, "three pebbles," stand indeed for the same aggregation of objects, but they by no means stand for the same physical fact. They are names of the same objects, but of those objects in two different states: though they *de*note the same things, their *con*notation is different. Three pebbles in two separate parcels, and three pebbles in one parcel, do not make the same impression on our senses; and the assertion that the very same pebbles may by an alteration of place and arrangement be made to produce either the one set of sensations or the other, though a very familiar proposition, is not an identical one. It is a truth known to us by early and constant experience: an inductive truth; and such truths are the foundation of the science of Number. The fundamental truths of that science all rest on the evidence of sense; they are proved by showing to our eyes and our fingers that any given number of objects, ten balls for example, may by separation and re-arrangement exhibit to our senses all the different sets of numbers the sum of which is equal to ten. All the improved methods of teaching arithmetic to children proceed on a knowledge of this fact. All who wish to carry the child's *mind* along with them in learning arithmetic; all who wish to teach numbers, and not mere ciphers--now teach it through the evidence of the senses, in the manner we have described.

We may, if we please, call the proposition "Three is two and one," a definition of the number three, and assert that arithmetic, as it has been asserted that geometry, is a science founded on definitions. But they are definitions in the geometrical sense, not the logical; asserting not the meaning of a term only, but along with it an observed matter of fact. The proposition, "A circle is a figure bounded by a line which has all its points equally distant from a point within it," is called the definition of a circle; but the proposition from which so many consequences follow, and which is really a first principle in geometry, is, that figures answering to this description exist. And thus we may call, "Three is two and one," a definition of three; but the calculations which depend on that proposition do not follow from the definition itself, but from an arithmetical theorem presupposed in it, namely, that collections of objects exist, which while they impress the senses thus, [Symbol:

three circles, two above one], may be separated into two parts, thus, [Symbol: two circles, a space, and a third circle]. This proposition being granted, we term all such parcels Threes, after which the enunciation of the above-mentioned physical fact will serve also for a definition of the word Three.

The Science of Number is thus no exception to the conclusion we previously arrived at, that the processes even of deductive sciences are altogether inductive, and that their first principles are generalizations from experience. It remains to be examined whether this science resembles geometry in the further circumstance, that some of its inductions are not exactly true; and that the peculiar certainty ascribed to it, on account of which its propositions are called Necessary Truths, is fictitious and hypothetical, being true in no other sense than that those propositions necessarily follow from the hypothesis of the truth of premises which are avowedly mere approximations to truth.

§ 3. The inductions of arithmetic are of two sorts: first, those which we have just expounded, such as One and one are two, Two and one are three, &c., which may be called the definitions of the various numbers, in the improper or geometrical sense of the word Definition; and secondly, the two following axioms: The sums of equals are equal, The differences of equals are equal. These two are sufficient; for the corresponding propositions respecting unequals may be proved from these, by a ***reductio ad absurdum***.

These axioms, and likewise the so-called definitions, are, as already shown, results of induction; true of all objects whatever, and, as it may seem, exactly true, without the hypothetical assumption of unqualified truth where an approximation to it is all that exists. The conclusions, therefore, it will naturally be inferred, are exactly true, and the science of number is an exception to other demonstrative sciences in this, that the absolute certainty which is predicable of its demonstrations is independent of all hypothesis.

On more accurate investigation, however, it will be found that, even in this case, there is one hypothetical element in the ratiocination. In all propositions concerning numbers, a condition is implied, without which none of them would be true; and that condition is an assumption which may be false. The condition is, that $1 = 1$; that all the numbers are numbers of the same or of equal units. Let this be doubtful, and not one of the propositions of arithmetic will hold true. How can we know that one pound and one pound make two pounds, if one of the pounds may be troy, and the other avoirdupois? They may not make two pounds of either, or of any weight. How can we know that a forty-horse power is always equal to itself, unless we assume that all horses are of equal strength? It is certain that 1 is always equal in ***number*** to 1; and where the mere number of objects, or of the parts of an object, without supposing them to be equivalent in any other respect, is all that is material, the conclusions of arithmetic, so far as they go to that alone, are true without mixture of hypothesis. There are a few such cases; as, for instance, an inquiry into the amount of the population of any country. It is indifferent to that inquiry whether they are grown people or children, strong or weak, tall or short; the only thing we want to ascertain is their number. But whenever, from equality or inequality of number, equality or inequality in any other respect is to be inferred, arithmetic carried into such inquiries becomes as hypothetical a science as geometry. All units must be assumed to be equal in that other respect; and this is never practically true, for one actual pound weight is not exactly equal to another, nor one mile's length to another; a nicer balance, or more accurate measuring instruments, would always detect some difference.

What is commonly called mathematical certainty, therefore, which comprises the twofold conception of unconditional truth and perfect accuracy, is not an attribute of all mathematical truths, but of those only which relate to pure Number, as distinguished from Quantity in the more enlarged sense; and only so long as we abstain from supposing that the numbers are a precise index to actual quantities. The certainty usually ascribed to the conclusions of geometry, and even to those of mechanics, is nothing whatever but certainty of inference. We can have full assurance of particular results under particular suppositions, but we cannot have the same assurance that these suppositions are accurately true, nor that they include all the data which may exercise an influence over the result in any given instance.

§ 4. It appears, therefore, that the method of all Deductive Sciences is hypothetical. They proceed by tracing the consequences of certain assumptions; leaving for separate consideration whether the assumptions are true or not, and if not exactly true, whether they are a sufficiently near approximation to the truth. The reason is obvious. Since it is only in questions of pure number that the assumptions are exactly true, and even there, only so long as no conclusions except purely numerical ones are to be founded on them; it must, in all other cases of deductive investigation, form a part of the inquiry, to determine how much the assumptions want of being exactly true in the case in hand. This is generally a matter of observation, to be repeated in every fresh case; or if it has to be settled by argument instead of observation, may require in every different case different evidence, and present every degree of difficulty from the lowest to the highest. But the other part of the process--namely, to determine what else may be concluded if we find, and in proportion as we find, the assumptions to be true--may be performed once for all, and the results held ready to be employed as the occasions turn up for use. We thus do all beforehand that can be so done, and leave the least possible work to be performed when cases arise and press for a decision. This inquiry into the inferences which can be drawn from assumptions, is what properly constitutes Demonstrative Science.

It is of course quite as practicable to arrive at new conclusions from facts assumed, as from facts observed; from fictitious, as from real, inductions. Deduction, as we have seen, consists of a series of inferences in this form--a is a mark of b, b of c, c of d, therefore a is a mark of d, which last may be a truth inaccessible to direct observation. In like manner it is allowable to say, ***Suppose*** that a were a mark of b, b of c, and c of d, a would be a mark of d, which last conclusion was not thought of by those who laid down the premises. A system of propositions as complicated as geometry might be deduced from assumptions which are false; as was done by Ptolemy, Descartes, and others, in their attempts to explain synthetically the phenomena of the solar system on the supposition that the apparent motions of the heavenly bodies were the real motions, or were produced in some way more or less different from the true one. Sometimes the same thing is knowingly done, for the purpose of showing the falsity of the assumption; which is called a ***reductio ad absurdum***. In such cases, the reasoning is as follows: a is a mark of b, and b of c; now if c were also a mark of d, a would be a mark of d; but d is known to be a mark of the absence of a; consequently a would be a mark of its own absence, which is a contradiction; therefore c is not a mark of d.

§ 5. It has even been held by some writers, that all ratiocination rests in the last resort on a ***reductio ad absurdum***; since the way to enforce assent to it, in case of obscurity, would be to show that if the conclusion be denied we must deny some one at least of the premisses, which, as they are all supposed true, would be a contradiction. And in accordance with this, many have thought that the peculiar nature of the evidence of ratiocination consisted in the impossibility of admitting the premisses and rejecting the conclusion without a contradiction in terms. This theory, however is inadmissible as an explanation of the grounds on which ratiocination itself rests. If any one denies the conclusion notwithstanding his admission of the premisses, he is not involved in any direct and express contradiction until he is compelled to deny some premiss; and he can only be forced to do this by a ***reductio ad absurdum***, that is, by another ratiocination: now, if he denies the validity of the reasoning process itself, he can no more be forced to assent to the second syllogism than to the first. In truth, therefore, no one is ever forced to a contradiction in terms: he can only be forced to a contradiction (or rather an infringement) of the fundamental maxim of ratiocination, namely, that whatever has a mark, has what it is a mark of; or, (in the case of universal propositions,) that whatever is a mark of anything, is a mark of whatever else that thing is a mark of. For in the case of every correct argument, as soon as thrown into the syllogistic form, it is evident without the aid of any other syllogism, that he who, admitting the premisses, fails to draw the conclusion, does not conform to the above axiom.

Without attaching exaggerated importance to the distinction now drawn, I think it enables us to characterize in a more accurate manner than is usually done, the nature of demonstrative evidence and of logical necessity. That is necessary, from which to withhold assent would be to violate the above axiom. And since the axiom can only be violated by assenting to premisses and rejecting a legitimate conclusion from them, nothing is necessary, except the connexion between a conclusion and premisses; of which doctrine, the whole of this and the preceding chapter are submitted as the proof.

We have now proceeded as far in the theory of Deduction as we can advance in the present stage of our inquiry. Any further insight into the subject requires that the foundation shall have been laid of the philosophic theory of Induction itself; in which theory that of deduction, as a mode of induction, which we have now shown it to be, will assume spontaneously the place which belongs to it, and will receive its share of whatever light may be thrown upon the great intellectual operation of which it forms so important a part.

We here, therefore, close the Second Book. The theory of Induction, in the most comprehensive sense of the term, will form the subject of the Third.

BOOK III. OF INDUCTION.

"According to the doctrine now stated, the highest, or rather the only proper object of physics, is to ascertain those established conjunctions of successive events, which constitute the order of the universe; to record the phenomena which it exhibits to our observations, or which it discloses to our experiments; and to refer these phenomena to their general laws."--D. STEWART, *Elements of the Philosophy of the Human Mind*, vol. ii. chap. iv. sect. 1.

CHAPTER I. PRELIMINARY OBSERVATIONS ON INDUCTION IN GENERAL.

§ 1. The portion of the present inquiry upon which we are now about to enter, may be considered as the principal, both from its surpassing in intricacy all the other branches, and because it relates to a process which has been shown in the preceding Book to be that in which the investigation of nature essentially consists. We have found that all Inference, consequently all Proof, and all discovery of truths not self-evident, consists of inductions, and the interpretation of inductions: that all our knowledge, not intuitive, comes to us exclusively from that source. What Induction is, therefore, and what conditions render it legitimate, cannot but be deemed the main question of the science of logic--the question which includes all others. It is, however, one which professed writers on logic have almost entirely passed over. The generalities of the subject have not been altogether neglected by metaphysicians; but, for want of sufficient acquaintance with the processes by which science has actually succeeded in establishing general truths, their analysis of the inductive operation, even when unexceptionable as to correctness, has not been specific enough to be made the foundation of practical rules, which might be for induction itself what the rules of the syllogism are for the interpretation of induction: while those by whom physical science has been carried to its present state of improvement--and who, to arrive at a complete theory of the process, needed only to generalize, and adapt to all varieties of problems, the methods which they themselves employed in their habitual pursuits--never until very lately made any serious attempt to philosophize on the subject, nor regarded the mode in which they arrived at their conclusions as deserving of study, independently of the conclusions themselves.

§ 2. For the purposes of the present inquiry, Induction may be defined, the operation of discovering and proving general propositions. It is true that (as already shown) the process of indirectly ascertaining individual facts, is as truly inductive as that by which we establish general truths. But it is not a different kind of induction; it is another form of the very same process: since, on the one hand, generals are but collections of particulars, definite in kind but indefinite in number; and on the other hand, whenever the evidence which we derive from observation of known cases justifies us in drawing an inference respecting even one unknown case, we should on the same evidence be justified in drawing a similar inference with respect to a whole class of cases. The inference either does not hold at all, or it holds in all cases of a certain description; in all cases which, in certain definable respects, resemble those we have observed.

If these remarks are just; if the principles and rules of inference are the same whether we infer general propositions or individual facts; it follows that a complete logic of the sciences would be also a complete logic of practical business and common life. Since there is no case of legitimate inference from experience, in which the conclusion may not legitimately be a general proposition; an analysis of the process by which general truths are arrived at, is virtually an analysis of all induction whatever. Whether we are inquiring into a scientific principle or into an individual fact, and whether we proceed by experiment or by ratiocination, every step in the train of inferences is essentially inductive, and the legitimacy of the induction depends in both cases on the same conditions.

True it is that in the case of the practical inquirer, who is endeavouring to ascertain facts not for the purposes of science but for those of business, such for instance as the advocate or the judge, the chief difficulty is one in which the principles of induction will afford him no assistance. It lies not in ***making*** his inductions but in the ***selection*** of them; in choosing from among all general propositions ascertained to be true, those which furnish marks by which he may trace whether the given subject possesses or not the predicate in question. In arguing a doubtful question of fact before a jury, the general propositions or principles to which the advocate appeals are mostly, in themselves, sufficiently trite, and assented to as soon as stated: his skill lies in bringing his case under those propositions or principles; in calling to mind such of the known or received maxims of probability as admit of application to the case in hand, and selecting from among them those best adapted to his object. Success is here dependent on natural or acquired sagacity, aided by knowledge of the particular subject, and of subjects allied with it. Invention, though it can be cultivated, cannot be reduced to rule; there is no science which will enable a man to bethink himself of that which will suit his purpose.

But when he ***has*** thought of something, science can tell him whether that which he has thought of will suit his purpose or not. The inquirer or arguer must be guided by his own knowledge and sagacity in the choice of the inductions out of which he will construct his argument. But the validity of the argument when constructed, depends on principles and must be tried by tests which are the same for all descriptions of inquiries, whether the result be to give A an estate, or to enrich science with a new general truth. In the one case and in the other, the senses, or testimony, must decide on the individual facts; the rules of the syllogism will determine whether, those facts being supposed correct, the case really falls within the formulae of the different inductions under which it has been successively brought; and finally, the legitimacy of the inductions themselves must be decided by other rules, and these it is now our purpose to investigate. If this third part of the operation be, in many of the questions of practical life, not the most, but the least arduous portion of it, we have seen that this is also the case in some great departments of the field of science; in all those which are principally deductive, and most of all in mathematics; where the inductions themselves are few in number, and so obvious and elementary that they seem to stand in no need of the evidence of experience, while to combine them so as to prove a given theorem or solve a problem, may call for the utmost powers of invention and contrivance with which our species is gifted.

If the identity of the logical processes which prove particular facts and those which establish general scientific truths, required any additional confirmation, it would be sufficient to consider that in many branches of science, single facts have to be proved, as well as principles; facts as completely individual as any that are debated in a court of justice; but which are proved in the same manner as the other truths of the science, and without disturbing in any degree the homogeneity of its method. A remarkable example of this is afforded by astronomy. The individual facts on which that science grounds its most important deductions, such facts as the magnitudes of the bodies of the solar system, their distances from one another, the figure of the earth, and its rotation, are scarcely any of them accessible to our means of direct observation: they are proved indirectly, by the aid of inductions founded on other facts which we can more easily reach. For example, the distance of the moon from the earth was determined by a very circuitous process. The share which direct observation had in the work consisted in ascertaining, at one and the same instant, the zenith distances of the moon, as seen from two points very remote from one another on the earth's surface. The ascertainment of these angular distances ascertained their supplements; and since the angle at the earth's centre subtended by the distance between the two places of observation was deducible by spherical trigonometry from the latitude and longitude of those places, the angle at the moon subtended by the same line became the fourth angle of a quadrilateral of which the other three angles were known. The four angles being thus ascertained, and two sides of the quadrilateral being radii of the earth; the two remaining sides and the diagonal, or in other words, the moon's distance from the two places of observation and from the centre of the earth, could be ascertained, at least in terms of the earth's radius, from elementary theorems of geometry. At each step in this demonstration we take in a new induction, represented, in the aggregate of its results, by a general proposition.

Not only is the process by which an individual astronomical fact was thus ascertained, exactly similar to those by which the same science establishes its general truths, but also (as we have shown to be the case in all legitimate reasoning) a general proposition might have been concluded instead of a single fact. In strictness, indeed, the result of the reasoning *is* a general proposition; a theorem respecting the distance, not of the moon in particular, but of any inaccessible object; showing in what relation that distance stands to certain other quantities. And although the moon is almost the only heavenly body the distance of which from the earth can really be thus ascertained, this is merely owing to the accidental circumstances of the other heavenly bodies, which render them incapable of affording such data as the application of the theorem requires; for the theorem itself is as true of them as it is of the moon.(53)

We shall fall into no error, then, if in treating of Induction, we limit our attention to the establishment of general propositions. The principles and rules of Induction, as directed to this end, are the principles and rules of all Induction; and the logic of Science is the universal Logic, applicable to all inquiries in which man can engage.

CHAPTER II. OF INDUCTIONS IMPROPERLY SO CALLED.

§ 1. Induction, then, is that operation of the mind, by which we infer that what we know to be true in a particular case or cases, will be true in all cases which resemble the former in certain assignable respects. In other words, Induction is the process by which we conclude that what is true of certain individuals of a class is true of the whole class, or that what is true at certain times will be true in similar circumstances at all times.

This definition excludes from the meaning of the term Induction, various logical operations, to which it is not unusual to apply that name.

Induction, as above defined, is a process of inference; it proceeds from the known to the unknown; and any operation involving no inference, any process in which what seems the conclusion is no wider than the premises from which it is drawn, does not fall within the meaning of the term. Yet in the common books of Logic we find this laid down as the most perfect, indeed the only quite perfect, form of induction. In those books, every process which sets out from a less general and terminates in a more general expression,--which admits of being stated in the form, "This and that A are B, therefore every A is B,"--is called an induction, whether anything be really concluded or not; and the induction is asserted to be not perfect, unless every single individual of the class A is included in the antecedent, or premiss: that is, unless what we affirm of the class has already been ascertained to be true of every individual in it, so that the nominal conclusion is not really a conclusion, but a mere reassertion of the premises. If we were to say, All the planets shine by the sun's light, from observation of each separate planet, or All the Apostles were Jews, because this is true of Peter, Paul, John, and every other apostle,--these, and such as these, would, in the phraseology in question, be called perfect, and the only perfect, Inductions. This, however, is a totally different kind of induction from ours; it is no inference from facts known to facts unknown, but a mere shorthand registration of facts known. The two simulated arguments which we have quoted, are not generalizations; the propositions purporting to be conclusions from them, are not really general propositions. A general proposition is one in which the predicate is affirmed or denied of an unlimited number of individuals; namely, all, whether few or many, existing or capable of existing, which possess the properties connoted by the subject of the proposition. "All men are mortal" does not mean all now living, but all men past, present, and to come. When the signification of the term is limited so as to render it a name not for any and every individual falling under a certain general description, but only for each of a number of individuals designated as such, and as it were counted off individually, the proposition, though it may be general in its language, is no general proposition, but merely that number of singular propositions, written in an abridged character. The operation may be very useful, as most forms of abridged notation are; but it is no part of the investigation of truth, though often bearing an important part in the preparation of the materials for that investigation.

§ 2. A second process which requires to be distinguished from Induction, is one to which mathematicians sometimes give that name: and which so far resembles Induction properly so called, that the propositions it leads to are really general propositions. For example, when we have proved with respect to the circle, that a straight line cannot meet it in more than two points, and when the same thing has been successively proved of the ellipse, the parabola, and the hyperbola, it may be laid down as an universal property of the sections of the cone. In this example there is no induction, because there is no inference: the conclusion is a mere summing up of what was asserted in the various propositions from which it is drawn. A case somewhat, though not altogether, similar, is the proof of a geometrical theorem by means of a diagram. Whether the diagram be on paper or only in the imagination, the demonstration (as formerly observed(54)) does not prove directly the general theorem; it proves only that the conclusion, which the theorem asserts generally, is true of the particular triangle or circle exhibited in the diagram; but since we perceive that in the same way in which we have proved it of that circle, it might also be proved of any other circle, we gather up into one general expression all the singular propositions susceptible of being thus proved, and embody them in an universal proposition. Having shown that the three angles of the triangle ABC are together equal to two right angles, we conclude that this is true of every other triangle, not because it is true of ABC, but for the same reason which proved it to be true of ABC. If this were to be called Induction, an appropriate name for it would be, induction by parity of reasoning. But the term cannot properly belong to it; the characteristic quality of Induction is wanting, since the truth obtained, though really general, is not believed on the evidence of particular instances. We do not conclude that all triangles have the property because some triangles have, but from the ulterior demonstrative evidence which was the ground of our conviction in the particular instances.

There are nevertheless, in mathematics, some examples of so-called induction, in which the conclusion does bear the appearance of a generalization grounded on some of the particular cases included in it. A mathematician, when he has calculated a sufficient number of the terms of an algebraical or arithmetical series to have ascertained what is called the *law* of the series, does not hesitate to fill up any number of the succeeding terms without repeating the calculations. But I apprehend he only does so when it is apparent from *a priori* considerations (which might be exhibited in the form of demonstration) that the mode of formation of the subsequent terms, each from that which preceded it, must be similar to the formation of the terms which have been already calculated. And when the attempt has been hazarded without the sanction of such general considerations, there are instances on record in which it has led to false results.

It is said that Newton discovered the binomial theorem by induction; by raising a binomial successively to a certain number of powers, and comparing those powers with one another until he detected the relation in which the algebraic formula of each power stands to the exponent of that power, and to the two terms of the binomial. The fact is not improbable: but a mathematician like Newton, who seemed to arrive *per saltum* at principles and conclusions that ordinary mathematicians only reached by a succession of steps, certainly could not have performed the comparison in question without being led by it to the *a priori* ground of the law; since any one who understands sufficiently the nature of multiplication to venture upon multiplying several lines of symbols at one operation, cannot but perceive that in raising a binomial to a power, the coefficients must depend on the laws of permutation and combination: and as soon as this is recognised, the theorem is demonstrated. Indeed, when once it was seen that the law prevailed in a few of the lower powers, its identity with the law of permutation would at once suggest the considerations which prove it to obtain universally. Even, therefore, such cases as these, are but examples of what I have called induction by parity of reasoning, that is, not really induction, because not involving inference of a general proposition from particular instances.

§ 3. There remains a third improper use of the term Induction, which it is of real importance to clear up, because the theory of induction has been, in no ordinary degree, confused by it, and because the confusion is exemplified in the most recent and most elaborate treatise on the inductive philosophy which exists in our language. The error in question is that of confounding a mere description of a set of observed phenomena, with an induction from them.

Suppose that a phenomenon consists of parts, and that these parts are only capable of being observed separately, and as it were piecemeal. When the observations have been made, there is a convenience (amounting for many purposes to a necessity) in obtaining a representation of the phenomenon as a whole, by combining, or as we may say, piecing these detached fragments together. A navigator sailing in the midst of the ocean discovers land: he cannot at first, or by any one observation, determine whether it is a continent or an island; but he coasts along it, and after a few days finds himself to have sailed completely round it: he then pronounces it an island. Now there was no particular time or place of observation at which he could perceive that this land was entirely surrounded by water: he ascertained the fact by a succession of partial observations, and then selected a general expression which summed up in two or three words the whole of what he so observed. But is there anything of the nature of an induction in this process? Did he infer anything that had not been observed, from something else which had? Certainly not. He had observed the whole of what the proposition asserts. That the land in question is an island, is not an inference from the partial facts which the navigator saw in the course of his circumnavigation; it is the facts themselves; it is a summary of those facts; the description of a complex fact, to which those simpler ones are as the parts of a whole.

Now there is, I conceive, no difference in kind between this simple operation, and that by which Kepler ascertained the nature of the planetary orbits: and Kepler's operation, all at least that was characteristic in it, was not more an inductive act than that of our supposed navigator.

The object of Kepler was to determine the real path described by each of the planets, or let us say by the planet Mars, (for it was of that body that he first established two of the three great astronomical truths which bear his name.) To do this there was no other mode than that of direct observation: and all which observation could do was to ascertain a great number of the successive places of the planet; or rather, of its apparent places. That the planet occupied successively all these positions, or at all events, positions which produced the same impressions on the eye, and that it passed from one of these to another insensibly, and without any apparent breach of continuity; thus much the senses, with the aid of the proper instruments, could ascertain. What Kepler did more than this, was to find what sort of a curve these different points would make, supposing them to be all joined together. He expressed the whole series of the observed places of Mars by what Dr. Whewell calls the general conception of an ellipse. This operation was far from being as easy as that of the navigator who expressed the series of his observations on successive points of the coast by the general conception of an island. But it is the very same sort of operation; and if the one is not an induction but a description, this must also be true of the other.

To avoid misapprehension, we must remark that Kepler, in one respect, performed a real act of induction; namely, in concluding that because the observed places of Mars were correctly represented by points in an imaginary ellipse, therefore Mars would continue to revolve in that same ellipse; and even in concluding that the position of the planet during the time which intervened between two observations, must have coincided with the intermediate points of the curve. But this really inductive operation requires to be carefully distinguished from the mere act of bringing the facts actually observed under a general description. So distinct are these two operations, that the one might have been performed without the other. Men might and did make correct inductions concerning the heavenly motions, before they had obtained correct general descriptions of them. It was known that the planets always moved in the same paths, long before it had been ascertained that those paths were ellipses. Astronomers early remarked that the same set of apparent positions returned periodically. When they obtained a new description of the phenomenon, they did not necessarily make any further induction, nor (which is the true test of a new general truth) add anything to the power of prediction which they already possessed.

§ 4. The descriptive operation which enables a number of details to be summed up in a single proposition, Dr. Whewell, by an aptly chosen expression, has termed the Colligation of Facts.(55) In most of his observations concerning that mental process I fully agree, and would gladly transfer all that portion of his book into my own pages. I only think him mistaken in setting up this kind of operation, which according to the old and received meaning of the term, is not induction at all, as the type of induction generally; and laying down, throughout his work, as principles of induction, the principles of mere colligation.

Dr. Whewell maintains that the general proposition which binds together the particular facts, and makes them, as it were, one fact, is not the mere sum of those facts, but something more, since there is introduced a conception of the mind, which did not exist in the facts themselves. "The particular facts," says he,(56) "are not merely brought together, but there is a new element added to the combination by the very act of thought by which they are combined.... When the Greeks, after long observing the motions of the planets, saw that these motions might be rightly considered as produced by the motion of one wheel revolving in the inside of another wheel, these wheels were creations of their minds, added to the facts which they perceived by sense. And even if the wheels were no longer supposed to be material, but were reduced to mere geometrical spheres or circles, they were not the less products of the mind alone,--something additional to the facts observed. The same is the case in all other discoveries. The facts are known, but they are insulated and unconnected, till the discoverer supplies from his own store a principle of connexion. The pearls are there, but they will not hang together till some one provides the string."

That a conception of the mind is introduced is indeed undeniable, and I willingly concede, that to hit upon the right conception is often a far more difficult and more meritorious achievement, than to prove its applicability when obtained. But a conception implies, and corresponds to, something conceived: and though the conception itself is not in the facts, but in our mind, it must be a conception *of* something which really is in the facts, some property which they actually possess, and which they would manifest to our senses, if our senses were able to take cognizance of them. If, for instance, the planet left behind it in space a visible track, and if the observer were in a fixed position at such a distance above the plane of the orbit as would enable him to see the whole of it at once, he would see it to be an ellipse; and if gifted with appropriate instruments, and powers of locomotion, he could prove it to be such by measuring its different dimensions. These things are indeed impossible to us, but not impossible in themselves; if they were so, Kepler's law could not be true.

Subject to the indispensable condition which has just been stated, I cannot perceive that the part which conceptions have in the operation of studying facts, has ever been overlooked or undervalued. No one ever disputed that in order to reason about anything we must have a conception of it; or that when we include a multitude of things under a general expression, there is implied in the expression a conception of something common to those things. But it by no means follows that the conception is necessarily pre-existent, or constructed by the mind out of its own materials. If the facts are rightly classed under the conception, it is because there is in the facts themselves something of which the conception is itself a copy; and which if we cannot directly perceive, it is because of the limited power of our organs, and not because the thing itself is not there. The conception itself is often obtained by abstraction from the very facts which, in Dr. Whewell's language, it is afterwards called in to connect. This he himself admits, when he observes, (which he does on several occasions,) how great a service would be rendered to the science of physiology by the philosopher "who should establish a precise, tenable, and consistent conception of life."(57) Such a conception **can** only be abstracted from the phenomena of life itself; from the very facts which it is put in requisition to connect. In other cases (no doubt) instead of collecting the conception from the very phenomena which we are attempting to colligate, we select it from among those which have been previously collected by abstraction from other facts. In the instance of Kepler's laws, the latter was the case. The facts being out of the reach of being observed, in any such manner as would have enabled the senses to identify directly the path of the planet, the conception requisite for framing a general description of that path could not be collected by abstraction from the observations themselves; the mind had to supply hypothetically, from among the conceptions it had obtained from other portions of its experience, some one which would correctly represent the series of the observed facts. It had to frame a supposition respecting the general course of the phenomenon, and ask itself, If this be the general description, what will the details be? and then compare these with the details actually observed. If they agreed, the hypothesis would serve for a description of the phenomenon: if not, it was necessarily abandoned, and another tried. It is such a case as this which gives rise to the doctrine that the mind, in framing the descriptions, adds something of its own which it does not find in the facts.

Yet it is a fact surely, that the planet does describe an ellipse; and a fact which we could see, if we had adequate visual organs and a suitable position. Not having these advantages, but possessing the conception of an ellipse, or (to express the meaning in less technical language) knowing what an ellipse was, Kepler tried whether the observed places of the planet were consistent with such a path. He found they were so; and he, consequently, asserted as a fact that the planet moved in an ellipse. But this fact, which Kepler did not add to, but found in, the motions of the planet, namely, that it occupied in succession the various points in the circumference of a given ellipse, was the very fact, the separate parts of which had been separately observed; it was the sum of the different observations.

Having stated this fundamental difference between my opinion and that of Dr. Whewell, I must add, that his account of the manner in which a conception is selected, suitable to express the facts, appears to me perfectly just. The experience of all thinkers will, I believe, testify that the process is tentative; that it consists of a succession of guesses; many being rejected, until one at last occurs fit to be chosen. We know from Kepler himself that before hitting upon the "conception" of an ellipse, he tried nineteen other imaginary paths, which, finding them inconsistent with the observations, he was obliged to reject. But as Dr. Whewell truly says, the successful hypothesis, though a guess, ought generally to be called, not a lucky, but a skilful guess. The guesses which serve to give mental unity and wholeness to a chaos of scattered particulars, are accidents which rarely occur to any minds but those abounding in knowledge and disciplined in intellectual combinations.

How far this tentative method, so indispensable as a means to the colligation of facts for purposes of description, admits of application to Induction itself, and what functions belong to it in that department, will be considered in the chapter of the present Book which relates to Hypotheses. On the present occasion we have chiefly to distinguish this process of Colligation from Induction properly so called: and that the distinction may be made clearer, it is well to advert to a curious and interesting remark, which is as strikingly true of the former operation, as it appears to me unequivocally false of the latter.

In different stages of the progress of knowledge, philosophers have employed, for the colligation of the same order of facts, different conceptions. The early rude observations of the heavenly bodies, in which minute precision was neither attained nor sought, presented nothing inconsistent with the representation of the path of a planet as an exact circle, having the earth for its centre. As observations increased in accuracy, and facts were disclosed which were not reconcileable with this simple supposition; for the colligation of those additional facts, the supposition was varied; and varied again and again as facts became more numerous and precise. The earth was removed from the centre to some other point within the circle; the planet was supposed to revolve in a smaller circle called an epicycle, round an imaginary point which revolved in a circle round the earth: in proportion as observation elicited fresh facts contradictory to these representations, other epicycles and other excentrics were added, producing additional complication; until at last Kepler swept all these circles away, and substituted the conception of an exact ellipse. Even this is found not to represent with complete correctness the accurate observations of the present day, which disclose many slight deviations from an orbit exactly elliptical. Now Dr. Whewell has remarked that these successive general expressions, though apparently so conflicting, were all correct: they all answered the purpose of colligation: they all enabled the mind to represent to itself with facility, and by a simultaneous glance, the whole body of facts at that time ascertained; each in its turn served as a correct description of the phenomena, so far as the senses had up to that time taken cognizance of them. If a necessity afterwards arose for discarding one of these general descriptions of the planet's orbit, and framing a different imaginary line, by which to express the series of observed positions, it was because a number of new facts had now been added, which it was necessary to combine with the old facts into one general description. But this did not affect the correctness of the former expression, considered as a general statement of the only facts which it was intended to represent. And so true is this, that, as is well remarked by M. Comte, these ancient generalizations, even the rudest and most imperfect of them, that of uniform movement in a circle, are so far from being entirely false, that they are even now habitually employed by astronomers when only a rough approximation to correctness is required. "L'astronomie moderne, en detruisant sans retour les hypotheses primitives, envisagees comme lois reelles du monde, a soigneusement maintenu leur valeur positive et permanente, la propriete de representer commodement les phenomenes quand il s'agit d'une premiere ebauche. Nos ressources a cet egard sont meme bien plus etendues, precisement a cause que nous ne nous faisons aucune illusion sur la realite des hypotheses; ce qui nous permet d'employer sans scrupule, en chaque cas, celle que nous jugeons la plus avantageuse."(58)

Dr. Whewell's remark, therefore, is philosophically correct. Successive expressions for the colligation of observed facts, or, in other words, successive descriptions of a phenomenon as a whole, which has been observed only in parts, may, though conflicting, be all correct as far as they go. But it would surely be absurd to assert this of conflicting inductions.

The scientific study of facts may be undertaken for three different purposes: the simple description of the facts; their explanation; or their prediction: meaning by prediction, the determination of the conditions under which similar facts may be expected again to occur. To the first of these three operations the name of Induction does not properly belong: to the other two it does. Now, Dr. Whewell's observation is true of the first alone. Considered as a mere description, the circular theory of the heavenly motions represents perfectly well their general features: and by adding epicycles without limit, those motions, even as now known to us, might be expressed with any degree of accuracy that might be required. The elliptical theory, as a mere description, would have a great advantage in point of simplicity, and in the consequent facility of conceiving it and reasoning about it; but it would not really be more true than the other. Different descriptions, therefore, may be all true: but not, surely, different explanations. The doctrine that the heavenly bodies moved by a virtue inherent in their celestial nature; the doctrine that they were moved by impact, (which led to the hypothesis of vortices as the only impelling force capable of whirling bodies in circles,) and the Newtonian doctrine, that they are moved by the composition of a centripetal with an original projectile force; all these are explanations, collected by real induction from supposed parallel cases; and they were all successively received by philosophers, as scientific truths on the subject of the heavenly bodies. Can it be said of these, as was said of the different descriptions, that they are all true as far as they go? Is it not clear that one only can be true in any degree, and the other two must be altogether false? So much for explanations: let us now compare different predictions: the first, that eclipses will occur whenever one planet or satellite is so situated as to cast its shadow upon another; the second, that they will occur whenever some great calamity is impending over mankind. Do these two doctrines only differ in the degree of their truth, as expressing real facts with unequal degrees of accuracy? Assuredly the one is true, and the other absolutely false.(59)

In every way, therefore, it is evident that to explain induction as the colligation of facts by means of appropriate conceptions, that is, conceptions which will really express them, is to confound mere description of the observed facts with inference from those facts, and ascribe to the latter what is a characteristic property of the former.

There is, however, between Colligation and Induction, a real correlation, which it is important to conceive correctly. Colligation is not always induction; but induction is always colligation. The assertion that the planets move in ellipses, was but a mode of representing observed facts; it was but a colligation; while the assertion that they are drawn, or tend, towards the sun, was the statement of a new fact, inferred by induction. But the induction, once made, accomplishes the purposes of colligation likewise. It brings the same facts, which Kepler had connected by his conception of an ellipse, under the additional conception of bodies acted upon by a central force, and serves therefore as a new bond of connexion for those facts; a new principle for their classification.

Further, that general description, which is improperly confounded with induction, is nevertheless a necessary preparation for induction; no less necessary than correct observation of the facts themselves. Without the previous colligation of detached observations by means of one general conception, we could never have obtained any basis for an induction, except in the case of phenomena of very limited compass. We should not be able to affirm any predicates at all, of a subject incapable of being observed otherwise than piecemeal: much less could we extend those predicates by induction to other similar subjects. Induction, therefore, always presupposes, not only that the necessary observations are made with the necessary accuracy, but also that the results of these observations are, so far as practicable, connected together by general descriptions, enabling the mind to represent to itself as wholes whatever phenomena are capable of being so represented.

§ 5. Dr. Whewell has replied at some length to the preceding observations, re-stating his opinions, but without (as far as I can perceive) adding anything to his former arguments. Since, however, mine have not had the good fortune to make any impression upon him, I will subjoin a few remarks, tending to shew more clearly in what our difference of opinion consists, as well as, in some measure, to account for it.

All the definitions of induction, by writers of authority, make it consist in drawing inferences from known cases to unknown; affirming of a class, a predicate which has been found true of some cases belonging to the class; concluding, because some things have a certain property, that other things which resemble them have the same property--or because a thing has manifested a property at a certain time, that it has and will have that property at other times.

It will scarcely be contended that Kepler's operation was an Induction in this sense of the term. The statement, that Mars moves in an elliptical orbit, was no generalization from individual cases to a class of cases. Neither was it an extension to all time, of what had been found true at some particular time. The whole amount of generalization which the case admitted of, was already completed, or might have been so. Long before the elliptic theory was thought of, it had been ascertained that the planets returned periodically to the same apparent places; the series of these places was, or might have been, completely determined, and the apparent course of each planet marked out on the celestial globe in an uninterrupted line. Kepler did not extend an observed truth to other cases than those in which it had been observed: he did not widen the **subject** of the proposition which expressed the observed facts. He left the subject as it was; the alteration he made was in the predicate. Instead of saying, the successive places of Mars are so and so, he summed them up in the statement, that the successive places of Mars are points in an ellipse. It is true, this statement, as Dr. Whewell says, was not the sum of the observations **merely**; it was the sum of the observations **seen under a new point of view**. (60) But it was not the sum of **more** than the observations, as a real induction is. It took in no cases but those which had been actually observed, or which could have been inferred from the observations before the new point of view presented itself. There was not that transition from known cases to unknown, which constitutes Induction in the original and acknowledged meaning of the term.

Old definitions, it is true, cannot prevail against new knowledge: and if the Keplerian operation, as a logical process, were really identical with what takes place in acknowledged induction, the definition of induction ought to be so widened as to take it in; since scientific language ought to adapt itself to the true relations which subsist between the things it is employed to designate. Here then it is that I join issue with Dr. Whewell. He does think the operations identical. He allows of no logical process in any case of induction, other than what there was in Kepler's case, namely, guessing until a guess is found which tallies with the facts: and accordingly, as we shall see hereafter, he rejects all canons of induction, because it is not by means of them that we guess. Dr. Whewell's theory of the logic of science would be very perfect, if it did not pass over altogether the question of Proof. But in my apprehension there is such a thing as proof, and inductions differ altogether from descriptions in their relation to that element. Induction is proof; it is inferring something unobserved from something observed: it requires, therefore, an appropriate test of proof; and to provide that test, is the special purpose of inductive logic. When, on the contrary, we merely collate known observations, and, in Dr. Whewell's phraseology, connect them by means of a new conception; if the conception does but serve to connect the observations, we have all we want. As the proposition in which it is embodied pretends to no other truth than what it may share with many other modes of representing the same facts, to be consistent with the facts is all it requires: it neither needs nor admits of proof; though it may serve to prove other things, inasmuch as, by placing the facts in mental connexion with other facts, not previously seen to resemble them, it assimilates the case to another class of phenomena, concerning which real Inductions have already been made. Thus Kepler's so-called law brought the orbit of Mars into the class ellipse, and by doing so, proved all the properties of an ellipse to be true of the orbit: but in this proof Kepler's law supplied the minor premiss, and not (as is the case with real Inductions) the major.

The mental operation which extracts from a number of detached observations certain general characters in which the observed phenomena resemble one another, or resemble other known facts, is what Bacon, Locke, and most subsequent metaphysicians, have understood by the word Abstraction. A general expression obtained by abstraction, connecting known facts by means of common characters, but without concluding from them to unknown, may, I think, with strict logical correctness, be termed a Description; nor do I know in what other way things can ever be described. My position, however, does not depend on the employment of that particular word; I am quite content to use Dr. Whewell's term Colligation, provided it be clearly seen that the process is not Induction, but something radically different.

What more may usefully be said on the subject of Colligation, or of the correlative expression invented by Dr. Whewell, the Explication of Conceptions, and generally on the subject of ideas and mental representations as connected with the study of facts, will find a more appropriate place in the Fourth Book, on the Operations Subsidiary to Induction: to which the reader must refer for the removal of any difficulty which the present discussion may have left.

CHAPTER III. OF THE GROUND OF INDUCTION.

§ 1. Induction properly so called, as distinguished from those mental operations, sometimes though improperly designated by the name, which I have attempted in the preceding chapter to characterize, may, then, be summarily defined as Generalization from Experience. It consists in inferring from some individual instances in which a phenomenon is observed to occur, that it occurs in all instances of a certain class; namely, in all which **resemble** the former, in what are regarded as the material circumstances.

In what way the material circumstances are to be distinguished from those which are immaterial, or why some of the circumstances are material and others not so, we are not yet ready to point out. We must first observe, that there is a principle implied in the very statement of what Induction is; an assumption with regard to the course of nature and the order of the universe: namely, that there are such things in nature as parallel cases; that what happens once, will, under a sufficient degree of similarity of circumstances, happen again, and not only again, but as often as the same circumstances recur. This, I say, is an assumption, involved in every case of induction. And, if we consult the actual course of nature, we find that the assumption is warranted. The universe, we find, is so constituted, that whatever is true in any one case, is true in all cases of a certain description; the only difficulty is, to find **what** description.

This universal fact, which is our warrant for all inferences from experience, has been described by different philosophers in different forms of language: that the course of nature is uniform; that the universe is governed by general laws; and the like. One of the most usual of these modes of expression, but also one of the most inadequate, is that which has been brought into familiar use by the metaphysicians of the school of Reid and Stewart. The disposition of the human mind to generalize from experience,--a propensity considered by these philosophers as an instinct of our nature,--they usually describe under some such name as "our intuitive conviction that the future will resemble the past." Now it has been well pointed out, that (whether the tendency be or not an original and ultimate element of our nature), Time, in its modifications of past, present, and future, has no concern either with the belief itself, or with the grounds of it. We believe that fire will burn to-morrow, because it burned to-day and yesterday; but we believe, on precisely the same grounds, that it burned before we were born, and that it burns this very day in Cochin-China. It is not from the past to the future, **as** past and future, that we infer, but from the known to the unknown; from facts observed to facts unobserved; from what we have perceived, or been directly conscious of, to what has not come within our experience. In this last predicament is the whole region of the future; but also the vastly greater portion of the present and of the past.

Whatever be the most proper mode of expressing it, the proposition that the course of nature is uniform, is the fundamental principle, or general axiom, of Induction. It would yet be a great error to offer this large generalization as any explanation of the inductive process. On the contrary, I hold it to be itself an instance of induction, and induction by no means of the most obvious kind. Far from being the first induction we make, it is one of the last, or at all events one of those which are latest in attaining strict philosophical accuracy. As a general maxim, indeed, it has scarcely entered into the minds of any but philosophers; nor even by them, as we shall have many opportunities of remarking, have its extent and limits been always very justly conceived. The truth is, that this great generalization is itself founded on prior generalizations. The obscurer laws of nature were discovered by means of it, but the more obvious ones must have been understood and assented to as general truths before it was ever heard of. We should never have thought of affirming that all phenomena take place according to general laws, if we had not first arrived, in the case of a great multitude of phenomena, at some knowledge of the laws themselves; which could be done no otherwise than by induction. In what sense, then, can a principle, which is so far from being our earliest induction, be regarded as our warrant for all the others? In the only sense, in which (as we have already seen) the general propositions which we place at the head of our reasonings when we throw them into syllogisms, ever really contribute to their validity. As Archbishop Whately remarks, every induction is a syllogism with the major premiss suppressed; or (as I prefer expressing it) every induction may be thrown into the form of a syllogism, by supplying a major premiss. If this be actually done, the principle which we are now considering, that of the uniformity of the course of nature, will appear as the ultimate major premiss of all inductions, and will, therefore, stand to all inductions in the relation in which, as has been shown at so much length, the major proposition of a syllogism always stands to the conclusion; not contributing at all to prove it, but being a necessary condition of its being proved; since no conclusion is proved for which there cannot be found a true major premiss.

The statement, that the uniformity of the course of nature is the ultimate major premiss in all cases of induction, may be thought to require some explanation. The immediate major premiss in every inductive argument, it certainly is not. Of that, Archbishop Whately's must be held to be the correct account. The induction, "John, Peter, &c., are mortal, therefore all mankind are mortal," may, as he justly says, be thrown into a syllogism by prefixing as a major premiss (what is at any rate a necessary condition of the validity of the argument) namely, that what is true of John, Peter, &c, is true of all mankind. But how come we by this major premiss? It is not self-evident; nay, in all cases of unwarranted generalization, it is not true. How, then, is it arrived at? Necessarily either by induction or ratiocination; and if by induction, the process, like all other inductive arguments, may be thrown into the form of a syllogism. This previous syllogism it is, therefore, necessary to construct. There is, in the long run, only one possible construction. The real proof that what is true of John, Peter, &c., is true of all mankind, can only be, that a different supposition would be inconsistent with the uniformity which we know to exist in the course of nature. Whether there would be this inconsistency or not, may be a matter of long and delicate inquiry; but unless there would, we have no sufficient ground for the major of the inductive syllogism. It hence appears, that if we throw the whole course of any inductive argument into a series of syllogisms, we shall arrive by more or fewer steps at an ultimate syllogism, which will have for its major premiss the principle, or axiom, of the uniformity of the course of nature.(61)

It was not to be expected that in the case of this axiom, any more than of other axioms, there should be unanimity among thinkers with respect to the grounds on which it is to be received as true. I have already stated that I regard it as itself a generalization from experience. Others hold it to be a principle which, antecedently to any verification by experience, we are compelled by the constitution of our thinking faculty to assume as true. Having so recently, and at so much length, combated a similar doctrine as applied to the axioms of mathematics, by arguments which are in a great measure applicable to the present case, I shall defer the more particular discussion of this controverted point in regard to the fundamental axiom of induction, until a more advanced period of our inquiry.(62) At present it is of more importance to understand thoroughly the import of the axiom itself. For the proposition, that the course of nature is uniform, possesses rather the brevity suitable to popular, than the precision requisite in philosophical, language: its terms require to be explained, and a stricter than their ordinary signification given to them, before the truth of the assertion can be admitted.

§ 2. Every person's consciousness assures him that he does not always expect uniformity in the course of events; he does not always believe that the unknown will be similar to the known, that the future will resemble the past. Nobody believes that the succession of rain and fine weather will be the same in every future year as in the present. Nobody expects to have the same dreams repeated every night. On the contrary, everybody mentions it as something extraordinary, if the course of nature is constant, and resembles itself, in these particulars. To look for constancy where constancy is not to be expected, as for instance, that a day which has once brought good fortune will always be a fortunate day, is justly accounted superstition.

The course of nature, in truth, is not only uniform, it is also infinitely various. Some phenomena are always seen to recur in the very same combinations in which we met with them at first; others seem altogether capricious; while some, which we had been accustomed to regard as bound down exclusively to a particular set of combinations, we unexpectedly find detached from some of the elements with which we had hitherto found them conjoined, and united to others of quite a contrary description. To an inhabitant of Central Africa, fifty years ago, no fact probably appeared to rest on more uniform experience than this, that all human beings are black. To Europeans, not many years ago, the proposition, All swans are white, appeared an equally unequivocal instance of uniformity in the course of nature. Further experience has proved to both that they were mistaken; but they had to wait fifty centuries for this experience. During that long time, mankind believed in an uniformity of the course of nature where no such uniformity really existed.

According to the notion which the ancients entertained of induction, the foregoing were cases of as legitimate inference as any inductions whatever. In these two instances, in which, the conclusion being false, the ground of inference must have been insufficient, there was, nevertheless, as much ground for it as this conception of induction admitted of. The induction of the ancients has been well described by Bacon, under the name of "Inductio per enumerationem simplicem, ubi non reperitur instantia contradictoria." It consists in ascribing the character of general truths to all propositions which are true in every instance that we happen to know of. This is the kind of induction which is natural to the mind when unaccustomed to scientific methods. The tendency, which some call an instinct, and which others account for by association, to infer the future from the past, the known from the unknown, is simply a habit of expecting that what has been found true once or several times, and never yet found false, will be found true again. Whether the instances are few or many, conclusive or inconclusive, does not much affect the matter: these are considerations which occur only on reflection: the unprompted tendency of the mind is to generalize its experience, provided this points all in one direction; provided no other experience of a conflicting character comes unsought. The notion of seeking it, of experimenting for it, of *interrogating* nature (to use Bacon's expression) is of much later growth. The observation of nature, by uncultivated intellects, is purely passive: they accept the facts which present themselves, without taking the trouble of searching for more: it is a superior mind only which asks itself what facts are needed to enable it to come to a sure conclusion, and then looks out for these.

But though we have always a propensity to generalize from unvarying experience, we are not always warranted in doing so. Before we can be at liberty to conclude that something is universally true because we have never known an instance to the contrary, we must have reason to believe that if there were in nature any instances to the contrary, we should have known of them. This assurance, in the great majority of cases, we cannot have, or can have only in a very moderate degree. The possibility of having it, is the foundation on which we shall see hereafter that induction by simple enumeration may in some remarkable cases amount practically to proof.(63) No such assurance, however, can be had, on any of the ordinary subjects of scientific inquiry. Popular notions are usually founded on induction by simple enumeration; in science it carries us but a little way. We are forced to begin with it; we must often rely on it provisionally, in the absence of means of more searching investigation. But, for the accurate study of nature, we require a surer and a more potent instrument.

It was, above all, by pointing out the insufficiency of this rude and loose conception of Induction, that Bacon merited the title so generally awarded to him, of Founder of the Inductive Philosophy. The value of his own contributions to a more philosophical theory of the subject has certainly been exaggerated. Although (along with some fundamental errors) his writings contain, more or less fully developed, several of the most important principles of the Inductive Method, physical investigation has now far outgrown the Baconian conception of Induction. Moral and political inquiry, indeed, are as yet far behind that conception. The current and approved modes of reasoning on these subjects are still of the same vicious description against which Bacon protested; the method almost exclusively employed by those professing to treat such matters inductively, is the very ***inductio per enumerationem simplicem*** which he condemns; and the experience which we hear so confidently appealed to by all sects, parties, and interests, is still, in his own emphatic words, ***mera palpatio***.

§ 3. In order to a better understanding of the problem which the logician must solve if he would establish a scientific theory of Induction, let us compare a few cases of incorrect inductions with others which are acknowledged to be legitimate. Some, we know, which were believed for centuries to be correct, were nevertheless incorrect. That all swans are white, cannot have been a good induction, since the conclusion has turned out erroneous. The experience, however, on which the conclusion rested was genuine. From the earliest records, the testimony of the inhabitants of the known world was unanimous on the point. The uniform experience, therefore, of the inhabitants of the known world, agreeing in a common result, without one known instance of deviation from that result, is not always sufficient to establish a general conclusion.

But let us now turn to an instance apparently not very dissimilar to this. Mankind were wrong, it seems, in concluding that all swans were white: are we also wrong, when we conclude that all men's heads grow above their shoulders, and never below, in spite of the conflicting testimony of the naturalist Pliny? As there were black swans, though civilized people had existed for three thousand years on the earth without meeting with them, may there not also be "men whose heads do grow beneath their shoulders," notwithstanding a rather less perfect unanimity of negative testimony from observers? Most persons would answer No; it was more credible that a bird should vary in its colour, than that men should vary in the relative position of their principal organs. And there is no doubt that in so saying they would be right: but to say why they are right, would be impossible, without entering more deeply than is usually done, into the true theory of Induction.

Again, there are cases in which we reckon with the most unfailing confidence upon uniformity, and other cases in which we do not count upon it at all. In some we feel complete assurance that the future will resemble the past, the unknown be precisely similar to the known. In others, however invariable may be the result obtained from the instances which have been observed, we draw from them no more than a very feeble presumption that the like result will hold in all other cases. That a straight line is the shortest distance between two points, we do not doubt to be true even in the region of the fixed stars. When a chemist announces the existence and properties of a newly-discovered substance, if we confide in his accuracy, we feel assured that the conclusions he has arrived at will hold universally, although the induction be founded but on a single instance. We do not withhold our assent, waiting for a repetition of the experiment; or if we do, it is from a doubt whether the one experiment was properly made, not whether if properly made it would be conclusive. Here, then, is a general law of nature, inferred without hesitation from a single instance; an universal proposition from a singular one. Now mark another case, and contrast it with this. Not all the instances which have been observed since the beginning of the world, in support of the general proposition that all crows are black, would be deemed a sufficient presumption of the truth of the proposition, to outweigh the testimony of one unexceptionable witness who should affirm that in some region of the earth not fully explored, he had caught and examined a crow, and had found it to be grey.

Why is a single instance, in some cases, sufficient for a complete induction, while in others, myriads of concurring instances, without a single exception known or presumed, go such a very little way towards establishing an universal proposition? Whoever can answer this question knows more of the philosophy of logic than the wisest of the ancients, and has solved the problem of induction.

CHAPTER IV. OF LAWS OF NATURE.

§ 1. In the contemplation of that uniformity in the course of nature, which is assumed in every inference from experience, one of the first observations that present themselves is, that the uniformity in question is not properly uniformity, but uniformities. The general regularity results from the co-existence of partial regularities. The course of nature in general is constant, because the course of each of the various phenomena that compose it is so. A certain fact invariably occurs whenever certain circumstances are present, and does not occur when they are absent; the like is true of another fact; and so on. From these separate threads of connexion between parts of the great whole which we term nature, a general tissue of connexion unavoidably weaves itself, by which the whole is held together. If A is always accompanied by D, B by E, and C by F, it follows that A B is accompanied by D E, A C by D F, B C by E F, and finally A B C by D E F; and thus the general character of regularity is produced, which, along with and in the midst of infinite diversity, pervades all nature.

The first point, therefore, to be noted in regard to what is called the uniformity of the course of nature, is, that it is itself a complex fact, compounded of all the separate uniformities which exist in respect to single phenomena. These various uniformities, when ascertained by what is regarded as a sufficient induction, we call in common parlance, Laws of Nature. Scientifically speaking, that title is employed in a more restricted sense, to designate the uniformities when reduced to their most simple expression. Thus in the illustration already employed, there were seven uniformities; all of which, if considered sufficiently certain, would in the more lax application of the term, be called laws of nature. But of the seven, three alone are properly distinct and independent; these being pre-supposed, the others follow of course: the three first, therefore, according to the stricter acceptation, are called laws of nature, the remainder not; because they are in truth mere *cases* of the three first; virtually included in them; said, therefore, to *result* from them: whoever affirms those three has already affirmed all the rest.

To substitute real examples for symbolical ones, the following are three uniformities, or call them laws of nature: the law that air has weight, the law that pressure on a fluid is propagated equally in all directions, and the law that pressure in one direction, not opposed by equal pressure in the contrary direction, produces motion, which does not cease until equilibrium is restored. From these three uniformities we should be able to predict another uniformity, namely, the rise of the mercury in the Torricellian tube. This, in the stricter use of the phrase, is not a law of nature.

It is a result of laws of nature. It is a *case* of each and every one of the three laws: and is the only occurrence by which they could all be fulfilled. If the mercury were not sustained in the barometer, and sustained at such a height that the column of mercury were equal in weight to a column of the atmosphere of the same diameter; here would be a case, either of the air not pressing upon the surface of the mercury with the force which is called its weight, or of the downward pressure on the mercury not being propagated equally in an upward direction, or of a body pressed in one direction and not in the direction opposite, either not moving in the direction in which it is pressed, or stopping before it had attained equilibrium. If we knew, therefore, the three simple laws, but had never tried the Torricellian experiment, we might *deduce* its result from those laws. The known weight of the air, combined with the position of the apparatus, would bring the mercury within the first of the three inductions; the first induction would bring it within the second, and the second within the third, in the manner which we characterized in treating of Ratiocination. We should thus come to know the more complex uniformity, independently of specific experience, through our knowledge of the simpler ones from which it results; although, for reasons which will appear hereafter, *verification* by specific experience would still be desirable, and might possibly be indispensable.

Complex uniformities which, like this, are mere cases of simpler ones, and have, therefore, been virtually affirmed in affirming those, may with propriety be called *laws*, but can scarcely, in the strictness of scientific speech, be termed Laws of Nature. It is the custom in science, wherever regularity of any kind can be traced, to call the general proposition which expresses the nature of that regularity, a *law*; as when, in mathematics, we speak of the law of decrease of the successive terms of a converging series. But the expression, *law of nature*, has generally been employed with a sort of tacit reference to the original sense of the word *law*, namely, the expression of the will of a superior. When, therefore, it appeared that any of the uniformities which were observed in nature, would result spontaneously from certain other uniformities, no separate act of creative will being supposed necessary for the production of the derivative uniformities, these have not usually been spoken of as laws of nature. According to another mode of expression, the question, What are the laws of nature? may be stated thus:--What are the fewest and simplest assumptions, which being granted, the whole existing order of nature would result?

Another mode of stating it would be thus: What are the fewest general propositions from which all the uniformities which exist in the universe might be deductively inferred?

Every great advance which marks an epoch in the progress of science, has consisted in a step made towards the solution of this problem. Even a simple colligation of inductions already made, without any fresh extension of the inductive inference, is already an advance in that direction. When Kepler expressed the regularity which exists in the observed motions of the heavenly bodies, by the three general propositions called his laws, he, in so doing, pointed out three simple suppositions which, instead of a much greater number, would suffice to construct the whole scheme of the heavenly motions, so far as it was known up to that time. A similar and still greater step was made when these laws, which at first did not seem to be included in any more general truths, were discovered to be cases of the three laws of motion, as obtaining among bodies which mutually tend towards one another with a certain force, and have had a certain instantaneous impulse originally impressed upon them. After this great discovery, Kepler's three propositions, though still called laws, would hardly, by any person accustomed to use language with precision, be termed laws of nature: that phrase would be reserved for the simpler laws into which Newton is said to have resolved them.

According to this language, every well-grounded inductive generalization is either a law of nature, or a result of laws of nature, capable, if those laws are known, of being predicted from them. And the problem of Inductive Logic may be summed up in two questions: how to ascertain the laws of nature; and how, after having ascertained them, to follow them into their results. On the other hand, we must not suffer ourselves to imagine that this mode of statement amounts to a real analysis, or to anything but a mere verbal transformation of the problem; for the expression, Laws of Nature, **means** nothing but the uniformities which exist among natural phenomena (or, in other words, the results of induction), when reduced to their simplest expression. It is, however, something, to have advanced so far, as to see that the study of nature is the study of laws, not *a* law; of uniformities, in the plural number: that the different natural phenomena have their separate rules or modes of taking place, which, though much intermixed and entangled with one another, may, to a certain extent, be studied apart: that (to resume our former metaphor) the regularity which exists in nature is a web composed of distinct threads, and only to be understood by tracing each of the threads separately; for which purpose it is often necessary to unravel some portion of the web, and exhibit the fibres apart. The rules of experimental inquiry are the contrivances for unravelling the web.

§ 2. In thus attempting to ascertain the general order of nature by ascertaining the particular order of the occurrence of each one of the phenomena of nature, the most scientific proceeding can be no more than an improved form of that which was primitively pursued by the human understanding, while undirected by science. When mankind first formed the idea of studying phenomena according to a stricter and surer method than that which they had in the first instance spontaneously adopted, they did not, conformably to the well meant but impracticable precept of Descartes, set out from the supposition that nothing had been already ascertained. Many of the uniformities existing among phenomena are so constant, and so open to observation, as to force themselves upon involuntary recognition. Some facts are so perpetually and familiarly accompanied by certain others, that mankind learnt, as children learn, to expect the one where they found the other, long before they knew how to put their expectation into words by asserting, in a proposition, the existence of a connexion between those phenomena. No science was needed to teach that food nourishes, that water drowns, or quenches thirst, that the sun gives light and heat, that bodies fall to the ground. The first scientific inquirers assumed these and the like as known truths, and set out from them to discover others which were unknown: nor were they wrong in so doing, subject, however, as they afterwards began to see, to an ulterior revision of these spontaneous generalizations themselves, when the progress of knowledge pointed out limits to them, or showed their truth to be contingent on some other circumstance not originally attended to. It will appear, I think, from the subsequent part of our inquiry, that there is no logical fallacy in this mode of proceeding; but we may see already that any other mode is rigorously impracticable: since it is impossible to frame any scientific method of induction, or test of the correctness of inductions, unless on the hypothesis that some inductions deserving of reliance have been already made.

Let us revert, for instance, to one of our former illustrations, and consider why it is that, with exactly the same amount of evidence, both negative and positive, we did not reject the assertion that there are black swans, while we should refuse credence to any testimony which asserted that there were men wearing their heads underneath their shoulders. The first assertion was more credible than the latter. But why more credible? So long as neither phenomenon had been actually witnessed, what reason was there for finding the one harder to be believed than the other? Apparently, because there is less constancy in the colours of animals, than in the general structure of their internal anatomy. But how do we know this? Doubtless, from experience. It appears, then, that we need experience to inform us, in what degree, and in what cases, or sorts of cases, experience is to be relied on. Experience must be consulted in order to learn from it under what circumstances arguments from it will be valid. We have no ulterior test to which we subject experience in general; but we make experience its own test. Experience testifies, that among the uniformities which it exhibits or seems to exhibit, some are more to be relied on than others; and uniformity, therefore, may be presumed, from any given number of instances, with a greater degree of assurance, in proportion as the case belongs to a class in which the uniformities have hitherto been found more uniform.

This mode of correcting one generalization by means of another, a narrower generalization by a wider, which common sense suggests and adopts in practice, is the real type of scientific Induction. All that art can do is but to give accuracy and precision to this process, and adapt it to all varieties of cases, without any essential alteration in its principle.

There are of course no means of applying such a test as that above described, unless we already possess a general knowledge of the prevalent character of the uniformities existing throughout nature. The indispensable foundation, therefore, of a scientific formula of induction, must be a survey of the inductions to which mankind have been conducted in unscientific practice; with the special purpose of ascertaining what kinds of uniformities have been found perfectly invariable, pervading all nature, and what are those which have been found to vary with difference of time, place, or other changeable circumstances.

§ 3. The necessity of such a survey is confirmed by the consideration, that the stronger inductions are the touchstone to which we always endeavour to bring the weaker. If we find any means of deducing one of the less strong inductions from stronger ones, it acquires, at once, all the strength of those from which it is deduced; and even adds to that strength; since the independent experience on which the weaker induction previously rested, becomes additional evidence of the truth of the better established law in which it is now found to be included. We may have inferred, from historical evidence, that the uncontrolled power of a monarch, of an aristocracy, or of the majority, will often be abused: but we are entitled to rely on this generalization with much greater assurance when it is shown to be a corollary from still better established facts; the very low degree of elevation of character ever yet attained by the average of mankind, and the little efficacy, for the most part, of the modes of education hitherto practised, in maintaining the predominance of reason and conscience over the selfish propensities. It is at the same time obvious that even these more general facts derive an accession of evidence from the testimony which history bears to the effects of despotism. The strong induction becomes still stronger when a weaker one has been bound up with it.

On the other hand, if an induction conflicts with stronger inductions, or with conclusions capable of being correctly deduced from them, then, unless on re-consideration it should appear that some of the stronger inductions have been expressed with greater universality than their evidence warrants, the weaker one must give way. The opinion so long prevalent that a comet, or any other unusual appearance in the heavenly regions, was the precursor of calamities to mankind, or to those at least who witnessed it; the belief in the veracity of the oracles of Delphi or Dodona; the reliance on astrology, or on the weather-prophecies in almanacs; were doubtless inductions supposed to be grounded on experience:(64) and faith in such delusions seems quite capable of holding out against a great multitude of failures, provided it be nourished by a reasonable number of casual coincidences between the prediction and the event. What has really put an end to these insufficient inductions, is their inconsistency with the stronger inductions subsequently obtained by scientific inquiry, respecting the causes on which terrestrial events really depend; and where those scientific truths have not yet penetrated, the same or similar delusions still prevail.

It may be affirmed as a general principle, that all inductions, whether strong or weak, which can be connected by a ratiocination, are confirmatory of one another: while any which lead deductively to consequences that are incompatible, become mutually each other's test, showing that one or other must be given up, or at least, more guardedly expressed. In the case of inductions which confirm each other, the one which becomes a conclusion from ratiocination rises to at least the level of certainty of the weakest of those from which it is deduced; while in general all are more or less increased in certainty. Thus the Torricellian experiment, though a mere case of three more general laws, not only strengthened greatly the evidence on which those laws rested, but converted one of them (the weight of the atmosphere) from a doubtful generalization into one of the best-established doctrines in the range of physical science.

If, then, a survey of the uniformities which have been ascertained to exist in nature, should point out some which, as far as any human purpose requires certainty, may be considered as quite certain and quite universal; then by means of these uniformities, we may be able to raise multitudes of other inductions to the same point in the scale. For if we can show, with respect to any induction, that either it must be true, or one of these certain and universal inductions must admit of an exception; the former generalization will attain the same certainty, and indefeasibleness within the bounds assigned to it, which are the attributes of the latter. It will be proved to be a law; and if not a result of other and simpler laws, it will be a law of nature.

There are such certain and universal inductions; and it is because there are such, that a Logic of Induction is possible.

CHAPTER V. OF THE LAW OF UNIVERSAL CAUSATION.

§ 1. The phenomena of nature exist in two distinct relations to one another; that of simultaneity, and that of succession. Every phenomenon is related, in an uniform manner, to some phenomena that coexist with it, and to some that have preceded or will follow it.

Of the uniformities which exist among synchronous phenomena, the most important, on every account, are the laws of number; and next to them those of space, or in other words, of extension and figure. The laws of number are common to synchronous and successive phenomena. That two and two make four, is equally true whether the second two follow the first two or accompany them. It is as true of days and years as of feet and inches. The laws of extension and figure, (in other words, the theorems of geometry, from its lowest to its highest branches,) are, on the contrary, laws of simultaneous phenomena only. The various parts of space, and of the objects which are said to fill space, coexist; and the unvarying laws which are the subject of the science of geometry, are an expression of the mode of their coexistence.

This is a class of laws, or in other words, of uniformities, for the comprehension and proof of which it is not necessary to suppose any lapse of time, any variety of facts or events succeeding one another. If all the objects in the universe were unchangeably fixed, and had remained in that condition from eternity, the propositions of geometry would still be true of those objects. All things which possess extension, or in other words, which fill space, are subject to geometrical laws. Possessing extension, they possess figure; possessing figure, they must possess some figure in particular, and have all the properties which geometry assigns to that figure. If one body be a sphere and another a cylinder, of equal height and diameter, the one will be exactly two-thirds of the other, let the nature and quality of the material be what it will. Again, each body, and each point of a body, must occupy some place or position among other bodies; and the position of two bodies relatively to each other, of whatever nature the bodies be, may be unerringly inferred from the position of each of them relatively to any third body.

In the laws of number, then, and in those of space, we recognise, in the most unqualified manner, the rigorous universality of which we are in quest. Those laws have been in all ages the type of certainty, the standard of comparison for all inferior degrees of evidence. Their invariability is so perfect, that we are unable even to conceive any exception to them; and philosophers have been led, although (as I have endeavoured to show) erroneously, to consider their evidence as lying not in experience, but in the original constitution of the intellect. If, therefore, from the laws of space and number, we were able to deduce uniformities of any other description, this would be conclusive evidence to us that those other uniformities possessed the same degree of rigorous certainty. But this we cannot do. From laws of space and number alone, nothing can be deduced but laws of space and number.

Of all truths relating to phenomena, the most valuable to us are those which relate to the order of their succession. On a knowledge of these is founded every reasonable anticipation of future facts, and whatever power we possess of influencing those facts to our advantage. Even the laws of geometry are chiefly of practical importance to us as being a portion of the premises from which the order of the succession of phenomena may be inferred. Inasmuch as the motion of bodies, the action of forces, and the propagation of influences of all sorts, take place in certain lines and over definite spaces, the properties of those lines and spaces are an important part of the laws to which those phenomena are themselves subject. Again, motions, forces or other influences, and times, are numerable quantities; and the properties of number are applicable to them as to all other things. But though the laws of number and space are important elements in the ascertainment of uniformities of succession, they can do nothing towards it when taken by themselves. They can only be made instrumental to that purpose when we combine with them additional premises, expressive of uniformities of succession already known. By taking, for instance, as premises these propositions, that bodies acted upon by an instantaneous force move with uniform velocity in straight lines; that bodies acted upon by a continuous force move with accelerated velocity in straight lines; and that bodies acted upon by two forces in different directions move in the diagonal of a parallelogram, whose sides represent the direction and quantity of those forces; we may by combining these truths with propositions relating to the properties of straight lines and of parallelograms, (as that a triangle is half of a parallelogram of the same base and altitude,) deduce another important uniformity of succession, viz. that a body moving round a centre of force describes areas proportional to the times. But unless there had been laws of succession in our premises, there could have been no truths of succession in our conclusions. A similar remark might be extended to every other class of phenomena really peculiar; and, had it been attended to, would have prevented many chimerical attempts at demonstrations of the indemonstrable, and explanations which do not explain.

It is not, therefore, enough for us that the laws of space, which are only laws of simultaneous phenomena, and the laws of number, which though true of successive phenomena do not relate to their succession, possess the rigorous certainty and universality of which we are in search. We must endeavour to find some law of succession which has those same attributes, and is therefore fit to be made the foundation of processes for discovering, and of a test for verifying, all other uniformities of succession. This fundamental law must resemble the truths of geometry in their most remarkable peculiarity, that of never being, in any instance whatever, defeated or suspended by any change of circumstances.

Now among all those uniformities in the succession of phenomena, which common observation is sufficient to bring to light, there are very few which have any, even apparent, pretension to this rigorous indefeasibility: and of those few, one only has been found capable of completely sustaining it. In that one, however, we recognise a law which is universal also in another sense; it is coextensive with the entire field of successive phenomena, all instances whatever of succession being examples of it. This law is the Law of Causation. The truth, that every fact which has a beginning has a cause, is coextensive with human experience.

This generalization may appear to some minds not to amount to much, since after all it asserts only this: "it is a law, that every event depends on some law." We must not, however, conclude that the generality of the principle is merely verbal; it will be found on inspection to be no vague or unmeaning assertion, but a most important and really fundamental truth.

§ 2. The notion of Cause being the root of the whole theory of Induction, it is indispensable that this idea should, at the very outset of our inquiry, be, with the utmost practicable degree of precision, fixed and determined. If, indeed, it were necessary for the purpose of inductive logic that the strife should be quelled, which has so long raged among the different schools of metaphysicians, respecting the origin and analysis of our idea of causation; the promulgation, or at least the general reception, of a true theory of induction, might be considered desperate, for a long time to come. But the science of the Investigation of Truth by means of Evidence, is happily independent of many of the controversies which perplex the science of the ultimate constitution of the human mind, and is under no necessity of pushing the analysis of mental phenomena to that extreme limit which alone ought to satisfy a metaphysician.

I premise, then, that when in the course of this inquiry I speak of the cause of any phenomenon, I do not mean a cause which is not itself a phenomenon; I make no research into the ultimate, or ontological cause of anything. To adopt a distinction familiar in the writings of the Scotch metaphysicians, and especially of Reid, the causes with which I concern myself are not ***efficient***, but ***physical*** causes. They are causes in that sense alone, in which one physical fact is said to be the cause of another. Of the efficient causes of phenomena, or whether any such causes exist at all, I am not called upon to give an opinion. The notion of causation is deemed, by the schools of metaphysics most in vogue at the present moment, to imply a mysterious and most powerful tie, such as cannot, or at least does not, exist between any physical fact and that other physical fact on which it is invariably consequent, and which is popularly termed its cause: and thence is deduced the supposed necessity of ascending higher, into the essences and inherent constitution of things, to find the true cause, the cause which is not only followed by, but actually ***produces***, the effect. No such necessity exists for the purposes of the present inquiry, nor will any such doctrine be found in the following pages. But neither will there be found anything incompatible with it. We are in no way concerned in the question. The only notion of a cause, which the theory of induction requires, is such a notion as can be gained from experience. The Law of Causation, the recognition of which is the main pillar of inductive science, is but the familiar truth, that invariability of succession is found by observation to obtain between every fact in nature and some other fact which has preceded it; independently of all consideration respecting the ultimate mode of production of phenomena, and of every other question regarding the nature of "Things in themselves."

Between the phenomena, then, which exist at any instant, and the phenomena which exist at the succeeding instant, there is an invariable order of succession; and, as we said in speaking of the general uniformity of the course of nature, this web is composed of separate fibres; this collective order is made up of particular sequences, obtaining invariably among the separate parts. To certain facts, certain facts always do, and, as we believe, will continue to, succeed. The invariable antecedent is termed the cause; the invariable consequent, the effect. And the universality of the law of causation consists in this, that every consequent is connected in this manner with some particular antecedent, or set of antecedents. Let the fact be what it may, if it has begun to exist, it was preceded by some fact or facts, with which it is invariably connected. For every event there exists some combination of objects or events, some given concurrence of circumstances, positive and negative, the occurrence of which is always followed by that phenomenon. We may not have found out what this concurrence of circumstances may be; but we never doubt that there is such a one, and that it never occurs without having the phenomenon in question as its effect or consequence. On the universality of this truth depends the possibility of reducing the inductive process to rules. The undoubted assurance we have that there is a law to be found if we only knew how to find it, will be seen presently to be the source from which the canons of the Inductive Logic derive their validity.

§ 3. It is seldom, if ever, between a consequent and a single antecedent, that this invariable sequence subsists. It is usually between a consequent and the sum of several antecedents; the concurrence of all of them being requisite to produce, that is, to be certain of being followed by, the consequent. In such cases it is very common to single out one only of the antecedents under the denomination of Cause, calling the others merely Conditions. Thus, if a person eats of a particular dish, and dies in consequence, that is, would not have died if he had not eaten of it, people would be apt to say that eating of that dish was the cause of his death. There needs not, however, be any invariable connexion between eating of the dish and death; but there certainly is, among the circumstances which took place, some combination or other on which death is invariably consequent: as, for instance, the act of eating of the dish, combined with a particular bodily constitution, a particular state of present health, and perhaps even a certain state of the atmosphere; the whole of which circumstances perhaps constituted in this particular case the **conditions** of the phenomenon, or in other words, the set of antecedents which determined it, and but for which it would not have happened. The real Cause, is the whole of these antecedents; and we have, philosophically speaking, no right to give the name of cause to one of them, exclusively of the others. What, in the case we have supposed, disguises the incorrectness of the expression, is this: that the various conditions, except the single one of eating the food, were not **events** (that is, instantaneous changes, or successions of instantaneous changes) but **states**, possessing more or less of permanency; and might therefore have preceded the effect by an indefinite length of duration, for want of the event which was requisite to complete the required concurrence of conditions: while as soon as that event, eating the food, occurs, no other cause is waited for, but the effect begins immediately to take place: and hence the appearance is presented of a more immediate and close connexion between the effect and that one antecedent, than between the effect and the remaining conditions. But though we may think proper to give the name of cause to that one condition, the fulfilment of which completes the tale, and brings about the effect without further delay; this condition has really no closer relation to the effect than any of the other conditions has. The production of the consequent required that they should all *exist* immediately previous, though not that they should all *begin* to exist immediately previous. The statement of the cause is incomplete, unless in some shape or other we introduce all the conditions. A man takes mercury, goes out of doors, and catches cold. We say, perhaps, that the cause of his taking cold was exposure to the air. It is clear, however, that his having taken mercury may have been a necessary condition of his catching cold; and though it might consist with usage to say that the cause of his attack was exposure to the air, to be accurate we ought to say that the cause was exposure to the air while under the effect of mercury.

If we do not, when aiming at accuracy, enumerate all the conditions, it is only because some of them will in most cases be understood without being expressed, or because for the purpose in view they may without detriment be overlooked. For example, when we say, the cause of a man's death was that his foot slipped in climbing a ladder, we omit as a thing unnecessary to be stated the circumstance of his weight, though quite as indispensable a condition of the effect which took place. When we say that the assent of the crown to a bill makes it law, we mean that the assent, being never given until all the other conditions are fulfilled, makes up the sum of the conditions, though no one now regards it as the principal one. When the decision of a legislative assembly has been determined by the casting vote of the chairman, we sometimes say that this one person was the cause of all the effects which resulted from the enactment. Yet we do not really suppose that his single vote contributed more to the result than that of any other person who voted in the affirmative; but, for the purpose we have in view, which is to insist on his share of the responsibility, the part which any other person had in the transaction is not material.

In all these instances the fact which was dignified by the name of cause, was the one condition which came last into existence. But it must not be supposed that in the employment of the term this or any other rule is always adhered to. Nothing can better shew the absence of any scientific ground for the distinction between the cause of a phenomenon and its conditions, than the capricious manner in which we select from among the conditions that which we choose to denominate the cause.

However numerous the conditions may be, there is hardly any of them which may not, according to the purpose of our immediate discourse, obtain that nominal pre-eminence. This will be seen by analysing the conditions of some one familiar phenomenon. For example, a stone thrown into water falls to the bottom. What are the conditions of this event? In the first place there must be a stone, and water, and the stone must be thrown into the water; but, these suppositions forming part of the enunciation of the phenomenon itself, to include them also among the conditions would be a vicious tautology, and this class of conditions, therefore, have never received the name of cause from any but the schoolmen, by whom they were called the *material* cause, *causa materialis*. The next condition is, there must be an earth: and accordingly it is often said, that the fall of a stone is caused by the earth; or by a power or property of the earth, or a force exerted by the earth, all of which are merely roundabout ways of saying that it is caused by the earth; or, lastly, the earth's attraction; which also is only a technical mode of saying that the earth causes the motion, with the additional particularity that the motion is *towards* the earth, which is not a character of the cause, but of the effect. Let us now pass to another condition. It is not enough that the earth should exist; the body must be within that distance from it, in which the earth's attraction preponderates over that of any other body. Accordingly we may say, and the expression would be confessedly correct, that the cause of the stone's falling is its being *within the sphere* of the earth's attraction. We proceed to a further condition. The stone is immersed in water: it is therefore a condition of its reaching the ground, that its specific gravity exceed that of the surrounding fluid, or in other words that it surpass in weight an equal volume of water. Accordingly any one would be acknowledged to speak correctly who said, that the cause of the stone's going to the bottom is its exceeding in specific gravity the fluid in which it is immersed.

Thus we see that each and every condition of the phenomenon may be taken in its turn, and, with equal propriety in common parlance, but with equal impropriety in scientific discourse, may be spoken of as if it were the entire cause. And in practice that particular condition is usually styled the cause, whose share in the matter is superficially the most conspicuous or whose requisiteness to the production of the effect we happen to be insisting on at the moment. So great is the force of this last consideration, that it sometimes induces us to give the name of cause even to one of the negative conditions. We say, for example, The army was surprised because the sentinel was off his post. But since the sentinel's absence was not what created the enemy, or put the soldiers asleep, how did it cause them to be surprised? All that is really meant is, that the event would not have happened if he had been at his duty. His being off his post was no producing cause, but the mere absence of a preventing cause: it was simply equivalent to his non-existence. From nothing, from a mere negation, no consequences can proceed. All effects are connected, by the law of causation, with some set of *positive* conditions; negative ones, it is true, being almost always required in addition. In other words, every fact or phenomenon which has a beginning, invariably arises when some certain combination of positive facts exists, provided certain other positive facts do not exist.

There is, no doubt, a tendency (which our first example, that of death from taking a particular food, sufficiently illustrates) to associate the idea of causation with the proximate antecedent *event*, rather than with any of the antecedent *states*, or permanent facts, which may happen also to be conditions of the phenomenon; the reason being that the event not only exists, but begins to exist, immediately previous; while the other conditions may have preexisted for an indefinite time. And this tendency shows itself very visibly in the different logical fictions which are resorted to, even by men of science, to avoid the necessity of giving the name of cause to anything which had existed for an indeterminate length of time before the effect. Thus, rather than say that the earth causes the fall of bodies, they ascribe it to a *force* exerted by the earth, or an *attraction* by the earth, abstractions which they can represent to themselves as exhausted by each effort, and therefore constituting at each successive instant a fresh fact, simultaneous with, or only immediately preceding, the effect. Inasmuch as the coming of the circumstance which completes the assemblage of conditions, is a change or event, it thence happens that an event is always the antecedent in closest apparent proximity to the consequent: and this may account for the illusion which disposes us to look upon the proximate event as standing more peculiarly in the position of a cause than any of the antecedent states. But even this peculiarity, of being in closer proximity to the effect than any other of its conditions, is, as we have already seen, far from being necessary to the common notion of a cause; with which notion, on the contrary, any one of the conditions, either positive or negative, is found, on occasion, completely to accord.(65)

The cause, then, philosophically speaking, is the sum total of the conditions, positive and negative taken together; the whole of the contingencies of every description, which being realized, the consequent invariably follows. The negative conditions, however, of any phenomenon, a special enumeration of which would generally be very prolix, may be all summed up under one head, namely, the absence of preventing or counteracting causes. The convenience of this mode of expression is mainly grounded on the fact, that the effects of any cause in counteracting another cause may in most cases be, with strict scientific exactness, regarded as a mere extension of its own proper and separate effects. If gravity retards the upward motion of a projectile, and deflects it into a parabolic trajectory, it produces, in so doing, the very same kind of effect, and even (as mathematicians know) the same quantity of effect, as it does in its ordinary operation of causing the fall of bodies when simply deprived of their support. If an alkaline solution mixed with an acid destroys its sourness, and prevents it from reddening vegetable blues, it is because the specific effect of the alkali is to combine with the acid, and form a compound with totally different qualities. This property, which causes of all descriptions possess, of preventing the effects of other causes by virtue (for the most part) of the same laws according to which they produce their own,(66) enables us, by establishing the general axiom that all causes are liable to be counteracted in their effects by one another, to dispense with the consideration of negative conditions entirely, and limit the notion of cause to the assemblage of the positive conditions of the phenomenon: one negative condition invariably understood, and the same in all instances (namely, the absence of all counteracting causes) being sufficient, along with the sum of the positive conditions, to make up the whole set of circumstances on which the phenomenon is dependent.

§ 4. Among the positive conditions, as we have seen that there are some to which, in common parlance, the term cause is more readily and frequently awarded, so there are others to which it is, in ordinary circumstances, refused. In most cases of causation a distinction is commonly drawn between something which acts, and some other thing which is acted upon; between an **agent** and a **patient**. Both of these, it would be universally allowed, are conditions of the phenomenon; but it would be thought absurd to call the latter the cause, that title being reserved for the former. The distinction, however, vanishes on examination, or rather is found to be only verbal; arising from an incident of mere expression, namely, that the object said to be ***acted upon***, and which is considered as the scene in which the effect takes place, is commonly included in the phrase by which the effect is spoken of, so that if it were also reckoned as part of the cause, the seeming incongruity would arise of its being supposed to cause itself. In the instance which we have already had, of falling bodies, the question was thus put:--What is the cause which makes a stone fall? and if the answer had been "the stone itself," the expression would have been in apparent contradiction to the meaning of the word cause. The stone, therefore, is conceived as the patient, and the earth (or, according to the common and most unphilosophical practice, some occult quality of the earth) is represented as the agent, or cause. But that there is nothing fundamental in the distinction may be seen from this, that it is quite possible to conceive the stone as causing its own fall, provided the language employed be such as to save the mere verbal incongruity. We might say that the stone moves towards the earth by the properties of the matter composing it; and according to this mode of presenting the phenomenon, the stone itself might without impropriety be called the agent; although, to save the established doctrine of the inactivity of matter, men usually prefer here also to ascribe the effect to an occult quality, and say that the cause is not the stone itself, but the ***weight*** or ***gravitation*** of the stone.

Those who have contended for a radical distinction between agent and patient, have generally conceived the agent as that which causes some state of, or some change in the state of, another object which is called the patient. But a little reflection will show that the licence we assume of speaking of phenomena as ***states*** of the various objects which take part in them, (an artifice of which so much use has been made by some philosophers, Brown in particular, for the apparent explanation of phenomena,) is simply a sort of logical fiction, useful sometimes as one among several modes of expression, but which should never be supposed to be the statement of a scientific truth. Even those attributes of an object which might seem with greatest propriety to be called states of the object itself, its sensible qualities, its colour, hardness, shape, and the like, are, in reality, (as no one has pointed out more clearly than Brown himself,) phenomena of causation, in which the substance is distinctly the agent, or producing cause, the patient being our own organs, and those of other sentient beings. What we call states of objects, are always sequences into which those the objects enter, generally as antecedents or causes; and things are never more active than in the production of those phenomena in which they are said to be acted upon. Thus, in the example of a stone falling to the earth, according to the theory of gravitation the stone is as much an agent as the earth, which not only attracts, but is itself attracted by, the stone. In the case of a sensation produced in our organs, the laws of our organization, and even those of our minds, are as directly operative in determining the effect produced, as the laws of the outward object. Though we call prussic acid the agent of a person's death, the whole of the vital and organic properties of the patient are as actively instrumental as the poison, in the chain of effects which so rapidly terminates his sentient existence. In the process of education, we may call the teacher the agent, and the scholar only the material acted upon; yet in truth all the facts which pre-existed in the scholar's mind exert either co-operating or counteracting agencies in relation to the teacher's efforts. It is not light alone which is the agent in vision, but light coupled with the active properties of the eye and brain, and with those of the visible object. The distinction between agent and patient is merely verbal: patients are always agents; in a great proportion, indeed, of all natural phenomena, they are so to such a degree as to react forcibly upon the causes which acted upon them: and even when this is not the case, they contribute, in the same manner as any of the other conditions, to the production of the effect of which they are vulgarly treated as the mere theatre. All the positive conditions of a phenomenon are alike agents, alike active; and in any expression of the cause which professes to be a complete one, none of them can with reason be excluded, except such as have already been implied in the words used for describing the effect; nor by including even these would there be incurred any but a merely verbal inconsistency.

§ 5. It now remains to advert to a distinction which is of first-rate importance both for clearing up the notion of cause, and for obviating a very specious objection often made against the view which we have taken of the subject.

When we define the cause of anything (in the only sense in which the present inquiry has any concern with causes) to be "the antecedent which it invariably follows," we do not use this phrase as exactly synonymous with "the antecedent which it invariably *has* followed in our past experience." Such a mode of conceiving causation would be liable to the objection very plausibly urged by Dr. Reid, namely, that according to this doctrine night must be the cause of day, and day the cause of night; since these phenomena have invariably succeeded one another from the beginning of the world. But it is necessary to our using the word cause, that we should believe not only that the antecedent always *has* been followed by the consequent, but that, as long as the present constitution of things endures, it always *will* be so. And this would not be true of day and night. We do not believe that night will be followed by day under all imaginable circumstances, but only that it will be so *provided* the sun rises above the horizon. If the sun ceased to rise, which, for aught we know, may be perfectly compatible with the general laws of matter, night would be, or might be, eternal. On the other hand, if the sun is above the horizon, his light not extinct, and no opaque body between us and him, we believe firmly that unless a change takes place in the properties of matter, this combination of antecedents will be followed by the consequent, day; that if the combination of antecedents could be indefinitely prolonged, it would be always day; and that if the same combination had always existed, it would always have been day, quite independently of night as a previous condition. Therefore is it that we do not call night the cause, nor even a condition, of day. The existence of the sun (or some such luminous body), and there being no opaque medium in a straight line(67) between that body and the part of the earth where we are situated, are the sole conditions; and the union of these, without the addition of any superfluous circumstance, constitutes the cause. This is what writers mean when they say that the notion of cause involves the idea of necessity. If there be any meaning which confessedly belongs to the term necessity, it is *unconditionalness*. That which is necessary, that which *must* be, means that which will be, whatever supposition we may make in regard to all other things. The succession of day and night evidently is not necessary in this sense. It is conditional on the occurrence of other antecedents. That which will be followed by a given consequent when, and only when, some third circumstance also exists, is not the cause, even though no case should have ever occurred in which the phenomenon took place without it.

Invariable sequence, therefore, is not synonymous with causation, unless the sequence, besides being invariable, is unconditional. There are sequences, as uniform in past experience as any others whatever, which yet we do not regard as cases of causation, but as conjunctions in some sort accidental. Such, to an accurate thinker, is that of day and night. The one might have existed for any length of time, and the other not have followed the sooner for its existence; it follows only if certain other antecedents exist; and where those antecedents existed, it would follow in any case. No one, probably, ever called night the cause of day; mankind must so soon have arrived at the very obvious generalization, that the state of general illumination which we call day would follow the presence of a sufficiently luminous body, whether darkness had preceded or not.

We may define, therefore, the cause of a phenomenon, to be the antecedent, or the concurrence of antecedents, on which it is invariably and ***unconditionally*** consequent. Or if we adopt the convenient modification of the meaning of the word cause, which confines it to the assemblage of positive conditions without the negative, then instead of "unconditionally," we must say, "subject to no other than negative conditions."

It is evident, that from a limited number of unconditional sequences, there will result a much greater number of conditional ones. Certain causes being given, that is, certain antecedents which are unconditionally followed by certain consequents; the mere coexistence of these causes will give rise to an unlimited number of additional uniformities. If two causes exist together, the effects of both will exist together; and if many causes coexist, these causes (by what we shall term hereafter the intermixture of their laws) will give rise to new effects, accompanying or succeeding one another in some particular order, which order will be invariable while the causes continue to coexist, but no longer. The motion of the earth in a given orbit round the sun, is a series of changes which follow one another as antecedents and consequents, and will continue to do so while the sun's attraction, and the force with which the earth tends to advance in a direct line through space, continue to coexist in the same quantities as at present. But vary either of these causes, and the unvarying succession of motions would cease to take place. The series of the earth's motions, therefore, though a case of sequence invariable within the limits of human experience, is not a case of causation. It is not unconditional.

This distinction between the relations of succession which so far as we know are unconditional, and those relations, whether of succession or of coexistence, which, like the earth's motions, or the succession of day and night, depend on the existence or on the coexistence of other antecedent facts--corresponds to the great division which Dr. Whewell and other writers have made of the field of science, into the investigation of what they term the Laws of Phenomena, and the investigation of causes; a phraseology, as I conceive, not philosophically sustainable, inasmuch as the ascertainment of causes, such causes as the human faculties *can* ascertain, namely, causes which are themselves phenomena, is, therefore, merely the ascertainment of other and more universal Laws of Phenomena. Yet the distinction, however incorrectly expressed, is not only real, but is one of the fundamental distinctions in science; indeed it is on this alone, as we shall hereafter find, that the possibility rests of framing a rigorous Canon of Induction.

§ 6. Does a cause always stand with its effect in the relation of antecedent and consequent? Do we not often say of two simultaneous facts that they are cause and effect--as when we say that fire is the cause of warmth, the sun and moisture the cause of vegetation, and the like? Since a cause does not necessarily perish because its effect has been produced, the two things do very generally coexist; and there are some appearances, and some common expressions, seeming to imply not only that causes may, but that they must, be contemporaneous with their effects. ***Cessante causa cessat et effectus***, has been a dogma of the schools: the necessity for the continued existence of the cause in order to the continuance of the effect, seems to have been once a generally received doctrine. Kepler's numerous attempts to account for the motions of the heavenly bodies on mechanical principles, were rendered abortive by his always supposing that the force which set those bodies in motion must continue to operate in order to keep up the motion which it at first produced. Yet there were at all times many familiar instances of the continuance of effects, long after their causes had ceased. A ***coup de soleil*** gives a person a brain fever: will the fever go off as soon as he is moved out of the sunshine? A sword is run through his body: must the sword remain in his body in order that he may continue dead? A ploughshare once made, remains a ploughshare, without any continuance of heating and hammering, and even after the man who heated and hammered it has been gathered to his fathers. On the other hand, the pressure which forces up the mercury in an exhausted tube must be continued in order to sustain it in the tube. This (it may be replied) is because another force is acting without intermission, the force of gravity, which would restore it to its level, unless counterpoised by a force equally constant. But again; a tight bandage causes pain, which pain will sometimes go off as soon as the bandage is removed. The illumination which the sun diffuses over the earth ceases when the sun goes down.

There is, therefore, a distinction to be drawn. The conditions which are necessary for the first production of a phenomenon, are occasionally also necessary for its continuance; but more commonly its continuance requires no condition except negative ones. Most things, once produced, continue as they are, until something changes or destroys them; but some require the permanent presence of the agencies which produced them at first. These may, if we please, be considered as instantaneous phenomena, requiring to be renewed at each instant by the cause by which they were at first generated. Accordingly, the illumination of any given point of space has always been looked upon as an instantaneous fact, which perishes and is perpetually renewed as long as the necessary conditions subsist. If we adopt this language we avoid the necessity of admitting that the continuance of the cause is ever required to maintain the effect. We may say, it is not required to maintain, but to reproduce the effect, or else to counteract some force tending to destroy it. And this may be a convenient phraseology. But it is only a phraseology. The fact remains, that in some cases (though these are a minority) the continuance of the conditions which produced an effect is necessary to the continuance of the effect.

As to the ulterior question, whether it is strictly necessary that the cause, or assemblage of conditions, should precede, by ever so short an instant, the production of the effect, (a question raised and argued with much ingenuity by a writer from whom I have quoted,(68)) I think the inquiry an unimportant one. There certainly are cases in which the effect follows without any interval perceptible by our faculties; and when there is an interval, we cannot tell by how many intermediate links imperceptible to us that interval may really be filled up. But even granting that an effect may commence simultaneously with its cause, the view I have taken of causation is in no way practically affected. Whether the cause and its effect be necessarily successive or not, causation is still the law of the succession of phenomena. Everything which begins to exist must have a cause; what does not begin to exist does not need a cause; what causation has to account for is the origin of phenomena, and all the successions of phenomena must be resolvable into causation. These are the axioms of our doctrine. If these be granted, we can afford, though I see no necessity for doing so, to drop the words antecedent and consequent as applied to cause and effect. I have no objection to define a cause, the assemblage of phenomena, which occurring, some other phenomenon invariably commences, or has its origin. Whether the effect coincides in point of time with, or immediately follows, the hindmost of its conditions, is immaterial. At all events it does not precede it; and when we are in doubt, between two coexistent phenomena, which is cause and which effect, we rightly deem the question solved if we can ascertain which of them preceded the other.

§ 7. It continually happens that several different phenomena, which are not in the slightest degree dependent or conditional on one another, are found all to depend, as the phrase is, on one and the same agent; in other words, one and the same phenomenon is seen to be followed by several sorts of effects quite heterogeneous, but which go on simultaneously one with another; provided, of course, that all other conditions requisite for each of them also exist. Thus, the sun produces the celestial motions, it produces daylight, and it produces heat. The earth causes the fall of heavy bodies, and it also, in its capacity of an immense magnet, causes the phenomena of the magnetic needle. A crystal of galena causes the sensations of hardness, of weight, of cubical form, of grey colour, and many others between which we can trace no interdependence. The purpose to which the phraseology of Properties and Powers is specially adapted, is the expression of this sort of cases. When the same phenomenon is followed (either subject or not to the presence of other conditions) by effects of different and dissimilar orders, it is usual to say that each different sort of effect is produced by a different property of the cause. Thus we distinguish the attractive or gravitative property of the earth, and its magnetic property: the gravitative, luminiferous, and calorific properties of the sun: the colour, shape, weight, and hardness of a crystal. These are mere phrases, which explain nothing, and add nothing to our knowledge of the subject; but, considered as abstract names denoting the connexion between the different effects produced and the object which produces them, they are a very powerful instrument of abridgment, and of that acceleration of the process of thought which abridgment accomplishes.

This class of considerations leads to a conception which we shall find to be of great importance, that of a Permanent Cause, or original natural agent. There exist in nature a number of permanent causes, which have subsisted ever since the human race has been in existence, and for an indefinite and probably an enormous length of time previous. The sun, the earth, and planets, with their various constituents, air, water, and the other distinguishable substances, whether simple or compound, of which nature is made up, are such Permanent Causes. These have existed, and the effects or consequences which they were fitted to produce have taken place, (as often as the other conditions of the production met,) from the very beginning of our experience. But we can give no account of the origin of the Permanent Causes themselves. Why these particular natural agents existed originally and no others, or why they are commingled in such and such proportions, and distributed in such and such a manner throughout space, is a question we cannot answer. More than this: we can discover nothing regular in the distribution itself; we can reduce it to no uniformity, to no law. There are no means by which, from the distribution of these causes or agents in one part of space, we could conjecture whether a similar distribution prevails in another. The coexistence, therefore, of Primeval Causes, ranks, to us, among merely casual concurrences: and all those sequences or coexistences among the effects of several such causes, which, though invariable while those causes coexist, would, if the coexistence terminated, terminate along with it, we do not class as cases of causation, or laws of nature: we can only calculate on finding these sequences or coexistences where we know by direct evidence, that the natural agents on the properties of which they ultimately depend, are distributed in the requisite manner. These Permanent Causes are not always objects; they are sometimes events, that is to say, periodical cycles of events, that being the only mode in which events can possess the property of permanence. Not only, for instance, is the earth itself a permanent cause, or primitive natural agent, but the earth's rotation is so too: it is a cause which has produced, from the earliest period, (by the aid of other necessary conditions,) the succession of day and night, the ebb and flow of the sea, and many other effects, while, as we can assign no cause (except conjecturally) for the rotation itself, it is entitled to be ranked as a primeval cause. It is, however, only the ***origin*** of the rotation which is mysterious to us: once begun, its continuance is accounted for by the first law of motion (that of the permanence of rectilinear motion once impressed) combined with the gravitation of the parts of the earth towards one another.

All phenomena without exception which begin to exist, that is, all except the primeval causes, are effects either immediate or remote of those primitive facts, or of some combination of them. There is no Thing produced, no event happening, in the known universe, which is not connected by an uniformity, or invariable sequence, with some one or more of the phenomena which preceded it; insomuch that it will happen again as often as those phenomena occur again, and as no other phenomenon having the character of a counteracting cause shall coexist. These antecedent phenomena, again, were connected in a similar manner with some that preceded them; and so on, until we reach, as the ultimate step attainable by us, either the properties of some one primeval cause, or the conjunction of several. The whole of the phenomena of nature were therefore the necessary, or in other words, the unconditional, consequences of some former collocation of the Permanent Causes.

The state of the whole universe at any instant, we believe to be the consequence of its state at the previous instant; insomuch that one who knew all the agents which exist at the present moment, their collocation in space, and their properties, in other words the laws of their agency, could predict the whole subsequent history of the universe, at least unless some new volition of a power capable of controlling the universe should supervene.(69) And if any particular state of the entire universe could ever recur a second time, all subsequent states would return too, and history would, like a circulating decimal of many figures, periodically repeat itself:--

Jam redit et virgo, redeunt Saturnia regna.... Alter erit tum Tiphys, et altera quae vehat Argo Delectos heroas; erunt quoque altera bella, Atque iterum ad Troiam magnus mittetur Achilles.

And though things do not really revolve in this eternal round, the whole series of events in the history of the universe, past and future, is not the less capable, in its own nature, of being constructed *a priori* by any one whom we can suppose acquainted with the original distribution of all natural agents, and with the whole of their properties, that is, the laws of succession existing between them and their effects: saving the more than human powers of combination and calculation which would be required, even in one possessing the data, for the actual performance of the task.

§ 8. Since everything which occurs is determined by laws of causation and collocations of the original causes, it follows that the coexistences which are observable among effects cannot be themselves the subject of any similar set of laws, distinct from laws of causation. Uniformities there are, as well of coexistence as of succession, among effects; but these must in all cases be a mere result either of the identity or of the coexistence of their causes: if the causes did not coexist, neither could the effects. And these causes being also effects of prior causes, and these of others, until we reach the primeval causes, it follows that (except in the case of effects which can be traced immediately or remotely to one and the same cause) the coexistences of phenomena can in no case be universal, unless the coexistences of the primeval causes to which the effects are ultimately traceable, can be reduced to an universal law: but we have seen that they cannot. There are, accordingly, no original and independent, in other words no unconditional, uniformities of coexistence between effects of different causes; if they coexist, it is only because the causes have casually coexisted. The only independent and unconditional coexistences which are sufficiently invariable to have any claim to the character of laws, are between different and mutually independent effects of the same cause; in other words, between different properties of the same natural agent. This portion of the Laws of Nature will be treated of in the latter part of the present Book, under the name of the Specific Properties of Kinds.

§ 9. It is proper in this place to advert to a doctrine at least as old as Dr. Reid, though propounded by him not as certain but as probable; which has been revived during the last few years in several quarters, and at present gives more signs of life than any other theory of causation at variance with that set forth in the preceding pages.

According to the theory in question, Mind, or, to speak more precisely, Will, is the only cause of phenomena. The type of Causation, as well as the exclusive source from which we derive the idea, is our own voluntary agency. Here, and here only (it is said) we have direct evidence of causation. We know that we can move our bodies. Respecting the phenomena of inanimate nature, we have no other direct knowledge than that of antecedence and sequence. But in the case of our voluntary actions, it is affirmed that we are conscious of power, before we have experience of results. An act of volition, whether followed by an effect or not, is accompanied by a consciousness of effort, "of force exerted, of power in action, which is necessarily causal, or causative." This feeling of energy or force, inherent in an act of will, is knowledge *a priori*; assurance, prior to experience, that we have the power of causing effects. Volition, therefore, it is asserted, is something more than an unconditional antecedent; it is a cause, in a different sense from that in which physical phenomena are said to cause one another: it is an Efficient Cause. From this the transition is easy to the further doctrine, that Volition is the *sole* Efficient Cause of all phenomena. "It is inconceivable that dead force could continue unsupported for a moment beyond its creation. We cannot even conceive of change or phenomena without the energy of a mind." "The word *action* itself," says another writer of the same school, "has no real significance except when applied to the doings of an intelligent agent. Let any one conceive, if he can, of any power, energy, or force, inherent in a lump of matter." Phenomena may have the semblance of being produced by physical causes, but they are in reality produced, say these writers, by the immediate agency of mind. All things which do not proceed from a human (or, I suppose, an animal) will, proceed, they say, directly from divine will. The earth is not moved by the combination of a centripetal and a projectile force; this is but a mode of speaking which serves to facilitate our conceptions. It is moved by the direct volition of an omnipotent being, in a path coinciding with that which we deduce from the hypothesis of these two forces.

As I have so often observed, the general question of the existence of Efficient Causes does not fall within the limits of our subject: but a theory which represents them as capable of being subjects of human knowledge, and which passes off as efficient causes what are only physical or phenomenal causes, belongs as much to Logic as to Metaphysics, and is a fit subject for discussion here.

To my apprehension, a volition is not an efficient, but simply a physical, cause. Our will causes our bodily actions in the same sense, and in no other, in which cold causes ice, or a spark causes an explosion of gunpowder. The volition, a state of our mind, is the antecedent; the motion of our limbs in conformity to the volition, is the consequent. This sequence I conceive to be not a subject of direct consciousness, in the sense intended by the theory. The antecedent, indeed, and the consequent, are subjects of consciousness. But the connexion between them is a subject of experience. I cannot admit that our consciousness of the volition contains in itself any *a priori* knowledge that the muscular motion will follow. If our nerves of motion were paralyzed, or our muscles stiff and inflexible, and had been so all our lives, I do not see the slightest ground for supposing that we should ever (unless by information from other people) have known anything of volition as a physical power, or been conscious of any tendency in feelings of our mind to produce motions of our body, or of other bodies. I will not undertake to say whether we should in that case have had the physical feeling which I suppose is meant when these writers speak of "consciousness of effort:" I see no reason why we should not; since that physical feeling is probably a state of nervous sensation beginning and ending in the brain, without involving the motory apparatus; but we certainly should not have designated it by any term equivalent to effort, since effort implies consciously aiming at an end, which we should not only in that case have had no reason to do, but could not even have had the idea of doing. If conscious at all of this peculiar sensation, we should have been conscious of it, I conceive, only as a kind of uneasiness, accompanying our feelings of desire.

Those against whom I am contending have never produced, and do not pretend to produce, any positive evidence(70) that the power of our will to move our bodies would be known to us independently of experience. What they have to say on the subject is, that the production of physical events by a will, seems to carry its own explanation with it, while the action of matter upon matter seems to require something else to explain it; and is even, according to them, "inconceivable" on any other supposition than that some will intervenes between the apparent cause and its apparent effect. They thus rest their case on an appeal to the inherent laws of our conceptive faculty; mistaking, as I apprehend, for the laws of that faculty its acquired habits, grounded on the spontaneous tendencies of its uncultured state. The succession between the will to move a limb and the actual motion, is one of the most direct and instantaneous of all sequences which come under our observation, and is familiar to every moment's experience from our earliest infancy; more familiar than any succession of events exterior to our bodies, and especially more so than any other case of the apparent origination (as distinguished from the mere communication) of motion. Now, it is the natural tendency of the mind to be always attempting to facilitate its conception of unfamiliar facts by assimilating them to others which are familiar. Accordingly, our voluntary acts, being the most familiar to us of all cases of causation, are, in the infancy and early youth of the human race, spontaneously taken as the type of causation in general, and all phenomena are supposed to be directly produced by the will of some sentient being. This original Fetichism I shall not characterize in the words of Hume, or of any follower of

Hume, but in those of a religious metaphysician, Dr. Reid, in order more effectually to shew the unanimity which exists on the subject among all competent thinkers.

"When we turn our attention to external objects, and begin to exercise our rational faculties about them, we find, that there are some motions and changes in them which we have power to produce, and that there are many which must have some other cause. Either the objects must have life and active power, as we have, or they must be moved or changed by something that has life and active power, as external objects are moved by us.

"Our first thoughts seem to be, that the objects in which we perceive such motion have understanding and active power as we have. 'Savages,' says the Abbe Raynal, 'wherever they see motion which they cannot account for, there they suppose a soul.' All men may be considered as savages in this respect, until they are capable of instruction, and of using their faculties in a more perfect manner than savages do."

"The Abbe Raynal's observation is sufficiently confirmed, both from fact, and from the structure of all languages.

"Rude nations do really believe sun, moon, and stars, earth, sea, and air, fountains, and lakes, to have understanding and active power. To pay homage to them, and implore their favour, is a kind of idolatry natural to savages.

"All languages carry in their structure the marks of their being formed when this belief prevailed. The distinction of verbs and participles into active and passive, which is found in all languages, must have been originally intended to distinguish what is really active from what is merely passive; and in all languages, we find active verbs applied to those objects, in which, according to the Abbe Raynal's observation, savages suppose a soul.

"Thus we say the sun rises and sets, and comes to the meridian, the moon changes, the sea ebbs and flows, the winds blow. Languages were formed by men who believed these objects to have life and active power in themselves. It was therefore proper and natural to express their motions and changes by active verbs.

"There is no surer way of tracing the sentiments of nations before they have records, than by the structure of their language, which, notwithstanding the changes produced in it by time, will always retain some signatures of the thoughts of those by whom it was invented. When we find the same sentiments indicated in the structure of all languages, those sentiments must have been common to the human species when languages were invented.

"When a few, of superior intellectual abilities, find leisure for speculation, they begin to philosophize, and soon discover, that many of those objects which at first they believed to be intelligent and active are really lifeless and passive. This is a very important discovery. It elevates the mind, emancipates from many vulgar superstitions, and invites to further discoveries of the same kind.

"As philosophy advances, life and activity in natural objects retires, and leaves them dead and inactive. Instead of moving voluntarily we find them to be moved necessarily; instead of acting, we find them to be acted upon; and Nature appears as one great machine, where one wheel is turned by another, that by a third; and how far this necessary succession may reach, the philosopher does not know."(71)

There is, then, a spontaneous tendency of the intellect to account to itself for all cases of causation by assimilating them to the intentional acts of voluntary agents like itself. This is the instinctive philosophy of the human mind in its earliest stage, before it has become familiar with any other invariable sequences than those between its own volitions and its voluntary acts. As the notion of fixed laws of succession among external phenomena gradually establishes itself, the propensity to refer all phenomena to voluntary agency slowly gives way before it. The suggestions, however, of daily life continuing to be more powerful than those of scientific thought, the original instinctive philosophy maintains its ground in the mind, underneath the growths obtained by cultivation, and keeps up a constant resistance to their throwing their roots deep into the soil. The theory against which I am contending derives its nourishment from that substratum. Its strength does not lie in argument, but in its affinity to an obstinate tendency of the infancy of the human mind.

That this tendency, however, is not the result of an inherent mental law, is proved by superabundant evidence. The history of science, from its earliest dawn, shows that mankind have not been unanimous in thinking either that the action of matter upon matter was **not** conceivable, or that the action of mind upon matter **was**. To some thinkers, and some schools of thinkers, both in ancient and in modern times, this last has appeared much more inconceivable than the former. Sequences entirely physical and material, as soon as they had become sufficiently familiar to the human mind, came to be thought perfectly natural, and were regarded not only as needing no explanation themselves, but as being capable of affording it to others, and even of serving as the ultimate explanation of things in general.

One of the most recent supporters of the Volitional theory has furnished an explanation, at once historically true and philosophically acute, of the failure of the Greek philosophers in physical inquiry, in which, as I conceive, he unconsciously depicts his own state of mind. "Their stumbling-block was one as to the nature of the evidence they had to expect for their conviction.... They had not seized the idea that they must not expect to understand the processes of outward causes, but only their results: and consequently, the whole physical philosophy of the Greeks was an attempt to identify mentally the effect with its cause, to feel after some not only necessary but natural connexion, where they meant by natural that which would *per se* carry some presumption to their own mind.... They wanted to see some *reason* why the physical antecedent should produce this particular consequent, and their only attempts were in directions where they could find such reasons."(72) In other words, they were not content merely to know that one phenomenon was always followed by another; they thought that they had not attained the true aim of science, unless they could perceive something in the nature of the one phenomenon, from which it might have been known or presumed *previous to trial* that it would be followed by the other: just what the writer, who has so clearly pointed out their error, thinks that he perceives in the nature of the phenomenon Volition. And to complete the statement of the case, he should have added that these early speculators not only made this their aim, but were quite satisfied with their success in it; not only sought for causes which should carry in their mere statement evidence of their efficiency, but fully believed that they had found such causes. The reviewer can see plainly that this was an error, because *he* does not believe that there exist any relations between material phenomena which can account for their producing one another: but the very fact of the persistency of the Greeks in this error, shows that their minds were in a very different state: they were able to derive from the assimilation of physical facts to other physical facts, the kind of mental satisfaction which we connect with the word explanation, and which the reviewer would have us think can only be found in referring phenomena to a will. When Thales and Hippo held that moisture was the universal cause, and eternal element, of which all other things were but the infinitely various sensible manifestations; when Anaximenes predicated the same thing of air, Pythagoras of numbers, and the like, they all thought that they had found a real explanation; and were content to rest in this explanation as ultimate. The ordinary sequences of the external universe appeared to them, no less than to their critic, to be inconceivable without the supposition of some universal agency to connect the antecedents with the consequents; but they did not think that Volition, exerted by minds, was the only agency which fulfilled this requirement. Moisture, or air, or numbers, carried to their minds a precisely similar impression of making that intelligible which was otherwise inconceivable, and gave the same full satisfaction to the demands of their conceptive faculty.

It was not the Greeks alone, who "wanted to see some reason why the physical antecedent should produce this particular consequent," some connexion "which would *per se* carry some presumption to their own mind." Among modern philosophers, Leibnitz laid it down as a self-evident principle that all physical causes without exception must contain in their own nature something which makes it intelligible that they should be able to produce the effects which they do produce. Far from admitting Volition as the only kind of cause which carried internal evidence of its own power, and as the real bond of connexion between physical antecedents and their consequents, he demanded some naturally and *per se* efficient physical antecedent as the bond of connexion between Volition itself and its effects. He distinctly refused to admit the will of a God as a sufficient explanation of anything except miracles; and insisted upon finding something that would account **better** for the phenomena of nature than a mere reference to divine volition.(73)

Again, and conversely, the action of mind upon matter (which, we are now told, not only needs no explanation itself, but is the explanation of all other effects), has appeared to some thinkers to be itself the grand inconceivability. It was to get over this very difficulty that the Cartesians invented the system of Occasional Causes. They could not conceive that thoughts in a mind could produce movements in a body, or that bodily movements could produce thoughts. They could see no necessary connexion, no relation *a priori*, between a motion and a thought. And as the Cartesians, more than any other school of philosophical speculation before or since, made their own minds the measure of all things, and refused, on principle, to believe that Nature had done what they were unable to see any reason why she must do, they affirmed it to be impossible that a material and a mental fact could be causes one of another. They regarded them as mere Occasions on which the real agent, God, thought fit to exert his power as a Cause. When a man wills to move his foot, it is not his will that moves it, but God (they said) moves it on the occasion of his will. God, according to this system, is the only efficient cause, not *qua* mind, or *qua* endowed with volition, but *qua* omnipotent. This hypothesis was, as I said, originally suggested by the supposed inconceivability of any real mutual action between Mind and Matter: but it was afterwards extended to the action of Matter upon Matter, for, on a nicer examination they found this inconceivable too, and therefore, according to their logic, impossible. The ***deus ex machina*** was ultimately called in to produce a spark on the occasion of a flint and steel coming together, or to break an egg on the occasion of its falling on the ground.

All this, undoubtedly, shows that it is the disposition of mankind in general, not to be satisfied with knowing that one fact is invariably antecedent and another consequent, but to look out for something which may seem to explain their being so--something ἄνευ οὗ τὸ αἴτιον οὐκ ἄν ποτ' εἴη αἴτιον. But we also see that this demand may be completely satisfied by an agency purely physical, provided it be much more familiar than that which it is invoked to explain. To Thales and Anaximenes, it appeared inconceivable that the antecedents which we see in nature, should produce the consequents; but perfectly natural that water, or air, should produce them. The writers whom I oppose declare this inconceivable, but can conceive that mind, or volition, is ***per se*** an efficient cause: while the Cartesians could not conceive even that, but peremptorily declared that no mode of production of any fact whatever was conceivable, except the direct agency of an omnipotent being. Thus giving additional proof of what finds new confirmation in every stage of the history of science: that both what persons can, and what they cannot, conceive, is very much an affair of accident, and depends altogether on their experience, and their habits of thought; that by cultivating the requisite associations of ideas, people may make themselves unable to conceive any given thing; and may make themselves able to conceive most things, however inconceivable these may at first appear: and the same facts in each person's mental history which determine what is or is not conceivable to him, determine also which among the various sequences in nature will appear to him so natural and plausible, as to need no other proof of their existence; to be evident by their own light, independent equally of experience and of explanation.

By what rule is any one to decide between one theory of this description and another? The theorists do not direct us to any external evidence; they appeal, each to his own subjective feelings. One says, the succession C, B, appears to me more natural, conceivable, and credible *per se* than the succession A, B; you are therefore mistaken in thinking that B depends upon A; I am certain, though I can give no other evidence of it, that C comes in between A and B, and is the real and only cause of B. The other answers--the successions C, B, and A, B, appear to me equally natural and conceivable, or the latter more so than the former: A is quite capable of producing B without any other intervention. A third agrees with the first in being unable to conceive that A can produce B, but finds the sequence D, B, still more natural than C, B, or of nearer kin to the subject matter, and prefers his D theory to the C theory. It is plain that there is no universal law operating here, except the law that each person's conceptions are governed and limited by his individual experience and habits of thought. We are warranted in saying of all three, what each of them already believes of the other two, namely, that they exalt into an original law of the human intellect and of outward nature, one particular sequence of phenomena, which appears to them more natural and more conceivable than other sequences, only because it is more familiar. And from this judgment I am unable to except the theory, that Volition is an Efficient Cause.

I am unwilling to leave the subject without adverting to the additional fallacy contained in the corollary from this theory; in the inference that because Volition is an efficient cause therefore it is the only cause, and the direct agent in producing even what is apparently produced by something else. Volitions are not known to produce anything directly except nervous action, for the will influences even the muscles only through the nerves. Though it were granted, then, that every phenomenon has an efficient, and not merely a phenomenal cause, and that volition, in the case of the peculiar phenomena which are known to be produced by it, is that efficient cause: are we therefore to say, with these writers, that since we know of no other efficient cause, and ought not to assume one without evidence, there *is* no other, and volition is the direct cause of all phenomena? A more outrageous stretch of inference could hardly be made. Because among the infinite variety of the phenomena of nature there is one, namely, a particular mode of action of certain nerves, which has for its cause, and as we are now supposing for its efficient cause, a state of our mind; and because this is the only efficient cause of which we are conscious, being the only one of which in the nature of the case we ***can*** be conscious, since it is the only one which exists within ourselves; does this justify us in concluding that all other phenomena must have the same kind of efficient cause with that one eminently special, narrow, and peculiarly human or animal, phenomenon? It is true there are cases in which, with acknowledged propriety, we generalize from a single instance to a multitude of instances. But they must be instances which resemble the one known instance, and not such as have no circumstance in common with it except that of being instances. I have, for example, no direct evidence that any creature is alive except myself: yet I attribute, with full assurance, life and sensation to other human beings and animals. But I do not conclude that all other things are alive merely because I am. I ascribe to certain other creatures a life like my own, because they manifest it by the same sort of indications by which mine is manifested. I find that their phenomena and mine conform to the same laws, and it is for this reason that I believe both to arise from a similar cause. Accordingly I do not extend the conclusion beyond the grounds for it. Earth, fire, mountains, trees, are remarkable agencies, but their phenomena do not conform to the same laws as my actions do, and I therefore do not believe earth or fire, mountains or trees, to possess animal life. But the supporters of the Volition Theory ask us to infer that volition causes everything, for no reason except that it causes one particular thing; although that one phenomenon, far from being a type of all natural phenomena, is eminently peculiar; its laws bearing scarcely any resemblance to those of any other phenomenon, whether of inorganic or of organic nature.(74)

CHAPTER VI. OF THE COMPOSITION OF CAUSES.

§ 1. To complete the general notion of causation on which the rules of experimental inquiry into the laws of nature must be founded, one distinction still remains to be pointed out: a distinction so radical, and of so much importance, as to require a chapter to itself.

The preceding discussions have rendered us familiar with the case in which several agents, or causes, concur as conditions to the production of an effect; a case, in truth, almost universal, there being very few effects to the production of which no more than one agent contributes. Suppose, then, that two different agents, operating jointly, are followed, under a certain set of collateral conditions, by a given effect. If either of these agents, instead of being joined with the other, had operated alone, under the same set of conditions in all other respects, some effect would probably have followed; which would have been different from the joint effect of the two, and more or less dissimilar to it. Now, if we happen to know what would be the effects of each cause when acting separately from the other, we are often able to arrive deductively, or *a priori*, at a correct prediction of what will arise from their conjunct agency. To enable us to do this, it is only necessary that the same law which expresses the effect of each cause acting by itself, shall also correctly express the part due to that cause, of the effect which follows from the two together. This condition is realised in the extensive and important class of phenomena commonly called mechanical, namely the phenomena of the communication of motion (or of pressure, which is tendency to motion) from one body to another. In this important class of cases of causation, one cause never, properly speaking, defeats or frustrates another; both have their full effect. If a body is propelled in two directions by two forces, one tending to drive it to the north, and the other to the east, it is caused to move in a given time exactly as far in *both* directions as the two forces would separately have carried it; and is left precisely where it would have arrived if it had been acted upon first by one of the two forces, and afterwards by the other. This law of nature is called, in dynamics, the principle of the Composition of Forces: and in imitation of that well-chosen expression, I shall give the name of the Composition of Causes to the principle which is exemplified in all cases in which the joint effect of several causes is identical with the sum of their separate effects.

This principle, however, by no means prevails in all departments of the field of nature. The chemical combination of two substances produces, as is well known, a third substance with properties entirely different from those of either of the two substances separately, or both of them taken together. Not a trace of the properties of hydrogen or of oxygen is observable in those of their compound, water. The taste of sugar of lead is not the sum of the tastes of its component elements, acetic acid and lead or its oxide; nor is the colour of green vitriol a mixture of the colours of sulphuric acid and copper. This explains why mechanics is a deductive or demonstrative science, and chemistry not. In the one, we can compute the effects of all combinations of causes, whether real or hypothetical, from the laws which we know to govern those causes when acting separately; because they continue to observe the same laws when in combination which they observed when separate: whatever would have happened in consequence of each cause taken by itself, happens when they are together, and we have only to cast up the results. Not so in the phenomena which are the peculiar subject of the science of chemistry. There, most of the uniformities to which the causes conformed when separate, cease altogether when they are conjoined; and we are not, at least in the present state of our knowledge, able to foresee what result will follow from any new combination, until we have tried the specific experiment.

If this be true of chemical combinations, it is still more true of those far more complex combinations of elements which constitute organised bodies; and in which those extraordinary new uniformities arise, which are called the laws of life. All organised bodies are composed of parts similar to those composing inorganic nature, and which have even themselves existed in an inorganic state; but the phenomena of life, which result from the juxtaposition of those parts in a certain manner, bear no analogy to any of the effects which would be produced by the action of the component substances considered as mere physical agents. To whatever degree we might imagine our knowledge of the properties of the several ingredients of a living body to be extended and perfected, it is certain that no mere summing up of the separate actions of those elements will ever amount to the action of the living body itself. The tongue, for instance, is, like all other parts of the animal frame, composed of gelatine, fibrin, and other products of the chemistry of digestion, but from no knowledge of the properties of those substances could we ever predict that it could taste, unless gelatine or fibrin could themselves taste; for no elementary fact can be in the conclusion, which was not first in the premisses.

There are thus two different modes of the conjunct action of causes; from which arise two modes of conflict, or mutual interference, between laws of nature. Suppose, at a given point of time and space, two or more causes, which, if they acted separately, would produce effects contrary, or at least conflicting with each other; one of them tending to undo, wholly or partially, what the other tends to do. Thus, the expansive force of the gases generated by the ignition of gunpowder tends to project a bullet towards the sky, while its gravity tends to make it fall to the ground. A stream running into a reservoir at one end tends to fill it higher and higher, while a drain at the other extremity tends to empty it. Now, in such cases as these, even if the two causes which are in joint action exactly annul one another, still the laws of both are fulfilled; the effect is the same as if the drain had been open for half an hour first,(75) and the stream had flowed in for as long afterwards. Each agent produced the same amount of effect as if it had acted separately, though the contrary effect which was taking place during the same time obliterated it as fast as it was produced. Here then, are two causes, producing by their joint operation an effect which at first seems quite dissimilar to those which they produce separately, but which on examination proves to be really the sum of those separate effects. It will be noticed that we here enlarge the idea of the sum of two effects, so as to include what is commonly called their difference, but which is in reality the result of the addition of opposites; a conception to which mankind are indebted for that admirable extension of the algebraical calculus, which has so vastly increased its powers as an instrument of discovery, by introducing into its reasonings (with the sign of subtraction prefixed, and under the name of Negative Quantities) every description whatever of positive phenomena, provided they are of such a quality in reference to those previously introduced, that to add the one is equivalent to subtracting an equal quantity of the other.

There is, then, one mode of the mutual interference of laws of nature, in which, even when the concurrent causes annihilate each other's effects, each exerts its full efficacy according to its own law, its law as a separate agent. But in the other description of cases, the agencies which are brought together cease entirely, and a totally different set of phenomena arise: as in the experiment of two liquids which, when mixed in certain proportions, instantly become a solid mass, instead of merely a larger amount of liquid.

§ 2. This difference between the case in which the joint effect of causes is the sum of their separate effects, and the case in which it is heterogeneous to them; between laws which work together without alteration, and laws which, when called upon to work together, cease and give place to others; is one of the fundamental distinctions in nature. The former case, that of the Composition of Causes, is the general one; the other is always special and exceptional. There are no objects which do not, as to some of their phenomena, obey the principle of the Composition of Causes; none that have not some laws which are rigidly fulfilled in every combination into which the objects enter. The weight of a body, for instance, is a property which it retains in all the combinations in which it is placed. The weight of a chemical compound, or of an organized body, is equal to the sum of the weights of the elements which compose it. The weight either of the elements or of the compound will vary, if they be carried farther from their centre of attraction, or brought nearer to it; but whatever affects the one affects the other. They always remain precisely equal. So again, the component parts of a vegetable or animal substance do not lose their mechanical and chemical properties as separate agents, when, by a peculiar mode of juxta-position, they, as an aggregate whole, acquire physiological or vital properties in addition. Those bodies continue, as before, to obey mechanical and chemical laws, in so far as the operation of those laws is not counteracted by the new laws which govern them as organised beings. When, in short, a concurrence of causes takes place which calls into action new laws bearing no analogy to any that we can trace in the separate operation of the causes, the new laws, while they supersede one portion of the previous laws, may co-exist with another portion, and may even compound the effect of those previous laws with their own.

Again, laws which were themselves generated in the second mode, may generate others in the first. Though there be laws which, like those of chemistry and physiology, owe their existence to a breach of the principle of Composition of Causes, it does not follow that these peculiar, or as they might be termed, ***heteropathic*** laws, are not capable of composition with one another. The causes which by one combination have had their laws altered, may carry their new laws with them unaltered into their ulterior combinations. And hence there is no reason to despair of ultimately raising chemistry and physiology to the condition of deductive sciences; for though it is impossible to deduce all chemical and physiological truths from the laws or properties of simple substances or elementary agents, they may possibly be deducible from laws which commence when these elementary agents are brought together into some moderate number of not very complex combinations. The Laws of Life will never be deducible from the mere laws of the ingredients, but the prodigiously complex Facts of Life may all be deducible from comparatively simple laws of life; which laws, (depending indeed on combinations, but on comparative-ly simple combinations, of antecedents) may, in more complex circumstances, be strictly compounded with one another, and with the physical and chemical laws of the ingredients. The details of the vital phenomena even now afford innumer-able exemplifications of the Composition of Causes; and in proportion as these phe-nomena are more accurately studied, there appears more reason to believe that the same laws which operate in the simpler combinations of circumstances do, in fact, continue to be observed in the more complex. This will be found equally true in the phenomena of mind; and even in social and political phenomena, the result of the laws of mind. It is in the case of chemical phenomena that the least progress has yet been made in bringing the special laws under general ones from which they may be deduced; but there are even in chemistry many circumstances to encourage the hope that such general laws will hereafter be discovered. The different actions of a chemical compound will never, undoubtedly, be found to be the sums of the actions of its separate elements; but there may exist, between the properties of the compound and those of its elements, some constant relation, which, if discoverable by a sufficient induction, would enable us to foresee the sort of compound which will result from a new combination before we have actually tried it, and to judge of what sort of elements some new substance is compounded before we have analysed it. The law of definite proportions, first discovered in its full generality by Dal-ton, is a complete solution of this problem in one, though but a secondary aspect, that of quantity: and in respect to quality, we have already some partial generaliza-tions sufficient to indicate the possibility of ultimately proceeding farther. We can predicate some common properties of the kind of compounds which result from the combination, in each of the small number of possible proportions, of any acid whatever with any base. We have also the curious law, discovered by Berthollet, that two soluble salts mutually decompose one another whenever the new combi-nations which result produce an insoluble compound, or one less soluble than the two former. Another uniformity is that called the law of isomorphism; the identity of the crystalline forms of substances which possess in common certain peculiarities of chemical composition. Thus it appears that even heteropathic laws, such laws of combined agency as are not compounded of the laws of the separate agencies, are yet, at least in some cases, derived from them according to a fixed principle. There may, therefore, be laws of the generation of laws from others dissimilar to them; and in chemistry, these undiscovered laws of the dependence of the properties of the compound on the properties of its elements, may, together with the laws of the elements themselves, furnish the premises by which the science is perhaps destined one day to be rendered deductive.

It would seem, therefore, that there is no class of phenomena in which the Composition of Causes does not obtain: that as a general rule, causes in combination produce exactly the same effects as when acting singly: but that this rule, though general, is not universal: that in some instances, at some particular points in the transition from separate to united action, the laws change, and an entirely new set of effects are either added to, or take the place of, those which arise from the separate agency of the same causes: the laws of these new effects being again susceptible of composition, to an indefinite extent, like the laws which they superseded.

§ 3. That effects are proportional to their causes is laid down by some writers as an axiom in the theory of causation; and great use is sometimes made of this principle in reasonings respecting the laws of nature, though it is incumbered with many difficulties and apparent exceptions, which much ingenuity has been expended in showing not to be real ones. This proposition, in so far as it is true, enters as a particular case into the general principle of the Composition of Causes: the causes compounded being, in this instance, homogeneous; in which case, if in any, their joint effect might be expected to be identical with the sum of their separate effects. If a force equal to one hundred weight will raise a certain body along an inclined plane, a force equal to two hundred weight will raise two bodies exactly similar, and thus the effect is proportional to the cause. But does not a force equal to two hundred weight, actually contain in itself two forces each equal to one hundred weight, which, if employed apart, would separately raise the two bodies in question? The fact, therefore, that when exerted jointly they raise both bodies at once, results from the Composition of Causes, and is a mere instance of the general fact that mechanical forces are subject to the law of Composition. And so in every other case which can be supposed. For the doctrine of the proportionality of effects to their causes cannot of course be applicable to cases in which the augmentation of the cause alters the **kind** of effect; that is, in which the surplus quantity super-added to the cause does not become compounded with it, but the two together generate an altogether new phenomenon. Suppose that the application of a certain quantity of heat to a body merely increases its bulk, that a double quantity melts it, and a triple quantity decomposes it: these three effects being heterogeneous, no ratio, whether corresponding or not to that of the quantities of heat applied, can be established between them. Thus the supposed axiom of the proportionality of effects to their causes fails at the precise point where the principle of the Composition of Causes also fails; viz. where the concurrence of causes is such as to determine a change in the properties of the body generally, and render it subject to new laws, more or less dissimilar to those to which it conformed in its previous state. The recognition, therefore, of any such law of proportionality, is superseded by the more comprehensive principle, in which as much of it as is true is implicitly asserted.

The general remarks on causation, which seemed necessary as an introduction to the theory of the inductive process, may here terminate. That process is essentially an inquiry into cases of causation. All the uniformities which exist in the succession of phenomena, and most of the uniformities in their coexistence, are either, as we have seen, themselves laws of causation, or consequences resulting from, and corollaries capable of being deduced from, such laws. If we could determine what causes are correctly assigned to what effects, and what effects to what causes, we should be virtually acquainted with the whole course of nature. All those uniformities which are mere results of causation, might then be explained and accounted for; and every individual fact or event might be predicted, provided we had the requisite data, that is, the requisite knowledge of the circumstances which, in the particular instance, preceded it.

To ascertain, therefore, what are the laws of causation which exist in nature; to determine the effects of every cause, and the causes of all effects,--is the main business of Induction; and to point out how this is done is the chief object of Inductive Logic.

CHAPTER VII. OF OBSERVATION AND EXPERIMENT.

§ 1. It results from the preceding exposition, that the process of ascertaining what consequents, in nature, are invariably connected with what antecedents, or in other words what phenomena are related to each other as causes and effects, is in some sort a process of analysis. That every fact which begins to exist has a cause, and that this cause must be found somewhere among the facts which immediately preceded the occurrence, may be taken for certain. The whole of the present facts are the infallible result of all past facts, and more immediately of all the facts which existed at the moment previous. Here, then, is a great sequence, which we know to be uniform. If the whole prior state of the entire universe could again recur, it would again be followed by the present state. The question is, how to resolve this complex uniformity into the simpler uniformities which compose it, and assign to each portion of the vast antecedent the portion of the consequent which is attendant on it.

This operation, which we have called analytical, inasmuch as it is the resolution of a complex whole into the component elements, is more than a merely mental analysis. No mere contemplation of the phenomena, and partition of them by the intellect alone, will of itself accomplish the end we have now in view. Nevertheless, such a mental partition is an indispensable first step. The order of nature, as perceived at a first glance, presents at every instant a chaos followed by another chaos. We must decompose each chaos into single facts. We must learn to see in the chaotic antecedent a multitude of distinct antecedents, in the chaotic consequent a multitude of distinct consequents. This, supposing it done, will not of itself tell us on which of the antecedents each consequent is invariably attendant. To determine that point, we must endeavour to effect a separation of the facts from one another, not in our minds only, but in nature. The mental analysis, however, must take place first. And every one knows that in the mode of performing it, one intellect differs immensely from another. It is the essence of the act of observing; for the observer is not he who merely sees the thing which is before his eyes, but he who sees what parts that thing is composed of. To do this well is a rare talent. One person, from inattention, or attending only in the wrong place, overlooks half of what he sees; another sets down much more than he sees, confounding it with what he imagines, or with what he infers; another takes note of the *kind* of all the circumstances, but being inexpert in estimating their degree, leaves the quantity of each vague and uncertain; another sees indeed the whole, but makes such an awkward division of it into parts, throwing things into one mass which require to be separated, and separating others which might more conveniently be considered as one, that the result is much the same, sometimes even worse, than if no analysis had been attempted at all. It would be possible to point out what qualities of mind, and modes of mental culture, fit a person for being a good observer; that, however, is a question not of Logic, but of the theory of Education, in the most enlarged sense of the term. There is not properly an Art of Observing. There may be rules for observing. But these, like rules for inventing, are properly instructions for the preparation of one's own mind; for putting it into the state in which it will be most fitted to observe, or most likely to invent. They are, therefore, essentially rules of self-education, which is a different thing from Logic. They do not teach how to do the thing, but how to make ourselves capable of doing it. They are an art of strengthening the limbs, not an art of using them.

The extent and minuteness of observation which may be requisite, and the degree of decomposition to which it may be necessary to carry the mental analysis, depend on the particular purpose in view. To ascertain the state of the whole universe at any particular moment is impossible, but would also be useless. In making chemical experiments, we do not think it necessary to note the position of the planets; because experience has shown, as a very superficial experience is sufficient to show, that in such cases that circumstance is not material to the result: and, accordingly, in the ages when men believed in the occult influences of the heavenly bodies, it might have been unphilosophical to omit ascertaining the precise condition of those bodies at the moment of the experiment. As to the degree of minuteness of the mental subdivision; if we were obliged to break down what we observe into its very simplest elements, that is, literally into single facts, it would be difficult to say where we should find them: we can hardly ever affirm that our divisions of any kind have reached the ultimate unit. But this, too, is fortunately unnecessary. The only object of the mental separation is to suggest the requisite physical separation, so that we may either accomplish it ourselves, or seek for it in nature; and we have done enough when we have carried the subdivision as far as the point at which we are able to see what observations or experiments we require. It is only essential, at whatever point our mental decomposition of facts may for the present have stopped, that we should hold ourselves ready and able to carry it farther as occasion requires, and should not allow the freedom of our discriminating faculty to be imprisoned by the swathes and bands of ordinary classification; as was the case with all early speculative inquirers, not excepting the Greeks, to whom it hardly ever occurred that what was called by one abstract name might, in reality, be several phenomena, or that there was a possibility of decomposing the facts of the universe into any elements but those which ordinary language already recognised.

§ 2. The different antecedents and consequents being, then, supposed to be, so far as the case requires, ascertained and discriminated from one another; we are to inquire which is connected with which. In every instance which comes under our observation, there are many antecedents and many consequents. If those antecedents could not be severed from one another except in thought, or if those consequents never were found apart, it would be impossible for us to distinguish (*a posteriori* at least) the real laws, or to assign to any cause its effect, or to any effect its cause. To do so, we must be able to meet with some of the antecedents apart from the rest, and observe what follows from them; or some of the consequents, and observe by what they are preceded. We must, in short, follow the Baconian rule of *varying the circumstances*. This is, indeed, only the first rule of physical inquiry, and not, as some have thought, the sole rule; but it is the foundation of all the rest.

For the purpose of varying the circumstances, we may have recourse (according to a distinction commonly made) either to observation or to experiment; we may either *find* an instance in nature, suited to our purposes, or, by an artificial arrangement of circumstances, *make* one. The value of the instance depends on what it is in itself, not on the mode in which it is obtained: its employment for the purposes of induction depends on the same principles in the one case and in the other; as the uses of money are the same whether it is inherited or acquired. There is, in short, no difference in kind, no real logical distinction, between the two processes of investigation. There are, however, practical distinctions to which it is of considerable importance to advert.

§ 3. The first and most obvious distinction between Observation and Experiment is, that the latter is an immense extension of the former. It not only enables us to produce a much greater number of variations in the circumstances than nature spontaneously offers, but also, in thousands of cases, to produce the precise *sort* of variation which we are in want of for discovering the law of the phenomenon; a service which nature, being constructed on a quite different scheme from that of facilitating our studies, is seldom so friendly as to bestow upon us. For example, in order to ascertain what principle in the atmosphere enables it to sustain life, the variation we require is that a living animal should be immersed in each component element of the atmosphere separately. But nature does not supply either oxygen or azote in a separate state. We are indebted to artificial experiment for our knowledge that it is the former, and not the latter, which supports respiration; and for our knowledge of the very existence of the two ingredients.

Thus far the advantage of experimentation over simple observation is universally recognised: all are aware that it enables us to obtain innumerable combinations of circumstances which are not to be found in nature, and so add to nature's experiments a multitude of experiments of our own. But there is another superiority (or, as Bacon would have expressed it, another prerogative) of instances artificially obtained over spontaneous instances,--of our own experiments over even the same experiments when made by nature,--which is not of less importance, and which is far from being felt and acknowledged in the same degree.

When we can produce a phenomenon artificially, we can take it, as it were, home with us, and observe it in the midst of circumstances with which in all other respects we are accurately acquainted. If we desire to know what are the effects of the cause A, and are able to produce A by means at our disposal, we can generally determine at our own discretion, so far as is compatible with the nature of the phenomenon A, the whole of the circumstances which shall be present along with it: and thus, knowing exactly the simultaneous state of everything else which is within the reach of A's influence, we have only to observe what alteration is made in that state by the presence of A.

For example, by the electric machine we can produce in the midst of known circumstances, the phenomena which nature exhibits on a grander scale in the form of lightning and thunder. Now let any one consider what amount of knowledge of the effects and laws of electric agency mankind could have obtained from the mere observation of thunder-storms, and compare it with that which they have gained, and may expect to gain, from electrical and galvanic experiments. This example is the more striking, now that we have reason to believe that electric action is of all natural phenomena (except heat) the most pervading and universal, which, therefore, it might antecedently have been supposed could stand least in need of artificial means of production to enable it to be studied; while the fact is so much the contrary, that without the electric machine, the voltaic battery, and the Leyden jar, we probably should never have suspected the existence of electricity as one of the great agents in nature; the few electric phenomena we should have known of would have continued to be regarded either as supernatural, or as a sort of anomalies and eccentricities in the order of the universe.

When we have succeeded in insulating the phenomenon which is the subject of inquiry, by placing it among known circumstances, we may produce further variations of circumstances to any extent, and of such kinds as we think best calculated to bring the laws of the phenomenon into a clear light. By introducing one well defined circumstance after another into the experiment, we obtain assurance of the manner in which the phenomenon behaves under an indefinite variety of possible circumstances. Thus, chemists, after having obtained some newly-discovered substance in a pure state, (that is, having made sure that there is nothing present which can interfere with and modify its agency,) introduce various other substances, one by one, to ascertain whether it will combine with them, or decompose them, and with what result; and also apply heat, or electricity, or pressure, to discover what will happen to the substance under each of these circumstances.

But if, on the other hand, it is out of our power to produce the phenomenon, and we have to seek for instances in which nature produces it, the task before us is very different. Instead of being able to choose what the concomitant circumstances shall be, we now have to discover what they are; which, when we go beyond the simplest and most accessible cases, it is next to impossible to do, with any precision and completeness. Let us take, as an exemplification of a phenomenon which we have no means of fabricating artificially, a human mind. Nature produces many; but the consequence of our not being able to produce it by art is, that in every instance in which we see a human mind developing itself, or acting upon other things, we see it surrounded and obscured by an indefinite multitude of unascertainable circumstances, rendering the use of the common experimental methods almost delusive. We may conceive to what extent this is true, if we consider, among other things, that whenever nature produces a human mind, she produces, in close connexion with it, also a body; that is, a vast complication of physical facts, in no two cases perhaps exactly similar, and most of which (except the mere structure, which we can examine in a sort of coarse way after it has ceased to act), are radically out of the reach of our means of exploration. If, instead of a human mind, we suppose the subject of investigation to be a human society or State, all the same difficulties recur in a greatly augmented degree.

We have thus already come within sight of a conclusion, which the progress of the inquiry will, I think, bring before us with the clearest evidence: namely, that in the sciences which deal with phenomena in which artificial experiments are impossible (as in the case of astronomy,) or in which they have a very limited range (as in physiology, mental philosophy, and the social science,) induction from direct experience is practised at a disadvantage generally equivalent to impracticability: from which it follows that the methods of those sciences, in order to accomplish anything worthy of attainment, must be to a great extent, if not principally, deductive. This is already known to be the case with the first of the sciences we have mentioned, astronomy; that it is not generally recognised as true of the others, is probably one of the reasons why they are still in their infancy.

§ 4. If what is called pure observation is at so great a disadvantage, compared with artificial experimentation, in one department of the direct exploration of phenomena, there is another branch in which the advantage is all on the side of the former.

Inductive inquiry having for its object to ascertain what causes are connected with what effects, we may begin this search at either end of the road which leads from the one point to the other: we may either inquire into the effects of a given cause, or into the causes of a given effect. The fact that light blackens chloride of silver might have been discovered either by experiments on light, trying what effect it would produce on various substances, or by observing that portions of the chloride had repeatedly become black, and inquiring into the circumstances. The effect of the urali poison might have become known either by administering it to animals, or by examining how it happened that the wounds which the Indians of Guiana inflict with their arrows prove so uniformly mortal. Now it is manifest from the mere statement of the examples, without any theoretical discussion, that artificial experimentation is applicable only to the former of these modes of investigation. We can take a cause, and try what it will produce: but we cannot take an effect, and try what it will be produced by. We can only watch till we see it produced, or are enabled to produce it by accident.

This would be of little importance, if it always depended on our choice from which of the two ends of the sequence we would undertake our inquiries. But we have seldom any option. As we can only travel from the known to the unknown, we are obliged to commence at whichever end we are best acquainted with. If the agent is more familiar to us than its effects, we watch for, or contrive, instances of the agent, under such varieties of circumstances as are open to us, and observe the result. If, on the contrary, the conditions on which a phenomenon depends are obscure, but the phenomenon itself familiar, we must commence our inquiry from the effect. If we are struck with the fact that chloride of silver has been blackened, and have no suspicion of the cause, we have no resource but to compare instances in which the fact has chanced to occur, until by that comparison we discover that in all those instances the substance had been exposed to light. If we knew nothing of the Indian arrows but their fatal effect, accident alone could turn our attention to experiments on the urali: in the regular course of investigation, we could only inquire, or try to observe, what had been done to the arrows in particular instances.

Wherever, having nothing to guide us to the cause, we are obliged to set out from the effect, and to apply the rule of varying the circumstances to the consequents, not the antecedents, we are necessarily destitute of the resource of artificial experimentation. We cannot, at our choice, obtain consequents, as we can antecedents, under any set of circumstances compatible with their nature. There are no means of producing effects but through their causes, and by the supposition the causes of the effect in question are not known to us. We have therefore no expedient but to study it where it offers itself spontaneously. If nature happens to present us with instances sufficiently varied in their circumstances, and if we are able to discover, either among the proximate antecedents or among some other order of antecedents, something which is always found when the effect is found, however various the circumstances, and never found when it is not; we may discover, by mere observation without experiment, a real uniformity in nature.

But though this is certainly the most favourable case for sciences of pure observation, as contrasted with those in which artificial experiments are possible, there is in reality no case which more strikingly illustrates the inherent imperfection of direct induction when not founded on experimentation. Suppose that, by a comparison of cases of the effect, we have found an antecedent which appears to be, and perhaps is, invariably connected with it: we have not yet proved that antecedent to be the cause, until we have reversed the process, and produced the effect by means of that antecedent. If we can produce the antecedent artificially, and if, when we do so, the effect follows, the induction is complete; that antecedent is the cause of that consequent.(76) But we have then added the evidence of experiment to that of simple observation. Until we had done so, we had only proved ***invariable*** antecedence, but not ***unconditional*** antecedence, or causation. Until it had been shown by the actual production of the antecedent under known circumstances, and the occurrence thereupon of the consequent, that the antecedent was really the condition on which it depended; the uniformity of succession which was proved to exist between them might, for aught we knew, be (like the succession of day and night) no case of causation at all; both antecedent and consequent might be successive stages of the effect of an ulterior cause. Observation, in short, without experiment (supposing no aid from deduction) can ascertain sequences and coexistences, but cannot prove causation.

In order to see these remarks verified by the actual state of the sciences, we have only to think of the condition of natural history. In zoology, for example, there is an immense number of uniformities ascertained, some of coexistence, others of succession, to many of which, notwithstanding considerable variations of the attendant circumstances, we know not any exception: but the antecedents, for the most part, are such as we cannot artificially produce; or if we can, it is only by setting in motion the exact process by which nature produces them; and this being to us a mysterious process, of which the main circumstances are not only unknown but unobservable, the name of experimentation would here be completely misapplied. Such are the facts: and what is the result? That on this vast subject, which affords so much and such varied scope for observation, we have not, properly speaking, ascertained a single cause, a single unconditional uniformity. We know not, in the case of most of the phenomena that we find conjoined, which is the condition of the other; which is cause, and which effect, or whether either of them is so, or they are not rather conjunct effects of causes yet to be discovered, complex results of laws hitherto unknown.

Although some of the foregoing observations may be, in technical strictness of arrangement, premature in this place, it seemed that a few general remarks on the difference between sciences of mere observation and sciences of experimentation, and the extreme disadvantage under which directly inductive inquiry is necessarily carried on in the former, were the best preparation for discussing the methods of direct induction; a preparation rendering superfluous much that must otherwise have been introduced, with some inconvenience, into the heart of that discussion. To the consideration of these methods we now proceed.

CHAPTER VIII. OF THE FOUR METHODS OF EXPERIMENTAL INQUIRY.

§ 1. The simplest and most obvious modes of singling out from among the circumstances which precede or follow a phenomenon, those with which it is really connected by an invariable law, are two in number. One is, by comparing together different instances in which the phenomenon occurs. The other is, by comparing instances in which the phenomenon does occur, with instances in other respects similar in which it does not. These two methods may be respectively denominated, the Method of Agreement, and the Method of Difference.

In illustrating these methods it will be necessary to bear in mind the two-fold character of inquiries into the laws of phenomena; which may be either inquiries into the cause of a given effect, or into the effects or properties of a given cause. We shall consider the methods in their application to either order of investigation, and shall draw our examples equally from both.

We shall denote antecedents by the large letters of the alphabet, and the consequents corresponding to them by the small. Let A, then, be an agent or cause, and let the object of our inquiry be to ascertain what are the effects of this cause. If we can either find, or produce, the agent A in such varieties of circumstances, that the different cases have no circumstance in common except A; then whatever effect we find to be produced in all our trials, is indicated as the effect of A. Suppose, for example, that A is tried along with B and C, and that the effect is *a b c*; and suppose that A is next tried with D and E, but without B and C, and that the effect is *a d e*.

Then we may reason thus: *b* and *c* are not effects of A, for they were not produced by it in the second experiment; nor are *d* and *e*, for they were not produced in the first. Whatever is really the effect of A must have been produced in both instances; now this condition is fulfilled by no circumstance except *a*. The phenomenon *a* cannot have been the effect of B or C, since it was produced where they were not; nor of D or E, since it was produced where they were not. Therefore it is the effect of A.

For example, let the antecedent A be the contact of an alkaline substance and an oil. This combination being tried under several varieties of circumstance, resembling each other in nothing else, the results agree in the production of a greasy and detersive or saponaceous substance: it is therefore concluded that the combination of an oil and an alkali causes the production of a soap. It is thus we inquire, by the Method of Agreement, into the effect of a given cause.

In a similar manner we may inquire into the cause of a given effect. Let *a* be the effect. Here, as shown in the last chapter, we have only the resource of observation without experiment: we cannot take a phenomenon of which we know not the origin, and try to find its mode of production by producing it: if we succeeded in such a random trial it could only be by accident. But if we can observe *a* in two different combinations, *a b c*, and *a d e*; and if we know, or can discover, that the antecedent circumstances in these cases respectively were A B C and A D E; we may conclude by a reasoning similar to that in the preceding example, that A is the antecedent connected with the consequent *a* by a law of causation. B and C, we may say, cannot be causes of *a*, since on its second occurrence they were not present; nor are D and E, for they were not present on its first occurrence. A, alone of the five circumstances, was found among the antecedents of *a* in both instances.

For example, let the effect *a* be crystallization. We compare instances in which bodies are known to assume crystalline structure, but which have no other point of agreement; and we find them to have one, and as far as we can observe, only one, antecedent in common: the deposition of a solid matter from a liquid state, either a state of fusion or of solution. We conclude, therefore, that the solidification of a substance from a liquid state is an invariable antecedent of its crystallization.

In this example we may go farther, and say, it is not only the invariable antecedent but the cause; or at least the proximate event which completes the cause. For in this case we are able, after detecting the antecedent A, to produce it artificially, and by finding that *a* follows it, verify the result of our induction. The importance of thus reversing the proof was strikingly manifested when by keeping a phial of water charged with siliceous particles undisturbed for years, a chemist (I believe Dr. Wollaston) succeeded in obtaining crystals of quartz; and in the equally interesting experiment in which Sir James Hall produced artificial marble, by the cooling of its materials from fusion under immense pressure: two admirable examples of the light which may be thrown upon the most secret processes of nature by well-contrived interrogation of her.

But if we cannot artificially produce the phenomenon A, the conclusion that it is the cause of *a* remains subject to very considerable doubt. Though an invariable, it may not be the unconditional antecedent of *a*, but may precede it as day precedes night or night day. This uncertainty arises from the impossibility of assuring ourselves that A is the *only* immediate antecedent common to both the instances. If we could be certain of having ascertained all the invariable antecedents, we might be sure that the unconditional invariable antecedent, or cause, must be found somewhere among them. Unfortunately it is hardly ever possible to ascertain all the antecedents, unless the phenomenon is one which we can produce artificially. Even then, the difficulty is merely lightened, not removed: men knew how to raise water in pumps long before they adverted to what was really the operating circumstance in the means they employed, namely, the pressure of the atmosphere on the open surface of the water. It is, however, much easier to analyse completely a set of arrangements made by ourselves, than the whole complex mass of the agencies which nature happens to be exerting at the moment of the production of a given phenomenon. We may overlook some of the material circumstances in an experiment with an electrical machine; but we shall, at the worst, be better acquainted with them than with those of a thunder-storm.

The mode of discovering and proving laws of nature, which we have now examined, proceeds on the following axiom: Whatever circumstance can be excluded, without prejudice to the phenomenon, or can be absent notwithstanding its presence, is not connected with it in the way of causation. The casual circumstances being thus eliminated, if only one remains, that one is the cause which we are in search of: if more than one, they either are, or contain among them, the cause: and so, ***mutatis mutandis***, of the effect. As this method proceeds by comparing differ-ent instances to ascertain in what they agree, I have termed it the Method of Agree-ment: and we may adopt as its regulating principle the following canon:--

FIRST CANON.

If two or more instances of the phenomenon under investigation have only one circumstance in common, the circumstance in which alone all the instances agree, is the cause (or effect) of the given phenomenon.

Quitting for the present the Method of Agreement, to which we shall almost immediately return, we proceed to a still more potent instrument of the investiga-tion of nature, the Method of Difference.

§ 2. In the Method of Agreement, we endeavoured to obtain instances which agreed in the given circumstance but differed in every other: in the present method we require, on the contrary, two instances resembling one another in every other respect, but differing in the presence or absence of the phenomenon we wish to study. If our object be to discover the effects of an agent A, we must procure A in some set of ascertained circumstances, as A B C, and having noted the effects pro-duced, compare them with the effect of the remaining circumstances B C, when A is absent. If the effect of A B C is *a b c*, and the effect of B C, *b c*, it is evident that the effect of A is *a*. So again, if we begin at the other end, and desire to investigate the cause of an effect *a*, we must select an instance, as *a b c*, in which the effect oc-curs, and in which the antecedents were A B C, and we must look out for another instance in which the remaining circumstances, *b c*, occur without *a*. If the ante-cedents, in that instance, are B C, we know that the cause of *a* must be A: either A alone, or A in conjunction with some of the other circumstances present.

It is scarcely necessary to give examples of a logical process to which we owe almost all the inductive conclusions we draw in daily life. When a man is shot through the heart, it is by this method we know that it was the gun-shot which killed him: for he was in the fulness of life immediately before, all circumstances being the same, except the wound.

The axioms implied in this method are evidently the following. Whatever an-tecedent cannot be excluded without preventing the phenomenon, is the cause, or a condition, of that phenomenon: Whatever consequent can be excluded, with no other difference in the antecedents than the absence of a particular one, is the effect of that one. Instead of comparing different instances of a phenomenon, to discover in what they agree, this method compares an instance of its occurrence with an instance of its non-occurrence, to discover in what they differ. The canon which is the regulating principle of the Method of Difference may be expressed as follows:--

SECOND CANON.

If an instance in which the phenomenon under investigation occurs, and an instance in which it does not occur, have every circumstance in common save one, that one occurring only in the former; the circumstance in which alone the two instances differ, is the effect, or cause, or a necessary part of the cause, of the phenomenon.

§ 3. The two methods which we have now stated have many features of resemblance, but there are also many distinctions between them. Both are methods of ***elimination.*** This term (employed in the theory of equations to denote the process by which one after another of the elements of a question is excluded, and the solution made to depend on the relation between the remaining elements only) is well suited to express the operation, analogous to this, which has been understood since the time of Bacon to be the foundation of experimental inquiry: namely, the successive exclusion of the various circumstances which are found to accompany a phenomenon in a given instance, in order to ascertain what are those among them which can be absent consistently with the existence of the phenomenon. The Method of Agreement stands on the ground that whatever can be eliminated, is not connected with the phenomenon by any law. The Method of Difference has for its foundation, that whatever can ***not*** be eliminated, ***is*** connected with the phenomenon by a law.

Of these methods, that of Difference is more particularly a method of artificial experiment; while that of Agreement is more especially the resource employed where experimentation is impossible. A few reflections will prove the fact, and point out the reason of it.

It is inherent in the peculiar character of the Method of Difference, that the nature of the combinations which it requires is much more strictly defined than in the Method of Agreement. The two instances which are to be compared with one another must be exactly similar, in all circumstances except the one which we are attempting to investigate: they must be in the relation of A B C and B C, or of *a b c* and *b c*. It is true that this similarity of circumstances needs not extend to such as are already known to be immaterial to the result. And in the case of most phenomena we learn at once, from the commonest experience, that most of the coexistent phenomena of the universe may be either present or absent without affecting the given phenomenon; or, if present, are present indifferently when the phenomenon does not happen, and when it does. Still, even limiting the identity which is required between the two instances, A B C and B C, to such circumstances as are not already known to be indifferent; it is very seldom that nature affords two instances, of which we can be assured that they stand in this precise relation to one another. In the spontaneous operations of nature there is generally such complication and such obscurity, they are mostly either on so overwhelmingly large or on so inaccessibly minute a scale, we are so ignorant of a great part of the facts which really take place, and even those of which we are not ignorant are so multitudinous, and therefore so seldom exactly alike in any two cases, that a spontaneous experiment, of the kind required by the Method of Difference, is commonly not to be found. When, on the contrary, we obtain a phenomenon by an artificial experiment, a pair of instances such as the method requires is obtained almost as a matter of course, provided the process does not last a long time. A certain state of surrounding circumstances existed before we commenced the experiment; this is B C. We then introduce A; say, for instance, by merely bringing an object from another part of the room, before there has been time for any change in the other elements. It is, in short, (as M. Comte observes,) the very nature of an experiment, to introduce into the pre-existing state of circumstances a change perfectly definite. We choose a previous state of things with which we are well acquainted, so that no unforeseen alteration in that state is likely to pass unobserved; and into this we introduce, as rapidly as possible, the phenomenon which we wish to study; so that in general we are entitled to feel complete assurance, that the pre-existing state, and the state which we have produced, differ in nothing except the presence or absence of that phenomenon. If a bird is taken from a cage, and instantly plunged into carbonic acid gas, the experimentalist may be fully assured (at all events after one or two repetitions) that no circumstance capable of causing suffocation had supervened in the interim, except the change from immersion in the atmosphere to immersion in carbonic acid gas. There is one doubt, indeed, which may remain in some cases of this description; the effect may have been produced not by the change, but by the means employed to produce the change. The possibility, however, of this last supposition generally admits of being conclusively tested by other experiments. It thus appears that in the study of the various kinds of phenomena which we can, by our voluntary agency, modify or control, we can in general satisfy the requisitions of the Method of Difference; but that by the spontaneous operations of nature those requisitions are seldom fulfilled.

The reverse of this is the case with the Method of Agreement. We do not here require instances of so special and determinate a kind. Any instances whatever, in which nature presents us with a phenomenon, may be examined for the purposes of this method; and if *all* such instances agree in anything, a conclusion of considerable value is already attained. We can seldom, indeed, be sure that the one point of agreement is the only one; but this ignorance does not, as in the Method of Difference, vitiate the conclusion; the certainty of the result, as far as it goes, is not affected. We have ascertained one invariable antecedent or consequent, however many other invariable antecedents or consequents may still remain unascertained. If A B C, A D E, A F G, are all equally followed by *a*, then *a* is an invariable consequent of A. If *a b c*, *a d e*, *a f g*, all number A among their antecedents, then A is connected as an antecedent, by some invariable law, with *a*. But to determine whether this invariable antecedent is a cause, or this invariable consequent an effect, we must be able, in addition, to produce the one by means of the other; or, at least, to obtain that which alone constitutes our assurance of having produced anything, namely, an instance in which the effect, *a*, has come into existence, with no other change in the pre-existing circumstances than the addition of A. And this, if we can do it, is an application of the Method of Difference, not of the Method of Agreement.

It thus appears to be by the Method of Difference alone that we can ever, in the way of direct experience, arrive with certainty at causes. The Method of Agreement leads only to laws of phenomena, (as some writers call them, but improperly, since laws of causation are also laws of phenomena): that is, to uniformities which either are not laws of causation, or in which the question of causation must for the present remain undecided. The Method of Agreement is chiefly to be resorted to, as a means of suggesting applications of the Method of Difference (as in the last example the comparison of A B C, A D E, A F G, suggested that A was the antecedent on which to try the experiment whether it could produce *a*); or as an inferior resource, in case the Method of Difference is impracticable; which, as we before showed, generally arises from the impossibility of artificially producing the phenomena. And hence it is that the Method of Agreement, though applicable in principle to either case, is more emphatically the method of investigation on those subjects where artificial experimentation is impossible; because on those it is, generally, our only resource of a directly inductive nature; while, in the phenomena which we can produce at pleasure, the Method of Difference generally affords a more efficacious process, which will ascertain causes as well as mere laws.

§ 4. There are, however, many cases in which, though our power of producing the phenomenon is complete, the Method of Difference either cannot be made available at all, or not without a previous employment of the Method of Agreement. This occurs when the agency by which we can produce the phenomenon is not that of one single antecedent, but of a combination of antecedents, which we have no power of separating from each other and exhibiting apart. For instance, suppose the subject of inquiry to be the cause of the double refraction of light. We can produce this phenomenon at pleasure, by employing any one of the many substances which are known to refract light in that peculiar manner. But if, taking one of those substances, as Iceland spar for example, we wish to determine on which of the properties of Iceland spar this remarkable phenomenon depends, we can make no use, for that purpose, of the Method of Difference; for we cannot find another substance precisely resembling Iceland spar except in some one property. The only mode, therefore, of prosecuting this inquiry is that afforded by the Method of Agreement; by which, in fact, through a comparison of all the known substances which have the property of doubly refracting light, it was ascertained that they agree in the circumstance of being crystalline substances; and though the converse does not hold, though all crystalline substances have not the property of double refraction, it was concluded, with reason, that there is a real connexion between these two properties; that either crystalline structure, or the cause which gives rise to that structure, is one of the conditions of double refraction.

Out of this employment of the Method of Agreement arises a peculiar modification of that method, which is sometimes of great avail in the investigation of nature. In cases similar to the above, in which it is not possible to obtain the precise pair of instances which our second canon requires--instances agreeing in every antecedent except A, or in every consequent except *a*; we may yet be able, by a double employment of the Method of Agreement, to discover in what the instances which contain A or *a*, differ from those which do not.

If we compare various instances in which *a* occurs, and find that they all have in common the circumstance A, and (as far as can be observed) no other circumstance, the Method of Agreement, so far, bears testimony to a connexion between A and *a*. In order to convert this evidence of connexion into proof of causation by the direct Method of Difference, we ought to be able in some one of these instances, as for example A B C, to leave out A, and observe whether by doing so, *a* is prevented. Now supposing (what is often the case) that we are not able to try this decisive experiment; yet, provided we can by any means discover what would be its result if we could try it, the advantage will be the same. Suppose, then, that as we previously examined a variety of instances in which *a* occurred, and found them to agree in containing A, so we now observe a variety of instances in which *a* does not occur, and find them agree in not containing A; which establishes, by the Method of Agreement, the same connexion between the absence of A and the absence of *a*, which was before established between their presence. As, then, it had been shown that whenever A is present *a* is present, so it being now shown that when A is taken away *a* is removed along with it, we have by the one proposition A B C, *a b c*, by the other B C, *b c*, the positive and negative instances which the Method of Difference requires.

This method may be called the Indirect Method of Difference, or the Joint Method of Agreement and Difference; and consists in a double employment of the Method of Agreement, each proof being independent of the other, and corroborating it. But it is not equivalent to a proof by the direct Method of Difference. For the requisitions of the Method of Difference are not satisfied, unless we can be quite sure either that the instances affirmative of *a* agree in no antecedent whatever but A, or that the instances negative of *a* agree in nothing but the negation of A. Now if it were possible, which it never is, to have this assurance, we should not need the joint method; for either of the two sets of instances separately would then be sufficient to prove causation. This indirect method, therefore, can only be regarded as a great extension and improvement of the Method of Agreement, but not as participating in the more cogent nature of the Method of Difference. The following may be stated as its canon:--

THIRD CANON.

If two or more instances in which the phenomenon occurs have only one circumstance in common, while two or more instances in which it does not occur have nothing in common save the absence of that circumstance; the circumstance in which alone the two sets of instances differ, is the effect, or cause, or a necessary part of the cause, of the phenomenon.

We shall presently see that the Joint Method of Agreement and Difference constitutes, in another respect not yet adverted to, an improvement upon the common Method of Agreement, namely, in being unaffected by a characteristic imperfection of that method, the nature of which still remains to be pointed out. But as we cannot enter into this exposition without introducing a new element of complexity into this long and intricate discussion, I shall postpone it to a subsequent chapter, and shall at once proceed to the statement of two other methods, which will complete the enumeration of the means which mankind possess for exploring the laws of nature by specific observation and experience.

§ 5. The first of these has been aptly denominated the Method of Residues. Its principle is very simple. Subducting from any given phenomenon all the portions which, by virtue of preceding inductions, can be assigned to known causes, the remainder will be the effect of the antecedents which had been overlooked, or of which the effect was as yet an unknown quantity.

Suppose, as before, that we have the antecedents A B C, followed by the consequents *a b c*, and that by previous inductions, (founded, we will suppose, on the Method of Difference,) we have ascertained the causes of some of these effects, or the effects of some of these causes; and are by this means apprised that the effect of A is *a*, and that the effect of B is *b*. Subtracting the sum of these effects from the total phenomenon, there remains *c*, which now, without any fresh experiment, we may know to be the effect of C. This Method of Residues is in truth a peculiar modification of the Method of Difference. If the instance A B C, *a b c*, could have been compared with a single instance A B, *a b*, we should have proved C to be the cause of *c*, by the common process of the Method of Difference. In the present case, however, instead of a single instance A B, we have had to study separately the causes A and B, and to infer from the effects which they produce separately, what effect they must produce in the case A B C where they act together.

Of the two instances, therefore, which the Method of Difference requires,--the one positive, the other negative,--the negative one, or that in which the given phenomenon is absent, is not the direct result of observation and experiment, but has been arrived at by deduction. As one of the forms of the Method of Difference, the Method of Residues partakes of its rigorous certainty, provided the previous inductions, those which gave the effects of A and B, were obtained by the same infallible method, and provided we are certain that C is the *only* antecedent to which the residual phenomenon *c* can be referred; the only agent of which we had not already calculated and subducted the effect. But as we can never be quite certain of this, the evidence derived from the Method of Residues is not complete unless we can obtain C artificially and try it separately, or unless its agency, when once suggested, can be accounted for, and proved deductively, from known laws.

Even with these reservations, the Method of Residues is one of the most important among our instruments of discovery. Of all the methods of investigating laws of nature, this is the most fertile in unexpected results; often informing us of sequences in which neither the cause nor the effect were sufficiently conspicuous to attract of themselves the attention of observers. The agent C may be an obscure circumstance, not likely to have been perceived unless sought for, nor likely to have been sought for until attention had been awakened by the insufficiency of the obvious causes to account for the whole of the effect. And *c* may be so disguised by its intermixture with *a* and *b*, that it would scarcely have presented itself spontaneously as a subject of separate study. Of these uses of the method, we shall presently cite some remarkable examples. The canon of the Method of Residues is as follows:--

FOURTH CANON.

Subduct from any phenomenon such part as is known by previous inductions to be the effect of certain antecedents, and the residue of the phenomenon is the effect of the remaining antecedents.

§ 6. There remains a class of laws which it is impracticable to ascertain by any of the three methods which I have attempted to characterize; namely, the laws of those Permanent Causes, or indestructible natural agents, which it is impossible either to exclude or to isolate; which we can neither hinder from being present, nor contrive that they shall be present alone. It would appear at first sight that we could by no means separate the effects of these agents from the effects of those other phenomena with which they cannot be prevented from coexisting. In respect, indeed, to most of the permanent causes, no such difficulty exists; since though we cannot eliminate them as coexisting facts, we can eliminate them as influencing agents, by simply trying our experiment in a local situation beyond the limits of their influence. The pendulum, for example, has its oscillations disturbed by the vicinity of a mountain: we remove the pendulum to a sufficient distance from the mountain, and the disturbance ceases: from these data we can determine by the Method of Difference, the amount of effect due to the mountain; and beyond a certain distance everything goes on precisely as it would do if the mountain exercised no influence whatever, which, accordingly, we, with sufficient reason, conclude to be the fact,

The difficulty, therefore, in applying the methods already treated of to determine the effects of Permanent Causes, is confined to the cases in which it is impossible for us to get out of the local limits of their influence. The pendulum can be removed from the influence of the mountain, but it cannot be removed from the influence of the earth: we cannot take away the earth from the pendulum, nor the pendulum from the earth, to ascertain whether it would continue to vibrate if the action which the earth exerts upon it were withdrawn. On what evidence, then, do we ascribe its vibrations to the earth's influence? Not on any sanctioned by the Method of Difference; for one of the two instances, the negative instance, is wanting. Nor by the Method of Agreement; for though all pendulums agree in this, that during their oscillations the earth is always present, why may we not as well ascribe the phenomenon to the sun, which is equally a coexistent fact in all the experiments? It is evident that to establish even so simple a fact of causation as this, there was required some method over and above those which we have yet examined.

As another example, let us take the phenomenon Heat. Independently of all hypothesis as to the real nature of the agency so called, this fact is certain, that we are unable to exhaust any body of the whole of its heat. It is equally certain, that no one ever perceived heat not emanating from a body. Being unable, then, to separate

Body and Heat, we cannot effect such a variation of circumstances as the foregoing three methods require; we cannot ascertain, by those methods, what portion of the phenomena exhibited by any body are due to the heat contained in it. If we could observe a body with its heat, and the same body entirely divested of heat, the Method of Difference would show the effect due to the heat, apart from that due to the body. If we could observe heat under circumstances agreeing in nothing but heat, and therefore not characterized also by the presence of a body, we could ascertain the effects of heat, from an instance of heat with a body and an instance of heat without a body, by the Method of Agreement; or we could determine by the Method of Difference what effect was due to the body, when the remainder which was due to the heat would be given by the Method of Residues. But we can do none of these things; and without them the application of any of the three methods to the solution of this problem would be illusory. It would be idle, for instance, to attempt to ascertain the effect of heat by subtracting from the phenomena exhibited by a body, all that is due to its other properties; for as we have never been able to observe any bodies without a portion of heat in them, the effects due to that heat might form a part of the very results, which we were affecting to subtract in order that the effect of heat might be shown by the residue.

If, therefore, there were no other methods of experimental investigation than these three, we should be unable to determine the effects due to heat as a cause. But we have still a resource. Though we cannot exclude an antecedent altogether, we may be able to produce, or nature may produce for us, some modification in it. By a modification is here meant, a change in it, not amounting to its total removal. If some modification in the antecedent A is always followed by a change in the consequent *a*, the other consequents *b* and *c* remaining the same; or, ***vice versa***, if every change in *a* is found to have been preceded by some modification in A, none being observable in any of the other antecedents; we may safely conclude that *a* is, wholly or in part, an effect traceable to A, or at least in some way connected with it through causation. For example, in the case of heat, though we cannot expel it altogether from any body, we can modify it in quantity, we can increase or diminish it; and doing so, we find by the various methods of experimentation or observation already treated of, that such increase or diminution of heat is followed by expansion or contraction of the body. In this manner we arrive at the conclusion, otherwise unattainable by us, that one of the effects of heat is to enlarge the dimensions of bodies; or what is the same thing in other words, to widen the distances between their particles.

A change in a thing, not amounting to its total removal, that is, a change which leaves it still the same thing it was, must be a change either in its quantity, or in some of its relations to other things, of which relations the principal is its position in space. In the previous example, the modification which was produced in the antecedent was an alteration in its quantity. Let us now suppose the question to be, what influence the moon exerts on the surface of the earth. We cannot try an experiment in the absence of the moon, so as to observe what terrestrial phenomena her annihilation would put an end to; but when we find that all the variations in the *position* of the moon are followed by corresponding variations in the time and place of high water, the place being always either the part of the earth which is nearest to, or that which is most remote from, the moon, we have ample evidence that the moon is, wholly or partially, the cause which determines the tides. It very commonly happens, as it does in this instance, that the variations of an effect are correspondent, or analogous, to those of its cause; as the moon moves further towards the east, the high water point does the same: but this is not an indispensable condition; as may be seen in the same example, for along with that high water point, there is at the same instant another high water point diametrically opposite to it, and which, therefore, of necessity, moves towards the west as the moon followed by the nearer of the tide waves advances towards the east: and yet both these motions are equally effects of the moon's motion.

That the oscillations of the pendulum are caused by the earth, is proved by similar evidence. Those oscillations take place between equidistant points on the two sides of a line, which, being perpendicular to the earth, varies with every variation in the earth's position, either in space or relatively to the object. Speaking accurately, we only know by the method now characterized, that all terrestrial bodies tend to the earth, and not to some unknown fixed point lying in the same direction. In every twenty-four hours, by the earth's rotation, the line drawn from the body at right angles to the earth coincides successively with all the radii of a circle, and in the course of six months the place of that circle varies by nearly two hundred millions of miles; yet in all these changes of the earth's position, the line in which bodies tend to fall continues to be directed towards it: which proves that terrestrial gravity is directed to the earth, and not, as was once fancied by some, to a fixed point of space.

The method by which these results were obtained, may be termed the Method of Concomitant Variations: it is regulated by the following canon:--

FIFTH CANON.

Whatever phenomenon varies in any manner whenever another phenomenon varies in some particular manner, is either a cause or an effect of that phenomenon, or is connected with it through some fact of causation.

The last clause is subjoined, because it by no means follows when two phenomena accompany each other in their variations, that the one is cause and the other effect. The same thing may, and indeed must happen, supposing them to be two different effects of a common cause: and by this method alone it would never be possible to ascertain which of the suppositions is the true one. The only way to solve the doubt would be that which we have so often adverted to, viz. by endeavouring to ascertain whether we can produce the one set of variations by means of the other. In the case of heat, for example, by increasing the temperature of a body we increase its bulk, but by increasing its bulk we do not increase its temperature; on the contrary, (as in the rarefaction of air under the receiver of an air-pump,) we generally diminish it: therefore heat is not an effect, but a cause, of increase of bulk. If we cannot ourselves produce the variations, we must endeavour, though it is an attempt which is seldom successful, to find them produced by nature in some case in which the pre-existing circumstances are perfectly known to us.

It is scarcely necessary to say, that in order to ascertain the uniform concomitance of variations in the effect with variations in the cause, the same precautions must be used as in any other case of the determination of an invariable sequence. We must endeavour to retain all the other antecedents unchanged, while that particular one is subjected to the requisite series of variations; or in other words, that we may be warranted in inferring causation from concomitance of variations, the concomitance itself must be proved by the Method of Difference.

It might at first appear that the Method of Concomitant Variations assumes a new axiom, or law of causation in general, namely, that every modification of the cause is followed by a change in the effect. And it does usually happen that when a phenomenon A causes a phenomenon *a*, any variation in the quantity or in the various relations of A, is uniformly followed by a variation in the quantity or relations of *a*. To take a familiar instance, that of gravitation. The sun causes a certain tendency to motion in the earth; here we have cause and effect; but that tendency is **towards** the sun, and therefore varies in direction as the sun varies in the relation of position; and moreover the tendency varies in intensity, in a certain numerical ratio to the sun's distance from the earth, that is, according to another relation of the sun. Thus we see that there is not only an invariable connexion between the sun and the earth's gravitation, but that two of the relations of the sun, its position with respect to the earth and its distance from the earth, are invariably connected as antecedents with the quantity and direction of the earth's gravitation. The cause of the earth's gravitating at all, is simply the sun; but the cause of its gravitating with a given intensity and in a given direction, is the existence of the sun in a given direction and at a given distance. It is not strange that a modified cause, which is in truth a different cause, should produce a different effect.

Although it is for the most part true that a modification of the cause is followed by a modification of the effect, the Method of Concomitant Variations does not, however, presuppose this as an axiom. It only requires the converse proposition; that anything on whose modifications, modifications of an effect are invariably consequent, must be the cause (or connected with the cause) of that effect; a proposition, the truth of which is evident; for if the thing itself had no influence on the effect, neither could the modifications of the thing have any influence. If the stars have no power over the fortunes of mankind, it is implied in the very terms, that the conjunctions or oppositions of different stars can have no such power.

Although the most striking applications of the Method of Concomitant Variations take place in the cases in which the Method of Difference, strictly so called, is impossible, its use is not confined to those cases; it may often usefully follow after the Method of Difference, to give additional precision to a solution which that has found. When by the Method of Difference it has first been ascertained that a certain object produces a certain effect, the Method of Concomitant Variations may be usefully called in to determine according to what law the quantity or the different relations of the effect follow those of the cause.

§ 7. The case in which this method admits of the most extensive employment, is that in which the variations of the cause are variations of quantity. Of such variations we may in general affirm with safety, that they will be attended not only with variations, but with similar variations, of the effect: the proposition, that more of the cause is followed by more of the effect, being a corollary from the principle of the Composition of Causes, which, as we have seen, is the general rule of causation; cases of the opposite description, in which causes change their properties on being conjoined with one another, being, on the contrary, special and exceptional. Suppose, then, that when A changes in quantity, *a* also changes in quantity, and in such a manner that we can trace the numerical relation which the changes of the one bear to such changes of the other as take place within our limits of observation. We may then, with certain precautions, safely conclude that the same numerical relation will hold beyond those limits. If, for instance, we find that when A is double, *a* is double; that when A is treble or quadruple, *a* is treble or quadruple; we may conclude that if A were a half or a third, *a* would be a half or a third, and finally, that if A were annihilated, *a* would be annihilated, and that *a* is wholly the effect of A, or wholly the effect of the same cause with A. And so with any other numerical relation according to which A and *a* would vanish simultaneously; as for instance if *a* were proportional to the square of A. If, on the other hand, *a* is not wholly the effect of A, but yet varies when A varies, it is probably a mathematical function not of A alone but of A and something else: its changes, for example, may be such as would occur if part of it remained constant, or varied on some other principle, and the remainder varied in some numerical relation to the variations of A. In that case, when A diminishes, *a* will seem to approach not towards zero, but towards some other limit: and when the series of variations is such as to indicate what that limit is, if constant, or the law of its variation if variable, the limit will exactly measure how much of *a* is the effect of some other and independent cause, and the remainder will be the effect of A (or of the cause of A).

These conclusions, however, must not be drawn without certain precautions. In the first place, the possibility of drawing them at all, manifestly supposes that we are acquainted not only with the variations, but with the absolute quantities, both of A and *a*. If we do not know the total quantities, we cannot, of course, determine the real numerical relation according to which those quantities vary. It is therefore an error to conclude, as some have concluded, that because increase of heat expands bodies, that is, increases the distance between their particles, therefore the distance is wholly the effect of heat, and that if we could entirely exhaust the body of its heat, the particles would be in complete contact. This is no more than a guess, and of the most hazardous sort, not a legitimate induction: for since we neither know how much heat there is in any body, nor what is the real distance between any two of its particles, we cannot judge whether the contraction of the distance does or does not follow the diminution of the quantity of heat according to such a numerical relation that the two quantities would vanish simultaneously.

In contrast with this, let us consider a case in which the absolute quantities are known; the case contemplated in the first law of motion; viz. that all bodies in motion continue to move in a straight line with uniform velocity until acted upon by some new force. This assertion is in open opposition to first appearances; all terrestrial objects, when in motion, gradually abate their velocity and at last stop; which accordingly the ancients, with their ***inductio per enumerationem simplicem***, imagined to be the law. Every moving body, however, encounters various obstacles, as friction, the resistance of the atmosphere, &c., which we know by daily experience to be causes capable of destroying motion. It was suggested that the whole of the retardation might be owing to these causes. How was this inquired into? If the obstacles could have been entirely removed, the case would have been amenable to the Method of Difference. They could not be removed, they could only be diminished, and the case, therefore, admitted only of the Method of Concomitant Variations. This accordingly being employed, it was found that every diminution of the obstacles diminished the retardation of the motion: and inasmuch as in this case (unlike the case of heat) the total quantities both of the antecedent and of the consequent were known; it was practicable to estimate, with an approach to accuracy, both the amount of the retardation and the amount of the retarding causes, or resistances, and to judge how near they both were to being exhausted; and it appeared that the effect dwindled as rapidly, and at each step was as far on the road towards annihilation, as the cause was. The simple oscillation of a weight suspended from a fixed point, and moved a little out of the perpendicular, which in ordinary circumstances lasts but a few minutes, was prolonged in Borda's experiments to more than thirty hours, by diminishing as much as possible the friction at the point of suspension, and by making the body oscillate in a space exhausted as nearly as possible of its air. There could therefore be no hesitation in assigning the whole of the retardation of motion to the influence of the obstacles: and since, after subducting this retardation from the total phenomenon, the remainder was an uniform velocity, the result was the proposition known as the first law of motion.

There is also another characteristic uncertainty affecting the inference that the law of variation which the quantities observe within our limits of observation, will hold beyond those limits. There is of course, in the first instance, the possibility that beyond the limits, and in circumstances therefore of which we have no direct experience, some counteracting cause might develop itself; either a new agent, or a new property of the agents concerned, which lies dormant in the circumstances we are able to observe. This is an element of uncertainty which enters largely into all our predictions of effects; but it is not peculiarly applicable to the Method of Concomitant Variations. The uncertainty, however, of which I am about to speak, is characteristic of that method; especially in the cases in which the extreme limits of our observation are very narrow, in comparison with the possible variations in the quantities of the phenomena. Any one who has the slightest acquaintance with mathematics, is aware that very different laws of variation may produce numerical results which differ but slightly from one another within narrow limits; and it is often only when the absolute amounts of variation are considerable, that the difference between the results given by one law and by another becomes appreciable. When, therefore, such variations in the quantity of the antecedents as we have the means of observing, are small in comparison with the total quantities, there is much danger lest we should mistake the numerical law, and be led to miscalculate the variations which would take place beyond the limits; a miscalculation which would vitiate any conclusion respecting the dependence of the effect upon the cause, that could be founded on those variations. Examples are not wanting of such mistakes. "The formulae," says Sir John Herschel,(77) "which have been empirically deduced for the elasticity of steam, (till very recently,) and those for the resistance of fluids, and other similar subjects," when relied on beyond the limits of the observations from which they were deduced, "have almost invariably failed to support the theoretical structures which have been erected on them."

In this uncertainty, the conclusion we may draw from the concomitant variations of *a* and A, to the existence of an invariable and exclusive connexion between them, or to the permanency of the same numerical relation between their variations when the quantities are much greater or smaller than those which we have had the means of observing, cannot be considered to rest on a complete induction. All that in such a case can be regarded as proved on the subject of causation is, that there is some connexion between the two phenomena; that A, or something which can influence A, must be *one* of the causes which collectively determine *a*. We may, however, feel assured that the relation which we have observed to exist between the variations of A and *a*, will hold true in all cases which fall between the same extreme limits; that is, wherever the utmost increase or diminution in which the result has been found by observation to coincide with the law, is not exceeded.

The four methods which it has now been attempted to describe, are the only possible modes of experimental inquiry, of direct induction *a posteriori*, as distinguished from deduction: at least, I know not, nor am able to imagine, any others. And even of these, the Method of Residues, as we have seen, is not independent of deduction; though, as it also requires specific experience, it may, without impropriety, be included among methods of direct observation and experiment.

These, then, with such assistance as can be obtained from Deduction, compose the available resources of the human mind for ascertaining the laws of the succession of phenomena. Before proceeding to point out certain circumstances, by which the employment of these methods is subjected to an immense increase of complication and of difficulty, it is expedient to illustrate the use of the methods by suitable examples drawn from actual physical investigations. These, accordingly, will form the subject of the succeeding chapter.

CHAPTER IX. MISCELLANEOUS EXAMPLES OF THE FOUR METHODS.

§ 1. I shall select, as a first example, an interesting speculation of one of the most eminent of theoretical chemists, Professor Liebig. The object in view, is to ascertain the immediate cause of the death produced by metallic poisons.

Arsenious acid, and the salts of lead, bismuth, copper, and mercury, if introduced into the animal organism, except in the smallest doses, destroy life. These facts have long been known, as insulated truths of the lowest order of generalization; but it was reserved for Liebig, by an apt employment of the first two of our methods of experimental inquiry, to connect these truths together by a higher induction, pointing out what property, common to all these deleterious substances, is the really operating cause of their fatal effect.

When solutions of these substances are placed in sufficiently close contact with many animal products, albumen, milk, muscular fibre, and animal membranes, the acid or salt leaves the water in which it was dissolved, and enters into combination with the animal substance: which substance, after being thus acted upon, is found to have lost its tendency to spontaneous decomposition, or putrefaction.

Observation also shows, in cases where death has been produced by these poisons, that the parts of the body with which the poisonous substances have been brought into contact, do not afterwards putrefy.

And, finally, when the poison has been supplied in too small a quantity to destroy life, eschars are produced, that is, certain superficial portions of the tissues are destroyed, which are afterwards thrown off by the reparative process taking place in the healthy parts.

These three sets of instances admit of being treated according to the Method of Agreement. In all of them the metallic compounds are brought into contact with the substances which compose the human or animal body; and the instances do not seem to agree in any other circumstance. The remaining antecedents are as different, and even opposite, as they could possibly be made; for in some the animal substances exposed to the action of the poisons are in a state of life, in others only in a state of organization, in others not even in that. And what is the result which follows in all the cases? The conversion of the animal substance (by combination with the poison) into a chemical compound, held together by so powerful a force as to resist the subsequent action of the ordinary causes of decomposition. Now, organic life (the necessary condition of sensitive life) consisting in a continual state of decomposition and recomposition of the different organs and tissues; whatever incapacitates them for this decomposition destroys life. And thus the proximate cause of the death produced by this description of poisons, is ascertained, as far as the Method of Agreement can ascertain it.

Let us now bring our conclusion to the test of the Method of Difference. Setting out from the cases already mentioned, in which the antecedent is the presence of substances forming with the tissues a compound incapable of putrefaction, (and *a fortiori* incapable of the chemical actions which constitute life,) and the consequent is death, either of the whole organism, or of some portion of it; let us compare with these cases other cases, as much resembling them as possible, but in which that effect is not produced. And, first, "many insoluble basic salts of arsenious acid are known not to be poisonous. The substance called alkargen, discovered by Bunsen, which contains a very large quantity of arsenic, and approaches very closely in composition to the organic arsenious compounds found in the body, has not the slightest injurious action upon the organism." Now when these substances are brought into contact with the tissues in any way, they do not combine with them; they do not arrest their progress to decomposition. As far, therefore, as these instances go, it appears that when the effect is absent, it is by reason of the absence of that antecedent which we had already good ground for considering as the proximate cause.

But the rigorous conditions of the Method of Difference are not yet satisfied; for we cannot be sure that these unpoisonous bodies agree with the poisonous substances in every property, except the particular one, of entering into a difficultly decomposable compound with the animal tissues. To render the method strictly applicable, we need an instance, not of a different substance, but of one of the very same substances, in circumstances which would prevent it from forming, with the tissues, the sort of compound in question; and then, if death does not follow, our case is made out. Now such instances are afforded by the antidotes to these poisons. For example, in case of poisoning by arsenious acid, if hydrated peroxide of iron is administered, the destructive agency is instantly checked. Now this peroxide is known to combine with the acid, and form a compound, which, being insoluble, cannot act at all on animal tissues. So, again, sugar is a well-known antidote to poisoning by salts of copper; and sugar reduces those salts either into metallic copper, or into the red suboxide, neither of which enters into combination with animal matter. The disease called painter's colic, so common in manufactories of white lead, is unknown where the workmen are accustomed to take, as a preservative, sulphuric-acid-lemonade (a solution of sugar rendered acid by sulphuric acid). Now diluted sulphuric acid has the property of decomposing all compounds of lead with organic matter, or of preventing them from being formed.

There is another class of instances, of the nature required by the Method of Difference, which seem at first sight to conflict with the theory. Soluble salts of silver, such for instance as the nitrate, have the same stiffening antiseptic effect on decomposing animal substances as corrosive sublimate and the most deadly metallic poisons; and when applied to the external parts of the body, the nitrate is a powerful caustic, depriving those parts of all active vitality, and causing them to be thrown off by the neighbouring living structures, in the form of an eschar. The nitrate and the other salts of silver ought, then, it would seem, if the theory be correct, to be poisonous; yet they may be administered internally with perfect impunity. From this apparent exception arises the strongest confirmation which the theory has yet received. Nitrate of silver, in spite of its chemical properties, does not poison when introduced into the stomach; but in the stomach, as in all animal liquids, there is common salt; and in the stomach there is also free muriatic acid. These substances operate as natural antidotes, combining with the nitrate, and if its quantity is not too great, immediately converting it into chloride of silver; a substance very slightly soluble, and therefore incapable of combining with the tissues, although to the extent of its solubility it has a medicinal influence, through an entirely different class of organic actions.

The preceding instances have afforded an induction of a high order of conclusiveness, illustrative of the two simplest of our four methods; although not rising to the maximum of certainty which the Method of Difference, in its most perfect exemplification, is capable of affording. For (let us not forget) the positive instance and the negative one which the rigour of that method requires, ought to differ only in the presence or absence of one single circumstance. Now, in the preceding argument, they differ in the presence or absence not of a single *circumstance*, but of a single *substance*: and as every substance has innumerable properties, there is no knowing what number of real differences are involved in what is nominally and apparently only one difference. It is conceivable that the antidote, the peroxide of iron for example, may counteract the poison through some other of its properties than that of forming an insoluble compound with it; and if so, the theory would fall to the ground, so far as it is supported by that instance. This source of uncertainty, which is a serious hindrance to all extensive generalizations in chemistry, is however reduced in the present case to almost the lowest degree possible, when we find that not only one substance, but many substances, possess the capacity of acting as antidotes to metallic poisons, and that all these agree in the property of forming insoluble compounds with the poisons, while they cannot be ascertained to agree in any other property whatsoever. We have thus, in favour of the theory, all the evidence which can be obtained by what we termed the Indirect Method of Difference, or the Joint Method of Agreement and Difference; the evidence of which, though it never can amount to that of the Method of Difference properly so called, may approach indefinitely near to it.

§ 2. Let the object be(78) to ascertain the law of what is termed ***induced*** electricity; to find under what conditions any electrified body, whether positively or negatively electrified, gives rise to a contrary electric state in some other body adjacent to it.

The most familiar exemplification of the phenomenon to be investigated, is the following. Around the prime conductors of an electrical machine, the atmosphere to some distance, or any conducting surface suspended in that atmosphere, is found to be in an electric condition opposite to that of the prime conductor itself. Near and around the positive prime conductor there is negative electricity, and near and around the negative prime conductor there is positive electricity. When pith balls are brought near to either of the conductors, they become electrified with the opposite electricity to it; either receiving a share from the already electrified atmosphere by conduction, or acted upon by the direct inductive influence of the conductor itself: they are then attracted by the conductor to which they are in opposition; or, if withdrawn in their electrified state, they will be attracted by any other oppositely charged body. In like manner the hand, if brought near enough to the conductor, receives or gives an electric discharge; now we have no evidence that a charged conductor can be suddenly discharged unless by the approach of a body oppositely electrified. In the case, therefore, of the electrical machine, it appears that the accumulation of electricity in an insulated conductor is always accompanied by the excitement of the contrary electricity in the surrounding atmosphere, and in every conductor placed near the former conductor. It does not seem possible, in this case, to produce one electricity by itself.

Let us now examine all the other instances which we can obtain, resembling this instance in the given consequent, namely, the evolution of an opposite electricity in the neighbourhood of an electrified body. As one remarkable instance we have the Leyden jar; and after the splendid experiments of Faraday in complete and final establishment of the substantial identity of magnetism and electricity, we may cite the magnet, both the natural and the electro-magnet, in neither of which is it possible to produce one kind of electricity by itself, or to charge one pole without charging an opposite pole with the contrary electricity at the same time. We cannot have a magnet with one pole: if we break a natural loadstone into a thousand pieces, each piece will have its two oppositely electrified poles complete within itself. In the voltaic circuit, again, we cannot have one current without its opposite. In the ordinary electric machine, the glass cylinder or plate, and the rubber, acquire opposite electricities.

From all these instances, treated by the Method of Agreement, a general law appears to result. The instances embrace all the known modes in which a body can become charged with electricity; and in all of them there is found, as a concomitant or consequent, the excitement of the opposite electric state in some other body or bodies. It seems to follow that the two facts are invariably connected, and that the excitement of electricity in any body has for one of its necessary conditions the possibility of a simultaneous excitement of the opposite electricity in some neighbouring body.

As the two contrary electricities can only be produced together, so they can only cease together. This may be shown by an application of the Method of Difference to the example of the Leyden jar. It needs scarcely be here remarked that in the Leyden jar, electricity can be accumulated and retained in considerable quantity, by the contrivance of having two conducting surfaces of equal extent, and parallel to each other through the whole of that extent, with a non-conducting substance such as glass between them. When one side of the jar is charged positively, the other is charged negatively, and it was by virtue of this fact that the Leyden jar served just now as an instance in our employment of the Method of Agreement. Now it is impossible to discharge one of the coatings unless the other can be discharged at the same time. A conductor held to the positive side cannot convey away any electricity unless an equal quantity be allowed to pass from the negative side: if one coating be perfectly insulated, the charge is safe. The dissipation of one must proceed *pari passu* with that of the other.

The law thus strongly indicated admits of corroboration by the Method of Concomitant Variations. The Leyden jar is capable of receiving a much higher charge than can ordinarily be given to the conductor of an electrical machine. Now in the case of the Leyden jar, the metallic surface which receives the induced electricity is a conductor exactly similar to that which receives the primary charge, and is therefore as susceptible of receiving and retaining the one electricity, as the opposite surface of receiving and retaining the other; but in the machine, the neighbouring body which is to be oppositely electrified is the surrounding atmosphere, or any body casually brought near to the conductor; and as these are generally much inferior in their capacity of becoming electrified, to the conductor itself, their limited power imposes a corresponding limit to the capacity of the conductor for being charged. As the capacity of the neighbouring body for supporting the opposition increases, a higher charge becomes possible: and to this appears to be owing the great superiority of the Leyden jar.

A further and most decisive confirmation by the Method of Difference, is to be found in one of Faraday's experiments in the course of his researches on the subject of induced electricity.

Since common or machine electricity, and voltaic electricity, may be considered for the present purpose to be identical, Faraday wished to know whether, as the prime conductor develops opposite electricity upon a conductor in its vicinity, so a voltaic current running along a wire would induce an opposite current upon another wire laid parallel to it at a short distance. Now this case is similar to the cases previously examined, in every circumstance except the one to which we have ascribed the effect. We found in the former instances that whenever electricity of one kind was excited in one body, electricity of the opposite kind must be excited in a neighbouring body. But in Faraday's experiment this indispensable opposition exists within the wire itself. From the nature of a voltaic charge, the two opposite currents necessary to the existence of each other are both accommodated in one wire; and there is no need of another wire placed beside it to contain one of them, in the same way as the Leyden jar must have a positive and a negative surface. The exciting cause can and does produce all the effect which its laws require, independently of any electric excitement of a neighbouring body. Now the result of the experiment with the second wire was, that no opposite current was produced. There was an instantaneous effect at the closing and breaking of the voltaic circuit; electric inductions appeared when the two wires were moved to and from one another; but these are phenomena of a different class. There was no induced electricity in the sense in which this is predicated of the Leyden jar; there was no sustained current running up the one wire while an opposite current ran down the neighbouring wire; and this alone would have been a true parallel case to the other.

It thus appears by the combined evidence of the Method of Agreement, the Method of Concomitant Variations, and the most rigorous form of the Method of Difference, that neither of the two kinds of electricity can be excited without an equal excitement of the other and opposite kind: that both are effects of the same cause; that the possibility of the one is a condition of the possibility of the other, and the quantity of the one an impassable limit to the quantity of the other. A scientific result of considerable interest in itself, and illustrating those three methods in a manner both characteristic and easily intelligible.(79)

§ 3. Our third example shall be extracted from Sir John Herschel's ***Discourse on the Study of Natural Philosophy***, a work replete with happily-selected exemplifications of inductive processes from almost every department of physical science, and in which alone, of all books which I have met with, the four methods of induction are distinctly recognised, though not so clearly characterized and defined, nor their correlation so fully shown, as has appeared to me desirable. The present example is described by Sir John Herschel as "one of the most beautiful specimens" which can be cited "of inductive experimental inquiry lying within a moderate compass;" the theory of dew, first promulgated by the late Dr. Wells, and now universally adopted by scientific authorities. The passages in inverted commas are extracted verbatim from the "Discourse."(80)

"Suppose ***dew*** were the phenomenon proposed, whose cause we would know. In the first place" we must determine precisely what we mean by dew: what the fact really is, whose cause we desire to investigate. "We must separate dew from rain, and the moisture of fogs, and limit the application of the term to what is really meant, which is, the spontaneous appearance of moisture on substances exposed in the open air when no rain or ***visible*** wet is falling." This answers to a preliminary operation which will be characterized in the ensuing book, treating of operations subsidiary to induction.(81) The state of the question being fixed, we come to the solution.

"Now, here we have analogous phenomena in the moisture which bedews a cold metal or stone when we breathe upon it; that which appears on a glass of water fresh from the well in hot weather; that which appears on the inside of windows when sudden rain or hail chills the external air; that which runs down our walls when, after a long frost, a warm moist thaw comes on." Comparing these cases, we find that they all contain the phenomenon which was proposed as the subject of investigation. Now "all these instances agree in one point, the coldness of the object dewed, in comparison with the air in contact with it." But there still remains the most important case of all, that of nocturnal dew: does the same circumstance exist in this case? "Is it a fact that the object dewed *is* colder than the air? Certainly not, one would at first be inclined to say; for what is to *make* it so? But ... the experiment is easy: we have only to lay a thermometer in contact with the dewed substance, and hang one at a little distance above it, out of reach of its influence. The experiment has been therefore made; the question has been asked, and the answer has been invariably in the affirmative. Whenever an object contracts dew, it *is* colder than the air."

Here then is a complete application of the Method of Agreement, establishing the fact of an invariable connexion between the deposition of dew on a surface, and the coldness of that surface compared with the external air. But which of these is cause, and which effect? or are they both effects of something else? On this subject the Method of Agreement can afford us no light: we must call in a more potent method. "We must collect more facts, or, which comes to the same thing, vary the circumstances; since every instance in which the circumstances differ is a fresh fact: and especially, we must note the contrary or negative cases, *i.e.*, where no dew is produced:" for a comparison between instances of dew and instances of no dew, is the condition necessary to bring the Method of Difference into play.

"Now, first, no dew is produced on the surface of polished metals, but it *is* very copiously on glass, both exposed with their faces upwards, and in some cases the under side of a horizontal plate of glass is also dewed." Here is an instance in which the effect is produced, and another instance in which it is not produced; but we cannot yet pronounce, as the canon of the Method of Difference requires, that the latter instance agrees with the former in all its circumstances except one; for the differences between glass and polished metals are manifold, and the only thing we can as yet be sure of is, that the cause of dew will be found among the circumstances by which the former substance is distinguished from the latter. But if we could be sure that glass, and the various other substances on which dew is deposited, have only *one* quality in common, and that polished metals and the other substances on which dew is *not* deposited have also nothing in common but the one circumstance, of *not* having the one quality which the others have; the requisitions of the Method of Difference would be completely satisfied, and we should recognise, in that quality of the substances, the cause of dew. This, accordingly, is the path of inquiry which is next to be pursued.

"In the cases of polished metal and polished glass, the contrast shows evidently that the *substance* has much to do with the phenomenon; therefore let the substance *alone* be diversified as much as possible, by exposing polished surfaces of various kinds. This done, a *scale of intensity* becomes obvious. Those polished substances are found to be most strongly dewed which conduct heat worst; while those which conduct well, resist dew most effectually." The complication increases; here is the Method of Concomitant Variations called to our assistance; and no other method was practicable on this occasion; for the quality of conducting heat could not be excluded, since all substances conduct heat in some degree. The conclusion obtained is, that *caeteris paribus* the deposition of dew is in some proportion to the power which the body possesses of resisting the passage of heat; and that this, therefore, (or something connected with this,) must be at least one of the causes which assist in producing the deposition of dew on the surface.

"But if we expose rough surfaces instead of polished, we sometimes find this law interfered with. Thus, roughened iron, especially if painted over or blackened, becomes dewed sooner than varnished paper: the kind of *surface*, therefore, has a great influence. Expose, then, the *same* material in very diversified states as to surface," (that is, employ the Method of Difference to ascertain concomitance of variations,) "and another scale of intensity becomes at once apparent; those *surfaces* which *part with their heat* most readily by radiation, are found to contract dew most copiously." Here, therefore, are the requisites for a second employment of the Method of Concomitant Variations; which in this case also is the only method available, since all substances radiate heat in some degree or other. The conclusion obtained by this new application of the method is, that **caeteris paribus** the deposition of dew is also in some proportion to the power of radiating heat; and that the quality of doing this abundantly (or some cause on which that quality depends) is another of the causes which promote the deposition of dew on the substance.

"Again, the influence ascertained to exist of **substance** and **surface** leads us to consider that of **texture**: and here, again, we are presented on trial with remarkable differences, and with a third scale of intensity, pointing out substances of a close firm texture, such as stones, metals, &c., as unfavourable, but those of a loose one, as cloth, velvet, wool, eiderdown, cotton, &c., as eminently favourable to the contraction of dew." The Method of Concomitant Variations is here, for the third time, had recourse to; and, as before, from necessity, since the texture of no substance is absolutely firm or absolutely loose. Looseness of texture, therefore, or something which is the cause of that quality, is another circumstance which promotes the deposition of dew; but this third cause resolves itself into the first, viz. the quality of resisting the passage of heat: for substances of loose texture "are precisely those which are best adapted for clothing, or for impeding the free passage of heat from the skin into the air, so as to allow their outer surfaces to be very cold, while they remain warm within;" and this last is, therefore, an induction (from fresh instances) simply **corroborative** of a former induction.

It thus appears that the instances in which much dew is deposited, which are very various, agree in this, and, so far as we are able to observe, in this only, that they either radiate heat rapidly or conduct it slowly: qualities between which there is no other circumstance of agreement, than that by virtue of either, the body tends to lose heat from the surface more rapidly than it can be restored from within. The instances, on the contrary, in which no dew, or but a small quantity of it, is formed, and which are also extremely various, agree (so far as we can observe) in nothing except in **not** having this same property. We seem, therefore, to have detected the characteristic difference between the substances on which dew is produced, and those on which it is not produced. And thus have been realized the requisitions of what we have termed the Indirect Method of Difference, or the Joint Method of Agreement and Difference. The example afforded of this indirect method, and of the manner in which the data are prepared for it by the Methods of Agreement and of Concomitant Variations, is the most important of all the illustrations of induction afforded by this interesting speculation.

We might now consider the question, on what the deposition of dew depends, to be completely solved, if we could be quite sure that the substances on which dew is produced differ from those on which it is not, in **nothing** but in the property of losing heat from the surface faster than the loss can be repaired from within. And though we never can have that complete certainty, this is not of so much importance as might at first be supposed; for we have, at all events, ascertained that even if there be any other quality hitherto unobserved which is present in all the substances which contract dew, and absent in those which do not, this other property must be one which, in all that great number of substances, is present or absent exactly where the property of being a better radiator than conductor is present or absent; an extent of coincidence which affords a strong presumption of a community of cause, and a consequent invariable coexistence between the two properties; so that the property of being a better radiator than conductor, if not itself the cause, almost certainly always accompanies the cause, and for purposes of prediction, no error is likely to be committed by treating it as if it were really such.

Reverting now to an earlier stage of the inquiry, let us remember that we had ascertained that, in every instance where dew is formed, there is actual coldness of the surface below the temperature of the surrounding air; but we were not sure whether this coldness was the cause of dew, or its effect. This doubt we are now able to resolve. We have found that, in every such instance, the substance must be one which, by its own properties or laws, would, if exposed in the night, become colder than the surrounding air. The coldness therefore, being accounted for independently of the dew, while it is proved that there is a connexion between the two, it must be the dew which depends on the coldness; or in other words, the coldness is the cause of the dew.

This law of causation, already so amply established, admits, however, of efficient additional corroboration in no less than three ways. First, by deduction from the known laws of aqueous vapour when diffused through air or any other gas; and though we have not yet come to the Deductive Method, we will not omit what is necessary to render this speculation complete. It is known by direct experiment that only a limited quantity of water can remain suspended in the state of vapour at each degree of temperature, and that this maximum grows less and less as the temperature diminishes. From this it follows, deductively, that if there is already as much vapour suspended as the air will contain at its existing temperature, any lowering of that temperature will cause a portion of the vapour to be condensed, and become water. But, again, we know deductively, from the laws of heat, that the contact of the air with a body colder than itself, will necessarily lower the temperature of the stratum of air immediately applied to its surface; and will therefore cause it to part with a portion of its water, which accordingly will, by the ordinary laws of gravitation or cohesion, attach itself to the surface of the body, thereby constituting dew. This deductive proof, it will have been seen, has the advantage of proving at once, causation as well as coexistence; and it has the additional advantage that it also accounts for the ***exceptions*** to the occurrence of the phenomenon, the cases in which, although the body is colder than the air, yet no dew is deposited; by showing that this will necessarily be the case when the air is so under-supplied with aqueous vapour, comparatively to its temperature, that even when somewhat cooled by the contact of the colder body, it can still continue to hold in suspension all the vapour which was previously suspended in it: thus in a very dry summer there are no dews, in a very dry winter no hoar frost. Here, therefore, is an additional condition of the production of dew, which the methods we previously made use of failed to detect, and which might have remained still undetected, if recourse had not been had to the plan of deducing the effect from the ascertained properties of the agents known to be present.

The second corroboration of the theory is by direct experiment, according to the canon of the Method of Difference. We can, by cooling the surface of any body, find in all cases some temperature, (more or less inferior to that of the surrounding air, according to its hygrometric condition), at which dew will begin to be deposited. Here, too, therefore, the causation is directly proved. We can, it is true, accomplish this only on a small scale; but we have ample reason to conclude that the same operation, if conducted in Nature's great laboratory, would equally produce the effect.

And, finally, even on that great scale we are able to verify the result. The case is one of those rare cases, as we have shown them to be, in which nature works the experiment for us in the same manner in which we ourselves perform it; introducing into the previous state of things a single and perfectly definite new circumstance, and manifesting the effect so rapidly that there is not time for any other material change in the pre-existing circumstances. "It is observed that dew is never copiously deposited in situations much screened from the open sky, and not at all in a cloudy night; but ***if the clouds withdraw even for a few minutes, and leave a clear opening, a deposition of dew presently begins***, and goes on increasing…. Dew formed in clear intervals will often even evaporate again when the sky becomes thickly overcast." The proof, therefore, is complete, that the presence or absence of an uninterrupted communication with the sky causes the deposition or non-deposition of dew. Now, since a clear sky is nothing but the absence of clouds, and it is a known property of clouds, as of all other bodies between which and any given object nothing intervenes but an elastic fluid, that they tend to raise or keep up the superficial temperature of the object by radiating heat to it, we see at once that the disappearance of clouds will cause the surface to cool; so that Nature, in this case, produces a change in the antecedent by definite and known means, and the consequent follows accordingly: a natural experiment which satisfies the requisitions of the Method of Difference.(82)

The accumulated proof of which the Theory of Dew has been found susceptible, is a striking instance of the fulness of assurance which the inductive evidence of laws of causation may attain, in cases in which the invariable sequence is by no means obvious to a superficial view.

§ 4. The last example will have conveyed to any one by whom it has been duly followed, so clear a conception of the use and practical management of three of the four methods of experimental inquiry, as to supersede the necessity of any further exemplification of them. The remaining method, that of Residues, not having found any place either in this or in the two preceding investigations, I shall extract from Sir John Herschel some examples of that method, with the remarks by which they are introduced.

"It is by this process, in fact, that science, in its present advanced state, is chiefly promoted. Most of the phenomena which Nature presents are very complicated; and when the effects of all known causes are estimated with exactness, and subducted, the residual facts are constantly appearing in the form of phenomena altogether new, and leading to the most important conclusions.

"For example: the return of the comet predicted by Professor Encke, a great many times in succession, and the general good agreement of its calculated with its observed place during any one of its periods of visibility, would lead us to say that its gravitation towards the sun and planets is the sole and sufficient cause of all the phenomena of its orbitual motion: but when the effect of this cause is strictly calculated and subducted from the observed motion, there is found to remain behind a *residual phenomenon*, which would never have been otherwise ascertained to exist, which is a small anticipation of the time of its reappearance, or a diminution of its periodic time, which cannot be accounted for by gravity, and whose cause is therefore to be inquired into. Such an anticipation would be caused by the resistance of a medium disseminated through the celestial regions; and as there are other good reasons for believing this to be a *vera causa*," (an actually existing antecedent,) "it has therefore been ascribed to such a resistance.

"M. Arago, having suspended a magnetic needle by a silk thread, and set it in vibration, observed, that it came much sooner to a state of rest when suspended over a plate of copper, than when no such plate was beneath it. Now, in both cases there were two *verae causae* (antecedents known to exist) "why it *should* come at length to rest, viz. the resistance of the air, which opposes, and at length destroys, all motions performed in it; and the want of perfect mobility in the silk thread. But the effect of these causes being exactly known by the observation made in the absence of the copper, and being thus allowed for and subducted, a residual phenomenon appeared, in the fact that a retarding influence was exerted by the copper itself; and this fact, once ascertained, speedily led to the knowledge of an entirely new and unexpected class of relations." This example belongs, however, not to the Method of Residues but to the Method of Difference, the law being ascertained by a direct comparison of the results of two experiments, which differed in nothing but the presence or absence of the plate of copper. To have made it exemplify the Method of Residues, the effect of the resistance of the air and that of the rigidity of the silk should have been calculated *a priori*, from the laws obtained by separate and foregone experiments."

"Unexpected and peculiarly striking confirmations of inductive laws frequently occur in the form of residual phenomena, in the course of investigations of a widely different nature from those which gave rise to the inductions themselves. A very elegant example may be cited in the unexpected confirmation of the law of the development of heat in elastic fluids by compression, which is afforded by the phenomena of sound. The inquiry into the cause of sound had led to conclusions respecting its mode of propagation, from which its velocity in the air could be precisely calculated. The calculations were performed; but, when compared with fact, though the agreement was quite sufficient to show the general correctness of the cause and mode of propagation assigned, yet the *whole* velocity could not be shown to arise from this theory. There was still a residual velocity to be accounted for, which placed dynamical philosophers for a long time in a great dilemma. At length Laplace struck on the happy idea, that this might arise from the *heat* developed in the act of that condensation which necessarily takes place at every vibration by which sound is conveyed. The matter was subjected to exact calculation, and the result was at once the complete explanation of the residual phenomenon, and a striking confirmation of the general law of the development of heat by compression, under circumstances beyond artificial imitation."

"Many of the new elements of chemistry have been detected in the investigation of residual phenomena. Thus Arfwedson discovered lithia by perceiving an excess of weight in the sulphate produced from a small portion of what he considered as magnesia present in a mineral he had analysed. It is on this principle, too, that the small concentrated residues of great operations in the arts are almost sure to be the lurking places of new chemical ingredients: witness iodine, brome, selenium, and the new metals accompanying platina in the experiments of Wollaston and Tennant. It was a happy thought of Glauber to examine what everybody else threw away."(83)

"Almost all the greatest discoveries in Astronomy," says the same author,(84) "have resulted from the consideration of residual phenomena of a quantitative or numerical kind.... It was thus that the grand discovery of the precession of the equinoxes resulted as a residual phenomenon, from the imperfect explanation of the return of the seasons by the return of the sun to the same apparent place among the fixed stars. Thus, also, aberration and nutation resulted as residual phenomena from that portion of the changes of the apparent places of the fixed stars which was left unaccounted for by precession. And thus again the apparent proper motions of the stars are the observed residues of their apparent movements outstanding and unaccounted for by strict calculation of the effects of precession, nutation, and aberration. The nearest approach which human theories can make to perfection is to diminish this residue, this ***caput mortuum*** of observation, as it may be considered, as much as practicable, and, if possible, to reduce it to nothing, either by showing that something has been neglected in our estimation of known causes, or by reasoning upon it as a new fact, and on the principle of the inductive philosophy ascending from the effect to its cause or causes."

The disturbing effects mutually produced by the earth and planets upon each other's motions were first brought to light as residual phenomena, by the difference which appeared between the observed places of those bodies, and the places calculated on a consideration solely of their gravitation towards the sun. It was this which determined astronomers to consider the law of gravitation as obtaining between all bodies whatever, and therefore between all particles of matter; their first tendency having been to regard it as a force acting only between each planet or satellite and the central body to whose system it belonged. Again, the catastrophists, in geology, be their opinion right or wrong, support it on the plea, that after the effect of all causes now in operation has been allowed for, there remains in the existing constitution of the earth a large residue of facts, proving the existence at former periods either of other forces, or of the same forces in a much greater degree of intensity. To add one more example: those who assert, what no one has ever shewn any real ground for believing, that there is in one human individual, one sex, or one race of mankind over another, an inherent and inexplicable superiority in mental faculties, could only substantiate their proposition by subtracting from the differences of intellect which we in fact see, all that can be traced by known laws either to the ascertained differences of physical organization, or to the differences which have existed in the outward circumstances in which the subjects of the comparison have hitherto been placed. What these causes might fail to account for, would constitute a residual phenomenon, which and which alone would be evidence of an ulterior original distinction, and the measure of its amount. But the assertors of such supposed differences have not provided themselves with these necessary logical conditions of the establishment of their doctrine.

The spirit of the Method of Residues being, it is hoped, sufficiently intelligible from these examples, and the other three methods having been so aptly exemplified in the inductive processes which produced the Theory of Dew, we may here close our exposition of the four methods, considered as employed in the investigation of the simpler and more elementary order of the combinations of phenomena.(85)

CHAPTER X. OF PLURALITY OF CAUSES; AND OF THE INTERMIXTURE OF EFFECTS.

§ 1. In the preceding exposition of the four methods of observation and experiment, by which we contrive to distinguish among a mass of coexistent phenomena the particular effect due to a given cause, or the particular cause which gave birth to a given effect; it has been necessary to suppose, in the first instance, for the sake of simplification, that this analytical operation is encumbered by no other difficulties than what are essentially inherent in its nature; and to represent to ourselves, therefore, every effect, on the one hand as connected exclusively with a single cause, and on the other hand as incapable of being mixed and confounded with any other coexistent effect. We have regarded *a b c d e*, the aggregate of the phenomena existing at any moment, as consisting of dissimilar facts, *a*, *b*, *c*, *d*, and *e*, for each of which one, and only one, cause needs be sought; the difficulty being only that of singling out this one cause from the multitude of antecedent circumstances, A, B, C, D, and E.

If such were the fact, it would be comparatively an easy task to investigate the laws of nature. But the supposition does not hold, in either of its parts. In the first place, it is not true that the same phenomenon is always produced by the same cause: the effect *a* may sometimes arise from A, sometimes from B. And, secondly, the effects of different causes are often not dissimilar, but homogeneous, and marked out by no assignable boundaries from one another: A and B may produce not *a* and *b*, but different portions of an effect *a*. The obscurity and difficulty of the investigation of the laws of phenomena is singularly increased by the necessity of adverting to these two circumstances; Intermixture of Effects, and Plurality of Causes. To the latter, being the simpler of the two considerations, we shall first direct our attention.

It is not true, then, that one effect must be connected with only one cause, or assemblage of conditions; that each phenomenon can be produced only in one way. There are often several independent modes in which the same phenomenon could have originated. One fact may be the consequent in several invariable sequences; it may follow, with equal uniformity, any one of several antecedents, or collections of antecedents. Many causes may produce motion: many causes may produce some kinds of sensation: many causes may produce death. A given effect may really be produced by a certain cause, and yet be perfectly capable of being produced without it.

§ 2. One of the principal consequences of this fact of Plurality of Causes is, to render the first of the inductive methods, that of Agreement, uncertain. To illustrate that method, we supposed two instances, A B C followed by *a b c*, and A D E followed by *a d e*. From these instances it might be concluded that A is an invariable antecedent of *a*, and even that it is the unconditional invariable antecedent, or cause, if we could be sure that there is no other antecedent common to the two cases. That this difficulty may not stand in the way, let us suppose the two cases positively ascertained to have no antecedent in common except A. The moment, however, that we let in the possibility of a plurality of causes, the conclusion fails. For it involves a tacit supposition, that *a* must have been produced in both instances by the same cause. If there can possibly have been two causes, those two may, for example, be C and E: the one may have been the cause of *a* in the former of the instances, the other in the latter, A having no influence in either case.

Suppose, for example, that two great artists, or great philosophers, that two extremely selfish, or extremely generous characters, were compared together as to the circumstances of their education and history, and the two cases were found to agree only in one circumstance: would it follow that this one circumstance was the cause of the quality which characterized both those individuals? Not at all; for the causes which may produce any type of character are innumerable; and the two persons might equally have agreed in their character, though there had been no manner of resemblance in their previous history.

This, therefore, is a characteristic imperfection of the Method of Agreement; from which imperfection the Method of Difference is free. For if we have two instances, A B C and B C, of which B C gives *b c*, and A being added converts it into *a b c*, it is certain that in this instance at least, A was either the cause of *a*, or an indispensable portion of its cause, even though the cause which produces it in other instances may be altogether different. Plurality of Causes, therefore, not only does not diminish the reliance due to the Method of Difference, but does not even render a greater number of observations or experiments necessary: two instances, the one positive and the other negative, are still sufficient for the most complete and rigorous induction. Not so, however, with the Method of Agreement. The conclusions which that yields, when the number of instances compared is small, are of no real value, except as, in the character of suggestions, they may lead either to experiments bringing them to the test of the Method of Difference, or to reasonings which may explain and verify them deductively.

It is only when the instances, being indefinitely multiplied and varied, continue to suggest the same result, that this result acquires any high degree of independent value. If there are but two instances, A B C and A D E, although these instances have no antecedent in common except A, yet as the effect may possibly have been produced in the two cases by different causes, the result is at most only a slight probability in favour of A; there may be causation, but it is almost equally probable that there was only a coincidence. But the oftener we repeat the observation, varying the circumstances, the more we advance towards a solution of this doubt. For if we try A F G, A H K, &c., all unlike one another except in containing the circumstance A, and if we find the effect *a* entering into the result in all these cases, we must suppose one of two things, either that it is caused by A, or that it has as many different causes as there are instances. With each addition, therefore, to the number of instances, the presumption is strengthened in favour of A. The inquirer, of course, will not neglect, if an opportunity present itself, to exclude A from some one of these combinations, from A H K for instance, and by trying H K separately, appeal to the Method of Difference in aid of the Method of Agreement. By the Method of Difference alone can it be ascertained that A is the cause of *a*; but that it is either the cause or another effect of the same cause, may be placed beyond any reasonable doubt by the Method of Agreement, provided the instances are very numerous, as well as sufficiently various.

After how great a multiplication, then, of varied instances, all agreeing in no other antecedent except A, is the supposition of a plurality of causes sufficiently re-butted, and the conclusion that *a* is the effect of A divested of the characteristic im-perfection and reduced to a virtual certainty? This is a question which we cannot be exempted from answering; but the consideration of it belongs to what is called the Theory of Probability, which will form the subject of a chapter hereafter. It is seen, however, at once, that the conclusion does amount to a practical certainty after a sufficient number of instances, and that the method, therefore, is not radically viti-ated by the characteristic imperfection. The result of these considerations is only, in the first place, to point out a new source of inferiority in the Method of Agree-ment as compared with other modes of investigation, and new reasons for never resting contented with the results obtained by it, without attempting to confirm them either by the Method of Difference, or by connecting them deductively with some law or laws already ascertained by that superior method. And, in the second place, we learn from this the true theory of the value of mere ***number*** of instances in inductive inquiry. The Plurality of Causes is the only reason why mere number is of any importance. The tendency of unscientific inquirers is to rely too much on number, without analysing the instances; without looking closely enough into their nature, to ascertain what circumstances are or are not eliminated by means of them. Most people hold their conclusions with a degree of assurance proportioned to the mere ***mass*** of the experience on which they appear to rest; not considering that by the addition of instances to instances, all of the same kind, that is, differing from one another only in points already recognised as immaterial, nothing what-ever is added to the evidence of the conclusion. A single instance eliminating some antecedent which existed in all the other cases, is of more value than the greatest multitude of instances which are reckoned by their number alone. It is necessary, no doubt, to assure ourselves, by a repetition of the observation or experiment, that no error has been committed concerning the individual facts observed; and until we have assured ourselves of this, instead of varying the circumstances, we cannot too scrupulously repeat the same experiment or observation without any change. But when once this assurance has been obtained, the multiplication of instances which do not exclude any more circumstances would be entirely useless, were it not for the Plurality of Causes.

It is of importance to remark, that the peculiar modification of the Method of

Agreement which, as partaking in some degree of the nature of the Method of Difference, I have called the Joint Method of Agreement and Difference, is not affected by the characteristic imperfection now pointed out. For, in the joint method, it is supposed not only that the instances in which *a* is, agree only in containing A, but also that the instances in which *a* is not, agree only in not containing A. Now, if this be so, A must be not only the cause of *a*, but the only possible cause: for if there were another, as for example B, then in the instances in which *a* is not, B must have been absent as well as A, and it would not be true that these instances agree *only* in not containing A. This, therefore, constitutes an immense advantage of the joint method over the simple Method of Agreement. It may seem, indeed, that the advantage does not belong so much to the joint method, as to one of its two premisses, (if they may be so called,) the negative premiss. The Method of Agreement, when applied to negative instances, or those in which a phenomenon does *not* take place, is certainly free from the characteristic imperfection which affects it in the affirmative case. The negative premiss, it might therefore be supposed, could be worked as a simple case of the Method of Agreement, without requiring an affirmative premiss to be joined with it. But although this is true in principle, it is generally altogether impossible to work the Method of Agreement by negative instances without positive ones: it is so much more difficult to exhaust the field of negation than that of affirmation. For instance, let the question be, what is the cause of the transparency of bodies; with what prospect of success could we set ourselves to inquire directly in what the multifarious substances which are *not* transparent, agree? But we might hope much sooner to seize some point of resemblance among the comparatively few and definite species of objects which *are* transparent; and this being attained, we should quite naturally be put upon examining whether the *absence* of this one circumstance be not precisely the point in which all opaque substances will be found to resemble.

The Joint Method of Agreement and Difference, therefore, or, as I have otherwise called it, the Indirect Method of Difference (because, like the Method of Difference properly so called, it proceeds by ascertaining how and in what the cases where the phenomenon is present, differ from those in which it is absent) is, after the direct Method of Difference, the most powerful of the remaining instruments of inductive investigation; and in the sciences which depend on pure observation, with little or no aid from experiment, this method, so well exemplified in the speculation on the cause of dew, is the primary resource, so far as direct appeals to experience are concerned.

§ 3. We have thus far treated Plurality of Causes only as a possible supposition, which, until removed, renders our inductions uncertain, and have only considered by what means, where the plurality does not really exist, we may be enabled to disprove it. But we must also consider it as a case actually occurring in nature, and which, as often as it does occur, our methods of induction ought to be capable of ascertaining and establishing. For this, however, there is required no peculiar method. When an effect is really producible by two or more causes, the process for detecting them is in no way different from that by which we discover single causes. They may (first) be discovered as separate sequences, by separate sets of instances. One set of observations or experiments shows that the sun is a cause of heat, another that friction is a source of it, another that percussion, another that electricity, another that chemical action is such a source. Or (secondly) the plurality may come to light in the course of collating a number of instances, when we attempt to find some circumstance in which they all agree, and fail in doing so. We find it impossible to trace, in all the cases in which the effect is met with, any common circumstance. We find that we can eliminate *all* the antecedents; that no one of them is present in all the instances, no one of them indispensable to the effect. On closer scrutiny, however, it appears that though no one is always present, one or other of several always is. If, on further analysis, we can detect in these any common element, we may be able to ascend from them to some one cause which is the really operative circumstance in them all. Thus it might, and perhaps will, be discovered, that in the production of heat by friction, percussion, chemical action, &c., the ultimate source is one and the same. But if (as continually happens) we cannot take this ulterior step, the different antecedents must be set down provisionally as distinct causes, each sufficient of itself to produce the effect.

We here close our remarks on the Plurality of Causes, and proceed to the still more peculiar and more complex case of the Intermixture of Effects, and the interference of causes with one another: a case constituting the principal part of the complication and difficulty of the study of nature; and with which the four only possible methods of directly inductive investigation by observation and experiment, are for the most part, as will appear presently, quite unequal to cope. The instrument of Deduction alone is adequate to unravel the complexities proceeding from this source; and the four methods have little more in their power than to supply premisses for, and a verification of, our deductions.

§ 4. A concurrence of two or more causes, not separately producing each its own effect, but interfering with or modifying the effects of one another, takes place, as has already been explained, in two different ways. In the one, which is exemplified by the joint operation of different forces in mechanics, the separate effects of all the causes continue to be produced, but are compounded with one another, and disappear in one total. In the other, illustrated by the case of chemical action, the separate effects cease entirely, and are succeeded by phenomena altogether different, and governed by different laws.

Of these cases the former is by far the more frequent, and this case it is which, for the most part, eludes the grasp of our experimental methods. The other and exceptional case is essentially amenable to them. When the laws of the original agents cease entirely, and a phenomenon makes its appearance, which, with reference to those laws, is quite heterogeneous; when, for example, two gaseous substances, hydrogen and oxygen, on being brought together, throw off their peculiar properties, and produce the substance called water; in such cases the new fact may be subjected to experimental inquiry, like any other phenomenon; and the elements which are said to compose it may be considered as the mere agents of its production; the conditions on which it depends, the facts which make up its cause.

The *effects* of the new phenomenon, the *properties* of water, for instance, are as easily found by experiment as the effects of any other cause. But to discover the *cause* of it, that is, the particular conjunction of agents from which it results, is often difficult enough. In the first place, the origin and actual production of the phenomenon are most frequently inaccessible to our observation. If we could not have learned the composition of water until we found instances in which it was actually produced from oxygen and hydrogen, we should have been forced to wait until the casual thought struck some one of passing an electric spark through a mixture of the two gases, or inserting a lighted taper into it, merely to try what would happen. Further, even if we could have ascertained, by the Method of Agreement, that oxygen and hydrogen were both present when water is produced, no experimentation on oxygen and hydrogen separately, no knowledge of their laws, could have enabled us deductively to infer that they would produce water. We require a specific experiment on the two combined.

Under these difficulties, we should generally have been indebted for our knowledge of the causes of this class of effects, not to any inquiry directed specifically towards that end, but either to accident, or to the gradual progress of experimentation on the different combinations of which the producing agents are susceptible; if it were not for a peculiarity belonging to effects of this description, that they often, under some particular combination of circumstances, reproduce their causes. If water results from the juxtaposition of hydrogen and oxygen whenever this can be made sufficiently close and intimate, so, on the other hand, if water itself be placed in certain situations, hydrogen and oxygen are reproduced from it: an abrupt termination is put to the new laws, and the agents reappear separately with their own properties as at first. What is called chemical analysis is the process of searching for the causes of a phenomenon among its effects, or rather among the effects produced by the action of some other causes upon it.

Lavoisier, by heating mercury to a high temperature in a close vessel containing air, found that the mercury increased in weight and became what was then called red precipitate, while the air, on being examined after the experiment, proved to have lost weight, and to have become incapable of supporting life or combustion. When red precipitate was exposed to a still greater heat, it became mercury again, and gave off a gas which did support life and flame. Thus the agents which by their combination produced red precipitate, namely the mercury and the gas, reappear as effects resulting from that precipitate when acted upon by heat. So, if we decompose water by means of iron filings, we produce two effects, rust and hydrogen: now rust is already known by experiments upon the component substances, to be an effect of the union of iron and oxygen: the iron we ourselves supplied, but the oxygen must have been produced from the water. The result therefore is that water has disappeared, and hydrogen and oxygen have appeared in its stead: or in other words, the original laws of these gaseous agents, which had been suspended by the superinduction of the new laws called the properties of water, have again started into existence, and the causes of water are found among its effects.

Where two phenomena, between the laws or properties of which considered in themselves no connexion can be traced, are thus reciprocally cause and effect, each capable in its turn of being produced from the other, and each, when it produces the other, ceasing itself to exist (as water is produced from oxygen and hydrogen, and oxygen and hydrogen are reproduced from water); this causation of the two phenomena by one another, each being generated by the other's destruction, is properly transformation. The idea of chemical composition is an idea of transformation, but of a transformation which is incomplete; since we consider the oxygen and hydrogen to be present in the water *as* oxygen and hydrogen, and capable of being discovered in it if our senses were sufficiently keen: a supposition (for it is no more) grounded solely on the fact, that the weight of the water is the sum of the separate weights of the two ingredients. If there had not been this exception to the entire disappearance, in the compound, of the laws of the separate ingredients; if the combined agents had not, in this one particular of weight, preserved their own laws, and produced a joint result equal to the sum of their separate results; we should never, probably, have had the notion now implied by the words chemical composition: and, in the fact of water produced from hydrogen and oxygen and hydrogen and oxygen produced from water, as the transformation would have been complete, we should have seen only a transformation.

In these cases, then, when the heteropathic effect (as we called it in a former chapter)(86) is but a transformation of its cause, or in other words, when the effect and its cause are reciprocally such, and mutually convertible into each other; the problem of finding the cause resolves itself into the far easier one of finding an effect, which is the kind of inquiry that admits of being prosecuted by direct experiment. But there are other cases of heteropathic effects to which this mode of investigation is not applicable. Take, for instance, the heteropathic laws of mind; that portion of the phenomena of our mental nature which are analogous to chemical rather than to dynamical phenomena; as when a complex passion is formed by the coalition of several elementary impulses, or a complex emotion by several simple pleasures or pains, of which it is the result without being the aggregate, or in any respect homogeneous with them. The product, in these cases, is generated by its various factors; but the factors cannot be reproduced from the product: just as a youth can grow into an old man, but an old man cannot grow into a youth. We cannot ascertain from what simple feelings any of our complex states of mind are generated, as we ascertain the ingredients of a chemical compound, by making it, in its turn, generate them. We can only, therefore, discover these laws by the slow process of studying the simple feelings themselves, and ascertaining synthetically, by experimenting on the various combinations of which they are susceptible, what they, by their mutual action upon one another, are capable of generating.

§ 5. It might have been supposed that the other, and apparently simpler variety of the mutual interference of causes, where each cause continues to produce its own proper effect according to the same laws to which it conforms in its separate state, would have presented fewer difficulties to the inductive inquirer than that of which we have just finished the consideration. It, presents, however, so far as direct induction apart from deduction is concerned, infinitely greater difficulties. When a concurrence of causes gives rise to a new effect, bearing no relation to the separate effects of those causes, the resulting phenomenon stands forth undisguised, inviting attention to its peculiarity, and presenting no obstacle to our recognising its presence or absence among any number of surrounding phenomena. It admits therefore of being easily brought under the canons of induction, provided instances can be obtained such as those canons require: and the non-occurrence of such instances, or the want of means to produce them artificially, is the real and only difficulty in such investigations; a difficulty not logical, but in some sort physical. It is otherwise with cases of what, in a preceding chapter, has been denominated the Composition of Causes. There, the effects of the separate causes do not terminate and give place to others, thereby ceasing to form any part of the phenomenon to be investigated; on the contrary, they still take place, but are intermingled with, and disguised by, the homogeneous and closely allied effects of other causes. They are no longer a, b, c, d, e, existing side by side, and continuing to be separately discernible; they are $+ a$, $- a$, $1/2\, b$, $- b$, $2\, b$, &c., some of which cancel one another, while many others do not appear distinguishably, but merge in one sum: forming altogether a result, between which and the causes whereby it was produced there is often an insurmountable difficulty in tracing by observation any fixed relation whatever.

The general idea of the Composition of Causes has been seen to be, that although two or more laws interfere with one another, and apparently frustrate or modify one another's operation, yet in reality all are fulfilled, the collective effect being the exact sum of the effects of the causes taken separately. A familiar instance is that of a body kept in equilibrium by two equal and contrary forces. One of the forces if acting alone would carry it in a given time a certain distance to the west, the other if acting alone would carry it exactly as far towards the east; and the result is the same as if it had been first carried to the west as far as the one force would carry it, and then back towards the east as far as the other would carry it, that is, precisely the same distance; being ultimately left where it was found at first.

All laws of causation are liable to be in this manner counteracted, and seemingly frustrated, by coming into conflict with other laws, the separate result of which is opposite to theirs, or more or less inconsistent with it. And hence, with almost every law, many instances in which it really is entirely fulfilled, do not, at first sight, appear to be cases of its operation at all. It is so in the example just adduced: a force, in mechanics, means neither more nor less than a cause of motion, yet the sum of the effects of two causes of motion may be rest. Again, a body solicited by two forces in directions making an angle with one another, moves in the diagonal; and it seems a paradox to say that motion in the diagonal is the sum of two motions in two other lines. Motion, however, is but change of place, and at every instant the body is in the exact place it would have been in if the forces had acted during alternate instants instead of acting in the same instant; (saving that if we suppose two forces to act successively which are in truth simultaneous, we must of course allow them double the time.) It is evident, therefore, that each force has had, during each instant, all the effect which belonged to it; and that the modifying influence which one of two concurrent causes is said to exercise with respect to the other, may be considered as exerted not over the action of the cause itself, but over the effect after it is completed. For all purposes of predicting, calculating, or explaining their joint result, causes which compound their effects may be treated as if they produced simultaneously each of them its own effect, and all these effects coexisted visibly.

Since the laws of causes are as really fulfilled when the causes are said to be counteracted by opposing causes, as when they are left to their own undisturbed action, we must be cautious not to express the laws in such terms as would render the assertion of their being fulfilled in those cases a contradiction. If, for instance, it were stated as a law of nature that a body to which a force is applied moves in the direction of the force, with a velocity proportioned to the force directly, and to its own mass inversely; when in point of fact some bodies to which a force is applied do not move at all, and those which do move are, from the very first, retarded by the action of gravity and other resisting forces, and at last stopped altogether; it is clear that the general proposition, though it would be true under a certain hypothesis, would not express the facts as they actually occur. To accommodate the expression of the law to the real phenomena, we must say, not that the object moves, but that it **tends** to move, in the direction and with the velocity specified. We might, indeed, guard our expression in a different mode, by saying that the body moves in that manner unless prevented, or except in so far as prevented, by some counteracting cause. But the body does not only move in that manner unless counteracted; it **tends** to move in that manner even when counteracted; it still exerts, in the original direction, the same energy of movement as if its first impulse had been undisturbed, and produces, by that energy, an exactly equivalent quantity of effect. This is true even when the force leaves the body as it found it, in a state of absolute rest; as when we attempt to raise a body of three tons weight with a force equal to one ton. For if, while we are applying this force, wind or water or any other agent supplies an additional force just exceeding two tons, the body will be raised; thus proving that the force we applied exerted its full effect, by neutralizing an equivalent portion of the weight which it was insufficient altogether to overcome. And if, while we are exerting this force of one ton upon the object in a direction contrary to that of gravity, it be put into a scale and weighed, it will be found to have lost a ton of its weight, or in other words, to press downwards with a force only equal to the difference of the two forces.

These facts are correctly indicated by the expression **tendency**. All laws of causation, in consequence of their liability to be counteracted, require to be stated in words affirmative of tendencies only, and not of actual results. In those sciences of causation which have an accurate nomenclature, there are special words which signify a tendency to the particular effect with which the science is conversant; thus **pressure**, in mechanics, is synonymous with tendency to motion, and forces are not reasoned on as causing actual motion, but as exerting pressure. A similar improvement in terminology would be very salutary in many other branches of science.

The habit of neglecting this necessary element in the precise expression of the laws of nature, has given birth to the popular prejudice that all general truths have exceptions; and much unmerited distrust has thence accrued to the conclusions of science, when they have been submitted to the judgment of minds insufficiently disciplined and cultivated. The rough generalizations suggested by common observation usually have exceptions; but principles of science, or in other words, laws of causation, have not. "What is thought to be an exception to a principle," (to quote words used on a different occasion,) "is always some other and distinct principle cutting into the former; some other force which impinges(87) against the first force, and deflects it from its direction. There are not a law and an exception to that law, the law acting in ninety-nine cases and the exception in one. There are two laws, each possibly acting in the whole hundred cases, and bringing about a common effect by their conjunct operation. If the force which, being the less conspicuous of the two, is called the ***disturbing*** force, prevails sufficiently over the other force in some one case, to constitute that case what is commonly called an exception, the same disturbing force probably acts as a modifying cause in many other cases which no one will call exceptions.

"Thus if it were stated to be a law of nature that all heavy bodies fall to the ground, it would probably be said that the resistance of the atmosphere, which prevents a balloon from falling, constitutes the balloon an exception to that pretended law of nature. But the real law is, that all heavy bodies ***tend*** to fall; and to this there is no exception, not even the sun and moon; for even they, as every astronomer knows, tend towards the earth, with a force exactly equal to that with which the earth tends towards them. The resistance of the atmosphere might, in the particular case of the balloon, from a misapprehension of what the law of gravitation is, be said to ***prevail over*** the law; but its disturbing effect is quite as real in every other case, since though it does not prevent, it retards the fall of all bodies whatever. The rule, and the so-called exception, do not divide the cases between them; each of them is a comprehensive rule extending to all cases. To call one of these concurrent principles an exception to the other, is superficial, and contrary to the correct principles of nomenclature and arrangement. An effect of precisely the same kind, and arising from the same cause, ought not to be placed in two different categories, merely as there does or does not exist another cause preponderating over it."(88)

§ 6. We have now to consider according to what method these complex effects, compounded of the effects of many causes, are to be studied; how we are enabled to trace each effect to the concurrence of causes in which it originated, and ascertain the conditions of its recurrence, the circumstances in which it maybe expected again to occur. The conditions of a phenomenon which arises from a composition of causes, may be investigated either deductively or experimentally.

The case, it is evident, is naturally susceptible of the deductive mode of investigation. The law of an effect of this description is a result of the laws of the separate causes on the combination of which it depends, and is therefore in itself capable of being deduced from these laws. This is called the method *a priori*. The other, or *a posteriori* method, professes to proceed according to the canons of experimental inquiry. Considering the whole assemblage of concurrent causes which produced the phenomenon, as one single cause, it attempts to ascertain that cause in the ordinary manner, by a comparison of instances. This second method subdivides itself into two different varieties. If it merely collates instances of the effect, it is a method of pure observation. If it operates upon the causes, and tries different combinations of them, in hopes of ultimately hitting the precise combination which will produce the given total effect, it is a method of experiment.

In order more completely to clear up the nature of each of these three methods, and determine which of them deserves the preference, it will be expedient (conformably to a favourite maxim of Lord Chancellor Eldon, to which, though it has often incurred philosophical ridicule, a deeper philosophy will not refuse its sanction) to "clothe them in circumstances." We shall select for this purpose a case which as yet furnishes no very brilliant example of the success of any of the three methods, but which is all the more suited to illustrate the difficulties inherent in them. Let the subject of inquiry be, the conditions of health and disease in the human body; or (for greater simplicity) the conditions of recovery from a given disease; and in order to narrow the question still more, let it be limited, in the first instance, to this one inquiry: Is, or is not some particular medicament (mercury, for instance) a remedy for that disease.

Now, the deductive method would set out from known properties of mercury, and known laws of the human body, and by reasoning from these, would attempt to discover whether mercury will act upon the body when in the morbid condition supposed, in such a manner as to restore health. The experimental method would simply administer mercury in as many cases as possible, noting the age, sex, temperament, and other peculiarities of bodily constitution, the particular form or variety of the disease, the particular stage of its progress, &c., remarking in which of these cases it produced a salutary effect, and with what circumstances it was on those occasions combined. The method of simple observation would compare instances of recovery, to find whether they agreed in having been preceded by the administration of mercury; or would compare instances of recovery with instances of failure, to find cases which, agreeing in all other respects, differed only in the fact that mercury had been administered, or that it had not.

§ 7. That the last of these three modes of investigation is applicable to the case, no one has ever seriously contended. No conclusions of value, on a subject of such intricacy, ever were obtained in that way. The utmost that could result would be a vague general impression for or against the efficacy of mercury, of no avail for guidance unless confirmed by one of the other two methods. Not that the results, which this method strives to obtain, would not be of the utmost possible value if they could be obtained. If all the cases of recovery which presented themselves, in an examination extending to a great number of instances, were cases in which mercury had been administered, we might generalize with confidence from this experience, and should have obtained a conclusion of real value. But no such basis for generalization can we, in a case of this description, hope to obtain. The reason is that which we have so often spoken of as constituting the characteristic imperfection of the Method of Agreement; Plurality of Causes. Supposing even that mercury does tend to cure the disease, so many other causes, both natural and artificial, also tend to cure it, that there are sure to be abundant instances of recovery, in which mercury has not been administered: unless, indeed, the practice be to administer it in all cases; on which supposition it will equally be found in the cases of failure.

When an effect results from the union of many causes, the share which each has in the determination of the effect cannot in general be great: and the effect is not likely, even in its presence or absence, still less in its variations, to follow, even approximatively, any one of the causes. Recovery from a disease is an event to which, in every case, many influences must concur. Mercury may be one such influence; but from the very fact that there are many other such, it will necessarily happen that although mercury is administered, the patient, for want of other concurring influences, will often not recover, and that he often will recover when it is not administered, the other favourable influences being sufficiently powerful without it. Neither, therefore, will the instances of recovery agree in the administration of mercury, nor will the instances of failure agree in its non-administration. It is much if, by multiplied and accurate returns from hospitals and the like, we can collect that there are rather more recoveries and rather fewer failures when mercury is administered than when it is not; a result of very secondary value even as a guide to practice, and almost worthless as a contribution to the theory of the subject.

§ 8. The inapplicability of the method of simple observation to ascertain the conditions of effects dependent on many concurring causes, being thus recognised; we shall next inquire whether any greater benefit can be expected from the other branch of the *a posteriori* method, that which proceeds by directly trying different combinations of causes, either artificially produced or found in nature, and taking notice what is their effect: as, for example, by actually trying the effect of mercury, in as many different circumstances as possible. This method differs from the one which we have just examined, in turning our attention directly to the causes or agents, instead of turning it to the effect, recovery from the disease. And since, as a general rule, the effects of causes are far more accessible to our study than the causes of effects, it is natural to think that this method has a much better chance of proving successful than the former.

The method now under consideration is called the Empirical Method; and in order to estimate it fairly, we must suppose it to be completely, not incompletely, empirical. We must exclude from it everything which partakes of the nature not of an experimental but of a deductive operation. If for instance we try experiments with mercury upon a person in health, in order to ascertain the general laws of its action upon the human body, and then reason from these laws to determine how it will act upon persons affected with a particular disease, this may be a really effectual method, but this is deduction. The experimental method does not derive the law of a complex case from the simpler laws which conspire to produce it, but makes its experiments directly upon the complex case. We must make entire abstraction of all knowledge of the simpler tendencies, the *modi operandi* of mercury in detail. Our experimentation must aim at obtaining a direct answer to the specific question, Does or does not mercury tend to cure the particular disease?

Let us see, therefore, how far the case admits of the observance of those rules of experimentation, which it is found necessary to observe in other cases. When we devise an experiment to ascertain the effect of a given agent, there are certain precautions which we never, if we can help it, omit. In the first place, we introduce the agent into the midst of a set of circumstances which we have exactly ascertained. It needs hardly be remarked how far this condition is from being realized in any case connected with the phenomena of life; how far we are from knowing what are all the circumstances which pre-exist in any instance in which mercury is administered to a living being. This difficulty, however, though insuperable in most cases, may not be so in all; there are sometimes (though I should think never in physiology) concurrences of many causes, in which we yet know accurately what the causes are. But when we have got clear of this obstacle we encounter another still more serious. In other cases, when we intend to try an experiment, we do not reckon it enough that there be no circumstance in the case, the presence of which is unknown to us. We require also that none of the circumstances which we do know, shall have effects susceptible of being confounded with those of the agent whose properties we wish to study. We take the utmost pains to exclude all causes capable of composition with the given cause; or if forced to let in any such causes, we take care to make them such, that we can compute and allow for their influence, so that the effect of the given cause may, after the subduction of those other effects, be apparent as a residual phenomenon.

These precautions are inapplicable to such cases as we are now considering. The mercury of our experiment being tried with an unknown multitude (or even let it be a known multitude) of other influencing circumstances, the mere fact of their being influencing circumstances implies that they disguise the effect of the mercury, and preclude us from knowing whether it has any effect or no. Unless we already knew what and how much is owing to every other circumstance, (that is, unless we suppose the very problem solved which we are considering the means of solving,) we cannot tell that those other circumstances may not have produced the whole of the effect, independently or even in spite of the mercury. The Method of Difference, in the ordinary mode of its use, namely by comparing the state of things following the experiment with the state which preceded it, is thus, in the case of intermixture of effects, entirely unavailing; because other causes than that whose effect we are seeking to determine, have been operating during the transition. As for the other mode of employing the Method of Difference, namely by comparing, not the same case at two different periods, but different cases, this in the present instance is quite chimerical. In phenomena so complicated it is questionable if two cases similar in all respects but one ever occurred; and were they to occur, we could not possibly know that they were so exactly similar.

Anything like a scientific use of the method of experiment, in these complicated cases, is therefore out of the question. We can in the most favourable cases only discover, by a succession of trials, that a certain cause is **very often** followed by a certain effect. For, in one of these conjunct effects, the portion which is determined by any one of the influencing agents, is generally, as we before remarked, but small; and it must be a more potent cause than most, if even the tendency which it really exerts is not thwarted by other tendencies in nearly as many cases as it is fulfilled.

If so little can be done by the experimental method to determine the conditions of an effect of many combined causes, in the case of medical science, still less is this method applicable to a class of phenomena, more complicated than even those of physiology, the phenomena of politics and history. There, Plurality of Causes exists in almost boundless excess, and the effects are, for the most part, inextricably interwoven with one another. To add to the embarrassment, most of the inquiries in political science relate to the production of effects of a most comprehensive description, such as the public wealth, public security, public morality, and the like: results liable to be affected directly or indirectly either in **plus** or in **minus** by nearly every fact which exists, or event which occurs, in human society. The vulgar notion, that the safe methods on political subjects are those of Baconian induction, that the true guide is not general reasoning, but specific experience, will one day be quoted as among the most unequivocal marks of a low state of the speculative faculties in any age in which it is accredited. Nothing can be more ludicrous than the sort of parodies on experimental reasoning which one is accustomed to meet with, not in popular discussion only, but in grave treatises, when the affairs of nations are the theme. "How," it is asked, "can an institution be bad, when the country has prospered under it?" "How can such or such causes have contributed to the prosperity of one country, when another has prospered without them?" Whoever makes use of an argument of this kind, not intending to deceive, should be sent back to learn the elements of some one of the more easy physical sciences. Such reasoners ignore the fact of Plurality of Causes in the very case which affords the most signal example of it. So little could be concluded, in such a case, from any possible collation of individual instances, that even the impossibility, in social phenomena, of making artificial experiments, a circumstance otherwise so prejudicial to directly inductive inquiry, hardly affords, in this case, additional reason of regret. For even if we could try experiments upon a nation or upon the human race, with as little scruple as M. Majendie tries them upon dogs or rabbits, we should never succeed in making two instances identical in every respect except the presence or absence of some one indefinite circumstance. The nearest approach to an experiment in the philosophical sense, which takes place in politics, is the introduction of a new operative element into national affairs by some special and assignable measure of government, such as the enactment or repeal of a particular law. But where there are so many influences at work, it requires some time for the influence of any new cause upon national phenomena to become apparent; and as the causes operating in so extensive a sphere are not only infinitely numerous, but in a state of perpetual alteration, it is always certain that before the effect of the new cause becomes conspicuous enough to be a subject of induction, so many of the other influencing circumstances will have changed as to vitiate the experiment.

Two, therefore, of the three possible methods for the study of phenomena resulting from the composition of many causes, being, from the very nature of the case, inefficient and illusory; there remains only the third,--that which considers the causes separately, and computes the effect from the balance of the different tendencies which produce it: in short, the deductive, or *a priori* method. The more particular consideration of this intellectual process requires a chapter to itself.

CHAPTER XI. OF THE DEDUCTIVE METHOD.

§ 1. The mode of investigation which, from the proved inapplicability of direct methods of observation and experiment, remains to us as the main source of the knowledge we possess or can acquire respecting the conditions, and laws of recurrence, of the more complex phenomena, is called, in its most general expression, the

Deductive Method; and consists of three operations: the first, one of direct induction; the second, of ratiocination; and the third, of verification.

I call the first step in the process an inductive operation, because there must be a direct induction as the basis of the whole; although in many particular investigations the place of the induction may be supplied by a prior deduction; but the premisses of this prior deduction must have been derived from induction.

The problem of the Deductive Method is, to find the law of an effect, from the laws of the different tendencies of which it is the joint result. The first requisite, therefore, is to know the laws of those tendencies; the law of each of the concurrent causes: and this supposes a previous process of observation or experiment upon each cause separately; or else a previous deduction, which also must depend for its ultimate premisses on observation or experiment. Thus, if the subject be social or historical phenomena, the premisses of the Deductive Method must be the laws of the causes which determine that class of phenomena; and those causes are human actions, together with the general outward circumstances under the influence of which mankind are placed, and which constitute man's position on the earth. The Deductive Method, applied to social phenomena, must begin, therefore, by investigating, or must suppose to have been already investigated, the laws of human action, and those properties of outward things by which the actions of human beings in society are determined. Some of these general truths will naturally be obtained by observation and experiment, others by deduction: the more complex laws of human action, for example, may be deduced from the simpler ones; but the simple or elementary laws will always, and necessarily, have been obtained by a directly inductive process.

To ascertain, then, the laws of each separate cause which takes a share in producing the effect, is the first desideratum of the Deductive Method. To know what the causes are, which must be subjected to this process of study, may or may not be difficult. In the case last mentioned, this first condition is of easy fulfilment. That social phenomena depend on the acts and mental impressions of human beings, never could have been a matter of any doubt, however imperfectly it may have been known either by what laws those impressions and actions are governed, or to what social consequences their laws naturally lead. Neither, again, after physical science had attained a certain development, could there be any real doubt where to look for the laws on which the phenomena of life depend, since they must be the mechanical and chemical laws of the solid and fluid substances composing the organised body and the medium in which it subsists, together with the peculiar vital laws of the different tissues constituting the organic structure. In other cases, really far more simple than these, it was much less obvious in what quarter the causes were to be looked for: as in the case of the celestial phenomena. Until, by combining the laws of certain causes, it was found that those laws explained all the facts which experience had proved concerning the heavenly motions, and led to predictions which it always verified, mankind never knew that those *were* the causes. But whether we are able to put the question before, or not until after, we have become capable of answering it, in either case it must be answered; the laws of the different causes must be ascertained, before we can proceed to deduce from them the conditions of the effect.

The mode of ascertaining those laws neither is, nor can be, any other than the fourfold method of experimental inquiry, already discussed. A few remarks on the application of that method to cases of the Composition of Causes, are all that is requisite.

It is obvious that we cannot expect to find the law of a tendency, by an induction from cases in which the tendency is counteracted. The laws of motion could never have been brought to light from the observation of bodies kept at rest by the equilibrium of opposing forces. Even where the tendency is not, in the ordinary sense of the word, counteracted, but only modified, by having its effects compounded with the effects arising from some other tendency or tendencies, we are still in an unfavourable position for tracing, by means of such cases, the law of the tendency itself. It would have been difficult to discover the law that every body in motion tends to continue moving in a straight line, by an induction from instances in which the motion is deflected into a curve, by being compounded with the effect of an accelerating force. Notwithstanding the resources afforded in this description of cases by the Method of Concomitant Variations, the principles of a judicious experimentation prescribe that the law of each of the tendencies should be studied, if possible, in cases in which that tendency operates alone, or in combination with no agencies but those of which the effect can, from previous knowledge, be calculated and allowed for.

Accordingly, in the cases, unfortunately very numerous and important, in which the causes do not suffer themselves to be separated and observed apart, there is much difficulty in laying down with due certainty the inductive foundation necessary to support the deductive method. This difficulty is most of all conspicuous in the case of physiological phenomena; it being impossible to separate the different agencies which collectively compose an organised body, without destroying the very phenomena which it is our object to investigate:

following life, in creatures we dissect, We lose it, in the moment we detect.

And for this reason I am inclined to the opinion, that physiology is embarrassed by greater natural difficulties, and is probably susceptible of a less degree of ultimate perfection, than even the social science; inasmuch as it is possible to study the laws and operations of one human mind apart from other minds, much less imperfectly than we can study the laws of one organ or tissue of the human body apart from the other organs or tissues.

It has been judiciously remarked that pathological facts, or, to speak in common language, diseases in their different forms and degrees, afford in the case of physiological investigation the most available equivalent to experimentation properly so called; inasmuch as they often exhibit to us a definite disturbance in some one organ or organic function, the remaining organs and functions being, in the first instance at least, unaffected. It is true that from the perpetual actions and reactions which are going on among all parts of the organic economy, there can be no prolonged disturbance in any one function without ultimately involving many of the others; and when once it has done so, the experiment for the most part loses its scientific value. All depends on observing the early stages of the derangement; which, unfortunately, are of necessity the least marked. If, however, the organs and functions not disturbed in the first instance, become affected in a fixed order of succession, some light is thereby thrown upon the action which one organ exercises over another; and we occasionally obtain a series of effects which we can refer with some confidence to the original local derangement; but for this it is necessary that we should know that the original derangement *was* local. If it was what is termed constitutional, that is, if we do not know in what part of the animal economy it took its rise, or the precise nature of the disturbance which took place in that part, we are unable to determine which of the various derangements was cause and which effect; which of them were produced by one another, and which by the direct, though perhaps tardy, action of the original cause.

Besides natural pathological facts, we can produce pathological facts artificially; we can try experiments, even in the popular sense of the term, by subjecting the living being to some external agent, such as the mercury of our former example. As this experimentation is not intended to obtain a direct solution of any practical question, but to discover general laws, from which afterwards the conditions of any particular effect may be obtained by deduction; the best cases to select are those of which the circumstances can be best ascertained: and such are generally not those in which there is any practical object in view. The experiments are best tried, not in a state of disease, which is essentially a changeable state, but in the condition of health, comparatively a fixed state. In the one, unusual agencies are at work, the results of which we have no means of predicting; in the other, the course of the accustomed physiological phenomena would, it may generally be presumed, remain undisturbed, were it not for the disturbing cause which we introduce.

Such, with the occasional aid of the method of Concomitant Variations, (the latter not less encumbered than the more elementary methods by the peculiar difficulties of the subject,) are our inductive resources for ascertaining the laws of the causes considered separately, when we have it not in our power to make trial of them in a state of actual separation. The insufficiency of these resources is so glaring, that no one can be surprised at the backward state of the science of physiology; in which indeed our knowledge of causes is so imperfect, that we can neither explain, nor could without specific experience have predicted, many of the facts which are certified to us by the most ordinary observation. Fortunately, we are much better informed as to the empirical laws of the phenomena, that is, the uniformities respecting which we cannot yet decide whether they are cases of causation or mere results of it. Not only has the order in which the facts of organization and life successively manifest themselves, from the first germ of existence to death, been found to be uniform, and very accurately ascertainable; but, by a great application of the Method of Concomitant Variations to the entire facts of comparative anatomy and physiology, the conditions of organic structure corresponding to each class of functions have been determined with considerable precision. Whether these organic conditions are the whole of the conditions, and indeed whether they are conditions at all, or mere collateral effects of some common cause, we are quite ignorant: nor are we ever likely to know, unless we could construct an organized body, and try whether it would live.

Under such disadvantages do we, in cases of this description, attempt the initial, or inductive step, in the application of the Deductive Method to complex phenomena. But such, fortunately, is not the common case. In general, the laws of the causes on which the effect depends may be obtained by an induction from comparatively simple instances, or, at the worst, by deduction from the laws of simpler causes so obtained. By simple instances are meant, of course, those in which the action of each cause was not intermixed or interfered with, or not to any great extent, by other causes whose laws were unknown. And only when the induction which furnished the premises to the Deductive Method rested on such instances, has the application of such a method to the ascertainment of the laws of a complex effect, been attended with brilliant results.

§ 2. When the laws of the causes have been ascertained, and the first stage of the great logical operation now under discussion satisfactorily accomplished, the second part follows; that of determining, from the laws of the causes, what effect any given combination of those causes will produce. This is a process of calculation, in the wider sense of the term; and very often involves processes of calculation in the narrowest sense. It is a ratiocination; and when our knowledge of the causes is so perfect, as to extend to the exact numerical laws which they observe in producing their effects, the ratiocination may reckon among its premises the theorems of the science of number, in the whole immense extent of that science. Not only are the highest truths of mathematics often required to enable us to compute an effect, the numerical law of which we already know; but, even by the aid of those highest truths, we can go but a little way. In so simple a case as the common problem of three bodies gravitating towards one another, with a force directly as their mass and inversely as the square of the distance, all the resources of the calculus have not hitherto sufficed to obtain any general solution but an approximate one. In a case a little more complex, but still one of the simplest which arise in practice, that of the motion of a projectile, the causes which affect the velocity and range (for example) of a cannon-ball may be all known and estimated; the force of the gunpowder, the angle of elevation, the density of the air, the strength and direction of the wind; but it is one of the most difficult of mathematical problems to combine all these, so as to determine the effect resulting from their collective action.

Besides the theorems of number, those of geometry also come in as premises, where the effects take place in space, and involve motion and extension, as in mechanics, optics, acoustics, astronomy. But when the complication increases, and the effects are under the influence of so many and such shifting causes as to give no room either for fixed numbers, or for straight lines and regular curves, (as in the case of physiological, to say nothing of mental and social phenomena,) the laws of number and extension are applicable, if at all, only on that large scale on which precision of details becomes unimportant; and although these laws play a conspicuous part in the most striking examples of the investigation of nature by the Deductive Method, as for example in the Newtonian theory of the celestial motions, they are by no means an indispensable part of every such process. All that is essential in it is, reasoning from a general law to a particular case, that is, determining by means of the particular circumstances of that case, what result is required in that instance to fulfil the law. Thus in the Torricellian experiment, if the fact that air has weight had been previously known, it would have been easy, without any numerical data, to deduce from the general law of equilibrium, that the mercury would stand in the tube at such a height that the column of mercury would exactly balance a column of the atmosphere of equal diameter; because, otherwise, equilibrium would not exist.

By such ratiocinations from the separate laws of the causes, we may, to a certain extent, succeed in answering either of the following questions: Given a certain combination of causes, what effect will follow? and, What combination of causes, if it existed, would produce a given effect? In the one case, we determine the effect to be expected in any complex circumstances of which the different elements are known: in the other case we learn, according to what law--under what antecedent conditions--a given complex effect will occur.

§ 3. But (it may here be asked) are not the same arguments by which the methods of direct observation and experiment were set aside as illusory when applied to the laws of complex phenomena, applicable with equal force against the Method of Deduction? When in every single instance a multitude, often an unknown multitude of agencies, are clashing and combining, what security have we that in our computation *a priori* have taken all these into our reckoning? How many must we not generally be ignorant of? Among those which we know, how probable that some have been overlooked; and even were all included, how vain the pretence of summing up the effects of many causes, unless we know accurately the numerical law of each,--a condition in most cases not to be fulfilled; and even when fulfilled, to make the calculation transcends, in any but very simple cases, the utmost power of mathematical science with its most modern improvements.

These objections have real weight, and would be altogether unanswerable, if there were no test by which, when we employ the Deductive Method, we might judge whether an error of any of the above descriptions had been committed or not. Such a test however there is: and its application forms, under the name of Verification, the third essential component part of the Deductive Method; without which all the results it can give have little other value than that of guess-work. To warrant reliance on the general conclusions arrived at by deduction, these conclusions must be found, on careful comparison, to accord with the results of direct observation wherever it can be had. If, when we have experience to compare with them, this experience confirms them, we may safely trust to them in other cases of which our specific experience is yet to come. But if our deductions have led to the conclusion that from a particular combination of causes a given effect would result, then in all known cases where that combination can be shown to have existed, and where the effect has not followed, we must be able to show (or at least to make a probable surmise) what frustrated it: if we cannot, the theory is imperfect, and not yet to be relied upon. Nor is the verification complete, unless some of the cases in which the theory is borne out by the observed result, are of at least equal complexity with any other cases in which its application could be called for.

It needs scarcely be observed, that,--if direct observation and collation of instances have furnished us with any empirical laws of the effect, whether true in all observed cases or only true for the most part,--the most effectual verification of which the theory could be susceptible would be, that it led deductively to those empirical laws; that the uniformities, whether complete or incomplete, which were observed to exist among the phenomena, were *accounted for* by the laws of the causes--were such as could not *but* exist if those be really the causes by which the phenomena are produced. Thus it was very reasonably deemed an essential requisite of any true theory of the causes of the celestial motions, that it should lead by deduction to Kepler's laws: which, accordingly, the Newtonian theory did.

In order, therefore, to facilitate the verification of theories obtained by deduction, it is important that as many as possible of the empirical laws of the phenomena should be ascertained, by a comparison of instances, conformably to the Method of Agreement: as well as (it must be added) that the phenomena themselves should be described, in the most comprehensive as well as accurate manner possible; by collecting from the observation of parts, the simplest possible correct expressions for the corresponding wholes: as when the series of the observed places of a planet was first expressed by a circle, then by a system of epicycles, and subsequently by an ellipse.

It is worth remarking, that complex instances which would have been of no use for the discovery of the simple laws into which we ultimately analyse their phenomena, nevertheless, when they have served to verify the analysis, become additional evidence of the laws themselves. Although we could not have got at the law from complex cases, still when the law, got at otherwise, is found to be in accordance with the result of a complex case, that case becomes a new experiment on the law, and helps to confirm what it did not assist to discover. It is a new trial of the principle in a different set of circumstances; and occasionally serves to eliminate some circumstance not previously excluded, and the exclusion of which might require an experiment impossible to be executed. This was strikingly conspicuous in the example formerly quoted, in which the difference between the observed and the calculated velocity of sound was ascertained to result from the heat extricated by the condensation which takes place in each sonorous vibration. This was a trial, in new circumstances, of the law of the development of heat by compression; and it added materially to the proof of the universality of that law. Accordingly any law of nature is deemed to have gained in point of certainty, by being found to explain some complex case which had not previously been thought of in connexion with it; and this indeed is a consideration to which it is the habit of scientific inquirers to attach rather too much value than too little.

To the Deductive Method, thus characterised in its three constituent parts, Induction, Ratiocination, and Verification, the human mind is indebted for its most conspicuous triumphs in the investigation of nature. To it we owe all the theories by which vast and complicated phenomena are embraced under a few simple laws, which, considered as the laws of those great phenomena, could never have been detected by their direct study. We may form some conception of what the method has done for us, from the case of the celestial motions; one of the simplest among the greater instances of the Composition of Causes, since (except in a few cases not of primary importance) each of the heavenly bodies may be considered, without material inaccuracy, to be never at one time influenced by the attraction of more than two bodies, the sun and one other planet or satellite, making with the reaction of the body itself, and the tangential force (as I see no objection to calling the force generated by the body's own motion, and acting in the direction of the tangent(89)) only four different agents on the concurrence of which the motions of that body depend; a much smaller number, no doubt, than that by which any other of the great phenomena of nature is determined or modified. Yet how could we ever have ascertained the combination of forces on which the motions of the earth and planets are dependent, by merely comparing the orbits, or velocities, of different planets, or the different velocities or positions of the same planet? Notwithstanding the regularity which manifests itself in those motions, in a degree so rare among the effects of a concurrence of causes; although the periodical recurrence of exactly the same effect, affords positive proof that all the combinations of causes which occur at all, recur periodically; we should not have known what the causes were, if the existence of agencies precisely similar on our own earth had not, fortunately, brought the causes themselves within the reach of experimentation under simple circumstances. As we shall have occasion to analyse, further on, this great example of the Method of Deduction, we shall not occupy any time with it here, but shall proceed to that secondary application of the Deductive Method, the result of which is not to prove laws of phenomena, but to explain them.

CHAPTER XII. OF THE EXPLANATION OF LAWS OF NATURE.

§ 1. The deductive operation by which we derive the law of an effect from the laws of the causes, of which the concurrence gives rise to it, may be undertaken either for the purpose of discovering the law, or of explaining a law already discovered. The word ***explanation*** occurs so continually and holds so important a place in philosophy, that a little time spent in fixing the meaning of it will be profitably employed.

An individual fact is said to be explained, by pointing out its cause, that is, by stating the law or laws of causation, of which its production is an instance. Thus, a conflagration is explained, when it is proved to have arisen from a spark falling into the midst of a heap of combustibles. And in a similar manner, a law or uniformity in nature is said to be explained, when another law or laws are pointed out, of which that law itself is but a case, and from which it could be deduced.

§ 2. There are three distinguishable sets of circumstances in which a law of causation may be explained from, or, as it also is often expressed, resolved into, other laws.

The first is the case already so fully considered; an intermixture of laws, producing a joint effect equal to the sum of the effects of the causes taken separately. The law of the complex effects is explained, by being resolved into the separate laws of the causes which contribute to it. Thus, the law of the motion of a planet is resolved into the law of the tangential force, which tends to produce an uniform motion in the tangent, and the law of the centripetal force, which tends to produce an accelerating motion towards the sun; the real motion being a compound of the two.

It is necessary here to remark, that in this resolution of the law of a complex effect, the laws of which it is compounded are not the only elements. It is resolved into the laws of the separate causes, together with the fact of their co-existence. The one is as essential an ingredient as the other; whether the object be to discover the law of the effect, or only to explain it. To deduce the laws of the heavenly motions, we require not only to know the law of a rectilineal and that of a gravitative force, but the existence of both these forces in the celestial regions, and even their relative amount. The complex laws of causation are thus resolved into two distinct kinds of elements: the one, simpler laws of causation, the other (in the aptly selected language of Dr. Chalmers) collocations; the collocations consisting in the existence of certain agents or powers, in certain circumstances of place and time. We shall hereafter have occasion to return to this distinction, and to dwell on it at such a length as dispenses with the necessity of further insisting on it here. The first mode, then, of the explanation of Laws of Causation, is when the law of an effect is resolved into the various tendencies of which it is the result, and into the laws of those tendencies.

§ 3. A second case is when, between what seemed the cause and what was supposed to be its effect, further observation detects an immediate link; a fact caused by the antecedent, and in its turn causing the consequent; so that the cause at first assigned is but the remote cause, operating through the intermediate phenomenon. A seemed the cause of C, but it subsequently appeared that A was only the cause of B, and that it is B which was the cause of C. For example: mankind were aware that the act of touching an outward object caused a sensation. It was, however, at last discovered, that after we have touched the object, and before we experience the sensation, some change takes place in a kind of thread called a nerve, which extends from our outward organs to the brain. Touching the object, therefore, is only the remote cause of our sensation; that is, not the cause, properly speaking, but the cause of the cause;--the real cause of the sensation is the change in the state of the nerve. Future experience may not only give us more knowledge than we now have of the particular nature of this change, but may also interpolate another link: between the contact (for example) of the object with our outward organs, and the production of the change of state in the nerve, there may take place some electric phenomenon; or some phenomenon of a nature not resembling the effects of any known agency. Hitherto, however, no such intermediate link has been discovered; and the touch of the object must be considered, provisionally at least, as the proximate cause of the affection of the nerve. The sequence, therefore, of a sensation of touch on contact with an object, is ascertained not to be an ultimate law; it is resolved, as the phrase is, into two other laws,--the law, that contact with an object produces an affection of the nerve; and the law, that an affection of the nerve produces sensation.

To take another example: the more powerful acids corrode or blacken organic compounds. This is a case of causation, but of remote causation; and is said to be explained when it is shown that there is an intermediate link, namely, the separation of some of the chemical elements of the organic structure from the rest, and their entering into combination with the acid. The acid causes this separation of the elements, and the separation of the elements causes the disorganization, and often the charring of the structure. So, again, chlorine extracts colouring matters, (whence its efficacy in bleaching,) and purifies the air from infection. This law is resolved into the two following laws. Chlorine has a powerful affinity for bases of all kinds, particularly metallic bases and hydrogen. Such bases are essential elements of colouring matters and contagious compounds: which substances, therefore, are decomposed and destroyed by chlorine.

§ 4. It is of importance to remark, that when a sequence of phenomena is thus resolved into other laws, they are always laws more general than itself. The law that A is followed by C, is less general than either of the laws which connect B with C and A with B. This will appear from very simple considerations.

All laws of causation are liable to be counteracted or frustrated, by the non-fulfilment of some negative condition: the tendency, therefore, of B to produce C may be defeated. Now the law that A produces B, is equally fulfilled whether B is followed by C or not; but the law that A produces C by means of B, is of course only fulfilled when B is really followed by C, and is therefore less general than the law that A produces B. It is also less general than the law that B produces C. For B may have other causes besides A; and as A produces C only by means of B, while B produces C whether it has itself been produced by A or by anything else, the second law embraces a greater number of instances, covers as it were a greater space of ground, than the first.

Thus, in our former example, the law that the contact of an object causes a change in the state of the nerve, is more general than the law that contact with an object causes sensation, since, for aught we know, the change in the nerve may equally take place when, from a counteracting cause, as for instance, strong mental excitement, the sensation does not follow; as in a battle, where wounds are often received without any consciousness of receiving them. And again, the law that change in the state of a nerve produces sensation, is more general than the law that contact with an object produces sensation; since the sensation equally follows the change in the nerve when not produced by contact with an object, but by some other cause; as in the well-known case, when a person who has lost a limb feels the same sensation which he has been accustomed to call a pain in the limb.

Not only are the laws of more immediate sequence into which the law of a remote sequence is resolved, laws of greater generality than that law is, but (as a consequence of, or rather as implied in, their greater generality) they are more to be relied on; there are fewer chances of their being ultimately found not to be universally true. From the moment when the sequence of A and C is shown not to be immediate, but to depend on an intervening phenomenon, then, however constant and invariable the sequence of A and C has hitherto been found, possibilities arise of its failure, exceeding those which can affect either of the more immediate sequences, A, B, and B, C. The tendency of A to produce C may be defeated by whatever is capable of defeating either the tendency of A to produce B, or the tendency of B to produce C; it is therefore twice as liable to failure as either of those more elementary tendencies; and the generalization that A is always followed by C, is twice as likely to be found erroneous. And so of the converse generalization, that C is always preceded and caused by A; which will be erroneous not only if there should happen to be a second immediate mode of production of C itself, but moreover if there be a second mode of production of B, the immediate antecedent of C in the sequence.

The resolution of the one generalization into the other two, not only shows that there are possible limitations of the former, from which its two elements are exempt, but shows also where these are to be looked for. As soon as we know that B intervenes between A and C, we also know that if there be cases in which the sequence of A and C does not hold, these are most likely to be found by studying the effects or the conditions of the phenomenon B.

It appears, then, that in the second of the three modes in which a law may be resolved into other laws, the latter are more general, that is, extend to more cases, and are also less likely to require limitation from subsequent experience, than the law which they serve to explain. They are more nearly unconditional; they are defeated by fewer contingencies; they are a nearer approach to the universal truth of nature. The same observations are still more evidently true with regard to the first of the three modes of resolution. When the law of an effect of combined causes is resolved into the separate laws of the causes, the nature of the case implies that the law of the effect is less general than the law of any of the causes, since it only holds when they are combined; while the law of any one of the causes holds good both then, and also when that cause acts apart from the rest. It is also manifest that the complex law is liable to be oftener unfulfilled than any one of the simpler laws of which it is the result, since every contingency which defeats any of the laws prevents so much of the effect as depends on it, and thereby defeats the complex law. The mere rusting, for example, of some small part of a great machine, often suffices entirely to prevent the effect which ought to result from the joint action of all the parts. The law of the effect of a combination of causes is always subject to the whole of the negative conditions which attach to the action of all the causes severally.

There is another and a still stronger reason why the law of a complex effect must be less general than the laws of the causes which conspire to produce it. The same causes, acting according to the same laws, and differing only in the proportions in which they are combined, often produce effects which differ not merely in quantity, but in kind. The combination of a centripetal with a projectile force, in the proportions which obtain in all the planets and satellites of our solar system, gives rise to an elliptical motion; but if the ratio of the two forces to each other were slightly altered, it is demonstrable that the motion produced would be in a circle, or a parabola, or an hyperbola: and it has been surmised that in the case of some comets one of these is really the fact. Yet the law of the parabolic motion would be resolvable into the very same simple laws into which that of the elliptical motion is revolved, namely, the law of the permanence of rectilineal motion, and the law of gravitation. If, therefore, in the course of ages, some circumstance were to manifest itself which, without defeating the law of either of those forces, should merely alter their proportion to one another, (such as the shock of a comet, or even the accumulating effect of the resistance of the medium in which astronomers have been led to surmise that the motions of the heavenly bodies take place;) the elliptical motion might be changed into a motion in some other conic section; and the complex law, that the heavenly motions take place in ellipses, would be deprived of its universality, though the discovery would not at all detract from the universality of the simpler laws into which that complex law is resolved. The law, in short, of each of the concurrent causes remains the same, however their collocations may vary; but the law of their joint effect varies with every difference in the collocations. There needs no more to show how much more general the elementary laws must be, than any of the complex laws which are derived from them.

§ 5. Besides the two modes which have been treated of, there is a third mode in which laws are resolved into one another; and in this it is self-evident that they are resolved into laws more general than themselves. This third mode is the ***subsumption*** (as it has been called) of one law under another: or (what comes to the same thing) the gathering up of several laws into one more general law which includes them all. The most splendid example of this operation was when terrestrial gravity and the central force of the solar system were brought together under the general law of gravitation. It had been proved antecedently that the earth and the other planets tend to the sun; and it had been known from the earliest times that terrestrial bodies tend towards the earth. These were similar phenomena; and to enable them both to be subsumed under one law, it was only necessary to prove that, as the effects were similar in quality, so also they, as to quantity, conform to the same rules. This was first shown to be true of the moon, which agreed with terrestrial objects not only in tending to a centre, but in the fact that this centre was the earth. The tendency of the moon towards the earth being ascertained to vary as the inverse square of the distance, it was deduced from this, by direct calculation, that if the moon were as near to the earth as terrestrial objects are, and the tangential force were suspended, the moon would fall towards the earth through exactly as many feet in a second as those objects do by virtue of their weight. Hence the inference was irresistible, that the moon also tends to the earth by virtue of its weight: and that the two phenomena, the tendency of the moon to the earth and the tendency of terrestrial objects to the earth, being not only similar in quality, but, when in the same circumstances, identical in quantity, are cases of one and the same law of causation. But the tendency of the moon to the earth and the tendency of the earth and planets to the sun, were already known to be cases of the same law of causation: and thus the law of all these tendencies, and the law of terrestrial gravity, were recognized as identical, or in other words, were subsumed under one general law, that of gravitation.

In a similar manner, the laws of magnetic phenomena have recently been subsumed under known laws of electricity. It is thus that the most general laws of nature are usually arrived at: we mount to them by successive steps. For, to arrive by correct induction at laws which hold under such an immense variety of circumstances, laws so general as to be independent of any varieties of space or time which we are able to observe, requires for the most part many distinct sets of experiments or observations, conducted at different times and by different people. One part of the law is first ascertained, afterwards another part: one set of observations teaches us that the law holds good under some conditions, another that it holds good under other conditions, by combining which observations we find that it holds good under conditions much more general, or even universally. The general law, in this case, is literally the sum of all the partial ones; it is the recognition of the same sequence in different sets of instances; and may, in fact, be regarded as merely one step in the process of elimination. That tendency of bodies towards one another, which we now call gravity, had at first been observed only on the earth's surface, where it manifested itself only as a tendency of all bodies towards the earth, and might, therefore, be ascribed to a peculiar property of the earth itself: one of the circumstances, namely, the proximity of the earth, had not been eliminated. To eliminate this circumstance required a fresh set of instances in other parts of the universe: these we could not ourselves create; and though nature had created them for us, we were placed in very unfavourable circumstances for observing them. To make these observations, fell naturally to the lot of a different set of persons from those who studied terrestrial phenomena, and had, indeed, been a matter of great interest at a time when the idea of explaining celestial facts by terrestrial laws was looked upon as the confounding of an indefeasible distinction. When, however, the celestial motions were accurately ascertained, and the deductive processes performed from which it appeared that their laws and those of terrestrial gravity corresponded, those celestial observations became a set of instances which exactly eliminated the circumstance of proximity to the earth; and proved that in the original case, that of terrestrial objects, it was not the earth, as such, that caused the motion or the pressure, but the circumstance common to that case with the celestial instances, namely, the presence of some great body within certain limits of distance.

§ 6. There are, then, three modes of explaining laws of causation, or, which is the same thing, resolving them into other laws. First, when the law of an effect of combined causes is resolved into the separate laws of the causes, together with the fact of their combination. Secondly, when the law which connects any two links, not proximate, in a chain of causation, is resolved into the laws which connect each with the intermediate links. Both of these are cases of resolving one law into two or more; in the third, two or more are resolved into one: when, after the law has been shown to hold good in several different classes of cases, we decide that what is true in each of these classes of cases, is true under some more general supposition, consisting of what all those classes of cases have in common. We may here remark that this last operation involves none of the uncertainties attendant on induction by the Method of Agreement, since we need not suppose the result to be extended by way of inference to any new class of cases, different from those by the comparison of which it was engendered.

In all these three processes, laws are, as we have seen, resolved into laws more general than themselves; laws extending to all the cases which the former extend to, and others besides. In the first two modes they are also resolved into laws more certain, in other words, more universally true than themselves; they are, in fact, proved not to be themselves laws of nature, the character of which is to be universally true, but *results* of laws of nature, which may be only true conditionally, and for the most part. No difference of this sort exists in the third case; since here the partial laws are, in fact, the very same law as the general one, and any exception to them would be an exception to it too.

By all the three processes, the range of deductive science is extended; since the laws, thus resolved, may be thenceforth deduced demonstratively from the laws into which they are resolved. As already remarked, the same deductive process which proves a law or fact of causation if unknown, serves to explain it when known.

The word explanation is here used in its philosophical sense. What is called explaining one law of nature by another, is but substituting one mystery for another; and does nothing to render the general course of nature other than mysterious: we can no more assign a *why* for the more extensive laws than for the partial ones. The explanation may substitute a mystery which has become familiar, and has grown to *seem* not mysterious, for one which is still strange. And this is the meaning of explanation, in common parlance. But the process with which we are here concerned often does the very contrary: it resolves a phenomenon with which we are familiar, into one of which we previously knew little or nothing; as when the common fact of the fall of heavy bodies is resolved into a tendency of all particles of matter towards one another. It must be kept constantly in view, therefore, that in science, those who speak of explaining any phenomenon mean (or should mean) pointing out not some more familiar, but merely some more general, phenomenon, of which it is a partial exemplification; or some laws of causation which produce it by their joint or successive action, and from which, therefore, its conditions may be determined deductively. Every such operation brings us a step nearer towards answering the question which was stated in a previous chapter as comprehending the whole problem of the investigation of nature, viz. What are the fewest assumptions, which being granted, the order of nature as it exists would be the result? What are the fewest general propositions from which all the uniformities existing in nature could be deduced?

The laws, thus explained or resolved, are sometimes said to be **accounted for**; but the expression is incorrect, if taken to mean anything more than what has been already stated. In minds not habituated to accurate thinking, there is often a confused notion that the general laws are the **causes** of the partial ones; that the law of general gravitation, for example, causes the phenomenon of the fall of bodies to the earth. But to assert this, would be a misuse of the word cause: terrestrial gravity is not an effect of general gravitation, but a **case** of it; that is, one kind of the particular instances in which that general law obtains. To account for a law of nature means, and can mean, nothing more than to assign other laws more general, together with collocations, which laws and collocations being supposed, the partial law follows without any additional supposition.

CHAPTER XIII. MISCELLANEOUS EXAMPLES OF THE EXPLANATION OF LAWS OF NATURE.

§ 1. Some of the most remarkable instances which have occurred since the great Newtonian generalization, of the explanation of laws of causation subsisting among complex phenomena, by resolving them into simpler and more general laws, are to be found among the speculations of Liebig in organic chemistry. These speculations, though they have not yet been sufficiently long before the world to entitle us positively to assume that no well-grounded objection can be made to any part of them, afford, however, so admirable an example of the spirit of the Deductive Method, that I may be permitted to present some specimens of them here.

It had been observed in certain cases, that chemical action is, as it were, contagious; that is to say, a substance which would not of itself yield to a particular chemical attraction, (the force of the attraction not being sufficient to overcome cohesion, or to destroy some chemical combination in which the substance was already held), will nevertheless do so if placed in contact with some other body which is in the act of yielding to the same force. Nitric acid, for example, does not dissolve pure platinum, which may "be boiled with this acid without being oxidized by it, even when in a state of such fine division that it no longer reflects light." But the same acid easily dissolves silver. Now if an alloy of silver and platinum be treated with nitric acid, the acid does not, as might naturally be expected, separate the two metals, dissolving the silver, and leaving the platinum; it dissolves both: the platinum as well as the silver becomes oxidized, and in that state combines with the undecomposed portion of the acid. In like manner, "copper does not decompose water, even when boiled in dilute sulphuric acid; but an alloy of copper, zinc, and nickel, dissolves easily in this acid with evolution of hydrogen gas." These phenomena cannot be explained by the laws of what is termed chemical affinity. They point to a peculiar law, by which the oxidation which one body suffers, causes another, in contact with it, to submit to the same change. And not only chemical composition, but chemical decomposition, is capable of being similarly propagated. The peroxide of hydrogen, a compound formed by hydrogen with a greater amount of oxygen than the quantity necessary to form water, is held together by a chemical attraction of so weak a nature, that the slightest circumstance is sufficient to decompose it; and it even, though very slowly, gives off oxygen and is reduced to water spontaneously (being, I presume, decomposed by the tendency of its oxygen to absorb heat and assume the gaseous state). Now it has been observed, that if this decomposition of the peroxide of hydrogen takes place in contact with some metallic oxides, as those of silver, and the peroxides of lead and manganese, it superinduces a corresponding chemical action upon those substances; they also give forth the whole or a portion of their oxygen, and are reduced to the metal or to the protoxide; although they do not undergo this change spontaneously, and there is no chemical affinity at work to make them do so. Other similar phenomena are mentioned by Liebig. "Now no other explanation," he observes, "of these phenomena can be given, than that a body in the act of combination or decomposition enables another body, with which it is in contact, to enter into the same state."

Here, therefore, is a law of nature of great simplicity, but which, owing to the extremely special and limited character of the phenomena in which alone it can be detected experimentally, (because in them alone its results are not intermixed and blended with those of other laws,) had been very little recognised by chemists, and no one could have ventured, on experimental evidence, to affirm it as a law common to all chemical action; owing to the impossibility of a rigorous employment of the Method of Difference where the properties of different kinds of substance are involved, an impossibility which we noticed and characterized in a previous chapter.(90) Now this extremely special and apparently precarious generalization has, in the hands of Liebig, been converted, by a masterly employment of the Deductive Method, into a law pervading all nature, in the same way as gravitation assumed that character in the hands of Newton; and has been found to explain, in the most unexpected manner, numerous detached generalizations of a more limited kind, reducing the phenomena concerned in those generalizations into mere cases of itself.

The contagious influence of chemical action is not a powerful force, and is only capable of overcoming weak affinities: we, may, therefore, expect to find it principally exemplified in the decomposition of substances which are held together by weak chemical forces. Now the force which holds a compound substance together is generally weaker, the more compound the substance is; and organic products are the most compound substances known, those which have the most complex atomic constitution. It is, therefore, upon such substances that the self-propagating power of chemical action is likely to exert itself in the most marked manner. Accordingly, first, it explains the remarkable laws of fermentation, and some of those of putrefaction. "A little leaven," that is, dough in a certain state of chemical action, impresses a similar chemical action upon "the whole lump." The contact of any decaying substance, occasions the decay of matter previously sound. Again, yeast is a substance actually in a process of decomposition from the action of air and water, evolving carbonic acid gas. Sugar is a substance which, from the complexity of its composition, has no great energy of coherence in its existing form, and is capable of being easily converted (by combination with the elements of water) into carbonic acid and alcohol. Now the mere presence of yeast, the mere proximity of a substance of which the elements are separating from each other, and combining with the elements of water, causes sugar to undergo the same change, giving out carbonic acid gas, and becoming alcohol. It is not the elements contained in the yeast which do this. "An aqueous infusion of yeast may be mixed with a solution of sugar, and preserved in vessels from which the air is excluded, without either experiencing the slightest change." Neither does the insoluble residue of the yeast, after being treated with water, possess the power of exciting fermentation. (Here we have the method of Difference). It is not the yeast itself, therefore; it is the yeast in a state of decomposition. The sugar, which would not decompose and oxidize by the mere presence of oxygen and water, is induced to do so when another oxidation is at work in the midst of it.

By the same principle Liebig is enabled to explain many cases of malaria; the pernicious influence of putrid substances; a variety of poisons; contagious diseases; and other phenomena. Of all substances, those composing the animal body are the most complex in their composition, and are in the least stable condition of union. The blood, in particular, is the most unstable compound known. It is, therefore, not surprising that gaseous or other substances, in the act of undergoing the chemical changes which constitute, for instance, putrefaction, should, when brought into contact with the tissues by respiration or otherwise, and still more when introduced by inoculation into the blood itself, impress upon some of the particles a chemical action similar to its own; which is propagated in like manner to other particles, until the whole system is placed in a state of chemical action more or less inconsistent with the chemical conditions of vitality.

Of the three modes in which we observed in the last chapter that the resolution of a special law into more general ones may take place, this speculation exemplifies the second. The laws explained are such as this, that yeast puts sugar into a state of fermentation. Between the remote cause, the presence of yeast, and the consequent fermentation of the sugar, there has been interpolated a proximate cause, the chemical action between the particles of the yeast and the elements of air and water. The special law is thus resolved into two others, more general than itself: the first, that yeast is decomposed by the presence of air and water; the second, that matter undergoing chemical action has a tendency to produce similar chemical action in other matter in contact with it. But while the investigation thus aptly exhibits the second mode of the resolution of a complex law, it no less happily exemplifies the third; the subsumption of special laws under a more general law, by gathering them up into one more comprehensive expression which includes them all. For the curious fact of the contagious nature of chemical action is only raised into a law of *all* chemical action by these very investigations; just as the Newtonian attraction was only recognised as a law of all matter when it was found to explain the phenomena of terrestrial gravity. Previously to Liebig's investigations, the property in question had only been observed in a few special cases of chemical action; but when his deductive reasonings have established that innumerable effects produced upon weak compounds, by substances none of whose known peculiarities would account for their having such a power, might be explained by considering the supposed special property to exist in all those cases, these numerous generalizations on separate substances are brought together into one law of chemical action in general: the peculiarities of the various substances being, in fact, eliminated, just as the Newtonian deduction eliminated from the instances of terrestrial gravity the circumstance of proximity to the earth.

§ 2. Another speculation of the same chemist, which, if it should ultimately be found to agree with all the facts of the extremely complicated phenomenon to which it relates, will constitute one of the finest examples of the Deductive Method on record, is his theory of respiration.

The facts of respiration, or in other words the special laws which it is attempted to explain from, and resolve into, more general ones, are, that the blood in passing through the lungs absorbs oxygen and gives out carbonic acid gas, changing thereby its colour from a blackish purple to a brilliant red. The absorption and exhalation are evidently chemical phenomena; and the carbon of the carbonic acid must have been derived from the body, that is, must have been absorbed by the blood from the substances with which it came into contact in its passage through the organism. Required to find the intermediate links--the precise nature of the two chemical actions which take place; first, the absorption of the carbon or of the carbonic acid by the blood, in its circulation through the body; next, the excretion of the carbon, or the exchange of the carbonic acid for oxygen, in its passage through the lungs.

Dr. Liebig believes himself to have found the solution of this ***vexata quaestio*** in a class of chemical actions in which scarcely any less acute and penetrating inquirer would have thought of looking for it.

Blood is composed of two parts, the serum and the globules. The serum absorbs and holds in solution carbonic acid in great quantity, but has no tendency either to part with it or to absorb oxygen. The globules, therefore, are concluded to be the portion of the blood which is operative in respiration. These globules contain a certain quantity of iron, which from chemical tests is inferred to be in the state of oxide.

Dr. Liebig recognised, in the known chemical properties of the oxides of iron, laws which, if followed out deductively, would lead to the prediction of the precise series of phenomena which respiration exhibits.

There are two oxides of iron, a protoxide and a peroxide. In the arterial blood the iron is in the form of peroxide: in the venous blood we have no direct evidence which of the oxides is present, but the considerations to be presently stated lead to the conclusion that it is the protoxide. As arterial and venous blood are in a perpetual state of alternate conversion into one another, the question arises, in what circumstances the protoxide of iron is capable of being converted into the peroxide, and *vice versa*. Now the protoxide readily combines with oxygen in the presence of water, forming the hydrated peroxide: these conditions it finds in passing through the lungs; it derives oxygen from the air, and finds water in the blood itself. This would already explain one portion of the phenomena of respiration. But the arterial blood, in quitting the lungs, is charged with hydrated peroxide: in what manner is the peroxide brought back to its former state?

The chemical conditions for the reduction of the hydrated peroxide into the state of protoxide, are precisely those which the blood meets with in circulating through the body; namely, contact with organic compounds.

Hydrated peroxide of iron, when treated with organic compounds (where no sulphur is present) gives forth oxygen and water, which oxygen, attracting the carbon from the organic substance, becomes carbonic acid; while the peroxide, being reduced to the state of protoxide, combines with the carbonic acid, and becomes a carbonate. Now this carbonate needs only come again into contact with oxygen and water to be decomposed; the carbonic acid being given off, and the protoxide, by the absorption of oxygen and water, becoming again the hydrated peroxide.

The mysterious chemical phenomena connected with respiration can now, by a beautiful deductive process, be completely explained. The arterial blood, containing iron in the form of hydrated peroxide, passes into the capillaries, where it meets with the decaying tissues, receiving also in its course certain non-azotised but highly carbonised animal products, in particular the bile. In these it finds the precise conditions required for decomposing the peroxide into oxygen and the protoxide. The oxygen combines with the carbon of the decaying tissues, and forms carbonic acid, which, though insufficient in amount to neutralize the whole of the protoxide, combines with a portion (one-fourth) of it, and returns in the form of a carbonate, along with the other three-fourths of the protoxide, through the venous system into the lungs. There it again meets with oxygen and water: the free protoxide becomes hydrated peroxide: the carbonate of protoxide parts with its carbonic acid, and by absorbing oxygen and water, enters also into the state of hydrated peroxide. The heat evolved in the transition from protoxide to peroxide, as well as in the previous oxidation of the carbon contained in the tissues, is considered by Liebig as the cause which sustains the temperature of the body. But into this portion of the speculation we need not enter.(91)

This example displays the second mode of resolving complex laws, by the interpolation of intermediate links in the chain of causation; and some of the steps of the deduction exhibit cases of the first mode, that which infers the joint effect of two or more causes from their separate effects; but to trace out in detail these exemplifications may be left to the intelligence of the reader. The third mode is not employed in this example, since the simpler laws into which those of respiration are resolved (the laws of the chemical action of the oxides of iron) were laws already known, and do not acquire any additional generality from their employment in the present case.

§ 3. The property which salt possesses of preserving animal substances from putrefaction is resolved by Liebig into two more general laws, the strong attraction of salt for water, and the necessity of the presence of water as a condition of putrefaction. The intermediate phenomenon which is interpolated between the remote cause and the effect, can here be not merely inferred but seen; for it is a familiar fact, that flesh upon which salt has been thrown is speedily found swimming in brine.

The second of the two factors (as they may be termed) into which the preceding law has been resolved, the necessity of water to putrefaction, itself affords an additional example of the Resolution of Laws. The law itself is proved by the

Method of Difference, since flesh completely dried and kept in a dry atmosphere does not putrefy, as we see in the case of dried provisions, and human bodies in very dry climates. A deductive explanation of this same law results from Liebig's speculations. The putrefaction of animal and other azotised bodies is a chemical process, by which they are gradually dissipated in a gaseous form, chiefly in that of carbonic acid and ammonia; now to convert the carbon of the animal substance into carbonic acid requires oxygen, and to convert the azote into ammonia requires hydrogen, which are the elements of water. The extreme rapidity of the putrefaction of azotised substances, compared with the gradual decay of non-azotised bodies (such as wood and the like) by the action of oxygen alone, he explains from the general law that substances are much more easily decomposed by the action of two different affinities upon two of their elements, than by the action of only one.

The purgative effect of salts with alkaline bases, when administered in concentrated solutions, is explained from the two following principles: Animal tissues (such as the stomach) do ***not*** absorb concentrated solutions of alkaline salts; and such solutions ***do*** dissolve the solids contained in the intestines. The simpler laws into which the complex law is here resolved, are the second of the two foregoing principles combined with a third, namely that the peristaltic contraction acts easily upon substances in a state of solution. The negative general proposition, that animal substances do not absorb these salts, contributes to the explanation by accounting for the absence of a counteracting cause, namely, absorption by the stomach, which in the case of other substances possessed of the requisite chemical properties, interferes to prevent them from reaching the substances which they are destined to dissolve.

§ 4. From the foregoing and similar instances, we may see the importance, when a law of nature previously unknown has been brought to light, or when new light has been thrown upon a known law by experiment, of examining all cases which present the conditions necessary for bringing that law into action; a process fertile in demonstrations of special laws previously unsuspected, and explanations of others already empirically known.

For instance, Faraday discovered by experiment, that voltaic electricity could be evolved from a natural magnet, provided a conducting body were set in motion at right angles to the direction of the magnet: and, this he found to hold not only of small magnets, but of that great magnet, the earth. The law being thus established experimentally, that electricity is evolved, by a magnet, and a conductor moving at right angles to the direction of its poles, we may now look out for fresh instances in which these conditions meet. Wherever a conductor moves or revolves at right angles to the direction of the earth's magnetic poles, there we may expect an evolution of electricity. In the northern regions, where the polar direction is nearly perpendicular to the horizon, all horizontal motions of conductors will produce electricity; horizontal wheels, for example, made of metal; likewise all running streams will evolve a current of electricity which will circulate round them; and the air thus charged with electricity may be one of the causes of the Aurora Borealis. In the equatorial regions, on the contrary, upright wheels placed parallel to the equator will originate a voltaic circuit, and waterfalls will naturally become electric.

For a second example; it has recently been found, chiefly by the researches of Professor Graham, that gases have a strong tendency to permeate animal membranes, and diffuse themselves through the spaces which such membranes inclose, notwithstanding the presence of other gases in those spaces. Proceeding from this general law, and reviewing a variety of cases in which gases lie contiguous to membranes, we are enabled to demonstrate or to explain the following more special laws: 1st. The human or animal body, when surrounded with any gas not already contained within the body, absorbs it rapidly; such, for instance, as the gases of putrefying matters: which helps to explain malaria. 2nd. The carbonic acid gas of effervescing drinks, evolved in the stomach, permeates its membranes, and rapidly spreads through the system, where, as suggested in a former note, it probably combines with the iron contained in the blood. 3rd. Alcohol taken into the stomach passes into vapour and spreads through the system with great rapidity; (which, combined with the high combustibility of alcohol, or in other words its ready combination with oxygen, may perhaps help to explain the bodily warmth immediately consequent on drinking spirituous liquors.) 4th. In any state of the body in which peculiar gases are formed within it, these will rapidly exhale through all parts of the body; and hence the rapidity with which, in certain states of disease, the surrounding atmosphere becomes tainted. 5th. The putrefaction of the interior parts of a carcase will proceed as rapidly as that of the exterior, from the ready passage outwards of the gaseous products. 6th. The exchange of oxygen and carbonic acid in the lungs is not prevented, but rather promoted, by the intervention of the membrane of the lungs and the coats of the blood vessels between the blood and the air. It is necessary, however, that there should be a substance in the blood with which the oxygen of the air may immediately combine; otherwise instead of passing into the blood, it would permeate the whole organism: and it is necessary that the carbonic acid, as it is formed in the capillaries, should also find a substance in the blood with which it can combine; otherwise it would leave the body at all points, instead of being discharged through the lungs.

§ 5. The following is a deduction which confirms, by explaining, the old but not undisputed empirical generalization, that soda powders weaken the human system. These powders, consisting of a mixture of tartaric acid with bicarbonate of soda, from which the carbonic acid is set free, must pass into the stomach as tartrate of soda. Now, neutral tartrates, citrates, and acetates of the alkalis are found, in their passage through the system, to be changed into carbonates; and to convert a tartrate into a carbonate requires an additional quantity of oxygen, the abstraction of which must lessen the oxygen destined for assimilation with the blood, on the quantity of which the vigorous action of the human system partly depends.

The instances of new theories agreeing with and explaining old empiricisms, are innumerable. All the just remarks made by experienced persons on human character and conduct, are so many special laws, which the general laws of the human mind explain and resolve. The empirical generalizations on which the operations of the arts have usually been founded, are continually justified and confirmed on the one hand, or corrected and improved on the other, by the discovery of the simpler scientific laws on which the efficacy of those operations depends. The effects of the rotation of crops, of the various manures, and other processes of improved agriculture, have been for the first time resolved in our own day into known laws of chemical and organic action, by Davy and Liebig. The processes of the medical art are even now mostly empirical: their efficacy is concluded, in each instance, from a special and most precarious experimental generalization: but as science advances in discovering the simple laws of chemistry and physiology, progress is made in ascertaining the intermediate links in the series of phenomena, and the more general laws on which they depend; and thus, while the old processes are either exploded, or their efficacy, in so far as real, explained, better processes, founded on the knowledge of proximate causes, are continually suggested and brought into use.(92) Many even of the truths of geometry were generalizations from experience before they were deduced from first principles. The quadrature of the cycloid is said to have been first effected by measurement, or rather by weighing a cycloidal card, and comparing its weight with that of a piece of similar card of known dimensions.

§ 6. To the foregoing examples from physical science, let us add another from mental. The following is one of the simple laws of mind: Ideas of a pleasurable or painful character form associations more easily and strongly than other ideas, that is, they become associated after fewer repetitions, and the association is more durable. This is an experimental law, grounded on the Method of Difference. By deduction from this law, many of the more special laws which experience shows to exist among particular mental phenomena may be demonstrated and explained:-- the ease and rapidity, for instance, with which thoughts connected with our passions or our more cherished interests are excited, and the firm hold which the facts relating to them have on our memory; the vivid recollection we retain of minute circumstances which accompanied any object or event that deeply interested us, and of the times and places in which we have been very happy or very miserable; the horror with which we view the accidental instrument of any occurrence which shocked us, or the locality where it took place, and the pleasure we derive from any memorial of past enjoyment; all these effects being proportional to the sensibility of the individual mind, and to the consequent intensity of the pain or pleasure from which the association originated. It has been suggested by the able writer of a biographical sketch of Dr. Priestley in a monthly periodical, that the same elementary law of our mental constitution, suitably followed out, would explain a variety of mental phenomena hitherto inexplicable, and in particular some of the fundamental diversities of human character and genius. Associations being of two sorts, either between synchronous, or between successive impressions; and the influence of the law which renders associations stronger in proportion to the pleasurable or painful character of the impressions, being felt with peculiar force in the synchronous class of associations; it is remarked by the writer referred to, that in minds of strong organic sensibility synchronous associations will be likely to predominate, producing a tendency to conceive things in pictures and in the concrete, richly clothed in attributes and circumstances, a mental habit which is commonly called Imagination, and is one of the peculiarities of the painter and the poet; while persons of more moderate susceptibility to pleasure and pain will have a tendency to associate facts chiefly in the order of their succession, and such persons, if they possess mental superiority, will addict themselves to history or science rather than to creative art. This interesting speculation the author of the present work has endeavoured, on another occasion, to pursue farther, and to examine how far it will avail towards explaining the peculiarities of the poetical temperament. It is at least an example which may serve, instead of many others, to show the extensive scope which exists for deductive investigation in the important and hitherto so imperfect Science of Mind.

§ 7. The copiousness with which I have exemplified the discovery and explanation of special laws of phenomena by deduction from simpler and more general ones, was prompted by a desire to characterize clearly, and place in its due position of importance, the Deductive Method; which in the present state of knowledge is destined henceforth irrevocably to predominate in the course of scientific investigation. A revolution is peaceably and progressively effecting itself in philosophy, the reverse of that to which Bacon has attached his name. That great man changed the method of the sciences from deductive to experimental, and it is now rapidly reverting from experimental to deductive. But the deductions which Bacon abolished were from premisses hastily snatched up, or arbitrarily assumed. The principles were neither established by legitimate canons of experimental inquiry, nor the results tested by that indispensable element of a rational Deductive Method, verification by specific experience. Between the primitive method of Deduction and that which I have attempted to characterize, there is all the difference which exists between the Aristotelian physics and the Newtonian theory of the heavens.

It would, however, be a mistake to expect that those great generalizations, from which the subordinate truths of the more backward sciences will probably at some future period be deduced by reasoning (as the truths of astronomy are deduced from the generalities of the Newtonian theory,) will be found, in all, or even in most cases, among truths now known and admitted. We may rest assured, that many of the most general laws of nature are as yet entirely unthought of; and that many others, destined hereafter to assume the same character, are known, if at all, only as laws or properties of some limited class of phenomena; just as electricity, now recognised as one of the most universal of natural agencies, was once known only as a curious property which certain substances acquired by friction, of first attracting and then repelling light bodies. If the theories of heat, cohesion, crystallization, and chemical action, are destined, as there can be little doubt that they are, to become deductive, the truths which will then be regarded as the ***principia*** of those sciences would probably, if now announced, appear quite as novel as the law of gravitation appeared to the cotemporaries of Newton; possibly even more so, since Newton's law, after all, was but an extension of the law of weight--that is, of a generalization familiar from of old, and which already comprehended a not inconsiderable body of natural phenomena. The general laws, of a similarly commanding character, which we still look forward to the discovery of, may not always find so much of their foundations already laid.

These general truths will doubtless make their first appearance in the character of hypotheses; not proved, nor even admitting of proof, in the first instance, but assumed as premisses for the purpose of deducing from them the known laws of concrete phenomena. But this, though their initial, cannot be their final state. To entitle an hypothesis to be received as one of the truths of nature, and not as a mere technical help to the human faculties, it must be capable of being tested by the canons of legitimate induction, and must actually have been submitted to that test. When this shall have been done, and done successfully, premisses will have been obtained from which all the other propositions of the science will thenceforth be presented as conclusions, and the science will, by means of a new and unexpected Induction, be rendered Deductive.

END OF VOL. I.

NOTES

1 In the later editions of Archbishop Whately's **Logic** and **Rhetoric** there are some expressions, which, though indefinite, resemble a disclaimer of the opinion here ascribed to him. If I have imputed that opinion to him erroneously, I am glad to find myself mistaken; but he has not altered the passages in which the opinion appeared to me to be conveyed, and which I still think inconsistent with the belief that Induction can be reduced to strict rules.

2 Archbishop Whately.

3 This important theory has recently been called in question by a writer of deserved reputation, Mr. Samuel Bailey; but I do not conceive that the grounds on which it has been admitted as an established doctrine for a century past, have been at all shaken by that gentleman's objections. I have elsewhere said what appeared to me necessary in reply to his arguments (Westminster Review, for October 1842.) It may be necessary to add, that some other processes of comparison than those described in the text (but equally the result of experience), appear occasionally to enter into our judgment of distances by the eye.

4 Computation or Logic, chap. ii.

5 In the original, "had, *or had not*." These last words, as involving a subtlety foreign to our present purpose, I have forborne to quote.

6 It would, perhaps, be more correct to say that inflected cases are names and something more; and that this addition prevents them from

being used as the subjects of propositions. But the purposes of our inquiry do not demand that we should enter with scrupulous accuracy into similar minutiae.

7 *Notare* to mark; *con*notare, to mark *along with*; to mark one thing **with** or **in addition to** another.

8 Archbishop Whately, who in the more recent editions of his Elements of Logic has aided in reviving the important distinction treated of in the text, proposes the term "Attributive" as a substitute for "Connotative," (p. 122, 9th ed.) The expression is, in itself, appropriate; but, as it has not the advantage of being connected with any verb, of so markedly distinctive a character as "to connote," it is not, I think, fitted to supply the place of the word Connotative in scientific use.

9 It would be well if this degeneracy of language took place only in the hands of the untaught vulgar; but some of the most remarkable instances are to be found in terms of art, and among technically educated persons, such as English lawyers. *Felony*, for example, is a law term, with the sound of which all are familiar; but there is no lawyer who would undertake to tell what a felony is, otherwise than by enumerating the various offences which are so called. Originally the word felony had a meaning; it denoted all offences, the penalty of which included forfeiture of lands or goods; but subsequent acts of parliament have declared various offences to be felonies without enjoining that penalty, and have taken away the penalty from others which continue nevertheless to be called felonies, insomuch that the acts so called have now no property whatever in common, save that of being unlawful and punishable.

10 Before quitting the subject of connotative names, it is proper to observe, that the first writer who, in our own times, has adopted

from the schoolmen the word *to connote*, Mr. Mill, in his Analysis of the Phenomena of the Human Mind, employs it in a signification different from that in which it is here used. He uses the word in a sense coextensive with its etymology, applying it to every case in which a name, while pointing directly to one thing, (which is consequently termed its signification,) includes also a tacit reference to some other thing. In the case considered in the text, that of concrete general names, his language and mine are the converse of one another. Considering (very justly) the signification of the name to lie in the attribute, he speaks of the word as *noting* the attribute, and *connoting* the things possessing the attribute. And he describes abstract names as being properly concrete names with their connotation dropped: whereas, in my view, it is the *de*notation which would be said to be dropped, what was previously connoted becoming the whole signification.

In adopting a phraseology at variance with that which so high an authority, and one which I am less likely than any other person to undervalue, has deliberately sanctioned, I have been influenced by the urgent necessity for a term exclusively appropriated to express the manner in which a concrete general name serves to mark the attributes which are involved in its signification. This necessity can scarcely be felt in its full force by any one who has not found by experience, how vain is the attempt to communicate clear ideas on the philosophy of language without such a word. It is hardly an exaggeration to say, that some of the most prevalent of the errors with which logic has been infected, and a large part of the cloudiness and confusion of ideas which have enveloped it, would, in all probability, have been avoided, if a term had been in common use to express exactly what I have signified by the term *to connote*. And the schoolmen, to whom we are indebted for the greater part of our logical language, gave us this also, and in this very sense. For although some of their general expressions countenance the use of the word in the more extensive and vague acceptation in which it is taken by Mr. Mill, yet when they had to define it specifically as a technical term, and to fix its meaning as such, with that admirable precision which always characterizes their definitions, they clearly explained that nothing was said to be connoted except *forms*, which word may generally, in their writings, be understood as synonymous with *attributes*.

Now, if the word *to connote*, so well suited to the purpose to which they applied it, be diverted from that purpose by being taken to fulfil another, for which it does not seem to me to be at all required; I am unable to find any expression to replace it, but such as are commonly employed in a sense so much more general, that it would be useless attempting to associate them peculiarly with this precise idea. Such are the words, to involve, to imply, &c. By employing these, I should fail of attaining the object for which alone the name is needed, namely, to distinguish this particular kind of involving and implying from all other kinds, and to assure to it the degree of habitual attention which its importance demands.

11 Or rather, all objects except itself and the percipient mind; for, as we shall see hereafter, to ascribe any attribute to an object necessarily implies a mind to perceive it.

12 *Philosophy of the Inductive Sciences*, vol. i. p. 40.

13 This doctrine is laid down in the clearest and strongest terms by M. Cousin, whose observations on the subject are the more worthy of attention, as, in consequence of the ultra-German and ontological character of his philosophy considered generally, they may be regarded as the admissions of an opponent.

"Nous savons qu'il existe quelque chose hors de nous, parceque nous ne pouvons expliquer nos perceptions sans les rattacher a des causes distinctes de nous-memes; nous savons de plus que ces causes, dont nous ne connaissons pas d'ailleurs l'essence, produisent les effets les plus variables, les plus divers, et meme les plus contraires, selon qu'elles rencontrent telle nature ou telle disposition du sujet. Mais savons-nous quelque chose de plus? et meme, vu le caractere indetermine des causes que nous concevons dans les corps, y a-t-il quelque chose de plus a savoir? Y a-t-il lieu de nous enquerir si nous percevons les choses telles qu'elles sont? Non evidemment.... Je ne dis pas que le probleme est insoluble, je dis qu'il est absurde et enferme une contradiction. *Nous* ne savons pas ce que ces causes sont en elles-memes, et la raison nous defend de chercher a le connaitre: mais il est bien evident *a priori*, qu'elles ne sont pas en elles-memes ce quelles sont par rapport a nous, puisque la presence du sujet modifie necessairement leur action. Supprimez tout sujet sentant, il est certain que ces causes agiraient encore puisqu'elles continueraient d'exister; mais elles agiraient autrement; elles seraient encore des qualites et des proprietes, mais qui ne resembleraient a rien de ce que nous connaissons. Le feu ne manifesterait plus aucune des proprietes que nous lui connaissons: que serait-il? C'est ce que nous ne saurons jamais. C'est d'ailleurs peut-etre un probleme qui ne repugne pas seulement a la nature de notre esprit, mais a l'essence meme des choses. Quand meme en effet on supprimerait par la pensee tous les sujets sentants, il faudrait encore admettre que nul corps ne manifesterait ses proprietes autrement qu'en relation avec un sujet quelconque, et dans ce cas ses proprietes ne seraient encore que relatives: en sorte qu'il me parait fort raisonnable d'admettre que les proprietes determinees des corps n'existent pas independamment d'un sujet quelconque, et que quand on demande si les proprietes de la matiere sont telles que nous les percevons, il faudrait voir auparavant si elles sont en tant que determinees, et dans quel sens il est vrai de dire qu'elles sont."--Cours d'Histoire de la Philosophie Morale au 18me siecle, 8me lecon.

14 An attempt, indeed, has been made by Reid and others, to establish that although some of the properties we ascribe to objects exist only in our sensations, others exist in the things themselves, being such as cannot possibly be copies of any impression upon the senses; and they ask, from what sensations our notions of extension and figure have been derived? The gauntlet thrown down by Reid was taken up by Brown, who, applying greater powers of analysis than had previously been applied to the notions of extension and figure, showed clearly what are the sensations from which those notions are derived, viz. sensations of touch, combined with sensations of a class previously too little adverted to by metaphysicians, those which have their seat in our muscular frame. Whoever wishes to be more particularly acquainted with this excellent specimen of metaphysical analysis, may consult the first volume of Brown's *Lectures*, or Mill's *Analysis of the Mind*.

On this subject also, M. Cousin may be quoted in favour of conclusions rejected by some of the most eminent thinkers of the school to which he belongs. M. Cousin recognises, in opposition to Reid, the essential *subjectivity* of our conceptions of the primary qualities of matter, as extension, solidity, &c., equally with those of colour, heat, and the remainder of what are called secondary qualities.--*Cours*, ut supra, 9me lecon.

15 Analysis of the Human Mind, i. 126 et seqq.

16 Dr. Whewell (*Of Induction*, p. 10) questions this statement, and asks, "Are we to say that a mole cannot dig the ground, except he has an idea of the ground, and of the snout and paws with which he digs it?" I thought it had been evident that I was here speaking of

rational digging, and not of digging by instinct.

17 "From hence also this may be deduced, that the first truths were
arbitrarily made by those that first of all imposed names upon
things, or received them from the imposition of others. For it is
true (for example) that *man is a living creature*, but it is for
this reason, that it pleased men to impose both these names on the
same thing."--*Computation or Logic*, ch. iii. sect. 8.

18 "Men are subject to err not only in affirming and denying, but also
in perception, and in silent cogitation.... Tacit errors, or the
errors of sense and cogitation, are made by passing from one
imagination to the imagination of another different thing; or by
feigning that to be past, or future, which never was, nor ever shall
be; as when, by seeing the image of the sun in water, we imagine the
sun itself to be there; or by seeing swords, that there has been or
shall be, fighting, because it uses to be so for the most part; or
when from promises we feign the mind of the promiser to be such and
such; or, lastly, when from any sign we vainly imagine something to
be signified which is not. And errors of this sort are common to all
things that have sense."--*Computation or Logic*, ch. v., sect. 1.

19 Ch. iii. sect. 3.

20 Book iv. ch. vii.

21 Καθόλου μὲν οὖν πᾶσα διαφορὰ προγινομένη τινὶ ἑτεροῖον ποιεῖ; ἀλλ'
αἱ μὲν κοινῶς τε καὶ ἰδίως (differences in the accidental properties) ἀλλοῖον
ποιοῦσιν; αἱ δὲ ἰδιαίτατα (differences in the essential properties) ἄλλο—Isag. cap.
iii.

22 Few among the great names in mental science have met with a harder
measure of justice from the present generation than Locke; the
unquestioned founder of the analytic philosophy of mind, but whose

doctrines were first caricatured, then, when the reaction arrived, cast off by the prevailing school even with contumely, and who is now regarded by one of the conflicting parties in philosophy as an apostle of heresy and sophistry, while among those who still adhere to the standard which he raised, there has been a disposition in later times to sacrifice his reputation in favour of Hobbes; a great writer, and a great thinker for his time, but inferior to Locke not only in sober judgment but even in profundity and original genius. Locke, the most candid of philosophers, and one whose speculations bear on every subject the strongest marks of having been wrought out from the materials of his own mind, has been mistaken for an unworthy plagiarist, while Hobbes has been extolled as having anticipated many of his leading doctrines. He did anticipate many of them, and the present is an instance in what manner it was generally done. They both rejected the scholastic doctrine of essences; but Locke understood and explained what these supposed essences really were; Hobbes, instead of explaining the distinction between essential and accidental properties, and between essential and accidental propositions, jumped over it, and gave a definition which suits at most only essential propositions, and scarcely those, as the definition of Proposition in general.

23 The always acute and often profound author of An Outline of Sematology (Mr. B. H. Smart) justly says, "Locke will be much more intelligible if, in the majority of places, we substitute 'the knowledge of' for what he calls 'the idea of' " (p. 10). Among the many criticisms on Locke's use of the word Idea, this is the only one which, as it appears to me, precisely hits the mark; and I quote it for the additional reason that it precisely expresses the point of difference respecting the import of Propositions, between my view and what I have spoken of as the Conceptualist view of them. Where a Conceptualist says that a name or a proposition expresses our Idea of a thing, I should generally say (instead of our Idea) our

Knowledge, or Belief, concerning the thing itself.

24 If we allow a differentia to what is not really a species. For the distinction of Kinds, in the sense explained by us, not being in any way applicable to attributes, it of course follows that although attributes may be put into classes, those classes can be admitted to be genera or species only by courtesy.

25 In the fuller discussion which Archbishop Whately has given to this subject in his later editions, he almost ceases to regard the definitions of names and those of things as, in any important sense, distinct. He seems (9th ed. p. 145) to limit the notion of a Real Definition to one which "explains anything *more* of the nature of the thing than is implied in the name;" (including under the word "implied," not only what the name connotes, but everything which can be deduced by reasoning from the attributes connoted). Even this, as he adds, is usually called, not a Definition, but a Description; and (as it seems to me) rightly so called. A Description, I conceive, can only be ranked among Definitions, when taken (as in the case of the zoological definition of man) to fulfil the true office of a Definition, by declaring the connotation given to a word in some special use, as a term of science or art; which special connotation of course would *not* be expressed by the proper definition of the word in its ordinary employment.

Mr. De Morgan, exactly reversing the doctrine of Archbishop Whately, understands by a Real Definition one which contains *less* than the Nominal Definition, provided only that what it contains is sufficient for distinction. "By *real* definition I mean such an explanation of the word, be it the whole of the meaning or only part, as will be sufficient to separate the things contained under that word from all others. Thus the following, I believe, is a complete definition of an elephant: An animal which naturally drinks by drawing the water into its nose, and then spirting it into its mouth."--*Formal Logic*, p. 36. Mr. De Morgan's general proposition and his example are at variance; for the peculiar mode of drinking of the elephant certainly forms no part of the meaning of the word elephant. It could not be said, because a person happened to be ignorant of this property, that he did not know what an elephant means.

26 In the only attempt which, so far as I know, has been made to refute the preceding argumentation, it is maintained that in the first form of the syllogism,

A dragon is a thing which breathes flame,
A dragon is a serpent,
Therefore some serpent or serpents breathe flame,

"there is just as much truth in the conclusion as there is in the premisses, or rather, no more in the latter than in the former. If the general name serpent includes both real and imaginary serpents, there is no falsity in the conclusion; if not, there is falsity in the minor premiss."

Let us, then, try to set out the syllogism on the hypothesis that the name serpent includes imaginary serpents. We shall find that it is now necessary to alter the predicates; for it cannot be asserted that an imaginary creature breathes flame: in predicating of it such a fact, we assert by the most positive implication that it is real and not imaginary. The conclusion must run thus, "Some serpent or serpents either do or are *imagined* to breathe flame." And to prove this conclusion by the instance of dragons, the premisses must be, A dragon is *imagined* as breathing flame, A dragon is a (real or imaginary) serpent: from which it undoubtedly follows, that there are serpents which are imagined to breathe flame; but the major premiss is not a definition, nor part of a definition; which is all that I am concerned to prove.

Let us now examine the other assertion--that if the word serpent stands for none but real serpents, the minor premiss (A dragon is a serpent) is false. This is exactly what I have myself said of the premiss, considered as a statement of fact: but it is not false as part of the definition of a dragon; and since the premisses, or one of them, *must* be false, (the conclusion being so,) the real premiss cannot be the definition, which is true, but the statement of fact, which is false.

27 "Few people" (I have said in another place) "have reflected how great a knowledge of Things is required to enable a man to affirm that any given argument turns wholly upon words. There is, perhaps, not one of the leading terms of philosophy which is not used in almost innumerable shades of meaning, to express ideas more or less widely different from one another. Between two of these ideas a sagacious and penetrating mind will discern, as it were intuitively, an unobvious link of connexion, upon which, though perhaps unable to give a logical account of it, he will found a perfectly valid argument, which his critic, not having so keen an insight into the Things, will mistake for a fallacy turning on the double meaning of a term. And the greater the genius of him who thus safely leaps over the chasm, the greater will probably be the crowing and vain-glory of the mere logician, who, hobbling after him, evinces his own superior wisdom by pausing on its brink, and giving up as desperate his proper business of bridging it over."

28 Contraries:
All A is B
No A is B

Subtraries:
Some A is B
Some A is not B

Contradictories:
All A is B
Some A is not B

Also contradictories:
No A is B
Some A is B

Respectively subalternate:
All A is B; No A is B
Some A is B; and Some A is not B

29 His conclusions are, "The first figure is suited to the discovery or proof of the properties of a thing; the second to the discovery or proof of the distinctions between things; the third to the discovery or proof of instances and exceptions; the fourth to the discovery, or exclusion, of the different species of a genus." The reference of syllogisms in the last three figures to the dictum de omni et nullo is, in Lambert's opinion, strained and unnatural: to each of the three belongs, according to him, a separate axiom, co-ordinate and of equal authority with that *dictum*, and to which he gives the names of *dictum de diverso* for the second figure, dictum de exemplo *for the third, and* dictum de reciproco for the fourth. See part i. or *Dianoiologie*, chap. iv. § 229 *et seqq.*

Mr. De Morgan's "Formal Logic, or the Calculus of Inference, Necessary and Probable," (a work published since the statement in the text was made,) far exceeds in elaborate minuteness Lambert's treatise on the syllogism. Mr. De Morgan's principal object is to bring within strict technical rules the cases in which a conclusion can be drawn from premises of a form usually classed as particular. He observes, very justly, that from the premises Most Bs are Cs, most Bs are As, it may be concluded with certainty that some As are Cs, since two portions of the class B, each of them comprising more than half, must necessarily in part consist of the same individuals. Following out this line of thought, it is equally evident that if we knew exactly what proportion the "most" in each of the premises bear to the entire class B, we could increase in a corresponding degree the definiteness of the conclusion. Thus if 60 per cent of B are included in C, and 70 per cent in A, 30 per cent at least must be common to both; in other words, the number of As which are Cs, and of Cs which are As, must be at least equal to 30 per cent of the class B. Proceeding on this conception of "numerically definite propositions," and extending it to such forms as these:--"45 Xs (or more) are each of them one of 70 Ys," or "45 Xs (or more), are no one of them to be found among 70 Ys," and examining what inferences admit of being drawn from the various combinations which may be made of premises of this description, Mr. De Morgan establishes universal formulae for such inferences; creating for that purpose not only a new technical language, but a formidable array of symbols analogous to those of algebra.

Since it is undeniable that inferences, in the cases examined by Mr. De Morgan, can legitimately be drawn, and that the ordinary theory takes no account of them, I will not say that it was not worth while to show in detail how these also could be reduced to formulae as rigorous as those of Aristotle. What Mr. De Morgan has done was worth doing once (perhaps more than once, as a school exercise); but I question if its results are worth studying and mastering for any practical purpose. The practical use of technical forms of reasoning is to bar out fallacies: but the fallacies which require to be guarded against in ratiocination properly so called, arise from the incautious use of the common forms of language; and the logician must track the fallacy into that territory, instead of waiting for it on a territory of his own. While he remains among propositions which have acquired the numerical precision of the Calculus of Probabilities, the enemy is left in possession of the only ground on which he can be formidable. The "quantification of the predicate," an invention to which Sir William Hamilton attaches so much importance as to have raised an angry dispute with Mr. De Morgan respecting its authorship, appears to me, I confess, as an accession to the art of Logic, of singularly small value. It is of course true, that "All men are mortal" is equivalent to "Every man is *some* mortal." But as mankind certainly will not be persuaded to "quantify" their predicates in common discourse, they want a logic which will teach them to reason correctly with propositions in the usual form, by furnishing them with a type of ratiocination to which propositions can be referred, retaining that form. Not to mention that the quantification of the predicate, instead of being a means of bringing out more clearly the meaning of the proposition, actually leads the mind out of the proposition, into another order of ideas. For when we say, All men are mortal, we simply mean to affirm the attribute mortality of all men; without thinking at all of the *class* mortal in the concrete, or troubling ourselves about whether it contains any other beings or not. It is only for some artificial purpose that we ever look at the proposition in the aspect in which the predicate also is thought of as a class-name, either including the subject only, or the subject and something more.

30 Supra, p. 129.

31 Logic, p. 239 (9th ed.)

32 It is hardly necessary to say, that I am not contending for any such

absurdity as that we *actually* "ought to have known" and considered the case of every individual man, past, present, and future, before affirming that all men are mortal: although this interpretation has been, strangely enough, put upon the preceding observations. There is no difference between me and Archbishop Whately, or any other defender of the syllogism, on the practical part of the matter; I am only pointing out an inconsistency in the logical theory of it, as conceived by almost all writers. I do not say that a person who affirmed, before the Duke of Wellington was born, that all men are mortal, *knew* that the Duke of Wellington was mortal; but I do say, that he *asserted* it; and I ask for an explanation of the apparent logical fallacy, of adducing in proof of the Duke of Wellington's mortality, a general statement which presupposes it. Finding no sufficient resolution of this difficulty in any of the writers on Logic, I have attempted to supply one.

33 Of Induction, p. 85.

34 For August 1846.

35 There is a striking passage in the Metaphysics of Aristotle (commencement of chap. iii.) on the necessity of beginning the study of a subject by a clear perception of its difficulties. Εστι τοῖς εὐπορῆσαι βουλομένοις προὔργου τὸ διαπορῆσαι καλῶς. ἡ γὰρ ὕστερον εὐπορία λύσις τῶν πρότερον ἀπορουμένων ἐστί. λύειν δὲ οὐκ ἔστιν ἀγνοοῦντα τὸν δεσμόν· ἀλλ' ἡ τῆς διανοίας ἀπορία δηλοῖ τοῦτο περὶ τοῦ πράγματος ... διὸ δεῖ τὰς δυσχερείας τεθεωρηκέναι πάσας πρότερον, τούτων τε χάριν καὶ διὰ τὸ τοὺς ζητοῦντας ἄνευ τοῦ διαπορῆσαι πρῶτον, ὁμοίους εἶναι τοῖς ποῖ δεῖ βαδίζειν ἀγνοοῦσι· καὶ πρὸς τούτοις, οὐδὲ εἴ ποτε τὸ ζητούμενον εὕρηκεν ἢ μὴ, γινώσκειν. τὸ γὰρ τέλος τούτῳ μὲν οὐ δῆλον, τῷ δὲ καλῶς προηπορηκότι δῆλον.

36 The reviewer misunderstands me when he supposes me to say that "the conclusion must be admitted *before* we can admit the major

premiss." What I say is, that there must be ground for admitting it *simultaneously*, or else the major premise is not proved.

37 Mechanical Euclid, pp. 149 *et seqq.*

38 We might, it is true, insert this property into the definition of parallel lines, framing the definition so as to require, *both* that when produced indefinitely they shall never meet, and *also* that any straight line which intersects one of them shall, if prolonged, meet the other. But by doing this we by no means get rid of the assumption; we are still obliged to take for granted the geometrical truth, that all straight lines in the same plane, which have the former of these properties, have also the latter. For if it were possible that they should not, that is, if any straight lines other than those which are parallel according to the definition, had the property of never meeting although indefinitely produced, the demonstrations of the subsequent portions of the theory of parallels could not be maintained.

39 Whewell's *Philosophy of the Inductive Sciences*, i. 130.

40 Dr. Whewell (*Of Induction* p. 84) thinks it unreasonable to contend that we know by experience, that our idea of a line exactly resembles a real line. "It does not appear," he says, "how we can compare our ideas with the realities, since we know the realities only by our ideas." We know the realities (I conceive) by our eyes. Dr. Whewell surely does not hold the "doctrine of perception by means of ideas," which Reid gave himself so much trouble to refute.

Dr. Whewell also says, that it does not appear why this resemblance of ideas to the sensations of which they are copies, should be spoken of as if it were a peculiarity of one class of ideas, those of space. My reply is, that I do not so speak of it. The peculiarity

I contend for is only one of degree. All our ideas of sensation of course resemble the corresponding sensations, but they do so with very different degrees of exactness and of reliability. No one, I presume, can recall in imagination a colour or an odour with the same distinctness and accuracy with which almost every one can mentally reproduce an image of a straight line or a triangle. To the extent, however, of their capabilities of accuracy, our recollections of colours or of odours may serve as subjects of experimentation, as well as those of lines and spaces, and may yield conclusions which will be true of their external prototypes. A person in whom, either from natural gift or from cultivation, the impressions of colour were peculiarly vivid and distinct, if asked which of two blue flowers was of the darkest tinge, though he might never have compared the two, or even looked at them together, might be able to give a confident answer on the faith of his distinct recollection of the colours; that is, he might examine his mental pictures, and find there a property of the outward objects. But in hardly any case except that of simple geometrical forms, could this be done by mankind generally, with a degree of assurance equal to that which is given by a contemplation of the objects themselves. Persons differ most widely in the precision of their recollection, even of forms: one person, when he has looked any one in the face for half a minute, can draw an accurate likeness of him from memory; another may have seen him every day for six months, and hardly know whether his nose is long or short. But everybody has a perfectly distinct mental image of a straight line, a circle, or a rectangle. And every one concludes confidently from these mental images to the corresponding outward things.

41 *Phil. Ind. Sc.* i. 59-61.

42 Ibid. 57.

43 Ibid. 54, 55.

44 "If all mankind had spoken one language, we cannot doubt that there would have been a powerful, perhaps a universal, school of philosophers, who would have believed in the inherent connexion between names and things, who would have taken the sound **man** to be the mode of agitating the air which is essentially communicative of the ideas of reason, cookery, bipedality, &c." De Morgan, Formal Logic, p. 246.

45 It would be difficult to name a man more remarkable at once for the greatness and the wide range of his mental accomplishments, than Leibnitz. Yet this eminent man gave as a reason for rejecting Newton's scheme of the solar system, that God **could not** make a body revolve round a distant centre, unless either by some impelling mechanism, or by miracle:--"Tout ce qui n'est pas explicable," says he in a letter to the Abbe Conti, "par la nature des creatures, est miraculeux. Il ne suffit pas de dire: Dieu a fait une telle loi de nature; donc la chose est naturelle. Il faut que la loi soit executable par les natures des creatures. Si Dieu donnait cette loi, par exemple, a un corps libre, de tourner a l'entour d'un certain centre, il faudrait ou qu'il y joignit d'autres corps qui par leur impulsion l'obligeassent de rester toujours dans son orbite circulaire, ou quil mit un ange a ses trousses, ou enfin il faudrait qu'il y concourut extraordinairement; car naturellement il s'ecartera par la tangente."-- **Works of Leibnitz**, ed. Dutens, iii. 446.

46 Phil. Ind. Sc. ii. 174.

47 Phil. Ind. Sc. i., 238.

48 Phil. Ind. Sc. i. 237.

49 Ibid. 213.

50 Ibid. 384, 385.

51 In his recent pamphlet (p. 81), Dr. Whewell greatly attenuates the opinion here quoted, reducing it to a surmise "that if we could conceive the composition of bodies distinctly, we might be able to see that it is necessary that the modes of their composition should be definite." The passage in the text asserts that we already see, or may and ought to see, this necessity; giving as the reason, that no other mode of combination is conceivable. That Dr. Whewell should ever have made this statement, is enough for the purposes of my illustration. To what he now says I have nothing to object. Undoubtedly, if we understood the ultimate molecular composition of bodies, we might find that their combining with one another in definite proportions is, in the present order of nature, a ***necessary consequence*** of that molecular composition; and has thus the only kind of necessity of which, in my view of the subject, any law of nature is susceptible. But in that case, the doctrine would be taken out of the class of axioms altogether. It would be no longer an ultimate principle, but a mere derivative law; regarded as necessary, not because self-evident, but because demonstrable.

52 The ***Quarterly Review*** for June 1841, contains an article of great ability on Dr. Whewell's two great works, the writer of which maintains, on the subject of axioms, the doctrine advanced in the text, that they are generalizations from experience, and supports that opinion by a line of argument strikingly coinciding with mine. When I state that the whole of the present chapter was written before I had seen the article, (the greater part, indeed, before it was published,) it is not my object to occupy the reader's attention

with a matter so unimportant as the degree of originality which may or may not belong to any portion of my own speculations, but to obtain for an opinion which is opposed to reigning doctrines, the recommendation derived from a striking concurrence of sentiment between two inquirers entirely independent of one another. I embrace the opportunity of citing from a writer of the extensive acquirements in physical and metaphysical knowledge and the capacity of systematic thought which the article evinces, passages so remarkably in unison with my own views as the following:--

"The truths of geometry are summed up and embodied in its definitions and axioms.... Let us turn to the axioms, and what do we find? A string of propositions concerning magnitude in the abstract, which are equally true of space, time, force, number, and every other magnitude susceptible of aggregation and subdivision. Such propositions, where they are not mere definitions, as some of them are, carry their inductive origin on the face of their enunciation.... Those which declare that two straight lines cannot inclose a space, and that two straight lines which cut one another cannot both be parallel to a third, are in reality the only ones which express characteristic properties of space, and these it will be worth while to consider more nearly. Now the only clear notion we can form of straightness is uniformity of direction, for space in its ultimate analysis is nothing but an assemblage of distances and directions. And (not to dwell on the notion of continued contemplation, *i.e.*, mental experience, as included in the very idea of uniformity; nor on that of transfer of the contemplating being from point to point, and of experience, during such transfer, of the homogeneity of the interval passed over) we cannot even propose the proposition in an intelligible form, to any one whose experience ever since he was born has not assured him of the fact. The unity of direction, or that we cannot march from a given point by more than one path direct to the same object, is matter of practical experience long before it can by possibility become matter of abstract thought. We cannot attempt mentally to exemplify the conditions of the assertion in an imaginary case opposed to it, without violating our habitual recollection of this experience, and defacing our mental picture of space as grounded on it. What but experience, we may ask, can possibly assure us of the homogeneity of the parts of distance, time, force, and measurable aggregates in general, on which the truth of the other axioms depends? As regards the latter axiom, after what has been said it must be clear that the very same course of remarks equally applies to its case, and that its truth is quite as much forced on the mind as that of the former by daily and hourly experience ... including always, be it observed, in our notion of experience, that which is gained by contemplation of the inward picture which the mind forms to itself in any proposed case, or which it arbitrarily selects as an example--such picture, in virtue of the extreme simplicity of these primary relations, being called up by the imagination with as much vividness and clearness as could be done by any external impression, which is the only meaning we can attach to the word intuition, as applied to such relations."

And again, of the axioms of mechanics:--"As we admit no such propositions, other than as truths inductively collected from observation, even in geometry itself, it can hardly be expected that, in a science of obviously contingent relations, we should acquiesce in a contrary view. Let us take one of these axioms and examine its evidence: for instance, that equal forces perpendicularly applied at the opposite ends of equal arms of a straight lever will balance each other. What but experience, we may ask, in the first place, can possibly inform us that a force so applied will have any tendency to turn the lever on its centre at all? or that force can be so transmitted along a rigid line perpendicular to its direction, as to act elsewhere in space than along its own line of action? Surely this is so far from being self-evident that it has even a paradoxical appearance, which is only to be removed by giving our lever thickness, material composition, and molecular powers. Again we conclude, that the two forces, being equal and applied under precisely similar circumstances, must, if they exert any effort at all to turn the lever, exert equal and opposite efforts: but what *a priori* reasoning can possibly assure us that they *do* act under precisely similar circumstances? that points which differ in place *are* similarly circumstanced as regards the exertion of force? that universal space may not have relations to universal force--or, at all events, that the organization of the material universe may not be such as to place that portion of space occupied by it in such relations to the forces exerted in it, as may invalidate the absolute similarity of circumstances assumed? Or we may argue, what have we to do with the notion of angular movement in the lever at all? The case is one of rest, and of quiescent destruction of force by force. Now how is this destruction effected? Assuredly by the counter-pressure which supports the fulcrum. But would not this destruction equally arise, and by the same amount of counteracting force, if each force simply pressed its own half of the lever against the fulcrum? And what can assure us that it is not so, except removal of one or other force, and consequent tilting of the lever? The other fundamental axiom of statics, that the pressure on the point of support is the sum of the weights ... is merely a scientific transformation and more refined mode of stating a coarse and obvious result of universal experience, viz. that the weight of a rigid body is the same, handle it or suspend it in what position or by what point we will, and that whatever sustains it sustains its total weight. Assuredly, as Mr. Whewell justly remarks, 'No one probably ever made a trial for the purpose of showing that the pressure on the support is equal to the sum of the weights' ... But it is precisely because in every action of his life from earliest infancy he has been continually making the trial, and seeing it made by every other living being about him, that he never dreams of staking its result on one additional attempt made with scientific accuracy. This would be as if a man should resolve to decide by experiment whether his eyes were useful for the purpose of seeing, by hermetically sealing himself up for half an hour in a metal case."

On the "paradox of universal propositions obtained by experience," the same writer says: "If there be necessary and universal truths expressible in propositions of axiomatic simplicity and obviousness, and having for their subject-matter the elements of all our experience and all our knowledge, surely these are the truths which, if experience suggest to us any truths at all, it ought to suggest most readily, clearly, and unceasingly. If it were a truth, universal and necessary, that a net is spread over the whole surface of every planetary globe, we should not travel far on our own without getting entangled in its meshes, and making the necessity of some means of extrication an axiom of locomotion.... There is, therefore, nothing paradoxical, but the reverse, in our being led by observation to a recognition of such truths, as ***general*** propositions, coextensive at least with all human experience. That they pervade all the objects of experience, must ensure their continual suggestion ***by*** experience; that they are true, must ensure that consistency of suggestion, that iteration of uncontradicted assertion, which commands implicit assent, and removes all occasion of exception; that they are simple, and admit of no misunderstanding, must secure their admission by every mind."

"A truth, necessary and universal, relative to any object of our knowledge, must verify itself in every instance where that object is before our contemplation, and if at the same time it be simple and intelligible, its verification must be obvious. The sentiment of such a truth cannot, therefore, but be present to our minds whenever that object is contemplated, and must therefore make a part of the mental picture or idea of that object which we may on any occasion summon before our imagination.... All propositions, therefore, become not only untrue but inconceivable, if ... axioms be violated in their enunciation."

Another high authority (if indeed it be another authority) may be cited in favour of the doctrine that axioms rest on the evidence of induction. "The axioms of geometry themselves may be regarded as in some sort an appeal to experience, not corporeal, but mental. When we say, the whole is greater than its part, we announce a general fact, which rests, it is true, on our ideas of whole and part; but, in abstracting these notions, we begin by considering them as subsisting in space, and time, and body, and again, in linear, and superficial, and solid space. Again, when we say, the equals of equals are equal, we mentally make comparisons, in equal spaces, equal times, &c., so that these axioms, however self-evident, are still general propositions so far of the inductive kind, that, independently of experience, they would not present themselves to the mind. The only difference between these and axioms obtained from extensive induction is this, that, in raising the axioms of geometry, the instances offer themselves spontaneously, and without the trouble of search, and are few and simple; in raising those of nature, they are infinitely numerous, complicated, and remote, so that the most diligent research and the utmost acuteness are required to unravel their web and place their meaning in evidence."--SIR J. HERSCHEL's Discourse on the Study of Natural Philosophy, pp. 95, 96.

53 Dr. Whewell thinks it improper to apply the term Induction to any operation not terminating in the establishment of a general truth. Induction, he says (in p. 15 of his pamphlet) "is not the same thing

as experience and observation. Induction is experience or observation **consciously** looked at in a **general** form. This consciousness and generality are necessary parts of that knowledge which is science." And he objects (p. 8) to the mode in which the word Induction is employed in this work, as an undue extension of that term "not only to the cases in which the general induction is consciously applied to a particular instance, but to the cases in which the particular instance is dealt with by means of experience in that rude sense in which experience can be asserted of brutes, and in which of course we can in no way imagine that the law is possessed or understood as a general proposition." This use of the term he deems a "confusion of knowledge with practical tendencies."

I disclaim, as strongly as Dr. Whewell can do, the application of such terms as induction, inference, or reasoning, to operations performed by mere instinct, that is, from an animal impulse, without the exertion of any intelligence. But I perceive no ground for confining the use of those terms to cases in which the inference is drawn in the forms and with the precautions required by scientific propriety. To the idea of Science, an express recognition and distinct apprehension of general laws as such, is essential: but nine-tenths of the conclusions drawn from experience in the course of practical life, are drawn without any such recognition: they are direct inferences from known cases, to a case supposed to be similar. I have endeavoured to shew that this is not only as legitimate an operation, but substantially the same operation, as that of ascending from known cases to a general proposition; (except that the latter process has one great security for correctness which the former does not possess). In Science, the inference must necessarily pass through the intermediate stage of a general proposition, because Science wants its conclusions for record, and not for instantaneous use. But the inferences drawn for the guidance of practical affairs, by persons who would often be quite incapable of expressing in unexceptionable terms the corresponding generalizations, may and frequently do exhibit intellectual powers quite equal to any which have ever been displayed in Science: and if these inferences are not inductive, what are they? The limitation imposed on the term by Dr. Whewell seems perfectly arbitrary; neither justified by any fundamental distinction between what he includes and what he desires to exclude, nor sanctioned by usage, at least from the time of Reid and Stewart, the principal legislators (as far as the English language is concerned) of modern metaphysical terminology.

54 Supra, p. 214.

55 Phil. Ind. Sc. ii. 213, 214.

56 Ibid.

57 Phil. Ind. Sc. ii. p. 173.

58 Cours de Philosophie Positive, vol. ii, p. 202.

59 Dr. Whewell, in his reply, contests the distinction here drawn, and maintains, that not only different descriptions, but different explanations of a phenomenon, may all be true. Of the three theories respecting the motions of the heavenly bodies, he says (p. 25): "Undoubtedly all these explanations may be true and consistent with each other, and would be so if each had been followed out so as to shew in what manner it could be made consistent with the facts. And this was, in reality, in a great measure done. The doctrine that the heavenly bodies were moved by vortices was successively modified, so that it came to coincide in its results with the doctrine of an inverse-quadratic centripetal force.... When this point was reached, the vortex was merely a machinery, well or ill devised, for

producing such a centripetal force, and therefore did not contradict the doctrine of a centripetal force. Newton himself does not appear to have been averse to explaining gravity by impulse. So little is it true that if one theory be true the other must be false. The attempt to explain gravity by the impulse of streams of particles flowing through the universe in all directions, which I have mentioned in the *Philosophy*, is so far from being inconsistent with the Newtonian theory, that it is founded entirely upon it. And even with regard to the doctrine, that the heavenly bodies move by an inherent virtue; if this doctrine had been maintained in any such way that it was brought to agree with the facts, the inherent virtue must have had its laws determined; and then it would have been found that the virtue had a reference to the central body; and so, the 'inherent virtue' must have coincided in its effect with the Newtonian force; and then, the two explanations would agree, except so far as the word 'inherent' was concerned. And if such a part of an earlier theory as this word *inherent* indicates, is found to be untenable, it is of course rejected in the transition to later and more exact theories, in Inductions of this kind, as well as in what Mr. Mill calls Descriptions. There is, therefore, still no validity discoverable in the distinction which Mr. Mill attempts to draw between descriptions like Kepler's law of elliptical orbits, and other examples of induction."

If the doctrine of vortices had meant, not that vortices existed, but only that the planets moved *in the same manner* as if they had been whirled by vortices; if the hypothesis had been merely a mode of representing the facts, not an attempt to account for them; if, in short, it had been only a Description; it would, no doubt, have been reconcileable with the Newtonian theory. The vortices, however, were not a mere aid to conceiving the motions of the planets, but a supposed physical agent, actively impelling them; a material fact, which might be true or not true, but could not be both true and not

true. According to Descartes' theory it was true, according to
Newton's it was not true. Dr. Whewell probably means that since the
phrases, centripetal and projectile force, do not declare the nature
but only the direction of the forces, the Newtonian theory does not
absolutely contradict any hypothesis which may be framed respecting
the mode of their production. The Newtonian theory, regarded as a
mere ***description*** of the planetary motions, does not; but the
Newtonian theory as an ***explanation*** of them does. For in what does
the explanation consist? In ascribing those motions to a general law
which obtains between all particles of matter, and in identifying
this with the law by which bodies fall to the ground; a kind of
motion which the vortices did not, and as it was rectilineal, could
not, explain. The one explanation, therefore, absolutely excludes
the other. Either the planets are not moved by vortices, or they do
not move by the law by which heavy bodies fall. It is impossible
that both opinions can be true. As well might it be said that there
is no contradiction between the assertions, that a man died because
somebody killed him, and that he died a natural death.

So, again, the theory that the planets move by a virtue inherent in
their celestial nature, is incompatible with either of the two
others; either that of their being moved by vortices, or that which
regards them as moving by a property which they have in common with
the earth and all terrestrial bodies. Dr. Whewell says, that the
theory of an inherent virtue agrees with Newton's when the word
inherent is left out, which of course it would be (he says) if
"found to be untenable." But leave that out, and where is the
theory? The word inherent ***is*** the theory. When that is omitted,
there remains nothing except that the heavenly bodies move by "a
virtue," ***i.e.*** by a power of some sort.

If Dr. Whewell is not yet satisfied, any other subject will serve
equally well to test his doctrine. He will hardly say that there is

no contradiction between the emission theory and the undulatory theory of light; or that there can be both one and two electricities; or that the hypothesis of the production of the higher organic forms by development from the lower, and the supposition of separate and successive acts of creation, are quite reconcileable; or that the theory that volcanoes are fed from a central fire, and the doctrines which ascribe them to chemical action at a comparatively small depth below the earth's surface, are consistent with one another, and all true as far as they go.

If different explanations of the same fact cannot both be true, still less, surely, can different predictions. Dr. Whewell quarrels (on what ground it is not necessary to consider) with the example I had chosen on this point, and thinks an objection to an illustration a sufficient answer to a theory. Examples not liable to his objection are easily found, if the proposition that conflicting predictions cannot both be true, can be made clearer by any examples. Suppose the phenomenon to be a newly-discovered comet, and that one astronomer predicts its return once in every 300 years--another, once in every 400: can they both be right? When Columbus predicted that by sailing constantly westward he should in time return to the point from which he set out, while others asserted that he could never do so except by turning back, were both he and his opponents true prophets? Were the predictions which foretold the wonders of railways and steamships, and those which averred that the Atlantic could never be crossed by steam navigation, nor a railway train propelled ten miles an hour, both (in Dr. Whewell's words) "true, and consistent with one another"?

Dr. Whewell sees no distinction between holding contradictory opinions on a question of fact, and merely employing different analogies to facilitate the conception of the same fact. The case of different Inductions belongs to the former class, that of different

Descriptions to the latter.

60 *Of Induction*, p. 33.

61 But though it is a condition of the validity of every induction that
there be uniformity in the course of nature, it is not a necessary
condition that the uniformity should pervade all nature. It is
enough that it pervades the particular class of phenomena to which
the induction relates. An induction concerning the motions of the
planets, or the properties of the magnet, would not be vitiated
though we were to suppose that wind and weather are the sport of
chance, provided it be assumed that astronomical and magnetic
phenomena are under the dominion of general laws. Otherwise the
early experience of mankind would have rested on a very weak
foundation; for in the infancy of science it could not be said to be
known that ***all*** phenomena are regular in their course.

Neither would it be correct to say that every induction by which we
infer any truth, implies the general fact of uniformity as
foreknown, even in reference to the kind of phenomena concerned. It
implies, ***either*** that this general fact is already known, ***or*** that
we may now know it: as the conclusion, The Duke of Wellington is
mortal, drawn from the instances A, B, and C, implies either that we
have already concluded all men to be mortal, or that we are now
entitled to do so from the same evidence. A vast amount of confusion
and paralogism respecting the grounds of Induction would be
dispelled by keeping in view these simple considerations.

62 Infra, chap. xxi.

63 Infra, chap. xxi, xxii.

64 Dr. Whewell (***Of Induction***, p. 16) will not allow these and similar

erroneous opinions to be called inductions; inasmuch as such superstitious fancies "were not collected from the facts by seeking a law of their occurrence, but were suggested by an imagination of the anger of superior powers, shown by such deviations from the ordinary course of nature." I conceive the question to be, not in what manner these notions were at first suggested, but by what evidence they have, from time to time, been supposed to be substantiated. If the believers in these erroneous opinions had been put on their defence, they would have referred to experience; to the comet which preceded the assassination of Julius Caesar, or to oracles and other prophecies known to have been fulfilled. It is by such appeals to facts that all analogous superstitions, even in our day, attempt to justify themselves; the supposed evidence of experience is what really gives them their hold on the mind. I quite admit that the influence of such coincidences would not be what it is, if strength were not lent to it by an antecedent presumption; but this is not peculiar to such cases; preconceived notions of probability form part of the explanation of many other cases of belief on insufficient evidence. The *a priori* prejudice does not prevent the erroneous opinion from being sincerely regarded as a legitimate conclusion from experience; but is, on the contrary, the very thing which predisposes the mind to that interpretation of experience.

Thus much in defence of the sort of examples objected to. But it would be easy to produce instances, equally adapted to the purpose, and in which no antecedent prejudice is at all concerned. "For many ages," says Archbishop Whately, "all farmers and gardeners were firmly convinced--and convinced of their knowing it by experience--that the crops would never turn out good unless the seed were sown during the increase of the moon." This was induction, but bad induction: just as a vicious syllogism is reasoning, but bad reasoning.

65 The assertion, that any and every one of the conditions of a phenomenon may be and is, on some occasions and for some purposes, spoken of as the cause, has been disputed by an intelligent reviewer of this work, (***Prospective Review*** for February 1850,) who maintains that "we always apply the word cause rather to that element in the antecedents which exercises *force*, and which would *tend* at all times to produce the same or a similar effect to that which, under certain conditions, it would actually produce." And he says, that "every one would feel" the expression, that the cause of a surprise was the sentinel's being off his post, to be incorrect; but that "the allurement or force which *drew* him off his post, might be so called, because in doing so it removed a resisting power which would have prevented the surprise." I cannot think that it would be wrong to say, that the event took place because the sentinel was absent, and yet right to say that it took place because he was bribed to be absent. Since the only direct effect of the bribe was his absence, the bribe could be called the remote cause of the surprise, only on the supposition that the absence was the proximate cause; nor does it seem to me that any one, who had not a theory to support, would use the one expression and reject the other.

The reviewer observes, that when a person dies of poison, his possession of bodily organs is a necessary condition, but that no one would ever speak of it as the cause. I admit the fact; but I believe the reason to be, that the occasion could never arise for so speaking of it; for when in the inaccuracy of common discourse we are led to speak of some one condition of a phenomenon as its cause, the condition so spoken of is always one which it is at least possible that the hearer may require to be informed of. The possession of bodily organs is a known condition, and to give that as the answer, when asked the cause of a person's death, would not

supply the information sought. Once conceive that a doubt could
exist as to his having bodily organs, or that he were to be compared
with some being who had them not, and cases may be imagined in which
it might be said that his possession of them was the cause of his
death. If Faust and Mephistopheles together took poison, it might be
said that Faust died because he was a human being, and had a body,
while Mephistopheles survived because he was a spirit.

It is for the same reason, that no one (as the reviewer remarks)
"calls the cause of a leap, the muscles or sinews of the body,
though they are necessary conditions; nor the cause of a
self-sacrifice, the knowledge which was necessary for it; nor the
cause of writing a book, that a man has time for it, which is a
necessary condition." These conditions (besides that they are
antecedent **states**, and not proximate antecedent **events**, and are
therefore never the conditions in closest apparent proximity to the
effect) are all of them so obviously implied, that it is hardly
possible there should exist that necessity for insisting on them,
which alone gives occasion for speaking of a single condition as if
it were the cause. Wherever this necessity exists in regard to some
one condition, and does not exist in regard to any other, I conceive
that it is consistent with usage, when scientific accuracy is not
aimed at, to apply the name cause to that one condition. If the only
condition which can be supposed to be unknown is a negative
condition, the negative condition may be spoken of as the cause. It
might be said that a person died for want of medical advice: though
this would not be likely to be said, unless the person was already
understood to be ill; and in order to indicate that this negative
circumstance was what made the illness fatal, and not the weakness
of his constitution, or the original virulence of the disease. It
might be said that a person was drowned because he could not swim;
the positive condition, namely that he fell into the water, being
already implied in the word drowned. And here let me remark, that

his falling into the water is in this case the only positive condition: all the conditions not expressly or virtually included in this (as that he could not swim, that nobody helped him, and so forth) are negative. Yet, if it were simply said that the cause of a man's death was falling into the water, there would be quite as great a sense of impropriety in the expression, as there would be if it were said that the cause was his inability to swim; because, though the one condition is positive and the other negative, it would be felt that neither of them was sufficient, without the other, to produce death.

With regard to the assertion that nothing is termed the cause, except the element which exerts active force; I waive the question as to the meaning of active force, and accepting the phrase in its popular sense, I revert to a former example, and I ask, would it be more agreeable to custom to say that a man fell because his foot slipped in climbing a ladder, or that he fell because of his weight--for his weight, and not the motion of his foot, was the active force which determined his fall. If a person walking out in a frosty day, stumbled and fell, it might be said that he stumbled because the ground was slippery, or because he was not sufficiently careful; but few people, I suppose, would say that he stumbled because he walked. Yet the only active force concerned was that which he exerted in walking: the others were mere negative conditions; but they happened to be the only ones which there could be any necessity to state; for he walked, most likely, in exactly his usual manner, and the negative conditions made all the difference. Again, if a person were asked why the army of Xerxes defeated that of Leonidas, he would probably say, because they were a thousand times the number; but I do not think he would say, it was because they fought; although that was the element of active force. The reviewer adds, "there are some conditions absolutely passive, and yet absolutely necessary to physical phenomena, viz., the relations of space and time; and to these no one ever applies the word cause without being immediately arrested by those who hear him." Even from this statement I am compelled to dissent. Few persons would feel it incongruous to say (for example) that a secret became known because it was spoken of when A. B. was within hearing; which is a condition of space; or that the cause why one of two particular trees is taller than the other, is that it has been longer planted; which is a condition of time.

66 There are a few exceptions; for there are some properties of objects which seem to be purely preventive; as the property of opaque bodies, by which they intercept the passage of light. This, as far as we are able to understand it, appears an instance not of one cause counteracting another by the same law whereby it produces its own effects, but of an agency which manifests itself in no other way than in defeating the effects of another agency. If we knew on what other relations to light, or on what peculiarities of structure, opacity depends, we might find that this is only an apparent, not a real, exception to the general proposition in the text. In any case it needs not affect the practical application. The formula which includes all the negative conditions of an effect in the single one of the absence of counteracting causes, is not violated by such cases as this; though, if all counteracting agencies were of this description, there would be no purpose served by employing the formula, since we should still have to enumerate specially the negative conditions of each phenomenon, instead of regarding them as implicitly contained in the positive laws of the various other agencies in nature.

67 I use the words "straight line" for brevity and simplicity. In reality the line in question is not exactly straight, for, from the effect of refraction, we actually see the sun for a short interval during which the opaque mass of the earth is interposed in a direct

line between the sun and our eyes; thus realizing, though but to a limited extent, the coveted desideratum of seeing round a corner.

68 The reviewer of Dr. Whewell in the **Quarterly Review**.

69 To the universality which mankind are agreed in ascribing to the Law of Causation, there is one claim of exception, one disputed case, that of the Human Will; the determinations of which, a large class of metaphysicians are not willing to regard as following the causes called motives, according to as strict laws as those which they suppose to exist in the world of mere matter. This controverted point will undergo a special examination when we come to treat particularly of the Logic of the Moral Sciences, (Book vi. ch. 2). In the meantime I may remark that these metaphysicians, who, it must be observed, ground the main part of their objection on the supposed repugnance of the doctrine in question to our consciousness, seem to me to mistake the fact which consciousness testifies against. What is really in contradiction to consciousness, they would, I think, on strict self-examination, find to be, the application to human actions and volitions of the ideas involved in the common use of the term Necessity; which I agree with them in objecting to. But if they would consider that by saying that a person's actions **necessarily** follow from his character, all that is really meant (for no more is meant in any case whatever of causation) is that he invariably **does** act in conformity to his character, and that any one who thoroughly knew his character could certainly predict how he would act in any supposable case; they probably would not find this doctrine either contrary to their experience or revolting to their feelings. And no more than this is contended for by any one but an Asiatic fatalist.

70 Unless we are to consider as such the following statement, by one of the writers quoted in the text: "In the case of mental exertion, the

result to be accomplished is ***preconsidered*** or meditated, and is therefore known ***a priori***, or before experience."--(Bowen's Lowell Lectures on the Application of Metaphysical and Ethical Science to the Evidence of Religion, Boston, 1849.) This is merely saying that when we will a thing we have an idea of it. But to have an idea of what we wish to happen, does not imply a prophetic knowledge that it will happen. Perhaps it will be said that the ***first time*** we exerted our will, when we had of course no experience of any of the powers residing in us, we nevertheless must already have known that we possessed them, since we cannot ***will*** that which we do not believe to be in our power. But the impossibility is perhaps in the words only, and not in the facts; for we may ***desire*** what we do not know to be in our power; and finding by experience that our bodies move according to our ***desire***, we may then, and only then, pass into the more complicated mental state which is termed will.

After all, even if we had an instinctive knowledge that our actions would follow our will, this, as Brown remarks, would prove nothing as to the nature of Causation. Our knowing, previous to experience, that an antecedent will be followed by a certain consequent, would not prove the relation between them to be anything ***more*** than antecedence and consequence.

71 Reid's ***Essays on the Active Powers***, Essay iv. ch. 3.

72 Prospective Review for February 1850.

73 Vide supra, p. 267, note.

74 In combating the theory, that Volition is the universal cause, I have purposely abstained from one of the strongest positive arguments against it--that volitions themselves obey causes, and even

external causes, namely, the inducements, or motives, which determine the will to act; because an objector might say that to employ this argument would be begging the question against the freedom of the will. Though it is not begging the question to affirm a doctrine, referring elsewhere for the proof of it, I am unwilling without necessity to build any part of my reasoning on a proposition which I am aware that those opposed to me in the present discussion do not admit.

75 I omit, for simplicity, to take into account the effect, in this latter case, of the diminution of pressure, in diminishing the flow of water through the drain; which evidently in no way affects the truth or applicability of the principle.

76 Unless, indeed, the consequent was generated not by the antecedent, but by the means we employed to produce the antecedent. As, however, these means are under our power, there is so far a probability that they are also sufficiently within our knowledge, to enable us to judge whether that could be the case or not.

77 Discourse on the Study of Natural Philosophy, p. 179.

78 For this speculation I am indebted to Mr. Alexander Bain.

79 This view of the necessary coexistence of opposite excitements involves a great extension of the original doctrine of two electricities. The early theorists assumed that, when amber was rubbed, the amber was made positive and the rubber negative to the same degree; but it never occurred to them to suppose that the existence of the amber charge was dependent on an opposite charge in the bodies with which the amber was contiguous, while the existence of the negative charge on the rubber was equally dependent on a contrary state of the surfaces that might accidentally be confronted

with it; that, in fact, in a case of electrical excitement by friction, four charges were the minimum that could exist. But this double electrical action is essentially implied in the explanation now universally adopted in regard to the phenomena of the common electric machine.

80 Pp. 159-162.

81 Infra, book iv., chap. ii. On Abstraction.

82 I must, however, remark, that this example, which seems to militate against the assertion we made of the comparative inapplicability of the Method of Difference to cases of pure observation, is really one of those exceptions which, according to a proverbial expression, prove the general rule. For this case, in which Nature, in her experiment, seems to have imitated the type of the experiments made by man, she has only succeeded in producing the likeness of man's most imperfect experiments; namely, those in which, though he succeeds in producing the phenomenon, he does so by employing complex means, which he is unable perfectly to analyse, and can form therefore no sufficient judgment what portion of the effects may be due, not to the supposed cause, but to some unknown agency of the means by which that cause was produced. In the natural experiment which we are speaking of, the means used was the clearing off a canopy of clouds; and we certainly do not know sufficiently in what this process consists, or on what it depends, to be certain a priori that it might not operate upon the deposition of dew independently of any thermometric effect at the earth's surface. Even, therefore, in a case so favourable as this to Nature's experimental talents, her experiment is of little value except in corroboration of a conclusion already attained through other means.

83 Discourse, pp. 156-8, and 171.

84 Outlines of Astronomy, p. 584.

85 Dr. Whewell, in his reply, expresses a very unfavourable opinion of
the utility of the Four Methods, as well as of the aptness of the
examples by which I have attempted to illustrate them. His words are
these (pp. 44-6):

"Upon these methods, the obvious thing to remark is, that they take
for granted the very thing which is most difficult to discover, the
reduction of the phenomena to formulae such as are here presented to
us. When we have any set of complex facts offered to us; for
instance, those which were offered in the cases of discovery which I
have mentioned,--the facts of the planetary paths, of falling bodies,
of refracted rays, of cosmical motions, of chemical analysis; and
when, in any of these cases, we would discover the law of nature
which governs them, or, if any one chooses so to term it, the
feature in which all the cases agree, where are we to look for our
A, B, C, and *a, b, c*? Nature does not present to us the cases in
this form; and how are we to reduce them to this form? You say,
when we find the combination of A B C with *a b c* and A B D with
a b d, then we may draw our inference. Granted; but when and where
are we to find such combinations? Even now that the discoveries are
made, who will point out to us what are the A, B, C, and *a, b, c*
elements of the cases which have just been enumerated? Who will tell
us which of the methods of inquiry those historically real and
successful inquiries exemplify? Who will carry these formulae through
the history of the sciences, as they have really grown up; and shew
us that these four methods have been operative in their formation;
or that any light is thrown upon the steps of their progress by
reference to these formulae?"

He adds that, in this work, the methods have not been applied "to a large body of conspicuous and undoubted examples of discovery, extending along the whole history of science," which ought to have been done in order that the methods might be shown to possess the "advantage" (which he claims as belonging to his own) of being those "by which all great discoveries in science have really been made."--(p. 66.)

There is a striking similarity between the objections here made against Canons of Induction, and what was alleged, in the last century, by as able men as Dr. Whewell, against the acknowledged Canon of Ratiocination. Those who protested against the Aristotelian Logic said of the Syllogism, what Dr. Whewell says of the Inductive Methods, that it "takes for granted the very thing which is most difficult to discover, the reduction of the argument to formulae such as are here presented to us." The grand difficulty, they said, is to obtain your syllogism, not to judge of its correctness when obtained. On the matter of fact, both they and Dr. Whewell are right. The greatest difficulty in both cases is first that of obtaining the evidence, and next, of reducing it to the form which tests its conclusiveness. But if we try so to reduce it without knowing ***to what***, we are not likely to make much progress. It is a more difficult thing to solve a geometrical problem, than to judge whether a proposed solution is correct: but if people were not able to judge of the solution when found, they would have little chance of finding it. And it cannot be pretended that to judge of an induction when found, is perfectly easy, is a thing for which aids and instruments are superfluous; for erroneous inductions, false inferences from experience, are quite as common, on some subjects much commoner, than true ones. The business of Inductive Logic is to provide rules and models (such as the Syllogism and its rules are for ratiocination) to which if inductive arguments conform, those arguments are conclusive, and not otherwise. This is what the Four Methods profess to be, and what I believe they are universally considered to be by experimental philosophers, who had practised all of them long before any one sought to reduce the practice to theory.

The assailants of the Syllogism had also anticipated Dr. Whewell in the other branch of his argument. They said that no discoveries were ever made by syllogism; and Dr. Whewell says, or seems to say, that none were ever made by the four Methods of Induction. To the former objectors, Archbishop Whately very pertinently answered, that their argument, if good at all, was good against the reasoning process altogether; for whatever cannot be reduced to syllogism, is not reasoning. And Dr. Whewell's argument, if good at all, is good against all inferences from experience. In saying that no discoveries were ever made by the four Methods, he affirms that none were ever made by observation and experiment; for assuredly if any were, it was by one or other of those methods.

This difference between us accounts for the dissatisfaction which my examples give him; for I did not select them with a view to satisfy any one who required to be convinced that observation and experiment are modes of acquiring knowledge: I confess that in the choice of them I thought only of illustration, and of facilitating the *conception* of the Methods by concrete instances. If it had been my object to justify the processes themselves as means of investigation, there would have been no need to look far off, or make use of recondite or complicated instances. As a specimen of a truth ascertained by the Method of Agreement, I might have chosen the proposition, "Dogs bark." This dog, and that dog, and the other dog, answer to A B C, A D E, A F G. The circumstance of being a dog, answers to A. Barking answers to *a*. As a truth made known by the Method of Difference, "Fire burns" might have sufficed. Before I touch the fire I am not burnt; this is B C; I touch it, and am burnt; this is A B C, *a* B C.

Such familiar experimental processes are not regarded as inductions by Dr. Whewell; but they are perfectly homogeneous with those by which, even on his own shewing, the pyramid of science is supplied with its base. In vain he attempts to escape from this truth by laying the most arbitrary restrictions on the choice of examples admissible as instances of Induction: they must neither be such as are still matter of discussion (p. 47), nor must any of them be drawn from mental and social subjects (p. 53), nor from ordinary observation and practical life (pp. 11-15). They must be taken exclusively from the generalizations by which scientific thinkers have ascended to great and comprehensive laws of natural phenomena. Now it is seldom possible, in these complicated inquiries, to go much beyond the initial steps, without calling in the instrument of Deduction, and the temporary aid of hypotheses; as I myself, in common with Dr. Whewell, have maintained against the purely empirical school. Since therefore such cases could not conveniently be selected to illustrate the principles of mere observation and experiment, Dr. Whewell takes advantage of their absence to represent the Experimental Methods as serving no purpose in scientific investigation; forgetting that if those methods had not supplied the first generalizations, there would have been no materials for his own conception of Induction to work upon.

His challenge, however, to point out which of the four methods are exemplified in certain important cases of scientific inquiry, is easily answered. "The planetary paths," as far as they are a case of induction at all, (see, on this point, the second chapter of the present Book) fall under the Method of Agreement. The law of "falling bodies," namely that they describe spaces proportional to the squares of the times, was historically a deduction from the first law of motion; but the experiments by which it was verified, and by which it might have been discovered, were examples of the Method of Agreement; and the apparent variation from the true law, caused by the resistance of the air, was cleared up by experiments *in vacuo*, constituting an application of the Method of Difference. The law of "refracted rays," (the constancy of the ratio between the sines of incidence and of refraction for each refracting substance) was ascertained by direct measurement, and therefore by the Method of Agreement. The "cosmical motions" were determined by highly complex processes of thought, in which Deduction was predominant, but the Methods of Agreement and of Concomitant Variations had a large part in establishing the empirical laws. Every case without exception of "chemical analysis" constitutes a well marked example of the Method of Difference. To any one acquainted with the subjects--to Dr. Whewell himself, there would not be the smallest difficulty in setting out "the A B C and *a b c* elements" of these cases.

If discoveries are ever made by observation and experiment without Deduction, the four methods are methods of discovery: but even if they were not methods of discovery, it would not be the less true that they are the sole methods of Proof; and in that character, even the results of Deduction are amenable to them. The great generalizations which begin as Hypotheses must end by being proved, and are in reality (as will be shown hereafter) proved by the Four Methods. Now it is with Proof, as such, that Logic is principally concerned. This distinction has indeed no chance of finding favour with Dr. Whewell; for it is the peculiarity of his system not to recognise, in cases of Induction, any necessity for proof. If, after assuming an hypothesis and carefully collating it with facts, nothing is brought to light inconsistent with it, that is, if experience does not *dis*prove it, he is content: at least until a simpler hypothesis, equally consistent with experience, presents itself. If this be Induction, doubtless there is no necessity for the four methods. But to suppose that it is so, appears to me a radical misconception of the nature of the evidence of physical truths.

86 *Ante*, p. 378.

87 It seems hardly necessary to say that the word ***impinges***, as a general term to express collision of forces, was here used by a figure of speech, and not as expressive of any theory respecting the nature of force.

88 *Essays on some Unsettled Questions of Political Economy*, Essay V.

89 There is no danger of confounding this acceptation of the term with the peculiar employment of the phrase "tangential force" in the theory of the planetary perturbations.

90 Supra, p. 420.

91 As corroborating the opinion that the protoxide of iron in the venous blood is only partially carbonated, the fact has been suggested, that the system shows great readiness to absorb an extra quantity of carbonic acid, as furnished in effervescing drinks. In such cases the acid must combine with something, and that something is not improbably the free protoxide. It would be worth ascertaining whether the protoxide itself or its carbonate has the greatest facility in absorbing oxygen and turning itself into hydrated peroxide in the lungs. If the carbonate, then the beneficial effect, on the animal economy, of drinks which give an artificial supply of carbonic acid to the system, would be, to that extent, deductively established.

92 It was an old generalization in surgery, that tight bandaging had a tendency to prevent or dissipate local inflammation. This sequence, being, in the progress of physiological knowledge, resolved into

more general laws, led to the important surgical invention made by Dr. Arnott, the treatment of local inflammation and tumours by means of an equable pressure, produced by a bladder partially filled with air. The pressure, by keeping back the blood from the part, prevents the inflammation, or the tumour, from being nourished; in the case of inflammation, it removes the stimulus, which the organ is unfit to receive: in the case of tumours, by keeping back the nutritive fluid it causes the absorption of matter to exceed the supply, and the diseased mass is gradually absorbed and disappears.

The Codes Of Hammurabi And Moses
W. W. Davies

QTY

The discovery of the Hammurabi Code is one of the greatest achievements of archaeology, and is of paramount interest, not only to the student of the Bible, but also to all those interested in ancient history...

Religion   **ISBN:** *1-59462-338-4*   **Pages:132**
MSRP $12.95

The Theory of Moral Sentiments
Adam Smith

QTY

This work from 1749. contains original theories of conscience amd moral judgment and it is the foundation for systemof morals.

Philosophy **ISBN:** *1-59462-777-0*   **Pages:536**
MSRP $19.95

Jessica's First Prayer
Hesba Stretton

QTY

In a screened and secluded corner of one of the many railway-bridges which span the streets of London there could be seen a few years ago, from five o'clock every morning until half past eight, a tidily set-out coffee-stall, consisting of a trestle and board, upon which stood two large tin cans, with a small fire of charcoal burning under each so as to keep the coffee boiling during the early hours of the morning when the work-people were thronging into the city on their way to their daily toil...

Pages:84

Childrens   **ISBN:** *1-59462-373-2*   *MSRP $9.95*

My Life and Work
Henry Ford

QTY

Henry Ford revolutionized the world with his implementation of mass production for the Model T automobile. Gain valuable business insight into his life and work with his own auto-biography... "We have only started on our development of our country we have not as yet, with all our talk of wonderful progress, done more than scratch the surface. The progress has been wonderful enough but..."

Pages:300

Biographies/   **ISBN:** *1-59462-198-5*   *MSRP $21.95*

The Art of Cross-Examination
Francis Wellman

QTY

I presume it is the experience of every author, after his first book is published upon an important subject, to be almost overwhelmed with a wealth of ideas and illustrations which could readily have been included in his book, and which to his own mind, at least, seem to make a second edition inevitable. Such certainly was the case with me; and when the first edition had reached its sixth impression in five months, I rejoiced to learn that it seemed to my publishers that the book had met with a sufficiently favorable reception to justify a second and considerably enlarged edition. ..

Reference   **ISBN:** *1-59462-647-2*

Pages:412

MSRP $19.95

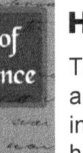

On the Duty of Civil Disobedience
Henry David Thoreau

QTY

Thoreau wrote his famous essay, On the Duty of Civil Disobedience, as a protest against an unjust but popular war and the immoral but popular institution of slave-owning. He did more than write—he declined to pay his taxes, and was hauled off to gaol in consequence. Who can say how much this refusal of his hastened the end of the war and of slavery ?

Law   **ISBN:** *1-59462-747-9*

Pages:48

MSRP $7.45

Dream Psychology Psychoanalysis for Beginners
Sigmund Freud

QTY

Sigmund Freud, born Sigismund Schlomo Freud (May 6, 1856 - September 23, 1939), was a Jewish-Austrian neurologist and psychiatrist who co-founded the psychoanalytic school of psychology. Freud is best known for his theories of the unconscious mind, especially involving the mechanism of repression; his redefinition of sexual desire as mobile and directed towards a wide variety of objects; and his therapeutic techniques, especially his understanding of transference in the therapeutic relationship and the presumed value of dreams as sources of insight into unconscious desires.

Psychology   **ISBN:** *1-59462-905-6*

Pages:196

MSRP $15.45

The Miracle of Right Thought
Orison Swett Marden

QTY

Believe with all of your heart that you will do what you were made to do. When the mind has once formed the habit of holding cheerful, happy, prosperous pictures, it will not be easy to form the opposite habit. It does not matter how improbable or how far away this realization may see, or how dark the prospects may be, if we visualize them as best we can, as vividly as possible, hold tenaciously to them and vigorously struggle to attain them, they will gradually become actualized, realized in the life. But a desire, a longing without endeavor, a yearning abandoned or held indifferently will vanish without realization.

Self Help   **ISBN:** *1-59462-644-8*

Pages:360

MSRP $25.45

The Rosicrucian Cosmo-Conception Mystic Christianity by *Max Heindel*   ISBN: *1-59462-188-8*   **$38.95**
The Rosicrucian Cosmo-conception is not dogmatic, neither does it appeal to any other authority than the reason of the student. It is: not controversial, but is: sent forth in the, hope that it may help to clear...   New Age/Religion Pages 646

Abandonment To Divine Providence by *Jean-Pierre de Caussade*   ISBN: *1-59462-228-0*   **$25.95**
"The Rev. Jean Pierre de Caussade was one of the most remarkable spiritual writers of the Society of Jesus in France in the 18th Century. His death took place at Toulouse in 1751. His works have gone through many editions and have been republished...   Inspirational/Religion Pages 400

Mental Chemistry by *Charles Haanel*   ISBN: *1-59462-192-6*   **$23.95**
Mental Chemistry allows the change of material conditions by combining and appropriately utilizing the power of the mind. Much like applied chemistry creates something new and unique out of careful combinations of chemicals the mastery of mental chemistry...   New Age Pages 354

The Letters of Robert Browning and Elizabeth Barret Barrett 1845-1846 vol II   ISBN: *1-59462-193-4*   **$35.95**
by *Robert Browning* and *Elizabeth Barrett*   Biographies Pages 596

Gleanings In Genesis (volume I) by *Arthur W. Pink*   ISBN: *1-59462-130-6*   **$27.45**
Appropriately has Genesis been termed "the seed plot of the Bible" for in it we have, in germ form, almost all of the great doctrines which are afterwards fully developed in the books of Scripture which follow...   Religion/Inspirational Pages 420

The Master Key by *L. W. de Laurence*   ISBN: *1-59462-001-6*   **$30.95**
In no branch of human knowledge has there been a more lively increase of the spirit of research during the past few years than in the study of Psychology, Concentration and Mental Discipline. The requests for authentic lessons in Thought Control, Mental Discipline and...   New Age/Business Pages 422

The Lesser Key Of Solomon Goetia by *L. W. de Laurence*   ISBN: *1-59462-092-X*   **$9.95**
This translation of the first book of the "Lernegton" which is now for the first time made accessible to students of Talismanic Magic was done, after careful collation and edition, from numerous Ancient Manuscripts in Hebrew, Latin, and French...   New Age/Occult Pages 92

Rubaiyat Of Omar Khayyam by *Edward Fitzgerald*   ISBN: *1-59462-332-5*   **$13.95**
Edward Fitzgerald, whom the world has already learned, in spite of his own efforts to remain within the shadow of anonymity, to look upon as one of the rarest poets of the century, was born at Bredfield, in Suffolk, on the 31st of March, 1809. He was the third son of John Purcell...   Music Pages 172

Ancient Law by *Henry Maine*   ISBN: *1-59462-128-4*   **$29.95**
The chief object of the following pages is to indicate some of the earliest ideas of mankind, as they are reflected in Ancient Law, and to point out the relation of those ideas to modern thought.   Religiom/History Pages 452

Far-Away Stories by *William J. Locke*   ISBN: *1-59462-129-2*   **$19.45**
"Good wine needs no bush, but a collection of mixed vintages does. And this book is just such a collection. Some of the stories I do not want to remain buried for ever in the museum files of dead magazine-numbers an author's not unpardonable vanity..."   Fiction Pages 272

Life of David Crockett by *David Crockett*   ISBN: *1-59462-250-7*   **$27.45**
"Colonel David Crockett was one of the most remarkable men of the times in which he lived. Born in humble life, but gifted with a strong will, an indomitable courage, and unremitting perseverance...   Biographies/New Age Pages 424

Lip-Reading by *Edward Nitchie*   ISBN: *1-59462-206-X*   **$25.95**
Edward B. Nitchie, founder of the New York School for the Hard of Hearing, now the Nitchie School of Lip-Reading, Inc, wrote "LIP-READING Principles and Practice". The development and perfecting of this meritorious work on lip-reading was an undertaking...   How-to Pages 400

A Handbook of Suggestive Therapeutics, Applied Hypnotism, Psychic Science   ISBN: *1-59462-214-0*   **$24.95**
by *Henry Munro*   Health/New Age/Health/Self-help Pages 376

A Doll's House: and Two Other Plays by *Henrik Ibsen*   ISBN: *1-59462-112-8*   **$19.95**
Henrik Ibsen created this classic when in revolutionary 1848 Rome. Introducing some striking concepts in playwriting for the realist genre, this play has been studied the world over.   Fiction/Classics/Plays 308

The Light of Asia by *sir Edwin Arnold*   ISBN: *1-59462-204-3*   **$13.95**
In this poetic masterpiece, Edwin Arnold describes the life and teachings of Buddha. The man who was to become known as Buddha to the world was born as Prince Gautama of India but he rejected the worldly riches and abandoned the reigns of power when... Religion/History/Biographies Pages 170

The Complete Works of Guy de Maupassant by *Guy de Maupassant*   ISBN: *1-59462-157-8*   **$16.95**
"For days and days, nights and nights, I had dreamed of that first kiss which was to consecrate our engagement, and I knew not on what spot I should put my lips..."   Fiction/Classics Pages 240

The Art of Cross-Examination by *Francis L. Wellman*   ISBN: *1-59462-309-0*   **$26.95**
Written by a renowned trial lawyer, Wellman imparts his experience and uses case studies to explain how to use psychology to extract desired information through questioning.   How-to/Science/Reference Pages 408

Answered or Unanswered? by *Louisa Vaughan*   ISBN: *1-59462-248-5*   **$10.95**
Miracles of Faith in China   Religion Pages 112

The Edinburgh Lectures on Mental Science (1909) by *Thomas*   ISBN: *1-59462-008-3*   **$11.95**
This book contains the substance of a course of lectures recently given by the writer in the Queen Street Hall, Edinburgh. Its purpose is to indicate the Natural Principles governing the relation between Mental Action and Material Conditions...   New Age/Psychology Pages 148

Ayesha by *H. Rider Haggard*   ISBN: *1-59462-301-5*   **$24.95**
Verily and indeed it is the unexpected that happens! Probably if there was one person upon the earth from whom the Editor of this, and of a certain previous history, did not expect to hear again...   Classics Pages 380

Ayala's Angel by *Anthony Trollope*   ISBN: *1-59462-352-X*   **$29.95**
The two girls were both pretty, but Lucy who was twenty-one who supposed to be simple and comparatively unattractive, whereas Ayala was credited, as her Bombwhat romantic name might show, with poetic charm and a taste for romance. Ayala when her father died was nineteen...   Fiction Pages 484

The American Commonwealth by *James Bryce*   ISBN: *1-59462-286-8*   **$34.45**
An interpretation of American democratic political theory. It examines political mechanics and society from the perspective of Scotsman James Bryce   Politics Pages 572

Stories of the Pilgrims by *Margaret P. Pumphrey*   ISBN: *1-59462-116-0*   **$17.95**
This book explores pilgrims religious oppression in England as well as their escape to Holland and eventual crossing to America on the Mayflower, and their early days in New England...   History Pages 268

www.**bookjungle**.com *email: sales@bookjungle.com fax: 630-214-0564 mail: Book Jungle PO Box 2226 Champaign, IL 61825*

QTY

The Fasting Cure *by Sinclair Upton*   ISBN: *1-59462-222-1* **$13.95** ☐
In the Cosmopolitan Magazine for May, 1910, and in the Contemporary Review (London) for April, 1910, I published an article dealing with my experiences in fasting. I have written a great many magazine articles, but never one which attracted so much attention... New Age/Self Help/Health Pages 164

Hebrew Astrology *by Sepharial*   ISBN: *1-59462-308-2* **$13.45** ☐
In these days of advanced thinking it is a matter of common observation that we have left many of the old landmarks behind and that we are now pressing forward to greater heights and to a wider horizon than that which represented the mind-content of our progenitors... Astrology Pages 144

Thought Vibration or The Law of Attraction in the Thought World   ISBN: *1-59462-127-6* **$12.95** ☐

by William Walker Atkinson   *Psychology/Religion Pages 144*

Optimism *by Helen Keller*   ISBN: *1-59462-108-X* **$15.95** ☐
Helen Keller was blind, deaf, and mute since 19 months old, yet famously learned how to overcome these handicaps, communicate with the world, and spread her lectures promoting optimism. An inspiring read for everyone... Biographies/Inspirational Pages 84

Sara Crewe *by Frances Burnett*   ISBN: *1-59462-360-0* **$9.45** ☐
In the first place, Miss Minchin lived in London. Her home was a large, dull, tall one, in a large, dull square, where all the houses were alike, and all the sparrows were alike, and where all the door-knockers made the same heavy sound... Childrens/Classic Pages 88

The Autobiography of Benjamin Franklin *by Benjamin Franklin*   ISBN: *1-59462-135-7* **$24.95** ☐
The Autobiography of Benjamin Franklin has probably been more extensively read than any other American historical work, and no other book of its kind has had such ups and downs of fortune. Franklin lived for many years in England, where he was agent... Biographies/History Pages 332

Name	
Email	
Telephone	
Address	
City, State ZIP	

☐ **Credit Card**   ☐ **Check / Money Order**

Credit Card Number	
Expiration Date	
Signature	

Please Mail to: Book Jungle
PO Box 2226
Champaign, IL 61825
or Fax to: 630-214-0564

ORDERING INFORMATION

web*: www.bookjungle.com*
email*: sales@bookjungle.com*
fax*: 630-214-0564*
mail*: Book Jungle PO Box 2226 Champaign, IL 61825*
or PayPal *to sales@bookjungle.com*

Please contact us for bulk discounts

DIRECT-ORDER TERMS

**20% Discount if You Order
Two or More Books**
Free Domestic Shipping!
Accepted: Master Card, Visa,
Discover, American Express

www.ingramcontent.com/pod-product-compliance
Lightning Source LLC
Chambersburg PA
CBHW080951020726
47505CB00009B/2152